FALLEN WITCH

SPELLBOUND MURDER BOOK 3

AMANDA BOOLOODIAN

My dad is my greatest cheerleader. Even before becoming an author he was my biggest supporter. Thank you for everything dad!

CHAPTER 1

MIRA COULD FEEL PRESSURE squeezing the building. She tried to tell herself it was her imagination, but she knew it was a losing battle.

The Borgo building. Why did Emmit have to live in the Borgo building? In the Ether, some monstrosity was wrapped around the building. How could that not affect the real world?

Trying to get the idea out of her mind was like trying to push away smoke.

The mirror reflected her pale face, but she was thankful it was winter and long sleeves hid the large bandage on her arm, covering stitches, which she also tried hard not to think about. From head to toe, scratches and cuts of various sizes peppered her skin, but thankfully, her arm was the only serious wound that remained from her last trip into the Ether.

She ran a brush through her hair again—anything to stall leaving the bathroom, which was her only sanctuary. The Reinfield men were professional and polite, but it was creepy to have someone else in the room with you everywhere you went. Especially when you slept.

It didn't feel right to complain about them, either. One of them had saved her life once already, but pockets of bad karma still floated around. It was either that or plain bad luck that led to a large beam that had nearly dropped on her head when she walked around the block.

Gabriel was really the one that saved her. He alerted Mira's bodyguard to the imminent danger, and the almost stranger had dragged her to safety.

However, Gabriel hadn't even called to check on her.

Mira's mood shifted from sad to seriously pissed off when she thought about that. Emmit had said Gabriel needed to take a step back, whatever that meant. She lost Gabriel and her family on the same day. The witches had shunned her, and even if he hadn't meant to do it, Gabriel had done the same.

Her only bright spot was a text she received from her sister. It said, 'Even if you are banished, you will always be my sister.'

The first time she read it, fear stabbed her straight through the heart. They were discussing banishment. It was bad enough being shunned—but with banishment, they try to bind the witch.

Well, they can try, Mira thought. She knew to be effective they'd need Tyler. Despite the fact that he hadn't woken up, the doctors had a positive outlook on Tyler's chances of recovery, but he was still going to have a difficult time. Mira was fairly certain he'd refuse to help, but after what he'd been through, it was a gamble.

For now, it was best to avoid the witches.

As expected, someone waited by the door the moment Mira stepped out of the bathroom. She tried not to let that depress her. She never knew what to say to them. She was trying to think of something when she noticed the man making furtive glances at the door.

"What's wrong, Mark?" Mira asked, fervently hoping he hadn't somehow been signaled by Gabriel. "You look uneasy."

"I think we should wait here," Mark said.

Mira frowned and moved toward the door.

"I really think we should stay here," he repeated.

Mira heard raised voices.

Emmit was very careful with his anger and tended to keep it bottled up. Butterflies swarmed in her stomach. There was only one person, besides herself, that got Emmit this worked up.

Gabriel.

Mira grinned and opened the door, listening to the argument. Mark hurried in front of her, checking his watch repeatedly. Thankfully, the plush carpet in the hallway dampened the sound of their approach. Her guard looked a little more frantic with each step.

"It's all right," she said softly before opening the door that led to the living room.

Emmit's apartment was a maze of corridors and rooms. She still had no idea where he slept or what half of the rooms were used for, if they were used at all, but she knew where the living room and kitchen were.

Mira hadn't seen or heard from Gabriel since they had returned from the Ether. Before then, actually, since Gabriel had been unconscious when they returned. Because of this, she didn't even hesitate when she entered the room.

Gabriel and Emmit were in a heated debate, but all she could do was beam now that Gabriel was back. They didn't notice her, but Ian, sitting on the couch, waved.

When Mira neared the couch, she felt the pressure that had been building around the two men. Despite the heated argument, the energy building around Emmit remained localized to him. The cold wave around Gabriel, usually haphazardly directed at Emmit in an unfocused sort of way, was now pent up around the angel.

Mira took a seat next to Ian and wondered briefly if Gabriel was learning control over his powers in this world.

"What are they arguing about?" Mira asked, keeping her voice low.

"No idea," Ian said. "I haven't heard from you since... well, since you got back. How are you doing?"

"Better," Mira said, "and Gabriel?"

"Who's your shadow?" Ian asked, avoiding the question and nodding to the man that stood behind the couch where Mira was sitting.

Mira didn't reply right away, feeling sad that Ian didn't want to answer. Her mind threw out awful options, and she couldn't help but wonder if Gabriel was upset with her over something.

"I'm surprised Gabriel hasn't said anything about the guard arrangement," Mira said, raising her voice slightly.

When Gabriel turned, the look of concern he gave her made her heart flutter. Once he looked her over, the concern melted and he turned back to Emmit.

"What's the problem?" Mira asked before the argument could start again. She had intended to ask what was wrong, but her thoughts were on what issue Gabriel must have with her.

"If you ask me," Gabriel said, stiffly, "he is."

"Gabe," Ian said, with a hint of warning in his voice.

Gabriel ran his hand through his hair and took a deep breath. "Right."

Whatever secret code the partners had, Mira must have missed it, because Gabriel's attitude toward Emmit didn't change, even after his temper faded away.

"What's it going to be?" Gabriel asked.

"I've told you everything of importance," Emmit said.

"You've given us nothing," Gabriel said. "Three people were discovered trapped in the Ether and we have at least three more missing. You are the only connection to the place."

"The faster you get to work, the faster you'll find what you're looking for," Emmit said. "I know nothing that will help."

Gabriel looked like he was going to go explode.

"Are you meeting with anyone today?" Mira asked.

Ian took the hint. "Yeah, that's what we had in mind. If you're feeling up to it, of course."

"Sure," Mira said, trying not to show too much eagerness at the idea of getting out of the apartment. "Give me a minute." She jumped up to grab her purse, forcing her bodyguard to rush to catch up.

When she returned to the living room, Gabriel, Ian, and Emmit were talking as though the previous fight hadn't taken place.

"I'm ready," she said, already moving toward the door.

The detectives looked almost as ready as she was to get out of there. When Mira noticed the bodyguard following, intent on leaving with them, she stopped.

"You can stay here, Mark," Mira said.

Like any other time she had told one of her bodyguards to leave, Mark ignored her.

"Really?" Mira said, trying to keep her frustration in check. "You're not coming with me."

Ian and Gabriel were waiting, front door open, standing in the hallway. When Mark moved with her toward the door again, Mira stopped and glared at Emmit.

"This isn't happening, Emmit," Mira said. She always felt awkward talking about her guard when the individual was in the room.

"You'll be with the detectives?" Emmit asked.

Mira could feel her face turn red as her animosity grew. "Mark nor any of the others are joining us today. You have no choice in this."

Irritation gathered around Emmit like a cloud. He glanced at the detectives in the hallway.

It wasn't until she saw Gabriel shrug that she realized Emmit was looking for a response from Gabriel, not her.

Mira shook her head and walked out, wondering how she could arrange it so she didn't have to come back. She stomped past Gabriel and Ian and jabbed at the elevator button, saying nothing to anyone. By the time they reached the car, her anger was still at a high pitch, but it felt good to be out of the building.

From one chaperone to another, she thought, stoking the fires. It was embarrassing, controlling, and she didn't like it.

"Who did you all want to see today?" Mira asked.

"There were three witches that were involved in bringing you back," Ian said. "I figured we'd start there."

Mira's heart sunk and the anger let go so depression could fill its place. "You haven't already spoken with them?"

"It's Gabe's first day back," Ian said.

"I'm glad to see you're feeling better," Mira said.

"Thanks," Gabriel said, not looking away from the road. "Do you know who the witches were?"

The quick change of subject took Mira off guard. It hurt that he didn't seem willing to talk with her.

"We should start with Mr. Singer," Mira said. What she didn't say was that she fervently hoped Mr. Singer would give her information about her own predicament. He would be the only one that might even consider talking with her at this point.

As they passed out of the cold steel city, Mira watched out the window. Mr. Singer, like most witches, preferred to live away from the city. Ian broke the awkward silence that was building up in the car by going over old details in the case. She didn't bother to add any input. It was all stuff they already knew and had already hashed out. Gabriel was willing to go over it all again, though.

The closer they traveled to Mr. Singer's house, the more anxious Mira grew. By the time they reached his gravel driveway, Mira was picking at her fingers and chewing her nails. She noticed Gabriel glancing at her in the rear-view mirror, but it was a fleeting look and Mira couldn't see his expression.

If it hadn't been so cold out, she would have considered staying in the car while the detectives went in and spoke with Mr. Singer.

"Come on," Ian said, not unkindly, when she was slow to walk to the house. "It's freezing out here."

"Is everything okay?" Gabriel asked.

There was no good reply to that, so she stood up a little straighter and went to the door.

The detectives stood aside for her to knock.

Mr. Singer opened the door immediately. He looked at Mira for a moment longer than comfortable before opening the door widely.

"Come in," Mr. Singer said. "I'm glad you detectives stopped by today. I have a few questions."

"We'll try to be of some help," Ian said. "We're hoping you can answer a few things for us as well."

"Would you like something to drink?" Mr. Singer asked. "I have tea, coffee, and water."

"No thank you," Ian said.

"Please, take a seat," Mr. Singer said, waving his arm at the couch in the living room. "Mira."

Mira jumped at the sound of her name. She hadn't been expecting him to address her right away.

"How is the spell on your detectives holding up?" he continued.

"Oh," Mira said, "it's still holding."

Ian shifted uncomfortably and his good-natured smile died at the reminder.

"Good to hear," Mr. Singer said. "Can I ask you to wait in the hallway? I think it will make the interview a little less awkward, don't you?"

Mira didn't dare look at Ian or Gabriel. "Sure," she mumbled, and then left the room feeling like a child being dismissed.

"We will be filling her in on everything," Gabriel said. "She is our connection to your world."

"That's no problem," Mr. Singer said.

"Then why—"

"Simply protocol," Mr. Singer replied, interrupting Gabriel. "The others won't ask, of course, but Mira may choose to do so on her own. I am glad to see you both well, however."

CHAPTER 2

MIRA STEPPED AROUND INTO the hallway and out of sight. She was grateful that no one could see her face. Why was this so hard? Well, she knew why, but she didn't know how things had ended up this way. She leaned back against the wall and closed her eyes before tears could fall.

While trying to bring herself under control, she missed the first part of the conversation.

"Andrea and Kevin are being taken care of by the community. They have no other relatives, but they are being cared for," Mr. Singer said. "Do you have any leads on their parents?"

"Not at this time," Ian said.

"Is it possible they were taken to the Ether as well?" Gabriel asked.

Mira could only imagine what Mr. Singer thought of that question. He took a lengthy pause before responding.

"I think at this point, Detective, anything is possible. You would be a better judge of that than anyone else."

"What can you tell us about the Ether?" Gabriel asked.

"I'm afraid I can't help you with that," Mr. Singer said. "I'm sure Mira has already told you everything that witches know."

"It's my understanding that you helped us back," Gabriel said. "For that, I'm eternally grateful. How was it done?"

"Once again," Mr. Singer said, "I'm afraid I can't help you with that. Mr. Harker was the one that brought you all back. We only cast a few simple spells and fueled the overarching ritual."

"I'm not sure I understand what that means," Gabriel said.

"The spells we cast did not connect to the Ether. They did not bring you back. What Mr. Harker did, I'm not sure, but you couldn't really call it a spell."

"What would you call it if not a spell?" Ian asked.

"There are many kinds of magic beyond witchcraft and sorcery," Mr. Singer said. "Witchcraft wasn't the only magic involved."

"But it needed witches?" Gabriel asked.

"It's possible another kind of magic would have worked— I'm not certain. You'd have to ask Mr. Harker about that," Mr. Singer said. "The only thing I can say is that no witch knows what's needed to go to the Ether."

"Then why call in the witches?" Ian asked.

"Witches have a lot of power. Even then, it took three of us. It probably couldn't have been done without Barney, either," Mr. Singer said. "He did seem to act as a tether to the other world."

"You say that no other witches have the knowledge to get into the Ether," Gabriel said.

"That's correct," Mr. Singer said.

"How do you know?" Gabriel asked.

"I'm sorry?" Mr. Singer said, sounding unsure what direction the conversation was taking.

"I'm sure you know all of the local witches, but could one of them have hidden the knowledge away? Or another witch from out of town, could they have brought the spell with them?"

"No." Mr. Singer's voice was adamant.

Mira had to admit, until a few days ago she had been just as sure as Mr. Singer sounded.

"How can you be certain?" Gabriel pressed.

"It has been centuries since a witch has gone to the Ether. I'm sure Mira told you, but before we stopped going there, our entire population had been severely diminished. It might have taken a few decades to scour the world of information on how to enter the Ether, but I assure you that the witches destroyed all of their spells and knowledge of the Ether."

"She has mentioned something similar," Gabriel said, "but the fact is someone has been going there. Even worse, something has been traveling in the other direction."

"Excuse me?" Mr. Singer said, his voice rising an octave. "I'm not sure I understand what you mean."

"Something from the Ether came back into this world," Gabriel said.

"This is not something that witches should be involved in," Mr. Singer said. "I'm going to have to ask you to not spread this rumor around."

"It's not a rumor," Gabriel said. "Like it or not, it's a fact. One of those things—"

"I'm afraid I don't know what things you are referring to," Mr. Singer said. "This has nothing to do with our community."

"Someone has taken witches over there," Gabriel said. "You've seen that with your own eyes. Tyler, Andrea, Kevin, and Mira are all witches that have been there."

"I saw four witches brought back to us," Mr. Singer said. "And for that, I'm grateful. Beyond that, I know nothing. No one in our community knows anything."

"John Parnell—"

"Is human," Mr. Singer said. "As is Barney. I don't know what the humans have been doing."

Mira winced. It sounded like Mr. Singer was reducing things to 'us versus them.' That was never a good sign in a supernatural community.

"I have another engagement this evening," Mr. Singer said. Mira heard him stand up. "If you'd like to come back another time, I'll be happy to see you again."

The couch squeaked as the detectives rose.

"Like it or not, Mr. Singer, someone is trying to collect witches," Gabriel said. "We will be asking more questions."

"Thank you for the warning, Detective. We will be vigilant and on guard," Mr. Singer said, leading them to the hallway where Mira still stood. He passed her without a glance and opened the door for them.

Ian gave Mr. Singer a card before leaving. Mira bowed her head, not wanting to look at anyone. However, when she turned to leave, she was brought up short.

"Miss Owens. Since you are here, may I have a word?" Mr. Singer made the question sound more like a demand.

Mira felt like she was being hollowed out.

"We'll meet you in the car," Ian said.

Gabriel looked as if he wanted to say something else, but changed his mind.

Mira stared at the door as it snapped shut. She was unsure of what to say.

Mr. Singer strode into the other room. The thought of leaving passed through Mira's mind. It was a tempting option, but with a sigh, Mira followed the witch.

"As you know, there will be a gathering at the next full moon," Mr. Singer said. "Until then, if you have any dealings with witches, I'd like today to be a model of what is expected."

"I haven't done anything," Mira said.

She hadn't meant to say it—she had meant to agree—but that wasn't what popped out.

Mr. Singer was bent over his kitchen counter writing something down.

"I'm afraid that isn't for me or you to decide," he said, scribbling furiously.

"But you have a say," Mira said. "I haven't done anything to deserve this."

"What we think we deserve and what we perceive the world is giving us are often different things." He ripped a piece of paper out of his notebook and gave it to her.

What we perceive the world is giving us? Mira was trying to follow his logic. She knew her karma had been falling, but she didn't think it had fallen far enough for the whole world to turn against her.

She stared blankly at the address on the paper.

"There are proceedings and protocols that are important for you to know. Go to that address; let them know you are picking up a package."

"Why?" Mira asked, dully.

"Miranda," Mr. Singer said, stressing her name.

She looked up at him for the first time since she'd been sent to the hall.

"There are important protocols that you must know in this type of situation. Please go pick up this package before allowing the detectives to start stirring up trouble with the other witches."

He seemed to be pleading with her without saying it. Was he asking her to help him while they were discussing banishing her?

"I'm afraid the detectives will do what they feel is necessary," Mira said, a tinge of coolness in her voice.

"Yes, well, you'll help them better by going to that address first," Mr. Singer said. "Do not let anyone else know we discussed anything beyond protocols for your situation."

"That's all we did discuss," Mira said.

"True. Let me see you out."

Mira stared at the paper wishing he had said something more. He held the door open for her.

"You understand not to contact the other witches, correct?" Mr. Singer asked.

Mira glared at him. "I'm going to visit Tyler."

"I understand. Under the circumstances, that's fine, as long as no other witches are there with you, aside from Tyler."

"This isn't fair," Mira said, bouncing from angry to bitter and back again.

She knew it was a stupid thing to say.

"I'm sure things will turn out best in the end," Mr. Singer said. "Good day, Miss Owens."

Mira stared at the paper as the door swung shut behind her. She started blindly toward the car.

"What's going on?" Gabriel asked.

Mira jumped, becoming unsteady, and a foot slid out from under her. Gabriel steadied her before she even realized she was going to fall. When she was on firmer footing, she shrugged away his arm. She didn't want to, but maybe keeping Gabriel at a distance would be a good idea.

Maybe it would hurt less.

"It's witch business," Mira said, not quite striding to the car in case she slid again.

"Are you in some sort of trouble?" Gabriel asked.

"Do you care?" Mira clenched her fists, wanting to take back the words.

"We should talk," Gabriel said, sounding as though he were trying not to get aggravated.

"I need to go pick something up," Mira said. Once she reached the car, she didn't wait for a response before sliding into the back seat.

Gabriel took his time getting into the car, but Mira was determined to avoid his gaze.

"Who's next on the list?" Ian asked.

"Mr. Singer asked me to pick something up before we go see any of the other witches," Mira said.

"That's really not his call," Gabriel said, turning the car around.

"I think I need to get it," Mira said. "It's important."

"Important to the case?" Gabriel asked.

"Maybe," Mira said. "It's information I need before I go to any other witch's house."

"Where do you need to go?" Ian asked, trying to sound upbeat. "I'm sure we can swing by."

Mira passed him the piece of paper.

Ian didn't say anything, but looked at the paper for a while before handing it to Gabriel.

"This could take a while," Gabriel said.

"If you drop me off downtown, I can get a ride," Mira said.

"Want me to drop you off first?" Gabriel asked.

It took Mira a moment to realize he wasn't talking to her.

"Yeah," Ian said, "I'll grab some lunch and get some other work done."

Ian and Gabriel started talking about another case they were working on and, although she was vaguely interested at first, Mira tuned them out after a while.

Mr. Singer's words still ran through her head, along with what it meant to be shunned.

The note mentioned that others could talk with her if she was there with Gabriel and Ian, but would they? If she stood outside the room like a chastised child, wouldn't that make her appear guilty of something?

She hadn't done anything wrong, she was sure of that. It was possible that karma was playing against her. Ian had fought the spell like hell until Gabriel was brought into the secret. When Gabriel had come back from the Ether unconscious, Mira had been exhausted and apparently losing more blood than she'd realized. Had Ian fought against the spell again?

After thinking about what she would have done in his place, especially with chaos reigning and no one willing to call an ambulance, she figured it was a certainty.

The car door opened, then shut, and Mira looked around, seeing the darkness of a parking garage.

"You certainly seem lost in thought," Gabriel said.

She realized they were alone; Ian was already getting into his car.

"Yeah, I guess so," Mira said.

"Jump up front and we can go."

When Mira stepped into the cold chill of the garage, she shivered—and not just from the cold. The memories of the last time she had been in the garage, in the Ether, were still with her.

"How do you park in here every day?" Mira asked.

"I didn't for a while," Gabriel said. "With all the earthquakes, there were a few people who started parking on the streets. It's hard to grab a spot."

When the car left the dim space, Mira felt relieved. They had faced their first real fight in the Ether in the reflection of that parking garage.

"Your first day back to work," Mira mused. "It's good to know that you're feeling better."

She saw him grip the steering wheel, and then relax again.

"I'm glad to find you okay as well," Gabriel said. "I thought I'd see you sooner."

"Same here," Mira said. "Especially after a falling beam nearly killed me. I expected to see you then."

"What happened?" Gabriel asked.

"Doesn't matter. I appreciate you alerting the guard, though."

"Was that yesterday?" Gabriel asked.

"Doesn't matter," Mira said, looking back out the window. "We're both back. Andrea and Kevin are safe. Tyler—well, he will get better."

"They keep me updated about his condition," Gabriel said. "I wish people would stop asking me questions about the whole thing."

"What do you tell them?" Mira asked.

"I tell them I don't remember anything. It seemed the safest way."

"And Ian, what does he tell people?"

"Just that he found me unconscious."

"I'm glad you're okay."

"And you," Gabriel said. "I was worried when I didn't see you. Ian didn't say much, but he mentioned you hurt your arm."

Mira wondered how much she should tell him. "The doctor was able to stitch me up."

"You needed stitches? How many?"

"I never asked. Quite frankly, it freaks me out that I have threads holding my skin together."

"Ian didn't mention it was that bad," Gabriel said.

"It's no big deal," Mira said, "besides, he was busy."

"With what?"

Mira grinned weakly, trying to lighten the mood. "The last thing I remember was him yelling at Emmit. That's enough to keep anyone busy."

"I can't believe you moved in with him," Gabriel said.

"What?" So much for trying to lighten the mood.

"I woke up in the hospital to find out that you were already shacked up with him." He sounded more hurt than angry.

"Shacked up?" Mira heard her voice go shrill, but she couldn't help it.

He gripped the steering wheel and relaxed again. "Sorry. It's none of my business."

Mira didn't know if she was going to cry from frustration, confusion, or dejection. Whatever it was, she didn't want it to happen in front of Gabriel.

She needed another spell. Fortitude again, maybe? Bliss?

The thought of Bliss brought the idea to a halt. This was something she needed to work through without spells.

"Sorry," he said again.

"Did you try to call either of us?"

"I called you at home a few times, only to find out you weren't there. Emmit reached me after I got out of the hospital."

Mira groaned inwardly. "What did he say?"

"He thanked me for helping you, said there were no hard feelings," the bitterness was thick in his voice, "and told me I could come visit."

"But you didn't visit," Mira said.

"I didn't want to be there," Gabriel said.

"Oh." It was all Mira could think of to say.

"Not at his place." He sounded like he was struggling not to seem upset. "He made sure I had a number to call in case I realized something might go wrong."

"I guess that's when he set up the whole bodyguard thing."

"He said he would, since I wasn't about to come over there."

Mira was quiet, wondering which direction she wanted things to go. She wanted to yell at both of them.

Gabriel was silent for a short time. "I wish things were different."

Frustration rose, and Gabriel's words had pushed her down a path. "They would have been if you had come over."

"He said you were going to be okay," Gabriel said. "That's what I needed to know."

"Well, at least you got what you wanted."

CHAPTER 3

MIRA WASN'T SURE THERE was a way to salvage this, and at the moment, she was so aggravated that she wasn't sure she wanted to salvage anything.

"I think what I wanted wasn't there." Gabriel said it so softly that Mira wasn't even sure she'd heard it correctly.

It was enough to raise Mira's blood pressure. "Funny, I was thinking the same thing, because by the time I woke up, you and Emmit had already arranged things, and I was saddled with a bodyguard."

"I assumed—"

"You did the same thing Emmit did," Mira snapped.

Gabriel slowed and turned into what looked like an art district, although one that had lost the shiny new feel.

"I didn't intend—"

"Just forget about it," Mira said, staring out the window.

"But—"

"This looks like the place," Mira said. "Stop here and I'll jump out."

"I don't think that's a good idea," Gabriel said. Despite his words, he was pulling to a stop on the crowded street.

Mira opened the door as soon as the car stopped and stared at the place Mr. Singer had sent her. She had been expecting a postal place. Instead, he had sent her to a used bookstore. Before going in, Mira double-checked the address. She stepped inside looking incredulous. Little bells hooked to the door jingled.

The shop looked small at first, but as Mira slowly walked between the densely lined shelves, she saw gaps in the shelving showing other open doorways.

"Can I help you?" someone asked.

After hearing the young, disinterested voice, she was sure she was in the wrong place.

Mira retraced her steps and found a counter close to the door. It was so covered in books that she hadn't even noticed the register.

"Um, I was supposed to pick up a package and I was given this address." Mira had no real hope of finding what she needed here.

The girl rolled her eyes and pulled open a drawer. "Go back to the next room, make a right, and follow the wall till you reach the door."

It was a normal key on an old-fashioned, plastic, avocado-green key chain that looked stolen from a hotel back in the seventies.

As Mira stepped into the next room, the doorbells jingled again. The girl up front started chatting away, but Mira ignored it. When Mira was forced to turn a corner, Gabriel caught up with her.

"What are you picking up here?" Gabriel asked.

"I have no idea," Mira said, looking at the spines of books, purposefully avoiding eye contact with Gabriel.

"Can we talk?" Gabriel asked.

"No," Mira said, still not letting him catch her eye. When she turned another corner, she spotted the door, which was a welcome sight. "This is what I'm looking for."

It was an old door with white paint peeling back to show other layers of paint.

The key had to be jiggled in the lock before it caught and turned. The door swung in, and Mira found herself walking into a room filled with the smoke and smell of incense.

Gauzy, multicolored strips of cloth hid the room's interior. Mira hesitated before pushing them aside, picturing all sorts of dangers, magical and otherwise, hidden in the room.

When Mira bumped against Gabriel, she realized she had taken a step back.

"Let me—"

Mira cut him off. "It's fine." She had to force herself to step forward again. It wasn't fear that made her want to stay where she was. The feeling of Gabriel directly behind her made her warm, and she wanted him to put his arms around her far more than she cared to admit. "I don't think Mr. Singer would send me anywhere dangerous. It would spoil all their fun of putting me on trial."

"Are you in some sort of trouble?" Gabriel asked, keeping his voice low.

"No," Mira said automatically as she pushed the fabric aside to a gloomy room beyond.

Out of the corner of her eye, she saw Gabriel rub his forehead, looking agitated. She ignored it, instead paying closer attention to the books in the room.

"So, you are in trouble," Gabriel said. "What for?"

"Do you really need to call me out every time I say something that's not true?"

"I told you, it's like fingernails running down a chalkboard when you lie."

There were fewer books in this room, and all of them that she saw looked ancient. Some sat alone on a shelf or little pedestal, while others shared a shelf with a few others, each spaced out so that they never touched. Mira took a closer look at one of the books. The title across the spine was in a runic language that looked familiar.

"So," Gabriel said quietly.

"So, what?" Mira asked, reaching out to stroke the spine of the aged book.

"What kind of trouble are you in?"

"Oh, he is a pretty one," came the deep voice of a man, hidden in the shadows. "Shut the door behind you. The last time a human wandered in here, they made such a mess of things."

"I was, uh, sent here to pick up a package?" Mira hadn't intended for it to come out as a question, but it did.

"So you're the one they've been talking about," the man said.

"Probably," she said in defeat.

As she approached the voice, the haze in the room thickened. She found herself in front of a large man, both in height and in width, with skin that appeared as dark as pitch in the dim light.

There was a book perched on a stand that caught her eye as she approached. Since he obviously knew who she was, she wasn't in a hurry to listen to what others might have been saying about her. The script across the cover was so worn that it was illegible, but something about it called to her. She reached out, but the sensation of pins and needles broke across her hand, forcing her to stop before touching it. Gabriel was a second behind, yanking her arm away.

Mira felt her heart beat faster at his touch and didn't rush to pull away.

"Oh, he's good," the man said, eyeing Gabriel. "Usually I stick to humans, but I think I'd stray back to supernaturals for a chance at you."

"You know I'm not human?" Gabriel asked, not responding to the rest.

"Oh, yes," came that rich voice, "but I haven't met anything like you before."

"Huh." Gabriel sounded disappointed.

"So," the man continued, "what are you, and are there more?"

Mira's eyes narrowed in on the man.

"I thought you couldn't ask that," Gabriel said.

"Oh, there's a lot you can do when you're on the fringes," the man said. "But when people need you, there's a lot they are willing to put up with."

"Who are you?" Mira asked.

"You can call me Chris," he said, then addressed Gabriel again, "but you can call me tonight."

"Sorry," Gabriel said, smoothly. "I'm unavailable."

"Oh, that is the story of my life," Chris said.

"Do you own this store?" Mira asked.

"I own the books," Chris said. "If you find yourself alone after the next new moon, you can call on Chris."

"If things go that way," Mira muttered, "I think they expect others not to help me. I'll have to go at it alone."

"Oh, that's the joy of being on the outside and having something they need," Chris said.

"I don't think I have anything they need," Mira said. "Nothing unique, anyway."

"Oh, honey, you are swimming in power, and that's not easy to come by," Chris said. "I'm not sure they could lock that strength away, even if they put a full thirteen together, unless your friend here will lend them his strength."

"Gabriel won't be," Mira said. "I mean, he wouldn't."

"No one may even get the chance to try if you don't get out from under that cloud," Chris said.

Mira blinked at him and stared, waiting for an explanation.

"The karma, honey. It's like a giant black weight pressing down. You're gonna have to clean that up."

"I thought it was getting better," Mira said.

"Oh," Chris said, nodding, "it's storing up something big for you. Better keep tall, blond, and gorgeous by your side."

"Can you see it?" Mira asked.

Chris cocked his head and gave her a little smile. "I have what you came for, right here." He picked a brown paper bag off the shelf next to him and handed it over.

Mira felt gloomy taking the package. Whatever it was, it couldn't be good.

"You have two days with this, and then you must return it," Chris said. "And bring your friend back with you. I like a big strong man around."

"All these books," Mira said, looking at another, "are they all about witches and witchcraft?"

"Just my little collection," Chris said.

"Are they for sale?" Mira asked.

"Occasionally," Chris said, "when I feel up to letting one go to a good home."

"Isn't all the smoke bad for them?" Mira asked.

"Not at all," Chris said. "The smoke is what keeps them hidden. It keeps all my darling books safe."

Mira had never heard such a thing. How would smoke hide anything?

"You run along," Chris said. "You have what you need. Mr. Singer will want you to read that carefully. More importantly, you're going to want to know what's in there."

"Thanks," Mira said, not feeling remotely convinced that she wanted to read whatever she had been given. Mr. Singer had been adamant that she know the protocols, but if there were enough of them to fill a book, she wasn't going to like it.

"Give the key to the girl, but if anyone asks, you don't know me, and you don't know this store," Chris said. For the first time, he sounded stern instead of playful. "See you in two days."

Mira couldn't help but glance at different titles on her way to the real store. She practically gulped in the fresh air.

She dropped the key off without a word and stepped out into the frigid winter. Gabriel led the way to the car. Thankfully, he was silent.

Mira ran her gloved hands over the package as Gabriel started the car and cranked up the heat.

"What's next?" Gabriel asked.

The paper crinkled in her hand as she squeezed it. "You can drop me off at Emmit's. I think I need to read this before we go see anyone else."

Gabriel sighed. "Why are you staying there?"

Mira looked at him sharply. It was the first time she'd really looked at him since entering the store.

"I guess it's none of my business." He put the car in gear and moved into the light traffic.

"Where else was I supposed to go?" Mira asked.

"Home?" Gabriel suggested.

"You think I should go home? It was easy enough for John to get in there once. I doubt he'll have any trouble a second time."

"Your parents' house? Maybe your sister's house? Hell, a hotel room would be better."

Mira gripped the package again before smoothing the brown paper back out. "I can't go to my family. I can't go anywhere. My store's been gone for almost two weeks now. That's a lot of money going out with nothing coming in. I don't even have a car."

"Why can't you go to your family?" Gabriel asked.

"I—" Mira stopped, not knowing how to continue. How do you tell someone you'd been shunned? It was so rare, and banishment hadn't been heard of in her lifetime. Even with all the trouble she had in college, they'd never contemplated banishing her. "Besides, the doctor has everything he needs there."

Gabriel was quiet for a few moments. "I feel like I'm missing a lot."

"It's not a big deal," Mira said.

Gabriel winced but said nothing. He drove them across the city to the towering skyscraper that held Emmit's apartment.

Mira embraced the silence. After a while, she took a chance and peeked into the bag. The book looked old with a blue cloth cover. What was the worst that could happen if she didn't read the book? She carefully closed the top and folded it down, making a hard crease before folding it again and again.

Mr. Singer and even Chris had been adamant that she read the book, but they couldn't make her read it. They couldn't make her jump through their hoops, right?

Then again, why not read it?

Gabriel slammed on his brakes and his arm shot out, catching her across the chest. Mira looked up, her heart pounding as she searched for whatever catastrophe was coming for her.

Horns blared from behind them, but Mira saw nothing.

Gabriel lowered his arm, but it was only to grab her hand. "Something's wrong."

"I gathered," Mira said over the increasingly persistent horn blaring.

Mira's heart was starting to slow, but the reprieve was brief. The world started to move. Mira's breath caught as she watched the skyscrapers sway. Ahead of them, where their car might have been if they hadn't stopped, a fireball billowed out of a store.

"Shit," Gabriel said, trying to look everywhere at once. "It had to be a gas line. Either that or a giant meth lab."

The ground stopped shuddering below them. The towers swayed slightly back into place. Some of the windows were broken out, but the buildings stood. In front of them, one store was engulfed in flames. The fire that had leapt across the street was hard at work on a parked car.

"It's done," Gabriel said. "At least I think it is. We're okay."

Mira shook and looked around, worried another unknown threat might jump out at her. Gabriel twisted in his seat and rubbed her hand. She realized she still had a death grip on his other hand. Although she loosened her grip, she wasn't ready to let go. It was a small comfort and she needed it.

Sirens were blaring from all directions. Looking behind them, she saw that cars were turning around in the street, ready to find another route or flee the city. Mira heard her cell phone ring in the depths of her purse, but she ignored it.

Little by little, she began to relax.

Gabriel's phone also began to ring. He dug around in his pocket, glanced at the screen, and then answered it with one hand, unwilling to let her go.

"Yes," he said.

He listened intently to the other end. Fire trucks were arriving in front of them, rushing in from the other direction.

"Got it," he said. "Yeah, we'll pick it up tomorrow."

Gabriel hung up, and his phone almost immediately rang again.

He let go of her hand and drew back. "It's Emmit." Gabriel jabbed at the screen as though trying to smash the little green symbol that flashed on it.

"What?" Gabriel growled into the phone.

Mira watched the devastation outside as an ambulance and police arrived.

"Yes, we're fine." There was a long pause, and then he said, "Right," and hung up.

"What did he want?" Mira asked.

"Wait here," Gabriel said.

He stepped out of the car and went to the officer that had driven around them and parked to block their path. Gabriel flashed his badge. There was a lot of pointing and some conversation. The officer spoke into his radio a few times, and then they watched the firemen work for a short time before Gabriel came back to the car.

Gabriel turned the car around and drove back the way they had come.

All the traffic lights were out, which was never good downtown.

They had crawled down a few streets before Mira spoke up.

"Thank you," she said.

"You're welcome," Gabriel said.

Neither of them looked at the other.

"I have a question," Gabriel said after a while. "When something like this occurs, does it release some of the negative karma that builds up?"

"A little," Mira said. "But nothing happened, so probably not a lot."

"Nothing happened? We were almost roasted."

"But we weren't."

"So, the only way to get rid of all this bad karma is to let bad things happen to you?"

"No. Some of it goes away on its own if it's not being actively increased. Good karma also helps reduce it."

"This must have reduced it some, right?"

"Like I said, it probably reduced it a little, but a giant metal beam almost crushed me the other day and this still happened. It doesn't get rid of enough to make a difference."

Gabriel was quiet until they were stopped by an officer directing traffic. "Tell me about these bodyguards Emmit has for you."

Mira shrugged. "They're not bad, but if Emmit doesn't call them off, I really am going to have to find somewhere else to stay."

"I'm not fond of Emmit, but I thought he had a good idea in keeping them around."

"It's creepy, especially when I wake up in the middle of the night and see them."

"What are they doing in your room?"

"They're always with me, except in the bathroom. Even then, I think they're listening at the door. This is the first break I've had from them since I woke up."

"You mentioned that earlier. Ian said you were okay when we got back. Nothing serious."

Mira sighed and rubbed her head, knowing she couldn't lie and just tell him she was fine. "I passed out before they called the ambulance. I was technically awake the next day, but I wasn't coherent."

"Passed out? I know you were tired, but—"

"Exhausted, dehydrated, and faint from blood loss. It all added up. After a transfusion and rest, I was better. Well, I was lucid, anyway."

CHAPTER 4

MIRA PEEKED AT GABRIEL and saw that he looked miserable. She quickly turned to look out the window again.

"Did you lose a lot of blood on the other side?" Gabriel asked.

"I don't remember. I guess so."

"Can they use it? I mean, are you safe here when those things in the Ether have your blood?"

"I don't think we have to worry about that," Mira said.

"But you said—"

"It's gone," Mira broke in. "I scorched the place." Memories welled up. The smell of burning flesh and blackened bodies threatened to swamp her before she could push it away. "They all died."

"I'm pretty sure they filled Lance's house. Its reflection, anyway."

"Lance's house isn't there anymore. In the Ether, I mean. There was part of a wall that survived. The rest is gone."

"Is that all I'm missing?" Gabriel asked.

Mira said nothing and was extremely grateful for the distraction when the officer let them start moving again.

"You said you couldn't go to your family." Gabriel seemed to be running down a mental list.

"That's right."

"Are you worried about them getting caught up in this? I mean, I wouldn't blame you if you were."

"I'm more worried they wouldn't open the door." Tiredness began to fog her mind. "My sister probably would, but she has kids. Like you said, I can't get them caught up in this."

"Why wouldn't they let you in?" Gabriel asked.

"You're not going to drop this, are you?"

"I'm a detective. This is what I do."

"Well, at least we know you're good at your job."

There were a few moments of silence, which Gabriel broke. "If you tell me what's going on, then maybe I can help."

"You can't," Mira said.

"It will at least give me an idea of what's happening. That'll keep me from doing or saying something stupid."

A ghost of a smile flickered across her face, but it was gone in a breath. "I've been shunned." It wasn't as blunt as she'd intended, but at least it was out there.

"What does that mean?" Gabriel asked.

"It means that no witch should talk to me. If I contact anyone, they're supposed to ignore me. I can be present if you and or Ian are there because it's part of the case. Aside from that, there shouldn't be any contact with other witches."

"They can't do that," Gabriel said.

Mira rolled her eyes. "Of course they can."

"Is that the trial thing Chris was talking about?"

"Sort of, although it sounds like they may be deciding then if they are banishing me or not."

Gabriel gripped the steering wheel. "And what does that mean?"

"Two hundred years ago, they would have bound my powers and chased me out of town with sticks and torches."

"And now?"

"They'll probably ask me to leave."

"What about your magic—would they bind that?"

Mira snorted. "They could try. Without Tyler helping, they wouldn't be able to."

"Chris mentioned something about thirteen witches together."

"They'd have to be desperate to try that. There are a few ways it could work, but every one of the thirteen has to really, really want it to happen, and if there isn't a good enough reason to justify it, the karmic backlash is big."

"Like what's happening with you because you bound Ian?"

"I'm not sure all of my bad karma has to do with Ian." The idea had been rolling around in the back of her mind since she had left Chris's store.

Gabriel stayed quiet, but glanced at her a few times while she tried to work her way through and around the idea.

"Ian isn't fighting the spell much anymore, though he did when you came back. I'm sure he beat hard against the spell at that point, but I don't think that lasted long. If you were still in the dark about everything, it might be getting close to what Chris described, but I get the feeling this is bigger than binding Ian should have caused."

"What else could cause it?" Gabriel asked.

"I'm not sure. Maybe the same thing the witches are so ticked off about."

"Which is?"

Mira closed her eyes and laid her head back on the seat. "I have no idea. It has to have something to do with the Ether."

"But nothing that has happened there has been your fault," Gabriel said.

Not knowing for sure if that was true or not, she said nothing.

"They can't do this to you," Gabriel said, picking up his earlier mantra.

"They can and they are," Mira said.

"What's Emmit doing about this?"

"Emmit? Nothing. He's not a witch."

"But he's a Harker, whatever the hell that means."

"It means nothing in a community of witches. He could say a few words to the council, but they can't do anything either. Witch business is witch business."

"Okay, then I'll go talk to them."

"There's nothing you can do, either."

"If I could do here what I can in the Ether, I could make them listen."

"Don't you dare! As far as they know, you're a human helping out. Emmit and Mr. Singer are the only ones who are aware you're something more. And Chris, I guess."

"They'll know what I am by the time I'm done."

Mira cracked a smile. "I know you're trying to help, but you can't—not really."

He fumed from the driver's seat.

Mira put a hand on his leg, as close to the knee as she could reach without it looking awkward. "I appreciate your sentiment, but let the witches do what they're going to do."

When she sat back, Gabriel grabbed her hand before it got far. This time, when she smiled at him, he looked back at her and matched her expression. Briefly, she gripped his hand before pulling away.

"Where are we going?" Mira asked, seeing that their slow progress was starting to move them out of the city. She watched for a while before closing her eyes and leaning back again.

"The elevator is out in your building," Gabriel said. "I figured we should grab a late lunch or early dinner before we decide to walk up twenty flights of stairs."

"Sounds good to me," Mira said, not opening her eyes. The noise of the catastrophe around them slowly began to fade away.

When Gabriel turned the car off, Mira jolted awake.

"Where are we?" Mira asked.

"The Landing," Gabriel said. "I think the only meals we've had together have been on the go or carry-out at your place, so I thought we'd try this instead."

The large lake behind the restaurant was covered with ice floating in sheets.

"I didn't even know this place was open in the winter," Mira said.

"There's no boat traffic, but it doesn't close for the off season," Gabriel said.

The cold air slapped Mira across the face when she stepped out of the car. Wind off the lake made the temperature feel even lower than it had been in the city. Inside, however, the restaurant was warmer than Mira had expected. The boat and lighthouse motif of the place made her long for summer.

Since the Landing was well known for boaters, their casual attire fit in, even in the dead of winter. After they were seated and given menus, the warmth of the room soaked in, making Mira yawn.

"Sorry I fell asleep." She momentarily worried that she had snored, but then figured it didn't really matter.

"It looked like you needed it," Gabriel said. "Besides, it gave me time to think a few things over."

Things had gotten so far skewed for her and Gabriel that Mira was a little worried about his train of thought.

"Have you considered leaving town?" Gabriel asked.

Mira's train completely derailed. "No."

He must have seen something in her face, because he rushed on. "Just until this mess has been sorted out. I don't want you to go—"

"Good," Mira said, "because I'm not."

"You'd be safe," Gabriel said.

"Karma isn't going to take a vacation just because I do."

"Someone could go with you," Gabriel said. "I'm sure Reinfield's men go where the job takes them."

"Great, so I can travel a hundred miles away, where I know no one, and have a stranger standing at the foot of my bed while I sleep. No thanks."

"I'll talk with Emmit. I didn't know that was going on."

"So far, it hasn't mattered what I've said. Emmit won't budge on it."

"Does he think someone is going to sneak up to his floor, break in, and then, what, walk through walls to avoid the guard at the door?"

"I've tried that," Mira said. "He reminded me that there are supernaturals that wouldn't be slowed down by walls."

That seemed to give Gabriel pause. "There are?"

"Yeah, in fact, I think one of the victims might have been able to do that."

"Who?"

"Karen Green, the banshee. I can't say for sure—it's only a rumor."

"I thought you all don't share rumors."

"Not anymore," Mira said. "We've learned a few lessons from the past. Still, witches pass grimoires down through the generations. They aren't all nice safe spells."

"I still don't think it's right for you to have to have Reinfield's men in your room," Gabriel said. "I'll talk to Emmit."

"I wish you better luck than I've had."

A waitress approached. While Gabriel chatted with the woman, Mira scanned the menu, before they ordered.

"He could be trying to overcompensate," Gabriel said when the waitress was out of hearing range.

"What?" Mira said, feeling like she'd missed something.

"Emmit. He could be trying to overcompensate for... you know."

"You mean trying to get me killed?"

"That wasn't intentional."

Mira raised her eyebrows. "You're on his side now?"

"God, no," Gabriel said. "I just meant, maybe the guards are his way of apologizing."

"It's possible," Mira said, not liking the new direction of conversation.

"Maybe he thinks you and he could—"

"There's not," Mira said. "He lost any chance of that when he told you I was already dead."

"Does he know that?"

"Yes." Mira twisted in her seat, wishing she could change the subject. "He's the one that said it, although I agreed with him."

Gabriel nodded and looked like he was trying to hide the fact that he was pleased.

"Can we change the subject?" Mira asked, trying not to sound like she was pleading.

"No."

Mira's mouth almost dropped open by the simple answer.

"Sorry," Gabriel said, quickly. "What I meant is that there's a reason why I wanted to know."

That sounded more promising to Mira, but she only nodded.

"I want to use you."

"What?" Mira was louder than intended.

"Shit, that came out wrong."

Mira put her elbows on the table and began to rub her temples with both hands.

"I want to use you against Emmit."

She sighed. "Do you think that sounds better?"

"Not really. Look, Emmit knows more about the Ether and this whole mess, but he won't tell me anything."

"And you want me to, what, seduce the answers out of him?"

"No. Don't even joke about that. I just want you to ask him the questions—with me there, of course. You may not get any further than I did, but I'd like us to try. If you don't mind, that is."

"We can do that," Mira said. "But can it be tomorrow?"

Gabriel smiled. "Of course. You look beat and I'm not far behind you. If I had known how bad you had been hurt in the Ether, I never would have dragged you out today."

"I was getting out of there today one way or the other," Mira said with a sleepy smile.

When the food arrived, Mira perked up a little. Food slowed down their conversation but didn't stop it.

"If you want to take it easy tomorrow, Ian and I can do the interviews on our own," Gabriel offered.

"I think you'll have better luck with me there." Mira's gaze went to her purse, where she had stowed the book. "Even if I'm standing in the corner."

"I'm sorry the witches are treating you this way," Gabriel said. "Are you sure there's nothing I can do?"

"If I find something, I'll let you know," Mira said.

"Are you going to read that whole book tonight?" Gabriel asked.

"I'm not even sure what it is," Mira said. "Not really, anyway."

She pushed her plate away before taking the book out of its bag. The cover was blue cloth, and there was no title on the cover or spine. Inside, was a title page with Shunned, Banished, and Bound written in type slightly larger than International Realignment for the Twentieth Century.

"It looks old," Gabriel said.

"It sounds like it was written over a hundred years ago," Mira said.

Flipping through the pages, she found a flower pressed between two pages. The page showed the beginning of a new chapter entitled Trial Preparation for Banishment.

The book snapped shut and Mira dropped it on the table before slumping back in her seat. "I can't believe this is happening."

"Am I allowed to read it?" Gabriel asked.

"I'm not sure there's any more trouble I could get into at this point."

Gabriel picked up the book and flipped through it, pausing here and there to scan a page. He, too, stopped at the flower.

"Does this represent anything?" Gabriel asked.

"Probably a bookmark left behind by the last poor witch who found need of the protocols." She added as much scorn as she could into the word, but felt that it still fell short.

"So it's not magical in any way?"

"Not by itself."

He scanned a few more pages before handing the book back. "There has to be a reason for all this."

Mira dropped the book back into the paper bag and shoved it in her purse. "I'm sure I've given them enough reasons over the years."

"Is there anything positive about this? The process, the results, the aftermath—does any of it have an upside?"

"I don't see how, but I guess I'll find out," Mira said. "Sorry to put a crimp in your day. I know you wanted to get more done."

"The earthquake would have stopped our interviews anyway."

"Do you think that the earthquakes are being caused by what's happening on the other side?" Mira asked.

"That world seems to be the reflection," Gabriel said, "but who knows really?"

The screech of the monster in the city of the Ether was vivid in Mira's mind. Each time, it had been accompanied by an earthquake. Was it crying because of the earthquake, or was the screeching causing it?

Gabriel paid for the meal, and when Mira tried to argue, he changed the subject.

"You said you and Emmit talked after you got back," Gabriel said.

It was enough to stop Mira's protests.

"Um, yeah, it seemed necessary since he had taken me in." Mira could feel her face heat up, so she led the way out of the restaurant, hoping to keep it hidden from Gabriel. Once outside, she wrapped her coat more tightly around herself.

"You said he lost any chance of being with you," Gabriel said.

Mira tried not to audibly sigh. Gabriel seemed intent on picking things apart. "I said that, yes."

"Have I?" Gabriel asked.

Mira stopped, ignoring the cold beating against her. "Have you... what?" She wanted to make sure she understood Gabriel before she stuck her foot in her mouth. It seemed as if he'd been saying things she hadn't expected all day.

"Have I lost any chance? You said it yourself. I did the same thing he did. When I woke up, I assumed the worst and left you alone."

It wasn't possible to take those words back. "Emmit almost got me killed because of his arrogance. You just..." She didn't know how to finish that. Saying he ticked her off didn't seem like the right direction for the conversation.

They stopped at his car, but neither of them reached for the door.

"I left you alone to deal with all this," Gabriel said. "And then there was the Ether."

"Why should the Ether be a factor?" Mira asked, trying to choose her words carefully.

"I don't really remember what happened. One moment we were there, and the next, I was waking up in the hospital. I feel like I let you down."

"That's crazy. You wouldn't even have been in the Ether if not for me. The only reason anyone survived is because you were there."

"I should have called you."

Mira agreed, but figured it probably wasn't the right thing to say. "You haven't lost your chance." She wouldn't have been able to forgive herself if she didn't tell him.

Gabriel broke the moment that had been stirring between them when he opened Mira's car door. "I should get you back."

CHAPTER 5

HAD SHE SAID SOMETHING wrong? He had asked the question. The big question. She had been waiting for this type of sign from him for ages. She'd told him he still had a chance, that he hadn't blown it, and she'd received nothing in return.

Traffic moving toward the city was light. Apparently, no one was in a rush to go back into a city that had been struck, once again, by an earthquake. There was still congestion in the streets, but the chaos had been extinguished.

"Did Ian get called back in to work?" Mira asked, trying to think of some sort of small talk.

"He was still on duty," Gabriel said.

"Do you think he'll be done in time for his date with Della tonight?"

"I think it will take a lot to make him miss his date. I'm not sure an earthquake would do the trick."

"I get the feeling that Della is thinking along the same lines." Della's anticipation of the date made Mira hopeful for the future. Della had planned on leaving work at a normal time tonight, which was a huge change for the lawyer.

"What about you?" Mira asked. "Do you have any plans for the night?"

The gaping silence after the question made Mira want to squirm in her seat, but she sat still and forced herself not to fill the silence.

"Not really." His words did nothing to fill the void left by his lack of response.

He had a date? Mira wondered if she should ask, but she didn't think she could pull off asking it in a joking, 'we're all good friends here,' kind of way.

"You?" he asked.

"The book."

"Oh, yeah."

"I think it'll keep me busy."

Gabriel drove into a parking structure nearby Emmit's apartment.

"You could drop me off out front if you need to be somewhere." The hint wasn't very subtle, Mira had to admit, but she was honestly curious as to what Gabriel had in mind for the night.

And why had he dropped their earlier conversation?

"I'm where I need to be," Gabriel said, not missing a beat this time.

Mira couldn't stop her lips from curling up, but she looked out the window, trying to hide the fact she was happy with his response.

"Do you think the elevator is fixed?" Mira asked.

"He sent me a text earlier," Gabriel said. "If it wasn't fixed, I would have found something else for us to do."

When Gabriel turned off the car, the chilled air began to slip in before the doors were even open.

Mira tugged her phone out of her purse before she got out of the car and saw that she hadn't received any messages from Emmit.

"I don't blame you," Mira said as she got out of the car. "I wasn't looking forward to them either."

"Ah, but you'd be stuck with me."

"I like being stuck with you." She wasn't too sure that she should have said it, but she was glad it was out.

"It just sucks that I have to take you back to his place."

Mira hugged her coat closer to her. It seemed that they were getting down to the real issue.

"But, it's for the best," Gabriel continued before she could say anything in her defense.

"Is it?" Mira asked, surprised by the sudden turnaround.

"Yeah, he can protect you when I can't."

"I'll be okay once I get back on my feet."

"How so?"

"I haven't done any magic since we've been back. If I put a few spells together, I can keep myself safe. At least for a while." In the back of her mind, a voice shrieked that she'd only be safe until the other witches cut her off. Although, she had sworn to others that her people couldn't bind her, she wasn't exactly sure. A week ago, she would have thought none of them could open a path to the Ether, either.

They waited for the light to turn green before they crossed the street. Gabriel was starting to pay close attention to the cars around them.

When the light turned green, Mira stepped off the curb and took two steps before she slid on the ice. She sucked in cold air in surprise, but Gabriel caught her as though it were a matter of course. Gabriel had her halfway across the street before her heart caught up with the fact that she was no longer falling.

"Thanks," she said when they were back on the sidewalk.

"Stay with him," Gabriel said.

"What?" It came out far too shrill, but she didn't care.

"Until we know John is gone, stay in Emmit's apartment."

"What? All day you've been complaining because I'm there."

"You're still a target. All the witches are, really. But John wanted you for a reason."

"Not five minutes ago you said it sucks that I was going back to Emmit's."

"It does, but it also keeps you safe, so stay with him."

Emotions bubbled over. It sounded as if he was trying to tell her what to do. Even worse, he seemed to be pushing her away.

Mira yanked the door of the building open, walked rigidly across the lobby, and then jabbed the button several times. She tried not to look at Gabriel, and when she caught a glance, she wished she had tried a lot harder. He seemed miserable.

Dammit, this wasn't her fault. She chided herself for wanting to tell him it was okay.

When the door opened, she was about to relent and let Gabriel off the hook, but there was a man in the elevator. He had been her first bodyguard and it looked like he'd drawn the short straw again. Seeing one of Reinfield's men only stoked her anger. The man held the door open, as though worried it might close before she got in.

She pummeled the button before he got the chance to push it for her.

"And you are?" Gabriel asked, eying the man up and down.

"Thomas," he said.

"Why were you waiting in the elevator, Thomas?" Gabriel asked.

Thomas nodded at Mira, who was glaring at both of them, and said nothing.

Mira's mouth turned into a cruel smile. "Thomas was waiting for me the moment I got out of bed the other day."

Gabriel frowned and seemed to give the man even more attention.

The doors opened and Mira rolled her eyes, shook her head, and went to the apartment. Another man waited at the apartment door, opening it before anyone else had the chance to do so.

Mira strode by and went to the living room, where she found Emmit, pacing.

"Where have you been?" Emmit asked, looking cross.

"Excuse me?" Mira dropped her purse on the table and put her hand on her hips.

"I'm sorry," Emmit said, changing his tone. "We lost track of you on your way out of town after the earthquake. I was concerned."

"What do you mean 'lost track of me'?"

"Not me personally," Emmit said.

Mira had had enough. "You had me followed?"

"In case you needed assistance," Emmit said.

"Next time, pick up a phone if you want to know where I am," Mira said.

"I reached out to Gabriel," Emmit said, glancing at the man.

"If you want to know where I am, ask me, not him," Mira said.

"I anticipated Gabriel might prefer that I reach out to him," Emmit said.

Mira glared from one man to the other. She wanted to yell at both of them, but she was afraid she'd be the one who would look like the idiot in the end.

"Whatever," Mira said at last. "Thank you for the ride, Gabriel." She snatched up her purse and started out of the room. When her shadow moved with her, she halted and crossed her arms. "Oh, no you don't, Thomas. You follow me and I'll curse you so bad you'll wish there was no tomorrow."

He remained impassive in his stance, but Mira could see the determination in his eyes.

She took a few more steps and stopped when she noticed movement again. Her hands balled into fists.

"Thomas," Emmit called. "May I have a word?"

Mira actually heard his sigh of relief and she finished storming off, feeling like her exit had lost its effectiveness when she'd threatened Thomas. It wasn't like it was his fault.

"You and I need to talk as well," Mira heard Gabriel say as she escaped.

Back in her room, she made sure to lock the door behind her. When the lock clicked, something broke loose inside her. Anger fell away, leaving resentment and depression in its wake. It didn't help that it felt awkward in the room now that she was alone. Putting the two men out of her head was difficult, but when she pulled the book out of her purse, she managed.

Mira dropped the book on her bed, though it dragged at her attention until she went to the bathroom, her sanctuary, where she found the only privacy she'd had in a few days.

Mr. Singer had pressed her to learn the protocols, but why should she? Looking back, Mira knew she hadn't done anything wrong except offer to help in the first place. John might be doing worse things had she not bound Ian.

It all boiled down to being in the Ether. Since she had been there, Mira knew how bad it was, and why witches should never be allowed to go to the Ether, but it wasn't like she had a choice. They had to see that, right?

Before she realized it, Mira needed to dry her eyes. She put a cold damp cloth on them for a few minutes and tried to shift her train of thought away from that great chasm of dreariness. It was time to pull herself back together.

There had to be a reason, a real reason, that Mr. Singer was doing this. He wasn't telling her everything, but he had sent her for the book.

When she wandered out of the bathroom, she was surprised at still finding herself alone. The book waited for her, so she flopped down on the bed next to it and started to read.

Dull was her first impression. It was also her second and third. It was written like a legal document, except without the legalese.

The person or persons implicated must have committed a breach that threatened exposure or is deemed inappropriate by the witches local or at large. Once a transgression is suspected, the accused can be shunned without evidence for no longer than one lunar cycle.

The book droned on and on. The witches' conclave had pummeled down each tradition, exception, and clause, and forced them to work together. Mira had expected to find out what it was she was supposed to be doing, but it appeared to be the one thing they left out. The only hint was on the marked page.

Once the accused is officially shunned, all witches must disregard the person or persons. Until the tribunal has gathered, the accused's existence is not to be realized. The local power has the authority to alter the severity of this action in extreme circumstances.

Mira sniffed and closed the book with a snap. She knew that you had to ignore someone shunned, but according to this, Mira no longer existed in the eyes of the witches. Unless Ian or Gabriel was around, which somehow made it worse.

Why in the hell should I bother to help if I don't exist? Why should I risk more negative karmic buildup?

Her heart felt squeezed. Then Mira thought about her mother. Even if she were found innocent at the tribunal, she'd never hear the end of it, and her dad, he must have been so disappointed in her at that point.

Seeing the severity of the protocols, Mira was surprised Robin had reached out to her at all. Her sister was straight and narrow, especially when it came to witchcraft, but Robin was willing to stand by Mira.

Mira toyed with the idea of opening the book again to see what happens when a shunned is allowed back into the fold, but it seemed as though the book already wanted the shunned to be non-existent.

I haven't done anything wrong. The idea burned through her and she snatched the book up, ready to throw it across the room. As she heaved the book back, a memory of Chris popped into her mind. He didn't seem like the type of guy to forgive for any damage to one of his books quickly.

Mira tried to rein in her frustrations and tossed the book gently on the bedside table. Looking around the room only aggravated her more. Home was where she belonged, not in Emmit's towering apartment.

However, home was no longer safe. The people after her wouldn't ignore her existence. In fact, they'd use the shunning to their advantage if they discovered it.

Maybe magic would make her feel better. Chris had mentioned that even with the full thirteen they might not be able to bind her power. It was hers, and since she no longer existed, they couldn't even try to take it away until the trial.

Mira may not be able to live at her apartment, but she planned on visiting. It was time to get back to what she was good at.

As Mira got ready the next day, she marveled that she'd woken up alone in her room. She had assumed one of Reinfield's men would have entered in the night. When she was ready to face the day, she found someone waiting for her in the hallway.

Mira couldn't remember the man's name, so settled for, "Good morning."

"Good morning, ma'am. If there is anything you need assistance with, please let me know."

"The only thing I need right now is breakfast." When Mira moved toward the kitchen, the man followed, but not as closely as many of the others, for which Mira was grateful.

They had just reached the door to the kitchen when cold energy began to vibrate the air erratically. Mira gripped her stomach and abandoned the thought of breakfast. Frowning, she moved to the living room.

For once, she wasn't greeted by raised voices of Emmit and Gabriel, but the men were definitely clashing.

"If I could have persuaded them, I would have already done so," Emmit said.

"You should try anyway," Gabriel said.

"What's going on this time?" Mira asked.

The two eased back from one another and the charged atmosphere began to diminish.

Emmit glanced up at Mira's guard and motioned the man away.

"I was trying to explain to Gabriel that the witches are not going to listen to me in this situation," Emmit said.

"What situation?" Mira asked.

"Yours," Gabriel said. "He could at least try to talk them around."

"What's done is done," Mira said, trying not to get upset at the reminder. "Leave the witches alone. To them, I don't exist."

"What's that supposed to mean?" Gabriel asked.

Mira shrugged. "I have no idea, but they'll meet fairly soon and it can get sorted out then."

"If you two will excuse me," Emmit said, "I have a busy day ahead of me."

"A busy day starting with us," Gabriel said.

Emmit raised an eyebrow and waited for an explanation.

"We have some questions to ask you," Gabriel said.

Mira hadn't noticed it happen, but once the two had stopped arguing, Emmit moved closer to Gabriel. Now he stood less than arm's length away. Gabriel was giving Emmit a cross look, but Gabriel didn't move.

"I'm sure we can make an appointment—"

"We really need to ask you some things," Mira cut in.

Agitation marred Emmit's face as he glared at Mira. "I did tell you before that people usually don't demand answers from me."

"But we are," Mira said, meeting and matching his aggravation, borrowing on the anger that had built up the previous night.

Emmit's face grew darker. "I don't see a reason—"

Gabriel stepped between them and crossed his arms. "Don't be an ass."

Emmit's eyes narrowed in on Gabriel. The room was still for the length of a breath before Emmit recomposed his expressionless face.

"Very well. This goes both ways, of course," Emmit said.

"What do you mean?" Mira asked.

"Neither of you has told me what happened the last time you were in the Ether."

CHAPTER 6

Y OU'RE LIVING IN THIS building, and you never talked to him about it?" Gabriel asked, turning to Mira. "Every time it was brought up, I got so ticked off that I never really said much," Mira admitted. "I figured he'd ask you, since I didn't tell him."

"Understandable," Gabriel said, "but still, the building may not be safe."

"Why wouldn't it be?" Emmit asked.

"The Ether isn't the same thing as this world," Mira said. "I didn't think what was happening there would matter."

"It probably doesn't," Gabriel said.

"There is not much in the Ether that can affect our world," Emmit said.

"The earthquakes and the heat wave weren't exactly a coincidence," Gabriel said.

"I said there isn't much that can affect us," Emmit said. "There are some ways for that world to project onto ours."

"See!" Gabriel snapped. "It's stuff like that that tells me there's a whole lot you aren't saying, and we need to know what it is."

"The things I know have no bearing on your case," Emmit said.

"How can you be sure?" Gabriel asked.

Emmit rubbed his temple. "The Ether is another world. Your case should remain firmly in this one."

"Not if we've ended up there twice already," Mira reasoned. "No one has gone into the Ether for centuries, and we've been there twice in the space of a couple of weeks. We need to know what you know."

Emmit sighed and flopped down into a chair. It was such a rare departure from his usual poised self that Mira almost felt sorry for him.

Almost.

"You are not the first in centuries to go into the Ether. You're not even the first this year," Emmit said. "Please, sit."

Mira took a seat, but it took a minute before Gabriel relaxed enough to join her on the couch. Mira could almost imagine him adjusting his wings as he rolled his shoulders before sitting.

"What I tell you is not to go beyond these walls," Emmit said. "Each of you must swear that you will not impart this information to anyone else. Not even your partner."

Gabriel rolled his eyes. "I swear."

Mira watched Emmit as he shook his head disparagingly at Gabriel. She had sworn to keep one of Emmit's secrets before, but Gabriel had forced the information out of her, through no fault of her own. Nothing had happened when she'd broken her promise.

Except the buildup of negative karma. After a few moments of contemplation, she dismissed the thought. She had done so much in the last two weeks that could cause bad karma that she couldn't blame it on breaking her promise to Emmit.

Still, it was something she wanted to think through, just in case.

"I'm afraid that isn't good enough," Emmit said to Gabriel. "Making a pact with a supernatural can be very different from making a promise to a human."

"How so?" Gabriel asked.

"Look at Ian," Mira said, still thinking over her decision. "He's bound by his promise to me."

"So, Emmit's going to bind us?" Gabriel asked.

"Not exactly," Mira said, "although that is always a possibility that you should consider before promising a supernatural anything. Other things are possible as well, depending on the supernatural you're dealing with."

"Supernaturals also take their promises more seriously," Emmit said. "Much like what Mira is doing now, they think things through before agreeing. It goes back to the days where knowing supernatural secrets could get you tortured or killed— if you were lucky."

"That's lucky?" Gabriel asked.

Emmit shrugged. "It depends on the alternatives. Since you are unfamiliar with the idea, follow Mira's lead."

When it came down to it, it was information Mira really needed to know. "I swear on my name and my family."

"That is a shortened version of a very old pact between supernaturals," Emmit said. "Basically, it means that if Mira breaks the promise, there will be consequences for her and her family."

Mira had never thought of it that way, but Emmit was right. The bad karma would be magnified and spread around. In centuries past, one supernatural might harm or kill another if they broke the promise. That was, if the secret sharer survived once others knew their secret.

Gabriel looked from one to the other. "That seems a little extreme."

"And yet, for many races it was vital that their secrets are kept," Emmit said.

"I get it." Gabriel appeared to mull the idea over and looked to Mira. Mira gave a small nod of encouragement. "Fine, I swear on my name and my family."

Emmit settled back into his chair and steepled his hands. "As I said, you were not the first to walk the Ether recently."

When his silence lasted too long, Mira pressed, "How do you know?"

"It is the reason I'm here," Emmit said. "It is also why I needed you to create the spell for me recently."

"Okay," Mira said, "but how did you know someone else was there? Did someone call and tell you?"

"The Ether is a world balanced on a knife blade. Changes can cause drastic effects. Myself, and those of my family, can sense when something occurs in the Ether and destroys the equilibrium."

So, this is one of the secrets of the Harkers'. No wonder he is always adamant that no one find out.

"Has the Ether always been so unsteady?" Mira asked.

Emmit nodded once. "I know what you are thinking, and yes, centuries ago something happened that nearly destroyed the world."

"What happened?" Mira asked.

"That is definitely not relevant to the here and now," Emmit said. "The Ether settled into a new rhythm and it is what you have recently seen."

"You came into town because of the Ether," Gabriel said. "You arrived around the time the murders started."

"About a week before they started," Emmit said.

"That looks pretty suspicious," Gabriel said.

"I can see how it would have been easy to tie the murders to my arrival, but the cause started before I arrived," Emmit said. "I was unaware of them until Mira's friend was taken, but, speaking of the murders is getting ahead of ourselves, I think."

"Go on, then," Mira said.

"Not long after my arrival, I discovered that someone had tried to clean the Ether."

"Did you go there?" Mira asked.

"If I entered the Ether I would never be able to return," Emmit said. "It is essentially a death sentence that would last an eternity."

"Death usually lasts that long," Gabriel said.

"What I mean," Emmit said, "is it would take that long for me to die. It would be a slow process."

Mira wrinkled her nose. His description made her wonder if Tyler had been going through something similar.

"How I learned is not important," Emmit said, "although, the end result was what caused me to seek out Mira's help. I didn't know about the first death at the time."

"Because?" Mira pressed.

"I can't be certain since I haven't spoken to all those involved—this is conjecture only. Once the witches tried to clean the Ether, the veil between the worlds became soft. Malleable, even."

"How do you know it was witches?" Mira asked. "Have you figured out who it was?"

"There are very few that could cross the border between our worlds," Emmit said. "The only groups with motive to do so would be the witches and the humans, but witches are the only ones with the ability. Anyway, because of the interference of the witches, I believe a group of misguided people were able to contact the other side."

"Using Barney?" Mira asked.

"There are other ways," Emmit said, "but it is probable that they went through Barney."

"If witches went to the Ether and saw the creatures there, why would they try to contact them again," Mira asked.

"John was human," Gabriel said. "So it was the humans that contacted the other side, wasn't it?"

"Yes," Emmit said. "The witches went to the Ether, weakening the path between worlds. It was the humans that reached out."

"Why would anyone want to clean the Ether?" Mira asked. "Why risk it with all those things there?"

"I doubt they saw any right away," Emmit said. "The people on the other side usually keep distance between themselves."

"But whatever the witches were doing drew them together?" Gabriel asked.

"Possibly, but I think the witches stepping into the Ether was enough to attract the attention of those that live there," Emmit said.

"Those things were what killed the witches a long time ago, weren't they?" Mira asked.

"Yes and no," Emmit said, "but we should stick with the present. With the people on the other side gathered together and with the way to our world reestablished, they reached out to the humans, probably through Barney."

"Why didn't they contact the witches?" Mira asked. "They were the ones actually going into the Ether."

Emmit hesitated. "The people on the other side wouldn't want to work with witches. It's also possible that they needed a certain type of mind. I guess they found that in John."

"And they got him to kill people?" Gabriel asked.

"Sacrifice, yes," Emmit said.

Gabriel's voice grew louder. "How could you think that wasn't related to the case?"

"There is nothing about what I am telling you that could help with your case. As I said, your job should stay firmly in this world."

"That's not up to you," Gabriel said with a barb in each word.

"Let's move on," Mira interrupted. "Why sacrifices?"

"My guess would be the energy involved," Emmit said. "With enough blood, it's possible to push the energy through to the other side."

"Why do they need it?" Gabriel asked. "We've seen what they eat—and it's not energy."

Emmit shifted in his seat, looking uncomfortable. "I've never seen the people from the other side, but I've heard them described numerous times."

"Numerous?" Mira asked.

"This is not the first time that witches have tried to access the Ether in my lifetime," Emmit said. "Nor is it the first time they've succeeded."

"I was always told that witches destroyed everything they knew about going to the Ether," Mira said.

"All witches are told that," Emmit said, "but it's difficult to wipe something like that out completely. There are always old grimoires being found. A few families also kept hold of the information and passed it down through the years in the hopes of gaining access again."

"Why, though?" Mira asked. "Why would anyone want to go there?"

"Have you performed any magic since you've returned from the Ether this time?" Emmit asked.

"No," she said, feeling a blush creep up. Her last spell had killed so many on the other side.

"While you were there, did you use any?" Emmit asked.

This time, Mira glared at him. "I didn't have much of a choice."

"Magic is much stronger there," Emmit said, ignoring her angst. "It deteriorates quickly, but while you have it, it's powerful. Not all of that goes away when you return. After your first visit to the Ether, did you notice the change when you returned?"

Mira remembered Della's response to the increase in power when Mira cast a spell.

Mira shrugged. "I didn't think much about it, since I didn't do much magic."

"You burned down a church," Emmit said.

"It wasn't a real church," Mira muttered.

"Why did they move to kidnapping people?" Gabriel asked.

"They specifically started kidnapping witches, and they will continue to do so." Emmit raised a hand as Gabriel attempted to respond. "Which you and your partner had already considered might happen. So again, it has no bearing on your case."

When Gabriel didn't interrupt, Emmit went on, "After the two of you entered the Ether, things changed again."

"We didn't do anything there except run and fight," Mira said. "Besides, what difference does it make if witches had already been there?"

"There is a great difference in power," Emmit said. "Now that Mira has entered the Ether more than once, the two of you together have more power than the local community of witches, even if you put them all together. But I don't think that was enough to change things. Nothing in the Ether took your power while there, although you burned some off, I'm sure."

Mira remembered how the power inside her magical items had slowly drained away during her first trip into the Ether.

"The difference was that you spilled blood in the Ether," Emmit said. "Both of you. That was enough to catch the attention of darker beings residing there."

"The thing with roots," Mira said, remembering the creature.

"Roots?" Emmit asked.

"We still have questions," Gabriel said.

"I'm certain that you do," Emmit said with a sigh, looking weary. "Any further and it's pure speculation. The people in the Ether have never had this much effect on the world, not for hundreds of years."

"We're still lost in the woods," Gabriel said. "Speculate. Take a guess at what happened next."

"Once we sent John back to the Ether, I guess the people from the Ether found a way to cross between the worlds. Worried that their gods might wake up, the people started stealing witches. They used the power from those they kidnapped to feed their gods in an effort to ensure the gods remained content and in hibernation."

"So, John thought he was sacrificing things to these gods?" Gabriel asked.

"Possibly," Emmit said with care.

"That's just dumb," Mira said. "There's no way John was worshiping anything from the Ether."

"It's possible that, to John, it was a convenient excuse," Emmit said, looking as if he were choosing each word carefully.

"An excuse to kill people?" Mira asked.

"Some people don't need much of an excuse to start killing," Gabriel said. "I've heard dumber reasons."

"Not just any people," Emmit said, "Supernaturals."

"But he's one of us," Mira said. "That doesn't make sense."

"He was human," Emmit said. "Prejudices against other beings probably made sense in his eyes."

"But Sally was human," Mira said.

"A human who was blackmailing him," Gabriel said.

Mira had forgotten that part.

"Now, in relation to your case, I'm sure you will find that there is nothing in what I've said that you didn't already know or suspect," Emmit said. "And since the law doesn't cover the hell that the Ether has become, nothing over there should have anything to do with your job."

"Why was Tyler working with you?" Mira asked.

Emmit beamed—the first time he smiled all day. "There are two witches in the area that are capable of opening a path into the Ether without assistance. He seemed the more likely suspect."

"But he wasn't involved, right?" Mira asked, hoping in her heart that Tyler wasn't the one that tried to clean the Ether.

"No," Emmit assured her, "and he was adamant that you not be involved. Since I needed insight into the witches, he assisted me."

"Why didn't he create the Balance spell for you?" Mira asked.

"There were several reasons," Emmit said, his smile softening. "Tyler knew a bit about the Ether, so I didn't want him anywhere near the place."

"And the other reasons?" Mira asked.

"I wanted to get to know you." Emmit looked at her as he had when they were together, and Mira felt her toes curl, hating herself for it.

Gabriel cleared his throat.

Emmit snapped his attention back to the angel.

"Did you find out who was going into the Ether?" Mira asked.

"Since you and Tyler were not involved, it would have to be multiple people working together," Emmit said.

"Do you think they've continued going back?" Gabriel asked.

"They might have at first," Emmit said, "but from the description of your visit, if the witches returned once the people from that side came together, the witches would be dead, or against returning to the Ether for their own safety."

"Or the witches could have been taken," Gabriel said.

Emmit frowned. "They are witches, so it's a definite possibility. I'm in the dark on your last visit. Was there any clue there were other witches around?"

"Only Tyler and the kids," Mira said.

"Uh, why don't I fill Emmit in on what we saw in the Ether," Gabriel suggested. "I know you don't want to talk about it."

"Not with him, anyway," Mira mumbled. "I'll grab breakfast. Are we going out today?" Mira asked Gabriel.

"Yeah, Ian is putting together a list of people to interview."

"I'll get ready to go, then." Mira glanced uncomfortably at Emmit before leaving the room.

CHAPTER 7

PUTTING EMMIT OUT OF her mind wasn't easy. She was starting to get over being mad at him, though she was still angry with herself for trusting him. He had given her no reason for her confidence. He had saved her once or twice, and Reinfield's men were useful to have around, but was that any reason to trust a person?

Well, yes, it was a good reason. Although there were still so many unknowns about Emmit that she should have been more careful. Especially once Gabriel and Ian warned her about Emmit.

Maybe she was being too hard on him. He had always been looking out for her, except when he'd given her up for dead.

Definitely not dating material, Mira told herself, but maybe still friend material.

At least he could be if she were able to move past his mistake.

Her feelings toward Gabriel were easier. The angel himself remained complicated, especially with the case involved and his tendency to save her life.

Being with Gabriel felt right. She smiled at the thought of this mess being over and having the chance to get to know him better. She warmed from the inside and got a tingly feeling, which disappeared the moment she got back into her room. The hateful book was waiting there. Knowing that she needed to finish reading it didn't help her feelings toward the thing.

When she wandered back to the living room, Gabriel and Emmit were standing together at the windows overlooking the city.

"I don't hear fighting," Mira mused. "Does that mean I need to give you all more time?"

"We don't fight," Gabriel said.

Mira crossed her arms and raised her eyebrows in disbelief.

"We disagree," Emmit said.

"Loudly," Gabriel admitted.

"I thought you didn't trust him," Mira said to Gabriel.

"That's true," Gabriel said. "With some things I don't."

Maybe it was because Emmit was from Europe, but he always seemed to stand far too close to Gabriel. He sometimes invaded her personal space as well, except those times he kept a carefully measured distance between him and herself, but she was certain that was for a whole other reason.

Or maybe it was her imagination.

"Is Emmit up to speed?" Mira asked.

"Yeah," Gabriel said.

"And the building?" Mira asked.

"I'm not certain," Emmit said. "I may need to delve a little deeper to see what these roots are that you mentioned."

"John said it was their god, or that some people called it a god."

Emmit tried to remain stoic, but he paled. "You think the elder god is fully awake in the Ether?"

"If that's what it was, it was definitely awake," Mira said.

"I need to know what happened before Gabriel arrived in the Ether," Emmit demanded.

Mira breathed deeply and pursed her lips. "Do you really?"

"Yes," Emmit said. "I need to know everything."

The last thing Mira wanted to think about was the stark fear that she felt alone with John in the Ether. "You want to know what happened to me while I was alone with John in the Ether with no wards, no protection, and no one to help." The words would hint at the helplessness she had felt, but couldn't manage to voice.

Emmit opened his mouth and closed it again. He looked torn.

Mira rubbed her forehead. Hadn't she just been telling herself that she might be giving Emmit too hard of a time? Yet, here she was doing it again.

"Look," she said, trying to release some of her anger. "There are only a few things you need to know. He was surprised by both you and Gabriel being there, and he was pissed off because he didn't want to be back in the Ether, but he felt you hadn't given him a choice."

"Does that mean he's still seeing visions, even though John himself is dead?" Emmit asked. He was slow and quiet in his speech, as if afraid to say something that might upset her.

"He seemed to still know or expect some stuff, but I got the impression the psychic power is even more erratic than it had been when John was alive. John also never saw the two of you when he looked into the future. Except..."

"Yes?" Emmit asked.

"When we were at Lance's—he saw you there."

Emmit thought that over. "Possibly because a large part of myself was in the Ether? If he could see me then, but couldn't later, that's the only thing I can think of." He appeared to think that over. "And John was upset to be back in the Ether?"

Mira glared. "Ticked off enough to push me down the stairs."

Emmit's face went blank.

"Although," she said after taking a steadying breath, "this is John we're talking about, so that could have happened anyway. He said Ether had changed and it was time for me to see Tyler— and that I had work to do. Then he showed me the massive creature in the city. He also pointed out there were other smaller things that moved around in the grass."

"I have no idea what those might be," Emmit said.

Mira shrugged.

"After that?" Emmit tried to encourage her to continue.

"I ran to my shop to get away from him. I tried a circle, and he told me Tyler had done the same thing. John said that no witch alive knew what they were doing, so the magic would fail. John also seemed surprised that you didn't tell us what he wanted to do with the witches."

"Anything else?" Emmit asked.

"No, Gabriel was there for the rest," Mira said.

"You were there for a while before he crossed over," Emmit said.

"Those are the only important things," Mira snapped.

Emmit started to say something else, but Gabriel interrupted, saying something too low for Mira to hear.

Mira transferred her scowl to Gabriel.

"Of course," Emmit said. "If you think of anything else, please tell me."

"Let's go," Gabriel said before Mira could say anything else. "Harker, I'm sure we'll be talking later."

"You're not going to have me followed again, are you?" Mira asked, not willing to leave when she still had some heat to burn off.

Emmit said nothing.

"Come on," Gabriel said after a moment.

"Whatever," Mira mumbled before leading Gabriel out the door and to the elevator.

One of Reinfield's men waited inside.

Mira watched the man for a moment, wondering if she should talk in front of him or not. Remembering that Emmit had sent her bodyguard out of the room before they'd discussed the Ether, she decided to bite back her words and let her anger simmer.

Gabriel, too, was quiet. When they left the building, Mira didn't notice anyone following them.

"What did you say to Emmit?" Mira asked, still checking for Reinfield's men, which she half expected to be hiding in the shadows.

"While you were out of the room, I told him everything that happened in the Ether," Gabriel said.

"I meant when we were on our way out, and you know it. Did you tell him I was telling the truth?"

"You weren't." Seeing the look on Mira's face, he rushed to continue, "I told him that you weren't in great shape and that he probably really didn't need to know anything else."

"Oh." Mira didn't feel completely pacified, but after dredging up what happened in the Ether, she knew there was no hope of a better mood.

"How was your reading?" Gabriel asked.

"Depressing," Mira said without thinking.

Gabriel's hand brushed her arm, but he lowered it quickly.

Did he want to comfort her? Mira wasn't against that, but at the same time, she didn't want him feeling sorry for her.

Mira gave him a weak smile. "Sorry, there's nothing nice to say about it. Until I have my trial with the witches, to them, I don't exist."

"It didn't seem that way yesterday. Mr. Singer spoke with you."

"To the witches, the only time I'm a real person is when I'm with you or Ian while working on the case."

"That's not fair," Gabriel said as they entered the parking garage.

"It doesn't have to be."

Gabriel unlocked the car and opened Mira's door, looking thoughtful. He didn't drive off even after he had the car started.

"What are you supposed to do before the trial?" Gabriel asked.

Mira pulled the book out and flipped to the hated passage. "It says, 'Until the tribunal has gathered, the accused's existence is not to be realized'. That's really the only thing I know."

Gabriel shook his head.

"I'm not quite finished with the book," Mira admitted. "After reading that, I set it aside for the night."

"I can see why," Gabriel said. "What about your family?"

"They're all witches. My sister texted me once anyway, but she won't risk her place in the coven or let her kids see her doing the wrong thing, so there's not much chance I'll hear from her again."

"But they're family."

"They're also witches. They probably figure it's only a few weeks and then everything will be fine again."

"I'm sorry," Gabriel said. "This sucks."

"It does." Mira stared out the window. "Do you talk with your family often?"

"Usually, I do but lately things have been a bit strained."

"They won't tell you anything about being an angel?"

"I'm beginning to think they don't know. I wouldn't have even found out if I hadn't gone to the Ether."

"Can they tell when people are lying?" Mira asked.

"Not that I've ever noticed. It used to freak them out when I was a kid and I told them people were lying. At least it did after they found out I was always right about it."

"It might not be an angel thing. Maybe it's a Gabriel thing," Mira said as she smiled at him. "Remember, you're still you."

"I'm adjusting."

"Maybe you could find other angels," Mira suggested. "They could help."

Gabriel smiled. "Do you think I should put out an ad?"

Mira grinned. "Sure, tell people you're looking for an angel and add a picture of yourself. I guarantee you'll get responses."

"That sounds like an online dating nightmare waiting to happen. I'll pass."

The atmosphere in the car lifted considerably and the tensions of the morning started to unwind. "You could still talk to other supernaturals about being an angel. And Ian, of course."

"It's good he knows," Gabriel said. "He's still a bit weird about stuff now and again, but I'm glad I told him."

"Is keeping Emmit's secret going to be a problem?" Mira asked.

"I'm still trying to process it all myself."

"Me too. Are we meeting up with Ian now?"

"Yeah. He's at the office. Are you going to be up to visiting more witches today?" Gabriel asked as they pulled to a stop in front of the station.

"As long as my family isn't on the list, I'll be okay. It would be too awkward on all sides. If you want to talk to them, count me out."

Gabriel texted his partner. "What Emmit told us did give me an idea. Is there any way to tell if a witch's power has increased?"

"You want to find who was in the Ether? If they're actively doing magic, I'd probably notice, but the chances of that are slim."

"Well, keep an eye out. If you're in another room, maybe you could poke around a bit," Gabriel suggested. "If you find anything, let me know."

"Unless you want to talk in code, I can't say anything about the Ether in front of Ian."

"Code words," Gabriel laughed. "I like it."

"Sure," Mira jibed. "If I say piranha, you know there's something wrong. Or," she said, bringing them back on track, "we can just wait until Ian isn't in earshot."

"Like, at dinner this evening?"

Mira tried not to grin like an idiot. "That sounds like the perfect time."

"Do you want to ride up front for the rest of the day?" Gabriel asked.

Mira followed his gaze and saw Ian approaching.

"I'll sit in the back. You and Ian have a case to discuss and I have a book to read."

Mira switched to the back seat, trying to spend as little time as possible in the cold.

"Thanks," Ian said, jumping into the passenger seat and rubbing his hands together in an effort to get them warm. "We've got a lot of driving today."

"Where to first?" Gabriel asked.

"Out to Aken." Ian started the GPS on his phone and Gabriel followed the instructions. "I was out there a few days ago, right after you left the hospital. There are a lot of werewolves in the area, according to Noah, but there's also one witch."

Mira sighed. "This is going to be a fun day."

"I take it you know the witch? That would be helpful," Ian said.

"Mary Messic," Mira said. "I've only been around her a few times, since she doesn't come to the meetings."

"Why not?" Ian asked.

"She hates everyone."

"She hates other witches?" Gabriel asked.

"And everyone else. Witches, humans, elves, everyone. The woman could cause a minotaur to run away with its tail between its legs."

Gabriel chuckled, but Ian turned in his seat. "Minotaur?"

"I've heard stories about her smoking fairies off her property and leaving dangerous things for pixies to pick up."

Ian's face soured. "What do you mean, 'smoking fairies'?"

"Kind of like you do with bees before you raid beehives," Mira said. "I've also heard that she uses bug spray on them, but I don't think she'd kill anyone."

"And pixies?" Ian asked, his voice sounding uneasy.

"If Ms. Messic hates supernaturals," Gabriel broke in, "she could be someone to keep an eye on."

"Oh, she hates humans, too," Mira said. "She lives near the werewolves since the area isn't highly populated and shifters mostly keep to themselves."

"My information says that she knows several of our victims," Ian said.

"She terrorizes indiscriminately," Mira said.

"Well," Ian said, "at least we can get her interview out of the way. Anything else you can tell us about her?"

"Not really," Mira said. "I've only met her a few times and wasn't in a hurry to meet her again. Why is she on the list?"

"Uh, it was just a connection. Anyway," Ian rushed to change the subject, "I thought we could stop by and check on Noah while we're there."

"Did you call him first?" Mira asked, turning her attention to her book.

"I figured we'd just drop by," Ian said.

Mira paged through the text. "Never a good idea with a werewolf."

"Why's that?" Ian asked.

"Noah will want to let you all in, in case you're there about Helen," Mira said. "If he has to shift to see you, you'd just make him cranky since you have no new information. Do you know what a cranky werewolf is like?"

"I guess I have an idea," Ian said, sounding somber. "At least after what happened at the conclave. But if there was a full moon at the last conclave, there can't be one now—unless some serious magical shit has screwed something up."

Mira rolled her eyes. "The phase of the moon has nothing to do with it. We've just passed a full moon."

"Where did the myth of the full moon come from?" Gabriel asked.

"I'm not sure, but it's good for them. In their wolf form, they only have to worry about being mistaken as a werewolf a few nights a month. Any other time and, like you, no one would consider them werewolves since they'd see the wolf when it wasn't a full moon."

"So either the werewolves made it up to keep themselves safe, or humans made it up to make themselves feel safe," Gabriel mused. "Interesting. Nothing is what I expect."

"Much like a cursing angel." Mira grinned and caught Gabriel's eye in the rear-view mirror.

It looked like he struggled not to smile himself.

Gabriel and Ian discussed their interviews for the day while Mira slumped down in the seat to read the rest of the protocols. She silently berated herself for not finishing the book last night. Had she realized she'd be facing Mary today, she'd have finished her homework.

Maybe visiting her family would have been better.

Imagining her sister or mother's frustrations about not being able to speak openly to Mira, made her second guess that idea.

It was possible they'd break all protocols, but if her mother did that, it would only mean that she'd harp on Mira about getting into trouble again.

For some reason, the idea made Mira smile sadly to herself. She'd like to think her mother would still talk with her.

Her father would say a few words of encouragement and then go on following the rules, saying they'd talk further when it was over. Robin might try to do something similar, but it would all depend on who else might be around.

Mira conceded that it would hurt too much to visit her family. She'd been given permission to visit Tyler, but since he wasn't conscious, it wasn't very helpful.

At least she still had Della. Thinking of her friend, Mira tugged out her cell phone and texted her.

How was your date?

She set her phone aside and continued to read, knowing Della would be too busy to respond right away.

Nothing about the book got any better, but luckily, she had almost made it through by the time they arrived at Mary's house.

The red brick house had a few steps up to a stark and small porch. Not wanting to be the one to knock, Mira hung back. Gabriel took her meaning and rang the bell.

There was a screech as though a cat had been stepped on.

Gabriel gave his partner a surreptitious look that was returned. They waited a minute before Gabriel tried again. This time a chime came from the house as expected.

"Was that really a cat?" Ian asked under his breath.

The door snapped open and an older woman, maybe still in her sixties, stood there expectantly, dressed in a severe suit.

Gabriel and Ian introduced themselves. As they spoke, Mary gave them an up and down look that might even have mirrored Mira's own when first meeting the detectives.

The detectives had that effect on many women, and despite all of Mary's cantankerous ways, she was still a woman.

When Mary spotted Mira, the situation went to hell.

CHAPTER 8

MARY SCREWED UP HER face ready for a fight. "How dare you bring her to my house? I won't have it!"

Mira unconsciously took a step back, but when she noticed what she'd done, she refused to take another.

"Ms. Owens is helping us on this investigation," Gabriel said.

"She'll contaminate my house!"

A flash of agitation passed quickly by Gabriel's face. "We'd be happy to ask our questions out here."

"Not with her!" Mary's voice was like a screech now. "Go away and don't come back." She slammed the door shut.

Feeling dejected, Mira went back to the car. Gabriel and Ian were a little more resolute and knocked on the door again.

Mira could hear Mary yell, "I know my rights!" before Mira shut the car door, blocking out the noise.

She could see Gabriel and Ian still talking through the door, but she didn't want to watch them, so she opened her book and pretended to read. Her eyes burned with unshed tears that her humiliation caused. If that happened every time, Mira didn't think she could continue.

Would the witches talk to the detectives without her around?

Mira had her notebook in hand before she realized it. When she first joined the case, she'd used Fortitude to help her through. Would that be enough this time?

Bliss.

A sigh of longing came out before Mira got her mind back on track. No more Bliss. Not ever.

Maybe with a boost, Fortitude would be enough. Mira thought the spell through and jotted down a few notes. A few minutes later, Gabriel slid into the front seat and turned to Mira.

He watched her silently, possibly to take in her mood. Mira didn't look up, keeping her face fixed on her notebook.

"You okay?" he asked.

Mira tapped the notebook with the back of her pen, still not looking up. "I'm fine."

"Why do you bother lying?"

"Why do you ask questions you know I'm going to lie about?" It was said as a simple statement, lacking any malice.

"I guess I was hoping you weren't upset." He waved at Ian, who quickly walked back to the car.

"Mary's a mean hag of a woman," Mira said as Ian got into the car. "She would have found something to yell about."

"I don't doubt that," Ian said. "I hope none of the others are like that."

Mira wanted to say that they wouldn't be that bad, but now she wasn't confident. Would they treat her that badly now that she'd been ostracized?

"She was the only person on the list that lives on this side of the city. The person is near Barney's apartment. His name is Levi Jaeger," Ian said, reading from his list.

"I don't know any witches by that name," Mira said absently, once again tapping the back of her pen on the notebook.

"He's not a witch," Ian said. "At least no one has said he is. I couldn't get much information on him, but Lance said that he knew most of the victims—one of the very few I've found that knew Dennis Simmons."

Mira's hand stopped twitching. "Does he know what's going on or who I am?"

"I wondered about that," Ian said. "If he didn't know, we'd get nothing out of him, even with you there, so I asked Lance to let him know we were coming and make sure he knew what was happening in the community."

"You really seem to be getting the hang of this," Gabriel said.

"I'm not supernatural, so I don't think they'd forgive a misstep easily," Ian said. "You two wouldn't have to deal with that."

"Gabriel would," Mira said.

"I figured that after so many people had been involved in the... incident, your secret would be out," Ian said.

"Is it?" Gabriel asked, looking back at Mira through the mirror.

"Mr. Singer and Emmit are the only ones that know," Mira said. "Unless you two have heard something."

"But there were so many people there," Ian said.

"It's not like he came out of the Ether with wings," Mira said. "Barney and the witches didn't notice him."

"We weren't the only ones over there," Gabriel reminded her.

"Tyler's still not awake," Mira said, "and he wouldn't say anything even if he was. Kevin is old enough to understand that he can't tell anyone, and Andrea calls you her guardian angel. Even when she talks about your wings and sword, they'll assume she's exaggerating due to trauma."

Gabriel glanced at Ian.

"I didn't say anything," Ian said. "I can't say anything to anyone, remember?"

It was the first time he hadn't been agitated about the subject of Mira binding him. Maybe he was coming around.

"You can talk to other supernaturals," Mira said.

"You're always with me when I do," Ian said.

"What about Della?" Mira asked.

"I didn't think about Della," Ian said. "Gabe isn't exactly on my mind when I'm with her."

Gabriel grinned.

"I wouldn't say anything, anyway," Ian said. "Not unless they already know, which only amounts to Mira and Emmit. Your secret is safe with me."

"I wasn't too worried about it," Gabriel said. "It does keep us on equal footing with the supernaturals."

"True," Ian said, sounding relieved that Gabriel would also have a hard time with other supernaturals. Mira had a feeling that Ian was worried about being an outsider.

"Is it possible Lance knows?" Gabriel asked.

"No idea," Mira said. "No one knows a lot about what vampires are capable of. He could have a knack for sensing supernaturals."

Mira turned back to her spell and reviewed the augmentations she'd written. This type of spell was something that she'd usually work through with Tyler. She knew what she had here was the beginning of something, but it was nowhere close to being finished.

When it was finished, she'd be able to handle anything.

She blinked at the paper, her mind frozen on the last thought. Then she ripped out the page and tore it to pieces. No one would have been able to read her codes anyway, but she still felt better with the idea obliterated.

"What's up?" Ian asked, turning in his seat.

"Notes for a spell," Mira said. "They were a mistake." She stowed the small pieces of paper in her purse and looked out the window. She missed seeing much of the world go by, since they were almost at their destination.

Mira had always hated the word 'projects' or Section 8. It was better than what some people called the area, but she preferred simply to say low-income housing. As a duplex, however, Levi's house was a step up from Barney's apartment building.

It didn't help that, at the moment, Mira had zero income and wouldn't have even been able to afford an apartment if not for Della and Emmit.

This time, the detectives let Mira take the lead. The light on the doorbell was exposed to the elements, the button having been badly damaged, so Mira knocked on the door.

A few moments later, there was a click, and the door opened wide.

"Hi," Mira said before really taking in the man in front of her. "I'm, uh... Mira and, um…" She trailed off, surprised to be facing a gorgeous person, clean cut and well built—not at all what she expected.

His looks weren't the issue though. Little alarm bells were going off in her head. As much as she wanted to watch Levi— and she could watch a man like that all day—she also wanted to run away. Possibly to hide under the covers.

"Are you Levi Jaeger?" Ian asked, taking over.

"I am," Levi said. His voice was as smooth as velvet. If it weren't for the fact that Mira was scared out of her mind, he would have caused her toes to curl even more than Emmit or Gabriel.

Ian introduced the group quickly before moving on. "Would you mind if we came in and asked you a few questions?"

Levi seemed to look around the three, making sure they were alone. "Sure." He stepped back from the door and beckoned them into the dark interior of his house.

Ian started to move forward, but Mira thrust out her arm, blocking his movement. "I, um, I'm not sure we should."

Even Levi's grin was both gorgeous and sinister. "You would be the witch."

"Um, yeah," Mira said, arm still out.

He winked at her. "I have that effect on witches. Come on in. I swear by my name and family, I'll do nothing unseemly."

After a moment, Gabriel nudged her from behind.

"Okay," Mira said carefully, wishing that she had a few spells ready to use.

From inside, the room was much brighter than Mira had first thought when she'd looked into the place. She stepped inside, trying to put Gabriel and Ian between herself and Levi, but the living room was too small, and she only accomplished jostling the detectives as they took seats in the living room.

After a few pleasantries, Ian and Gabriel settled into their routine, starting with Dennis. As they spoke, Mira sat rigid, her eyes darting around the room. She chided herself for being this way, but she couldn't seem to settle down. The way Levi leered at her wasn't helping. It made her predicament embarrassing since he seemed to know what she was going through.

After talking briefly of Dennis, the detectives moved onto the other names on the list.

"I knew Karen well," Levi said.

For the first time since seeing him, Mira felt less threatened. Talking about Karen had changed Levi's demeanor drastically.

The detectives noted the reaction as well.

"Tell us about your relationship with Karen," Ian said.

"Her people and ours always got along," Levi said.

"Your people?" Ian asked.

Mira nudged Ian hard in the side.

"Right," Ian mumbled, "sorry."

Levi appeared amused. "I wouldn't expect that kind of courtesy from a witch. Not to me, at any rate."

Mira shrugged. "You're one of us."

Levi chuckled, and Mira blushed.

"A supernatural, I mean," she corrected. "I didn't mean witch."

"Thank you," Levi said, looking sincere, although thoroughly amused.

The ground shook slightly, and Mira caught sight of Levi's TV wobbling.

"Another quake," Ian said uneasily.

"A small one, at least," Levi said. "I gave up trying to keep anything on the walls."

"So," Gabriel cut in, "you got along with Karen?"

"Yes," Levi said, still watching Mira, "we were friends."

Feeling uncomfortable, Mira looked around the room while the interview continued. She wasn't sure what the detectives were getting out of the conversation, but she was finding out very little. He didn't seem to know anyone else and wasn't saying anything useful, at least to her knowledge.

As the interview wound down, she felt relieved.

"Your place of employment wasn't on file," Ian said as they stood to leave. "Do you mind telling us what you do for a living?"

"For the past two years, very little," Levi said. "There are too many witches—or people with a high concentration of witch blood in their ancestry—around here."

"And they'll stop you from working?" Ian asked.

"Their reactions tend to put employers off," Levi said.

"Why live in the area, then?" Ian asked.

The question wiped any trace of amusement off Levi's face, and at first, Mira didn't think he was going to answer. "A close family member needs specialized treatment."

Mira took a step back when he spoke as the terror rose in her.

"There are medical specialists here," Levi said tersely. "If a witch is around, she even gets poor treatment in the hospital. I need to look after her and didn't want to leave her alone."

"I'm sorry to hear that," Ian said.

Levi rose, signifying the end of the interview. Once Mira's feet realized going away would be amazing, she hurried to the door.

On the porch, she hesitated. "Before we go, I'd like a minute to talk to Levi." No one looked more surprised by this than the now aggravated Levi did. "Alone," Mira added pointedly when neither of the men moved.

Ian nodded, but Gabriel didn't look convinced. He took a hard look at Levi, before saying, "Just a minute," reluctantly.

"You're going to ask me about it, aren't you," Levi snapped.

Mira's heart beat faster and she had to stop herself from backing away. "What? No." She took a steadying breath, causing the cold air to cloud. "I don't know what this is, but you seem like a decent guy."

"Yeah, right," he ridiculed.

Anger started to bubble up in Mira, but fear blocked its path. "It doesn't seem to be anything you're doing. I think it's what you are."

"Just go," Levi said.

"If you're interested, I can do something to block that."

Levi glared but said nothing.

"It wouldn't change anything about you—it would just make it so witches don't have that reaction. If nothing else, the person in the hospital might get better treatment if I could make her something."

His eyes tried to bore holes into her.

"Anyway," Mira said, "I just wanted to offer." She backed down the steps, not turning her back to Levi until she reached the bottom.

She was a yard away before he called out.

"Why?"

Confused, Mira turned. When she laid eyes on Levi, the need to run was fully renewed. "What do you mean?"

"Why would a witch help me?"

"Because no one deserves to be treated this way," she said, motioning toward him. "At least not without a good reason."

"How do you know there's not one?"

"You haven't done anything to me that would cause me to feel like this. It's what you are or maybe what I am that's doing this. That shouldn't mean you have to hide away."

"You don't know anything about it. Not really."

"You're right," Mira said, backing away again, feeling slightly better with each step she took away from Levi. "I don't. It was, um, nice to meet you." She hurried back to the car and practically jumped in.

When she was safe inside, she realized that she was breathing heavily.

"Jeez, Mira," Ian said. "I'm sure the guy is good looking and all, but I wouldn't have expected that from you."

Gabriel gave him a death glare and put the car into gear.

"What?" Her voice came out squeaky as the residual fear began to break down.

"Nothing," Ian said. "Forget I said anything."

"You thought... you thought I liked him?" Mira said incredulously. "He scared the crap out of me."

"How?" Ian asked. "He didn't do anything."

"I don't think he did it on purpose. He wasn't lying when he said witches react to him." She felt heat rush to her face as the words came out, but she wanted to make herself clear. "If you two weren't there, I would have been gone the second he opened the door."

"Really?" Ian said.

It chaffed a little that Ian aimed the question at Gabriel, using him as a lie detector, when she was right there.

Gabriel nodded. "Apparently. We should drop by the station and check in."

"What could cause a witch to react like that?" Ian asked, ignoring his partner trying to change the subject.

"I have no idea," Mira said. "I'm not even sure I want to know."

"You were tripping over yourself on the way out," Ian said, sounding accusatory. "But then you stayed back to talk to him."

Mira pulled out her phone, trying to give herself something to concentrate on besides fear. "I offered to help," Mira mumbled.

"Help what?" Ian asked.

Mira shrugged. "It's not his fault that witches react that way. Maybe I could make something to stop people treating him that way. Instinct told me to run, but logic said I was being stupid."

"That was really nice of you."

Mira tried not to take offense that Ian sounded surprised. "The person in the hospital might be better off as well."

"What are you going to make?"

"Nothing," Mira said. "He probably thought I was trying to trick him or something."

"He's probably been cursed one too many times," Ian said.

The idea tumbled around. "I didn't think of that. You may be right. You're getting to know witches."

"That's not witches," Ian said. "That's people. Most people, anyway. Human nature; hurt it before it hurts you."

"For a small earthquake, this one seems to have caused a lot more traffic," Gabriel said.

He hadn't taken much interest in the conversation about Levi, and Mira wasn't put off by letting the conversation go.

CHAPTER 9

MAYBE WE SHOULD STOP somewhere for lunch," Ian said.

"Sure," Gabriel said. "We're close to Harmon's and the lunch rush is probably long over."

"The day feels like it should be over," Mira said, stretching in the back seat. "It's been going on forever."

"I think talking to Mary did that," Ian said. "You said she hates humans, too?"

"Like I said, she really hates everyone," Mira said.

"She knew John, didn't she?" Gabriel asked.

"I'm sure she did," Mira said, "but then, most of the community knew John."

"What can you tell us about him?" Gabriel asked. "I mean, before he became what he is now."

"He was fairly personable," Mira said. "It seems awful to say that now."

"Who was he friends with?" Gabriel asked, steering the conversation.

"Barney. Of course, you've heard about that." Mira sifted through all of her recollections about John. "He was also close to William."

"That still seems like something we should look into a little more," Gabriel said. "William's a witch hunter, after all, and witches are disappearing."

"It seems like a natural place to start," Ian said.

"Witch hunters today are just people that recognize witches. I've told you, it doesn't mean they actually hunt witches," Mira said.

"It doesn't mean they don't hunt them, either," Gabriel said.

Mira opened her mouth to argue, but closed it again. Gabriel wasn't wrong, but it was incredibly hard for her to believe William would hurt anyone. Then again, Mira had once thought the same about John.

"This all started with John, who happens to be human. It makes sense to dig deeper," Ian said. "John was one of the first people I interviewed, and he stayed pretty high on my list of suspects after talking with him."

"Why's that?" Mira asked, genuinely curious about what he'd seen that she had missed.

"The fact that he was being blackmailed by Sally was enough," Ian said as they pulled into Harmon's parking lot. "But he was also lying about what Sally was blackmailing him about."

"What did he say?" Mira asked.

"He rambled about lack of due diligence in an insurance policy. He said it cost the company a lot of money."

"I could see why he wouldn't want that to get out," Gabriel said.

"When I followed up, I learned the company didn't have to pay out," Ian said. "There's no reason to put up with blackmail over that."

"Makes sense he was high on the list," Gabriel said.

After the car was shut off, the three quickly made their way through the frigid air and into the blissfully warm restaurant.

Mimi was in the dining room and greeted them warmly before showing them to their seat.

"I was so sorry to hear about your store," Mimi said as Mira slid into the booth. "Ian mentioned it, and then your partner filled me in."

"Did she?" Mira said, surprised. She hadn't spoken much with her partner after their last visit to the store with the insurance adjusters.

It struck Mira that now she couldn't talk to her friend. If she'd still had the store, being shunned would have made it almost impossible for her to work.

"Her catering is picking up," Mimi said. "She's supplying my pies now and they've never sold better."

Gabriel sat next to Mira and her focus shifted to his close proximity.

"I'll send someone over to take your order," Mimi said.

Mira was too intent on the warmth generated by Gabriel to make much small talk. Once they placed their orders, the conversation returned to John, which distracted her.

"Did John have any other close friends?" Gabriel asked.

Mira pictured John at the conclaves, and everything he did took on a new sinister element in her remembrance. "It's hard to think about John the way he was before. He talked to just about everyone, but I can't say he was particularly close to anyone else in the community."

"Well, at least we have a direction to go in. Do you know where William would be this time of day?" Gabriel asked.

"I'm not sure," Mira said. "I think he gets home around four. Want me to call him?"

"No," Gabriel said. "Let's just meet him there."

Mira didn't like the idea of surprising William like that, but she didn't say anything.

"I wish we knew what Sally had been blackmailing John about," Gabriel said.

"Did Martin know anything?" Mira asked.

"The boyfriend? Not that I'm aware of," Gabriel said.

"His interviews were all at the station, so I never asked about the supernatural," Ian said. "I tried to, but the interviews are recorded. I guess that counts as telling someone. He's human, right? Would he even know about the supernatural stuff?"

"I didn't think Sally would tell him about the supernatural. They hadn't known each other that long." Mira shifted uncomfortably in her seat. "Although, I also didn't think Sally was capable of blackmail."

"It's worth following up on—we can track him down later today. I'm sure we have his typical routines in the file. What makes you think he might know about the blackmail?"

"Someone mentioned that Karen didn't like Sally or her boyfriend," Mira said. "If Sally was blackmailing Karen, then it makes sense that Karen would hate her. But why Martin?"

"Association," Ian suggested.

"Maybe, but why mention him at all?" Mira said. "It's not like he ever came to a meeting."

"Good point," Gabriel said as their food arrived.

Once the waiter was gone, Ian picked the conversation back up. "What happens if Martin gets arrested? If he knows about the supernatural stuff, I mean."

Mira shrugged. "I know there're ways of dealing with it. It depends on the person, though. I saw a supernatural get arrested and the local council decided not to do anything to keep him from talking, despite him ranting about all kinds of things about the community."

Ian stopped with his food halfway to his mouth. "That sounds like something they'd stop." He dropped his fork. "I mean, christ, your community bound me and I'm a damned cop."

"Oh, they bound his powers—they even let me help with that." Mira smiled at the thought of getting some of her bad karma released at the time. "But he couldn't prove anything. Not that anyone bothered to check. He sounded like a lunatic, so they let him keep talking."

"What happened to him?" Ian asked.

"He's in prison for another year or so," Mira said, not wanting to think of the day the man would be set free.

"But no one did anything about what he was saying?" Ian asked, unwilling to let it go.

"No," Mira said as she tried to control her temper. She really didn't want to think about her college years. "I think he started out in the mental ward at prison, but I heard he was only there for a short time. He must have shut up at some point."

Ian didn't ask anything else, but he still didn't look very happy.

Gabriel broke the tense silence before it could build up steam. "So, we're seeing William and Martin. I'll pay, and then we can go."

He reached for the check and bumped a glass of water. It wouldn't be right to say the water went everywhere as the glass fell—its direction was absolute.

Straight into Mira's lap.

"Oh, shit," Gabriel said, grabbing napkins to try to stop at least some of the spill, but it was too late. His face was turning red. "I'm sorry."

Mira tried not to sigh and counted herself lucky that it had only been water. "It's no big deal. I'll just... go clean up." Mira tried not to slide across the seat so she wouldn't get wetter, and then made a beeline to the restrooms, relieved to find hand dryers.

Once she was as dry as she could get without taking off her clothes, she joined Gabriel and Ian. The mad dash to the car outside wasn't fast enough for Mira, who was really feeling the chill.

In the car, she shivered in the back seat, keeping her discomfort to herself.

"I'm sorry again," Gabriel said, glancing at her in the rear-view mirror.

"It's my own bad luck. No big deal."

"Do you want to make a trip to Emmit's?"

"It's too far out of the way. Don't worry about it. I'll dry."

Gabriel looked as though he was going to say more, but Ian cut in. "Where are we going first?"

"We'll go see William," Gabriel said. "He lives with his parents, right?"

"Yes," Mira said.

"We can talk to them as well," Gabriel said. "Are they witch hunters as well?"

"Yeah, the witch hunter trait runs in families. Not always, but most of the time."

"But William's human, isn't he?" Ian asked. "In the same way Barney, Sally, and John are?"

"Yes." Mira was surprised to find that talking about Sally didn't hurt quite as much as it previously had. Her friend, in the way Mira had known her, was slipping away.

If the others sensed her melancholy mood, they kept it to themselves.

When they pulled up in front of William's house, Mira had second thoughts about what she was doing. William was a friend. Sure, he was closer to Tyler than to her, but he was still a friend. She knew what this might look like—the witch blaming the witch hunter.

She had to remind herself that it wasn't like that. Mira wasn't bringing the detectives here to interrogate him, only to get more information.

It wasn't until she had that sorted in her head that Mira was ready to follow Gabriel and Ian's lead and exit the car. As soon as she got out of the car, the two detectives headed straight for the door, talking low enough that she couldn't hear.

At the porch, Gabriel stopped and turned to Mira. "Be careful on the ice." He took two steps toward her before losing his own footing and sliding into Mira, knocking them both to the ground.

Mira ended up on her back in the snow with her limbs tangled together with Gabriel's.

"Smooth," Ian chuckled. "Anyone hurt?"

Gabriel sighed and pushed himself up to his knees. "This doesn't work well if I'm the one you need to be protected from."

Mira sat up. She had landed softly in the snow and didn't mind finding herself on the ground with Gabriel. She smiled inwardly at the idea and let Gabriel pull her to her feet.

"Are you all right?" Gabriel asked.

"Yeah," Mira said, happy she could say that without lying to him. She brushed the snow off herself before joining Ian at the door.

Before Ian could knock, William was at the door. "Hi, I thought I heard someone outside." He opened the door wide. "Come in."

Mira dusted the last of the snow off and kicked some of it off her boots as well before following the others inside.

"I have to say," William continued as he led them farther into the living room, "I'm surprised to see you all here."

"Sorry to stop in unexpectedly," Mira said. "It's nice to see a friendly face."

William gave her a wary smile. "Dad mentioned that you were having trouble with some of the witches. Everything okay?"

"As well as can be expected," Mira said. "It'll sort itself out soon." She wished fervently that she could believe what she said.

Apparently, Gabriel did as well. He was developing an odd tick each time she lied. It was as though he was trying to hide a wince by blinking rapidly.

"Can I get you all anything?" William asked.

"No, thank you," Ian said. "We just wanted to ask you a few questions."

"I still haven't seen Barney. Any word?" William asked. He gestured for them to sit.

Mira wanted to tell him that Barney was safe, but the seer was in hiding and the fewer people that knew where he was the better.

"Actually, we're hoping you can tell us a little more about John," Ian said.

William's concerned smile seemed to freeze on his face. "I'm not sure what I can tell you that you don't already know."

"Were you friends with John?" Ian asked.

William shifted. "I thought I was. I'm still having a hard time believing he's the one behind all this."

Mira felt sorry for William as the detectives peppered him with questions. It was interesting to see Ian asking most of the questions and seeing that each time William lied, Gabriel was able to add a few follow up questions that had William filling in more details. Mira could tell he was trying to distance himself from the memory of John.

She didn't blame him.

It wasn't until the questions came around to Sally that Mira also grew uncomfortable.

"They had some sort of falling out," William said when they asked if John and Sally were friends. "It happened months before Sally died, though. John never told me what happened, but he didn't like her afterward. After a few weeks passed, they were at least able to be civil to each other."

"And you don't know what they fell out over?" Gabriel pressed.

"He never said, but I think it had to do with John starting to hang out with other people in the community," William said.

"What makes you think that?" Gabriel asked.

William shrugged. "He never really spent time with other supernaturals outside of the meetings, but around the time John and Sally started not getting along, John was spending time with Don."

"Who's Don?" Ian asked.

"I don't know his last name," William admitted. "He's one of the coven witches. They don't like being around me much."

"Were you surprised to see John become friends with the witches?" Ian asked.

William thought about that for a while. "John talked with pretty much everyone at the meetings, but I had never known him to be friends with any of the other supernaturals in everyday life. That could just be me, though. We weren't really close, and I've only known him for a few years."

Mira was starting to feel uncomfortable hearing William talk about John in almost friendly terms. She was having a hard time picturing him any other way than what he had been that moment he'd shot Emmit in her apartment. To her, John was a monster even before he was possessed by one.

It was also difficult to see William become more and more uncomfortable. He was obviously relieved when the detectives were ready to go.

The only other thing he said to Mira was goodbye, and that seemed half-hearted. It was disheartening to see her ring of friends getting smaller.

She wondered briefly what it would be like when Tyler woke up. Even if he decided to side with the witches and not talk to her, she'd still like to see him open his eyes.

"We have the name Don," Ian said when they were back in the car. While Gabriel drove, Ian flipped through his notes. "I think I've seen the name Donald. Mira, does it sound familiar?"

"Not to me. Robin or Mr. Singer would know," Mira said.

"This might be him," Ian said, scanning the page. "Sybil's brother. His middle name is Donald."

"Let's call Mr. Singer and see if there's anyone else who goes by that name," Gabriel said. "We can swing around and see Don tomorrow."

Traffic around them grew slower as they entered the smaller city streets.

"That leaves Martin for tonight," Ian said.

"We can drop Mira off first," Gabriel said.

"Are you sure?" Mira was surprised that she was being dropped off so soon.

"He's human," Ian reminded her. "You don't have to stick around for this one."

Mira had thought it would be her and Gabriel dropping Ian off tonight, not the other way around.

Honks bounced and echoed off the surrounding buildings as traffic came to a stop.

Mira leaned forward to see what was causing the issue. "Was there an accident?"

"Looks like," Ian said. "There's someone on scene."

Much like Levi's neighborhood, there weren't many people outside. Except for the cars and the people near the intersection ahead, the sidewalks appeared empty.

Movement off to the side caught Mira's attention.

Was that scale or fur? Mira froze. "Did you see that?"

"See what?" Gabriel asked.

Mira scrambled for her seatbelt, not taking her eyes off the spot where the creature disappeared.

"It's not possible." Mira finally made her fingers work and unbuckled herself.

"What's not?"

"I think we need to know what happened up there," Mira's voice wavered. She had her hand on the door handle, but was having trouble making herself get out of the car.

"What's wrong?" Gabriel asked. He appeared uneasy and he was looking around.

"One of those things. I could have sworn one of those things was here." Only one of 'those things' would cause Mira's reaction, so she didn't bother explaining further.

"That's not possible," Gabriel said.

Mira bit her lip. "I hope you're right." She forced her shaking body to move quickly out of the car.

Gabriel's yell of, "Don't!" was cut off by the slamming of the car door. Mira ran across the sidewalk and was surprised and somewhat disappointed that nothing tripped her up.

"Mira!" Gabriel was attempting to yell without attracting attention.

Mira ignored him and ran into the alley. She had to see—had to know.

The alley was exactly as she expected it would be. Halfway through, she realized why. She'd been here before—a few times. She'd had to pass this way sometimes when she had trouble parking her car.

Even more recently, she'd walked through here a few weeks ago in the middle of the night, while her store burned.

"Stop!" Gabriel called.

Mira stumbled, surprised that her legs followed his command and stopped. When she caught her balance, she turned to glare at Gabriel, who was quickly running straight for her.

CHAPTER 10

E HADN'T ACTUALLY CAUSED her to stop, had he?

"What—"

Mira was cut off when something slammed into her side, and she rushed from surprise to pain before she hit the ground. A scaled foot with talons struck the ground in front of her face. She squeezed her eyes shut, expecting claws or fangs at any moment. Pressure bore down on her and she couldn't help but cry out.

Death didn't come.

Gabriel reached her side and the weight lifted. He turned her over, his face all stony seriousness while his eyes showed her own fear mirrored.

The smell of burnt tar cut through her confusion. She was afraid to take her eyes off of Gabriel, even as other feet pounded through the alley.

"Did it get her?" someone asked.

"You could have killed her," Gabriel said.

"I assure you, Detective Flint, I wouldn't have risked it if I wasn't certain."

"Who are you?" Gabriel yelled, breaking eye contact with Mira.

He glared at a man standing over them. The stranger wore jeans and an old brown leather coat that looked ready to fall apart.

"I'll take care of this," the man said. "Get her out of here."

Gabriel jumped up and got into the man's face. "You shot at her!"

Mira felt dazed and looked around. Beside her, she saw the thing that she has followed into the alley.

Scales and fur. When she looked closer, she saw what appeared to be an arm had grown out of the thing's side and its head was distorted.

It was also dead. Black blood oozed out around her.

The idea of the foul muck touching her made her try to backpedal. She immediately bumped into Gabriel's leg.

"Gabriel," she squeaked, trying to grind herself into his legs in an effort to move away.

"Shit," Gabriel muttered, dragging her to her feet.

Agony spread across her arm, which felt damp in her coat. Stitches, she told herself, you just tore them open. It was a flighty thought, quickly to be replaced by stubbornly trying to stay standing until the vertigo passed. Gabriel's arm was wrapped around her, securing her in place, but he was shaking.

"I'll make sure a doctor meets up with you," the man said. "She might need it."

"You're coming with us," Gabriel snarled.

"No." The man put a hand on Gabriel's shoulder as though he were an old friend. "She's alive, but shaken. I'll take care of this."

Gabriel pulled Mira a little closer and she winced as new pains were discovered.

"Where are you hurt?" Gabriel asked, lowing his voice, but sounding tense.

"I think I ripped open the stitches in my arm." She was unsure about the man. Seeing him more clearly now, he was maybe in his late forties, with a little gray seeping from his scalp.

"Anywhere else?" Gabriel asked.

Mira didn't know where to start. "Not as bad as my arm."

"I should stay here," Gabriel said. "I'll text Ian and he'll pick you up."

"No," the older man said again.

"They're Reinfield's men," Mira whispered.

"That doesn't make me feel any better," Gabriel said. "Can you walk?"

Mira gritted her teeth and then told the truth even though she didn't want to admit it. "I—I'm not sure if I can by myself."

Gabriel's stony expression broke, revealing fear and concern. "To hell with this. They can do... whatever. Come on. I've got you."

Mira wrapped an arm around Gabriel's waist and they awkwardly walked to the main street. Gabriel didn't turn around to see what was taking place behind them, but continued to the curb where he stopped and looked her over. Mira didn't see Ian, but Gabriel didn't seem worried.

Mira started to shake and turned to look at the mouth of the alley.

"As soon as we get someplace warm, I'll look at your arm." Gabriel checked the street at incoming traffic. "Here he is."

Gabriel eased her into the backseat and circled around the car to join her from the other side.

"What the hell happened?" Ian asked, appearing aggravated.

Mira eased out of her coat.

"Shit," Gabriel said, quickly pulling her sleeve up.

"The hospital isn't far," Ian said, all traces of irritation gone.

"We're going to Emmit's apartment," Mira said.

Ian curled up his nose. "Gabe?"

"Yeah," Gabriel said, taking off his coat and shirt. "There's a doctor meeting us there." He tried to catch Mira's eye, but she felt dazed.

"She looks pale," Ian said.

"She'll be fine," Gabriel said, "but getting there faster is better."

Mira heard a tearing noise and looked over. "You're going to run out of shirts." Sadly, he was wearing another shirt under that one.

One of these days...

"They need to be replaced anyway. This is going to hurt."

Mira took a deep breath. She gritted her teeth as Gabriel wound the cloth tightly around her arm.

"How's that?" he asked.

"Not as bad as I thought."

Gabriel looked around. "Drop us off out front. I'll get a ride or something, just let me know where you leave my car."

"I can park it and come up," Ian said.

"It's no problem. I've got this." As he said it, he put his arm around Mira and drew closer to her.

He was calm now, and Mira took comfort in that.

She closed her eyes and leaned her head against his chest at the same time the car pulled to a stop.

There hadn't even been time to enjoy it.

Gabriel helped Mira out of the car and tried to hurry her into the building. In this part of town, there were people on the streets, but the cold kept their time outside brief.

The cold sliced through Mira like a knife. She wrapped her arms around herself. Gabriel threw his coat over her shoulders and got her moving again.

Mira felt a little better than she had in the alley. Once Reinfield's men had them ensconced in the elevator, Mira took stock of herself.

"I think I got blood on your coat," she said.

"Don't worry about it."

She tugged her jeans away from her leg where blood was making the fabric cling.

"Damnit," Gabriel said, squatting down to try to pull up the leg of her jeans.

"It's just a cut," Mira said, but she didn't try to push him away. "I think that thing—"

"Not here," Gabriel said, nodding slightly to the man staring straight forward who was undoubtedly her bodyguard.

"It's a cut," Mira repeated.

The door chimed and opened.

The man stepped outside and waited beside the door. "Can I assist you into the apartment?"

"I've got her," Gabriel said.

The man said nothing, but opened the front door for them.

"Take her to the second door on the left," Emmit said stiffly when they walked in. "Then, you and I are going to have a chat."

"Not now, Emmit," Gabriel said.

Mira sighed. "I just want to—"

Emmit cut Mira off. "The second door on the left."

Mira stopped and glared at him.

Emmit stared blankly at her for a few moments, and then his voice softened. "Sorry, I've been worried. The doctor wants to see you. He's already in there."

Mira shook her head and moved down the hall, not letting go of Gabriel. Emmit sounded more than a little perturbed. She didn't think she wanted him alone in the same room as Gabriel.

The doctor greeted her and started his examination at the same time.

"It looks like you've been busy. I've got some local anesthetic I'm going to give you," the doctor said.

Gabriel led Mira to the bed. He looked around the room much like Reinfield's men did, checking all the corners to make sure there was nothing waiting.

"It looks like you're in good hands," he said while the doctor gave her the injections. "I'm going to talk with Emmit. I'm not sure how much he knows."

"He knows very little," Emmit said at the door.

"While that starts to work," the doctor said, ignoring everyone but Mira, "I'm going to cut your shirt off."

"Why—"

"It will be better than risking it dragging along your arm."

"Okay," she said with a sigh. She had purposefully chosen one of her favorite shirts since she knew she'd be spending the day with Gabriel. She smiled weakly at the angel. "Looks like we're going shopping together."

"I'm getting no information from Reinfield's men beyond them saying, there was an incident," Emmit said.

"I thought they told you everything," Gabriel said.

Mira bit her lip. The doctor had a large pair of scissors in hand and she wondered how bad the skin under her shirt looked this evening. She'd been rolling on the ground more often than any adult should, so there were bound to be some blotchy bruises.

"They usually do," Emmit said. "This time, you're telling me."

"Once this is off," the doctor said as he snipped along the neckline, "we'll do the same with your jeans."

That, she knew she didn't want either of the men to see. Her hip was likely still bruised and turning green along the edges.

"It's probably best they didn't say anything," Gabriel said.

Mira cleared her throat.

"Start from the beginning of the incident," Emmit said.

"Excuse me," Mira called out. They both turned to her, though the doctor kept clipping as though nothing was happening.

"Yes?" Emmit asked.

"Can I get a little privacy?"

Emmit's forehead crinkled in confusion. "Why?"

"Are you kidding me?" Mira asked, the shirt already cut down her back—the doctor had started at the top and was working his way down the arm.

"I've seen you before," Emmit said. "There's—"

"That's enough," Gabriel said, grabbing Emmit's arm and pulling him to the door. "Let's go."

Once he nudged Emmit out, he turned around. "Do you need anything?"

"There's a robe in my bathroom, would you mind getting someone to grab it?"

"I meant the last time she was injured," Emmit said to Gabriel's back. "I wasn't talking about—"

"I'll make sure it's waiting in the hall for you," Gabriel said, closing the door.

"Thank you," Mira called.

Mira heard Gabriel's voice, muffled by the thick doors. It sounded as though he said the word idiot, causing her to smile again.

"Your other arm appears to be uninjured," the doctor said. "You can pull the shirt off that way. I'm going to start at the bottom of your jeans. Usually I have assistance on this, but with the short notice, I wasn't able to reach anyone."

"I can take my own jeans off," Mira said, standing and taking the shirt the rest of the way off. Before the doctor could argue, she stripped the rest of the way.

The doctor made quick work with her arm, admonishing her for being so active and rough while still injured.

Mira kept her head turned and her eyes shut tight the whole time. She wasn't a fan of needles.

He let her know that stitching the skin multiple times raised the chance of scarring, but he would do everything he could to prevent that.

After her arm was sewn up and covered, she opened her eyes again. The doctor had just started cleaning the cut on her leg when the yelling started.

Trying to ignore it was like trying not to pay attention to someone bouncing a balloon against your head repeatedly. It wasn't painful, and it really didn't worry her much, but still, it was seriously aggravating.

"Thank you," she said as the doctor finished bandaging her leg. "I appreciate everything you've done for me this last week."

Mira's eye twitched as the noise in the other room rose again before dying away.

"I have some pain medicine called in to the pharmacy. I'm certain Mr. Harker's, eh, employees will pick them up."

The arguing grew louder again. Mira stood and strode out of the room. She yanked the door open, and her cheeks turned red when the man in the hall held out her robe while trying to remain professional.

Mira snatched the robe from him. "Thank you," she said as she turned and tugged it over one arm before gently maneuvering her arm through the other sleeve.

"I'll leave instructions," the doctor called.

She cinched up her robe and marched to the living room, where the noise had once again died away.

"What is with you two?" Mira snapped.

They both gave her their best innocent looks, which made her roll her eyes.

"Whatever," she said under her breath. She moved to the couch and made herself comfortable, while ensuring the silky fabric of the robe covered everything it should.

"Shouldn't you be resting?" Emmit asked.

"I'm not sure anyone could sleep when you two are nearby in the same room. Emmit knows everything?" she asked Gabriel.

"Yeah," Gabriel said.

"So, who was the guy in jeans?"

Emmit stared accusingly at Gabriel. "I thought I knew everything."

"He's the guy that shot the... whatever the hell it was in the alley. I didn't describe any of the men to you—why would I bother with one just because he wore jeans."

"It explains why I didn't get any information until after you arrived," Emmit said. "Was he wearing a brown leather coat?"

"Yeah," Mira said.

"I feel much better about him shooting in your direction. You've been lucky enough to meet Reinfield himself," Emmit said. "He doesn't miss his shots."

"The man who runs the concierge service?" Gabriel asked.

"He has other people for that. Reinfield is more specialized," Emmit said. "I'd quite like to know why he's in town."

"Apparently, he's killing monsters," Mira said. "There's something seriously wrong if that thing came from the Ether."

"There's no way it came from this world," Gabriel said.

"John must have pulled it here at some point," Emmit said. "It's the only logical reason for the creature to be here."

"What if there are more of them?" Mira asked.

"If there are, I'll hear about it at the station," Gabriel said. "In fact, I need to get over there now."

"Are we doing more interviews?" Mira asked. "If you wait for me to get dressed, I'll go with you."

"Not today," Gabriel said. "Get some rest. We'll see about tomorrow."

"Are you—"

"I'm sure," Gabriel interrupted. "It might be best to stay in for a few days anyway. At least until we're sure nothing else from the Ether has slipped through."

She could feel herself being shoved aside and the thought thoroughly depressed her. "And tonight?"

The fact that Gabriel looked confused for a few seconds made her feel even worse. He'd apparently already forgotten that he'd asked her out.

"Another time," Gabriel said.

"No problem," Mira said, trying not to let her face or voice expose the despondency she was starting to feel.

"I need to return that book tomorrow," Mira said.

"I'm sure Emmit will be happy to help," Gabriel said.

The fact that he looked dejected didn't make her feel any better.

"Of course," Emmit said. "I'll assist with anything you need."

"How are you now?" Gabriel asked.

"Fine," Mira said, not feeling a bit sorry when she saw Gabriel flinch. "In fact, I should get dressed. I have some errands to run."

"Maybe you should—"

"I'll see you around," Mira said, cutting him off. She left before he had time to debate.

Once out of sight from the living room, she slowed down her pace, wanting to catch what they said after she left, while at the same time telling herself she didn't care.

They didn't say more than a few words to each other, and she couldn't make them out.

Which is good, she told herself. It doesn't matter what they said.

Her guard was waiting for her at her door. As she approached, he entered the room. When Mira walked in, he was returning from the bathroom, doing his usual security sweep.

"No monsters under the bed?" Mira asked.

"Not at the moment," he said. "Is there anything I can assist you with?"

"No thanks, I'm good." What she needed help with was something he could do nothing about.

"I'll be in the hall if you need anything."

She nodded and sat on the corner of her bed. Two days out of the tower and she was already sent back. The building felt like a prison that had forgotten to put bars in the windows.

Looking glumly around the room, she saw that someone had left her purse, clothes—even the cut shirt—and Gabriel's coat on the dresser.

Right away, she saw that there was a good chance Gabriel's coat was ruined. The jeans she'd wash and hope for the best. She inspected the shirt, noticing a large patch of black on the side. She curled her nose up at what had to be the beast's blood.

Knowing that thing had bled on her made her skin crawl. All thoughts fled her mind, except getting to the shower as quickly as she could. She dropped her clothes off on the floor, not actually wanting to take time to stop and remove anything. In the bathroom, she turned the water up as hot as she could stand and showered while trying to keep her injured arm out of the water.

It wasn't an easy feat.

Another set of hands would have been ideal, but whose would they be? She lathered her hair with one hand and thought wistfully of Gabriel, until she remembered that he'd blown off their date that evening.

It had been a date, right? When he asked her about tonight, she had no doubt that's what it was, but now she didn't feel sure.

As much as she hated to think it, Emmit was out of the question. She had no doubts that he would help her wash everything from head to toe, and she was even more certain that she'd enjoy every minute of it. At least until the morning when she'd hate herself.

Emmit was handsome, rich—although she had no idea where his money came from—and he liked her. Nevertheless, it all felt temporary and fleeting. Even when thinking about Emmit, thoughts of anything being long term never came to mind. She couldn't even fathom the prospect.

Gabriel was different. She couldn't wait until this disaster was over with. After John was in jail or in the ground—she didn't much care which—and after the witches started talking to her again, then maybe things would slow down. If life were normal, with a car, job, and simple days, she'd get the chance to know if there was something real with Gabriel.

There were already feelings building between the two of them, but maybe it was one sided. As she thought about all the times he'd saved her, she feared he'd think being with her wasn't worth the drama.

That was probably why he called tonight off, seeing as she almost got mauled in the middle of the day by some creature from another dimension.

She turned off the water and struggled to dry off one handed.

Hell, I'm too much drama for me. He's only doing the smart thing.

By the time she was dressed, she was exhausted, but she didn't want to go to sleep yet after announcing that she had things to do. Gabriel wasn't going to let her help with the case at the moment, but that didn't mean she couldn't be of any help at all.

CHAPTER 11

GRABBING HER PURSE, SHE wandered in the living room in search of Emmit. The room felt larger when no one was in there beyond herself and her shadow.

"Do you know where Emmit is?" Mira asked the bodyguard.

There was a long pause where he said nothing. She wondered for a moment if he had been told not to answer her, but that was crazy.

Finally, he said, "In his office. Past the kitchen to the right."

"What's your name?" Mira asked on the way.

"Eric, ma'am."

"You can call me Mira."

"Yes, ma'am."

"Or Miranda, if you want to be all formal."

"Yes, ma'am."

"You're going to call me ma'am or Ms. Owens, aren't you?" she asked as she reached what she figured was the door to Emmit's office.

"Yes, ma'am."

When she looked at him, he grinned. "It's for the best," he said. "Please, let me."

He didn't give her a chance to say no. Eric knocked once before stepping in and doing a cursory sweep of the room.

"Thank you, Eric," Emmit said. "I'm sure you're due a break. Mira, please come in and take a seat."

The office was nothing like she'd imagined. There was a desk in the corner, but it looked mostly unused. Instead, a long table with books and stacks of paper stood centrally in the room.

A soft leather couch and a few chairs were set up next to tall windows and she went there to settle in. She enjoyed the feeling of suede when she sat. It was as though the couch would encompass her.

Emmit joined her but said nothing.

"This is a little awkward," she said after a while.

"I wish it wasn't the case," Emmit said.

"What are you working on?" Mira asked, nodding to the table that dominated the room.

"Research, mostly," Emmit said. "The pathways to the Ether haven't been this thin since the witches stopped using them. If what you and Gabriel have described is true, then the issue has gone too far to be fixed by ordinary means."

"Ordinary and the Ether don't go well together. It sounds all wrong."

"As it should."

"Do you know what happened last time?" Mira asked, leaning her head against the couch. "When the witches disappeared?"

"It's my understanding the Ether was a beautiful place then—almost the opposite of what it is now. It was a gleaming, pure reflection of this world. Witches didn't discover the realm, it was shown to them, but they used it often. The time they spent there made them more powerful. For many, it became like an addiction."

Mira knew addiction well, so she said nothing.

"It didn't take long before the witches became out of hand in this world."

"Out of hand, how?" Mira asked.

"They had enough power to do as they pleased. People lived in fear of the witches."

"I didn't know that. I thought they just started disappearing."

"They did disappear. Slowly, at first, and then all who entered the Ether never returned. History is what people make of it. The witches that survived were not proud of what had occurred, so they choose to erase many of the facts."

"What happened to them?"

Emmit looked at nothing for a few moments, as though trying to piece together the past. "It's hard to know for sure. The supernatural community was small at the time. Werewolves and vampires had been hunted almost to extinction. Elves were unknown, sorcerers were living on their own—virtually hidden from the entire world—and any mythological creature that couldn't pass as human stayed well away from civilization."

"What do you think happened?" Mira asked, not wanting to let the subject drop.

"People with power, especially if some are misusing that power, create many enemies."

"That's understandable, but with so few supernaturals around, who—"

"Humans."

"But that's..." Mira tried to absorb the idea, but was having difficulty. "I mean, if the witches were so powerful, how could the humans do anything?"

"How are they doing it now?" Emmit asked.

Mira sat quietly, trying to see the flaws. "They're using magic, but it's not only humans."

"This is true, but the humans are involved."

"They have witches helping them now—what did they have back then? Was it... Was it those things? Like the monster that attacked me today?"

"They wouldn't have helped," Emmit said. "When you were in the Ether, you saw the creature covering this building. I think that was what the humans used."

"John said some people called it a god."

"Some do. The elder gods became nothing more than a sentient parasite in the Ether. Thousands of witches have been sacrificed to it throughout the ages. The power of magic keeps it alive and growing, and there will always be humans that want to put an end to those that wield more power than they do."

"How was this stopped last time?" Mira asked.

"Humans had no idea what they'd created. The polarity of the Ether was flipped. Eventually, witches stopped coming for fear they wouldn't return, but the walls between the worlds were so thin that the elder gods could feel the power remaining in our world. I suspect the witches that went to the Ether no longer tasted as good. "

Mira cringed at the thought. "It tried to get through?"

"Yes," Emmit said. "Although I can't be sure there was only one. It was much smaller than what you've described, but possibly more powerful since it had fresher food. Then again, this one has been fed."

"The ones John killed." Mira felt ill to think that Sally had been murdered to feed this thing.

"And Tyler. From what Gabriel described, there were others as well."

"I didn't see anyone but Tyler and the kids."

"He felt it prudent to spare you those details."

Mira felt heavy and closed her eyes, but nightmarish visions of what might have been in that house greeted her. "The kids?" she asked, not sure if she wanted to hear anymore.

"They weren't used for that purpose. I'm not sure why they were being held."

"How do we stop it?" Mira asked.

Emmit looked at the table covered in books and paper. "I thought if I left, the power draw wouldn't be as great, but that is no longer the case. The walls are too thin and there is strong power here, other than mine, to draw on."

"Why didn't you tell us this before?" Mira asked.

Emmit gave her a weak smile. "I wanted to keep you out of it as much as possible. For many reasons, not all of them good ones."

"And Gabriel?"

"Gabriel is too important to risk. He'll watch out for you, but this whole world might need him in the end."

"Why?"

"Angels are hard to come by and greatly needed. You could say they keep a kind of balance in this world."

Mira's trouble with Gabriel sounded minuscule by comparison.

"He'll need you as well."

Not believing that for even a moment, she cleared her throat and tried to shift gears away from Gabriel. "Now that you've told me, how do we stop this thing?"

"I'm sure I'll find an answer soon," Emmit said smoothly.

"Anything I can do to help?"

"Not until I know what I'm doing."

"Would you let me know if I could do anything?"

Emmit smiled at her. "Possibly."

Mira shook her head. "Out of curiosity, why are you letting me know about this now?"

"Witches are good at keeping track of things if they want to. Spell books are passed down for hundreds of years, rewritten as needed. Even if you change a spell, families are usually able to trace things to the source."

"You want me to check spell books?"

"That wouldn't hurt, but I'm afraid the witches in the past wouldn't have wanted to record this knowledge. The reason I'm letting you know now is so that you'll write it down. Keep track of the information. The truth needs to be passed down in case it's needed again."

"Are you sure?"

"I am. Who knows, maybe one of your descendants will help a future Harker."

"Why are you the one doing this?"

He smiled again. "People always wonder what type of supernatural the Harkers are."

Mira lifted her head, feeling suddenly alert. She definitely wanted to know the same.

"The truth is I'm a Harker. It's not only who I am, but also what I am. My family has prevented, stopped, and even eradicated many conflicts in the past. It was my ancestor that sealed off the Ether the last time."

"How come no one knows that?"

"Some do. Lance has seen some of the work that the Harkers have done."

"Are there many Harkers?" Mira realized what she asked and rushed to correct herself. "You don't have to answer that, of course. I mean, I know you have a sister, but I didn't know if there were any other Harkers out in the world."

"There are very few for good reason," he said.

"Why's that?" Mira asked.

"The witches, vampires, and werewolves weren't the only ones to let themselves get out of control."

"Oh," Mira said, surprised, "I've never heard anything about it."

"History is what you make it," Emmit repeated his earlier sentiment.

Mira's head whirled with information, and she felt even more tired than she previously had. "Thank you for telling me."

"You may not want to thank me in the end," Emmit said. "I should get back to work, and you look as though you could use some rest."

Mira nodded. "I need to do some stuff first."

"Someone has delivered the prescription the doctor left for you."

"I need to go to my apartment."

Emmit looked uncomfortable. "I'm not certain that's wise. We don't know where John might be."

"Since I doubt anyone will let me out of here alone, I'm sure someone will be with me."

"Reinfield's men are only human. At least most of them."

"Last time I was home an angel and a Harker couldn't stop John."

"All the more reason for you to stay here," Emmit said. "If you make a list, we can have someone go over and get anything you need."

"Not a chance," Mira said. "What I'm after they'd never be able to find."

Emmit frowned and drummed his fingers on the arm of the couch.

"In case you missed it," Mira said, starting to get aggravated, "I wasn't asking. It was more of a 'heads up, I'm going out.'"

"Would it be possible to wait until tomorrow?" Emmit asked. "It'll allow time for Reinfield's men to double check the area."

Mira opened her mouth to argue out of reflex, but her arm was starting to ache, and an evening curled up in her room with Alchemy and Oracle sounded ideal. "I do have another errand that I have to run tomorrow. I guess it wouldn't hurt to wait." It wasn't as if she had the energy to cast any spells that night anyway.

"Thank you," Emmit said. "I'd love to join you, if you don't mind."

"We'll see."

Mira assumed the pain in her arm was what woke her up, but her cell phone started ringing again. Despite the one AM call time, Mira jumped out of bed, feeling alert.

Normally, Mira never slept with the phone volume up, but she'd fostered a small hope that her sister or mother may chance a late-night call.

The number was unknown to Mira, but she answered anyway. "Hello."

"Is this Mira Owens?"

Her tiny ray of hope burned out. "It is."

"I'm sorry to bother you so late, but your friend Tyler is awake and asking for you. Normally, we would wait, but he is quite insistent that he see you tonight and refuses to rest."

Tyler has been 'resting' for days, Mira thought. He's probably aggravated about the missed time. It's definitely his way.

There was a knock at the door.

"Tell him I'm on my way," Mira said.

When she hung up, the door cracked open. In a low voice, a man asked, "Is there anything you need assistance with, Ms. Owens?"

"Yes," Mira said, not bothering to be quiet. "I need a ride to the hospital."

The man looked alarmed and stepped into the room, already searching for hidden threats. "Are you inj—"

"It's not for me. I need to go see my friend." Mira snapped on a light and began to rush through getting ready.

Tonight's bodyguard wasn't comfortable leaving the room. That's what I get for surprising the man in the middle of the night, Mira thought distractedly. He was probably intending on doing nothing more than seeing how long he could stand without blinking.

Lesson learned; never startle your own bodyguard. Mira ground her teeth, waiting for the man to clear the bathroom.

Once again, she told herself this was going too far. There was no way she could continue living with someone who shadowed her at all times of the day and night.

Then she remembered the creature that had attacked her.

Maybe a few more days wouldn't hurt.

"Is the car ready?" she asked as she grabbed her purse and phone.

"There is a vehicle waiting for us out front."

She glanced around her bedroom one last time, always feeling that she was missing something when she rushed.

Alchemy tried to trip her up, but didn't follow her out of the room.

Emmit waited for her at the front door.

"Did the hospital call you, too?" Mira asked.

"No," Emmit said. "I was fortunate enough to get the message, however. May I accompany you?"

Tyler had asked for her, but she figured having Emmit along wouldn't hurt. They were also friends, after all.

"Of course," Mira said.

The elevator stood waiting for them, and in a few minutes, they were on their way across town.

For some reason, Mira felt satisfied that her bodyguard for the night had been left at the apartment. Sure, two men were in the front seat that could serve the same purpose, but they were probably more worried about Emmit.

He paid the bills, after all.

The city center still thrived, even when the late hours of the night tripped over and became the early hours of the morning. As they moved away from the tall buildings, the night turned lonely and forlorn.

"How is your arm this morning?" Emmit asked.

"Not bad," Mira lied, figuring as soon as she got home she would take one of the pain pills prescribed. She could rough it until then.

"It's amazing that when someone is around a person like Gabriel, they become worse at lying instead of better."

Mira turned to deny it, but saw the grin that played on Emmit's face. She couldn't help but match it.

Lights flared behind Emmit, illuminating the truck. Then metal and glass crunched in, swallowing Emmit.

Mira's heart didn't have time to catch up. She was slung around like a rag doll, smashing into airbags as the car was thrown around.

Glass flew around her and she squeezed her eyes shut tight. Movement slowed, stopped, and then nothing but the sound of an engine remained. Mira didn't move—there hadn't been any time for panic or fear, only shock. If she moved now, she was certain that pain would shortly follow.

Doors slammed.

Good, she thought someone's here. They can get help. She dared to open her eyes.

In the seat in front of her, the man didn't move. She could only bear to look at the driver for a few moments. She turned to Emmit and cried out.

The side of the truck and the roof had been pushed over him. His seat had collapsed back, which probably saved his life.

She hoped it had saved his life.

"Emmit?"

Only his upper body was visible. His head was turned toward her, but his eyes were shut.

"Emmit!" Mira began fumbling to remove her seatbelt but was having trouble finding it. Her hands were shaking. They didn't want to work.

Her car door was wrenched open as she unclipped her belt.

She arched forward to reach Emmit, but hands grabbed her arm and pulled her out.

Someone hooked their arms under hers and dragged her backward, away from the wreckage. With each step the person took, Mira could see more of the scene.

A garbage truck had hit them on the driver's side.

Sirens rose in the distance and she hoped the empty streets would help the emergency crew to reach them quickly.

Mira was dropped unceremoniously on the ground, where she smacked her head on concrete. White lights popped behind her closed eyes.

"Hey! Hey! Open your eyes, damn you!"

Mira blinked a few times, letting the figure come into view.

She screamed.

"Yeah, I have that effect on people," said the scarred face. "Get up."

John's face was covered in burn scars, but that wasn't what caused her stomach to revolt. The creature was still using John's body, despite the fact that his shell looked beyond being dead.

"You're hard to get at," John said, kicking her leg lightly. "Now, we've got to go."

Mira was still trying to wrap her mind around what had happened.

"Come on," John grabbed her under the arms and tried to drag her to her feet.

"I'm not going with you," Mira said. In the back of her mind, she knew that she wasn't protesting or being as forceful as she should, but that part of her was being blocked out by the confusion and shock of the incident.

He struggled for a while longer before dropping her. "Dammit, get up already! You stupid—"

John stopped and looked around, apparently startled. Then he reached for her again.

Her brain kicked into low gear, realizing that it was a dead man reaching out for her. She pushed herself onto her elbows and scuttled to the side.

"Stupid witch," he spat. "That's okay, though. If you won't come with me now, then you're going to come to me later."

"What?" Mira asked, tears running down her face.

"That's right, Princess. You're going to ditch your guards and leave your tower. If you don't, the witch in the hospital is dead, your angel friend will be taken away, and then we'll move on to your family."

"What?"

Nothing John was saying was soaking in.

The sound of metal scraping against metal made John's head whip around to the accident.

"I'm out of time. You've got my number. You should, anyway, it hasn't even been an hour since I called."

"You—"

"When I call, you'll come, or I'll make you regret it."

He disappeared.

Mira laid, stunned, on what she hoped was the sidewalk. The cold seeped through her clothes. Seconds ticked by as she tried to comprehend what had just happened.

"Mira!"

Thoughts of John tore away like cobwebs. "Gabriel?" She didn't yell—she was too dazed and too cold to yell. Even the concept of raising her voice made her head ache.

"Shit."

Feet pounded toward her and she leveraged herself up to a sitting position.

Gabriel appeared over her. He took off his coat, which he immediately tossed over Mira. It didn't take her body long to soak up the warmth Gabriel had left behind.

"Lie down," Gabriel said, somehow maintaining a professional composure.

"Where did you come from?" Mira asked.

His calmness broke. "I— I tried to call... I didn't make it in time. I tried—"

The sound of metal bending out of shape made Gabriel look up.

"Tell me where it hurts," he said, more adamant this time.

Mira had to think about the question. She was feeling light headed, and the world didn't seem real anymore. Could it be real if John was in it?

"Mira, answer me," Gabriel insisted.

"I think... I think I'm cold. Help me up."

"Not a chance, you could be hurt. There's an ambulance on the way."

"There are a million airbags in that vehicle and it's freezing. I only hit my head on the concrete when..." She didn't want to finish that statement. It still seemed unreal.

"Mira!" It was a roar more than a yell.

Mira cringed, wondering what fresh hell was about to be bestowed on her.

"Jesus, Harker," Gabriel snapped. "Shut the hell up."

Gabriel had barely got out his name before Emmit appeared beside them.

"She's alive?" Emmit asked, barely disguising his fury.

When she moved to stand, Gabriel moved closer and her way up was barred.

"You're going to scare her. Back off," Gabriel said.

But Mira wasn't scared of Emmit. All fear was reserved for John. Still, hot energy poured over her and she decided the wisest decision would be to stay on the ground.

"Go help the others," Gabriel said.

"No." Emmit's voice was a dark dam ready to burst. "I can't be found on the scene."

"You're leaving?" Gabriel asked through clenched teeth.

"I will momentarily, now that I see she is alive."

"It's not life threatening," Gabriel said. "At least as far as I can tell."

"Where were you?" Emmit asked. "Someone did this and you were nowhere."

"Go to hell," Gabriel said. "And if you're going to leave, do it. The ambulance is almost here."

"Give me a moment," Emmit said, trying to bring his anger under control.

"Not a chance."

"You're a cop," Emmit snapped. "Go check on the others."

Gabriel glared up at him and they stared at each other. Mira had no idea what passed unspoken between them.

"I'll be right back," Gabriel said. "One minute."

Emmit crouched down next to her and took her hand, but he watched Gabriel until he was well away.

Then he looked at her, slowly taking in every inch of her as though he was able to look beyond her clothes to the skin beneath.

"Are you badly injured?" Emmit asked, his voice softer than she'd expected.

"No, but I'm cold. Help me up."

"We should take Gabriel's advice on this. Wait until a professional can check on you."

"Emmit Harker, if you don't help me up right now, I'll—I'll—"

Emmit watched her, eyebrows raised, waiting for the end of the sentence.

Threatening to curse Emmit seemed ludicrous, so Mira changed tactics. "Just help me up."

"You have some fire in you." A small smile appeared as Emmit took Mira's hand and pulled her up, but he watched her carefully.

Mira clutched at Gabriel's coat and wrapped it around her once she was steady.

"I'm not sure what happened tonight," Emmit said, "but I will find out."

Mira was going to tell him about John, but her brain and mouth seemed to be disagreeing on that course of action.

The sirens were almost to them.

"I'll be nearby," Emmit said.

He was gone the moment the words left his mouth.

CHAPTER 12

DREAMS CAME AND WENT. Angels and demons fighting. The mysterious Chris, smoking his pipe while watching Mira run, trying to escape John.

Sometimes, she fought alongside the demon, sometimes the angel. There were times when they both battled against her and she stood no hope.

When she clawed her way out of a twisted dream—one where she and John stood over Gabriel and laughed—she opened her eyes to a brightly lit room. Sadly, it was one completely unfamiliar to her.

When she moved, muscles protested and she groaned.

Memories from the night before came out of hiding. The night had become a string of flashing lights and commotion. One of Reinfield's men had died on the scene and the other had been injured.

Mira was the only one left from the accident that hadn't been forced to go to the hospital, but the EMTs checked her out on the scene.

Another person was found dead as well. The other driver hadn't been wearing his seatbelt. Mira wondered if John had forced the man to drive, or if the man had been working with John.

The driver would never be able to tell them.

When Gabriel took her away from the mess, Mira had fallen asleep as he drove carefully through the city. She remembered waking up and going into a house and...

And that's it, I guess, Mira thought.

She tried to stretch, but her body was one big ache made worse when she spread her arms wide.

Noises from another room forced Mira out of bed, despite not being happy with the movement. She was still fully dressed from last night, minus shoes.

Mira practically tiptoed across the room and slowly opened the door, only to find a short empty hallway, at the end of which she found Gabriel, humming while cooking.

"Oh good," Gabriel said when he noticed her. "You're up."

"Yeah." Mira didn't remember the decision to go to Gabriel's, but her heart warmed at the idea that she was there.

"How are you feeling this morning?"

"Sore," Mira admitted.

"I've got something for that. And lunch is almost ready."

"Thanks."

"Don't thank me yet—we still need to talk about last night."

Mira wrinkled her nose at the suggestion and looked around. "You have a nice house."

"Thanks." Gabriel tipped a sandwich out of the pan and onto a plate before sliding it across the counter to her.

"This smells good."

"I think you'll like it. Let's take a seat."

The kitchen had a breakfast table next to two large side-by-side windows. Mira could only see a fence and sky when she looked out, but at least the sun was shining.

"Do you remember everything that happened last night?"

"Yeah. Up to the point I fell asleep, anyway. How is..." She realized she didn't know the other passengers' names and her stomach dropped.

"Harker is fine, if that's what you're worried about. He's called a few times."

"Not Emmit. The others."

"You already know about the driver. The passenger has a broken arm and he's bruised pretty badly."

Mira pictured her driver and turned inward. "I can't believe... I mean..." She closed her eyes and took a deep breath, trying not to think about it.

"It was a bad wreck. We're lucky it didn't kill everyone involved."

Mira nodded.

"The authorities are looking into the accident. Harker is digging deeper, but can't seem to find anything about the driver to indicate this was anything other than an accident. The only thing out of place is Tyler. He never woke up."

Mira shook her head.

"I, on the other hand, think you know something. I found you a dozen yards away, and it didn't look like you got there on your own."

"It was John." Mira didn't see the point in trying to hide the fact.

"Jesus. That asshole has more lives than a cat."

"He was burned pretty badly, but he's still going."

More for something to do rather than hunger, Mira started to eat lunch, which was even better than it smelled.

"What did he want?" Gabriel asked.

Mira twisted uncomfortably in her seat. That part was the thing she really didn't want to discuss.

"He wanted you," Gabriel guessed.

"Yes," Mira said with a sigh. "I'm supposed to meet him tomorrow."

"His brain must be starting to die if he thinks you'll meet or go anywhere near him."

"Right," Mira said halfheartedly.

Gabriel drummed his fingers on the table. "Why does he think you'll come?"

"Tyler. He said he'd kill Tyler and..." Mira faltered. Did she want Gabriel to know John had threatened him as well? "And go after my family."

"And?" Gabriel asked.

She had no idea if he'd heard the lie by omission or if he was just that good at reading people. "He said he'd take you away."

Gabriel shook his head. "Tyler's easy to look after—Harker can put some people on it, I'm sure. We can get word to your family as well. I think the community will help."

"And you?"

Gabriel looked at her as if she was crazy. "If he comes near either of us, I'll shoot him. This time, I won't stop until he stops moving."

Mira knew that was easy to say, but much harder to put into practice.

When their plates were empty, Gabriel stacked them and put them next to the sink.

"I can do the dishes if you want," Mira said, following him.

"They can wait. You should put some shoes on. I have nightmares about you not wearing shoes."

Mira wiggled her toes. "I'm not sure where you put them."

"Under the bed. You should grab your stuff, too. We need to get over to Harker's place."

Mira's shoulders sagged at the thought.

"We won't be there long." Gabriel's voice dropped the professional edge he'd been using since she woke. "Unless you want to be there longer, of course."

That was enough to perk Mira up. "Are we doing more interviews today?"

Gabriel had a worried look in his eyes. "Not today. We're moving you out of Harker's place and into here."

"Here, as in your house?"

"There are two extra bedrooms, so you can take your pick— or stay in one and we can set the other up for your workshop. There's also space in the garage you can use. I'm not sure where you can hide stuff, but I bet we can come up with something."

"You want me to move in with you?"

He seemed to be losing steam. "If you'd rather stay at Harker's place I'm sure he has other rooms I can use."

"No!" Mira said much more quickly than she intended. "No, but maybe I should move back home."

"I can sleep on the couch."

Mira's lips sprung up in the corners. "Are you planning on following me around?"

"Yes," he said, completely serious. "I'm not going to be so far away again. And relying on others..." he trailed off, as he seemed to forget what he was going to say. "Anyway, I'm sticking close by."

"You can't blame yourself for last night," Mira said, reading between the lines. "The creature living inside John appears to be getting desperate."

Gabriel said nothing.

Mira felt that words would be wasted trying to convince him further. "Does Emmit know you want me to move out? After last night, I'm surprised he hasn't tracked me down yet."

"I thought it best to tell Harker face to face." Gabriel grinned, but managed to hide it quickly.

"That should be a fun conversation," Mira said.

"In the end, it's your choice."

"My choice to have you follow me around?"

"That's my choice," Gabriel said. "Your choice is whether I get the couch, my own bed, or if I have to sleep outside your apartment in my car."

Mira liked how he casually left out Emmit's apartment.

Gabriel being beside her, that was something she could live with—wanted to live with—but there was no way she'd admit it.

"Let's give your bed a shot," she said.

He grinned. "That sounds more promising than I intended."

She couldn't help but return the smile. "Good."

Butterflies swarmed Mira's stomach while they looked at each other. Her breathing became shallower and faster.

The phone rang, killing the moment.

"That'll be Harker." Gabriel made no move to answer the phone. Instead, he looked pointedly down to her feet.

She wriggled her toes again in response.

"Shoes," he said. "Then we can go before Harker ruptures something."

Emmit wasn't happy, but didn't react quite the way Mira had anticipated.

He calmly asked to speak to Gabriel for a while alone, so Mira just shrugged and went to pack her things.

When she entered the room, she could only stare around. She'd been here less than a week, but somehow she had burrowed into the place. How could she dig her way out?

Figuring the bathroom to be the most difficult part, since she had used it as her only true sanctuary away from people, she skipped it and started with the closet.

How did she have so many clothes? She swore the hangers spontaneously created them somehow. After she folded a few outfits and laid them out on the bed, she second-guessed her packing. It wasn't a permanent move any more than staying in Emmit's apartment. What would Gabriel think if she hauled tons of stuff over to his house?

The other issue was luggage. She had a few bags to pack things around in and nothing more.

Mira sorted through her belongings. She'd just have to explain to Emmit that she'd return for the rest. Even though her apartment wasn't in use, she could still store her stuff there.

Packing only what she needed for the next few days was a quick process. Rising and falling energy could be felt in the living room, but the two weren't shouting.

Maybe it was an improvement?

Instead of interrupting, Mira wound her way through the hallways, crossing the kitchen and letting herself into Emmit's study.

John wanted strength, and since she had the most, it raised a big fat target on her back. He wasn't going to let her go.

Emmit had the only information she knew of about the Ether.

The table was long and crowded with materials. At first, she only walked around it, searching for a trace of anything that might look familiar. At the far end, she decided to delve into the mess. She carefully opened the nearest book, finding a language so far different from her own that even the letters didn't make any sense.

Moving on, she found where Emmit must have been working. The surrounding books had some symbols of witchcraft, some English, and another in Latin.

More importantly, she found his notes.

Emmit wrote in a mixture of Latin and English. Since college was a few years in the past, and Mira hadn't seen a lick of Latin since, she could only make rough translations of what he was saying. His drawings, however, were more intelligible.

The first illustration showed a double circle, much like the one that she had used when she'd cast the Balance spell for him. This one had runes along the outside. From what she could see, there was no matching potion to go with it, so she assumed he must be intending straight circle magic.

On the next page, she found another double circle, much smaller, with three points surrounding, but this one didn't even have runes around it.

Mira wondered briefly if this was the way to open a pathway to the Ether. Emmit mentioned that if he went to the other side, he could fix the problem, but then he'd be stuck there. Maybe this was a way around it.

A steady flow of energy from both Emmit and Gabriel distracted Mira. Sighing, she looked at all the research piled up on the table, knowing she'd never understand even a quarter of what laid there.

What she could do was stop Emmit and Gabriel from aggravating the hell out of each other, even if just for a short interval.

Mira closed the door behind her, ready to intervene. When she entered the living room, however, she found she was alone. After a few moments, she revised the thought to almost alone. Eric, one of Reinfield's men, stood rigidly next to the entryway. She chewed on her lip, wondering if she should approach the man.

It seemed almost wrong not to.

"Hi, Eric," Mira said, walking slowly over.

"Good afternoon. Is there anything I can assist you with?"

"Do you ever get tired of saying that?"

He didn't say anything, but he grinned.

"Can I ask you something?"

"Certainly."

She wrung her hands. "It's about last night."

Eric shifted his stance.

"About the driver." Mira looked at her hands and tried not to tear up. "Did he have any family?"

Eric didn't say anything.

"I just wanted to—I don't know—do something I guess. Not that there's anything I really could do."

"Mr. Harker and Detective Flint are on their way upstairs," Eric said.

"Oh," Mira said, feeling her chest tighten. "Okay. I guess I'll get my bag."

She was almost out of the room when she got a response, although not the one she wanted.

"Let me help you with that." Eric strode across the room and passed her. Mira had to walk fast to keep up. Once in her room, he looked around before closing the door.

Mira felt a little leery. It wasn't like she actually knew the man, and she had essentially caused his coworker—maybe even friend—to die in an awful accident.

He twisted an earpiece out of his ear and cupped it in his hand. "We don't really talk about this kind of thing, but Ronnie was a good guy and he wouldn't want you to be concerned."

Mira tried to swallow past the lump in her throat, but wasn't having any luck.

"We know the risks of our job. Ronnie's family is well taken care of by Mr. Reinfield. We'll watch your back and make sure this guy doesn't get to you."

"I'm not worried about that."

"We are."

She nodded at looked at her hands again, gripping each other until they turned white. "So, there's nothing I can do?"

"We've got this." Eric, using exaggerated movements to make sure she noticed, reinserted the earpiece. "Do you have anything additional?"

She glanced around the room and noticed the protocols on the nightstand. She grabbed it and put it in her purse.

"I think I have everything. Thank you."

He smiled and opened the door for her.

Mira jumped when Emmit appeared in the doorframe. Her heart raced at the sudden appearance.

Eric stood more rigid.

"Is everything all right?" Emmit asked, glancing at Eric before turning his attention to Mira.

"Of course," Mira said. "Sorry I snagged one of the guards, but I'm not feeling great and needed help with my bag."

Emmit relaxed slightly. "I should have thought of that."

"And I wanted to see if someone could bring Alchemy and Oracle to Gabriel's. Although, I could pick them up now with some help."

"I'll ensure they make it there immediately."

"What did you do with Gabriel?"

"Let me get your bag." Emmit nodded at Eric and took the bag, and then put an arm around Mira to escort her. "Gabriel is in the living room."

"What were you all doing?" Mira asked.

"Making arrangements," Emmit said.

"Arguing, you mean."

Emmit ignored the remark. "I might need to leave unexpectedly, and I wanted to make sure all would be well in my absence."

"You can't go," Mira said.

Emmit stiffened again. "I'm sorry."

"I mean, if you're going..." She paused, and then glanced at Eric, who was following fairly close behind. "If you're thinking of going to where Gabriel and I went, don't." When he didn't respond, she added, "Please. You can't just disappear."

Emmit moved in front of her and pulled her into a gentle but insistent hug, which she returned, worried she wouldn't see him again.

Someone sighed, and Mira pictured Gabriel seeing them like this. She couldn't see around Emmit, but who else could it be?

Emmit didn't seem to care. "The best I can do is promise to talk with you or Gabriel again, sometime soon. You know how to reach me if you ever need to, and you'll always have a room here if you want."

Mira nodded and pulled away. For a moment, she didn't think Emmit was going to let go. When he did relinquish her, it was with reluctance.

He put an arm around her back again and continued to the living room. Mira was glad Gabriel wasn't in the hall.

"Gabriel is correct in this instance. This move will keep you safer. Although," he added in a louder voice as they entered the living room, "I'd prefer you both stay here."

"You'll know where we'll be," Gabriel said. "Do you have everything you need?"

"It's been a long day," Emmit said. "I'll have the rest of your belongings sent over."

They said their goodbyes in the entryway, and before she knew it, Mira was out of the building. Standing in front, she looked up at the towering building as though saying goodbye again.

"You're good with the move, right?" Gabriel asked.

Mira lowered her gaze and smiled at him. "It never felt like I belonged here."

"And with me? Do you feel like you belong at my house?"

"I think it'll be interesting to find out."

CHAPTER 13

MIRA HELD THE BOOK, safely wrapped in its envelope, in her hands, and looked through the windows at the used bookstore. The same girl worked the counter.

"I'm sure Chris would understand if you weren't up to returning it today," Gabriel said.

Mira gave him a skeptical look. "Do you actually believe that?"

"Yeah, okay. Maybe not." Gabriel looked around the street. "Let's get inside."

Mira couldn't help but look around as well. "Is something going to happen?"

"We're going to get colder. Come on."

Gabriel opened the door for her and Mira veered straight to the girl behind the counter.

"Excuse me," Mira had to say to get the girl's attention.

The girl rolled her eyes up, not bothering to move her head to look at Mira and said, "Uhh," making sure she sounded put upon before grabbing the key. Then she saw Gabriel and sat up a little straighter. "Here you go." She handed the key to Gabriel, who smiled broadly at her.

"Thank you," he said as Mira walked off.

The towers of books made Mira uncomfortably aware of earthquake possibilities. She had to remind herself that with

Gabriel here, she should be safe. As she wound through the building, a treacherous little part of herself said, like last night? But Mira assumed that today's change in living arrangements was in response to last night. He wanted to keep her safe.

Last night definitely hadn't been his fault.

At the door, Gabriel passed the key over to Mira. Behind it, they found the same fabric blocking the view of the room to the outside world.

Then she hesitated.

Chris saw far more than anyone else she knew. Emmit may appear to look into her, but Chris saw everything that made her the witch she was. He saw the power and the karma. What else did he see?

She went to wrap her hand in Gabriel's, as she had so many times in the Ether, but she stopped herself. Instead, she plunged inside to hide the twitch of her arm.

"Hmmm," came the voice in the darkness as Gabriel shut the door behind them. "I see you brought tall, blond, and gorgeous with you. I trust you have my book?"

Mira once again tried to look at every book as she passed. There weren't many of them, as books were given space to breathe in the room, but some of the titles weren't easy to comprehend

"I do," Mira said, pulling the book out of her purse as she tried to read a book with a title made out of runes.

"And what did you think?" Chris asked.

"I think it sucks and this whole shunning thing is crap." Mira was surprised it came out that way, but something about Chris made her want to tell it as she saw it. Maybe because he was on the outside looking in, same as she was at the moment.

"Oh, you blind little witch," Chris said.

"Hey!" Mira snapped.

Gabriel put a hand on her shoulder, and she crossed her arms instead of ranting.

"What's she supposed to be seeing?" Gabriel asked.

Chris sighed. "Singer assumed he was making it easy." Louder, he said, "You don't exist."

"Yeah," Mira scoffed, "that's the part that sucks."

"I don't know what you did to get where you are," Chris said, "but I do know that if Singer is giving you this, it's because what you may have to do next is going to break a whole lot of rules."

Mira thought about what she had to do next. Stay alive? Find John, maybe? None of it seemed too bad.

"So what happens if she breaks a bunch of rules?" Gabriel asked.

"She doesn't exist, cutie pie. Nothing counts to the witches."

"So, she can do what she wants?"

"Well, the community will see her. They have their own rules, but they won't interfere with the witch side of things. There's always the humans, too, of course. You can't get caught breaking human rules. At least not the big ones."

"Interesting," Gabriel said.

"Did Mr. Singer give you any hints as to what he thinks I'll be doing?" Mira asked.

"Once upon a time he might have," Chris said with a sigh. "But the world moves on. The point may be moot with that black cloud weighing you down."

"Is it bad?" Mira asked.

"Honey, you're supposed to be making it smaller, not bigger."

"There's no way it's getting worse, is it? I haven't done..." Ronnie. Reinfield's employees may not blame her, but the universe probably didn't care a fig for that.

"You're looking a little pale," Chris said with a wide, malevolent grin. "Was it something I said?"

Would putting an end to John help or hurt?

"Your books," Mira said, turning to look around the room. "They're rare, right?

"Some of them," Chris said, carefully.

"And the others?" Mira asked.

"One of a kind," Chris said, sounding leery.

"Do you have anything about the Ether?" Mira asked.

"We don't need anything about that place," Gabriel said. "Do we?"

Mira walked around the room, looking at the books, careful not to touch any while waiting for Chris to answer.

"I don't know," Mira said. "Last week, I wouldn't have thought so. A few weeks before that I wouldn't even have contemplated the idea."

"I guess there's a point to that," Gabriel said before turning to Chris. "Do you have anything?"

"Why would you think anyone has books on the Ether?" Chris asked.

"Because someone has to," Mira said. "We—"

"Saw something that came from that world," Gabriel interrupted.

"How do you know it came from there?" Chris asked.

"Scales and fur," Gabriel said. "Claws on more legs than most creatures in this world."

"Bleeding some sort of black tar-like fluid," Mira added.

"But how do you know something like that came from the Ether?" Chris asked.

"It attacked her. Some guy shot it," Gabriel said.

"Who?" Chris asked, far too quickly.

"Harker said his name might be Reinfield," Mira said.

Chris fumbled around and started something burning next to him—incense, from the smell of it—and fanned himself. "Reinfield and a Harker? Is the Harker the brother or the sister?"

"Brother," Mira said.

"Be still my heart," Chris said. "And with those two in town, they might just stop my heart altogether."

"Do you know them?" Mira asked.

"Not really. Just rumors and stories, mostly dug out of old books," Chris said. "If they're here, the Ether is an issue. I thought things were feeling a little thin."

"To know that much, you must have something on the Ether," Mira said.

"One book," Chris said. "But it will do you no good. I've never found anyone that can read it."

"Can I see?" Mira asked.

"On the pedestal at the end of the aisle," Chris said after a short pause.

Mira went to the pedestal and looked at the blood-red book. On the cover, a double circle with three points around it was embossed in silver on the cover.

"Do you mind if I look through it?" Mira asked.

"Since you asked, you may," Chris said.

Mira carefully opened the cover. She turned a few old pages, examining the writing. "It's gibberish."

"Yes," Chris said. "It sometimes takes people that way."

Latin, runes, Arabic, Mandarin and a whole host of other languages showed on the page. She read one or two of the words she knew, 'house' and 'story,' then turned the page. On the next, she saw nothing legible, so she flipped to the previous page to try to find something else decipherable.

She let the page drop from her hands and took a step back, bumping into Gabriel. "The page changed."

"It doesn't like it when someone tries to read it," Chris said.

"Doesn't like it?" Gabriel asked. "It's a book."

"That's what I assumed," Chris said.

"May I?" Gabriel asked.

"Be gentle," Chris said in teasing voice.

Gabriel stared at the page that Mira had open. He studied it for a few moments, and then turned the page, concentrating hard. Frowning, he glanced up at Chris, then to the page, studying it once again.

"What is it that you see?" Chris asked.

"What?" Gabriel asked, tearing his eyes away from the page.

"What do you see?" Chris repeated, leaning forward.

Gabriel shrugged and closed the book. "Nothing I can make sense of."

Chris made a huffy sigh and sat back once again.

"Can we buy the book? Or borrow it?" Mira asked.

"Oh, no. That one stays where it is. It doesn't even like to leave its pedestal."

"We should go," Gabriel said. Putting his hand on the small of Mira's back, he gently urged her forward.

"You sure?" Chris asked. "You're welcome to spend the evening."

"Like I said, I'm not available," he said.

"I don't mind sharing," Chris said.

"I do," Gabriel said. "We'll see you around."

They wound their way out of the store, dropping off the key on the way. Mira breathed the cold air in deeply when she reached the outdoors, trying to rid her lungs of the smoke while Gabriel hurried her mutely to the car.

Mira checked her phone and found a string of texts from Della. She made herself busy with that, but after a while, Gabriel's silence started to worry her.

She sought to fill the void. "I was hoping to get a chance at studying that book. I doubt he'd make me the same offer of spending the night, though."

"We should talk about something else," Gabriel said.

"Why?" Mira asked.

"I mean something to take our minds off the case and off... well, off of all the weirdness."

"Weirdness?" Mira tried not to take his comment personally.

"Yeah, I think I need a night of normalcy."

"As in no magic?" She tried not to sound accusatory, but that made her voice flat.

"No Ether, no monsters, and no murderers trying to kill us. And no angel crap."

"And magic?"

"Can we just be Gabriel and Mira tonight?"

"I'm a witch. You just asked me to move in with you, and now you want no magic?"

"Magic is fine, as long as it has nothing to do with monsters or the Ether. Or angels."

Mira shifted uncomfortably in her seat and went back to reading her texts. Sadly, she found something along a similar theme. Della was starting to get worried about Ian not being comfortable with magic.

Maybe it was something in the air.

"Sorry," Gabriel said after a while. "I didn't mean I didn't want you around. I love that you're here."

"Is there something wrong?" Mira asked, not looking up from her phone.

He hesitated.

Mira saw that he seemed worried. "Was it something I did?"

"No." Gabriel rushed. "I think Chris, the smoke, and that book all just got to me."

He wasn't saying something. Mira didn't have to have his lie-detector skills to know it. She texted Della, saying she was worried Gabriel could be having the same issue.

It only took a few seconds for Della to respond. We need to fix this!

Any ideas how? Mira texted back.

A night of magic? Show them it's natural?

Mira thought that over. She knew that for Gabriel, at least, it wouldn't work. How about the opposite?

I'm not going to hide who I am.

Mira sighed. What you are, Della, is a smart outgoing woman who just happens to do magic. We can show them we have a normal side.

I have no idea what that even looks like.

For once, Mira was the one that felt confident. No supernaturals, no talking about their case, and no magic unless it's necessary.

"Everything okay?" Gabriel asked.

"It's fine," Mira said. "Just talking with Della."

Are you and Gabriel...

Mira grinned. Hopefully.

Double? Della asked.

Gabriel and Ian were friends, so Mira figured they had to talk about stuff other than work when they were together. It might just work.

Dinner?

"Did you have anything planned for tonight?" Mira asked.

"I thought we'd be moving more stuff," Gabriel said. "I didn't think we'd have time to do much tonight."

"How about dinner with Ian and Della?"

"That sounds perfect."

"I need to shower first, though," Mira said. "All that smoke is still clinging to me."

The idea of having a 'normal' night probably didn't mean the same thing to Ian and Gabriel as it did for Della and Mira. Magic was a part of their everyday lives. Although, Mira would be the first to admit that she had gone a long time without doing any magic.

Since it had been so long, the couples were starting the evening out at Della's house. That gave Mira the excuse she'd needed to raid her apartment.

Walking up the stairs to the apartment felt eerie. Mira couldn't help but grip the banister and look around for any nasty surprises that might try to befall her. The last time she had been at her apartment in this world, she had been kidnapped and taken to the Ether by a crazed monster masquerading as John.

Mira had unlocked the door and was turning the knob when Gabriel's hand fell on hers, stopping her from opening the door. He didn't say anything, only looked around, as though studying the surroundings before going inside.

"What's wrong?" Mira asked.

"It feels off, is all," Gabriel said, keeping his voice low.

Mira jumped and yanked her hand away when her cell phone rang. Embarrassed by her skittishness, she fumbled in her pocket for the phone.

"Hello?" she said, stepping away from the door, which Gabriel was still holding.

"I thought that I would be accompanying you to visit your apartment." Emmit's British accent held a barb.

"Are you following me?" Mira asked, looking around again. She spent more time gazing into shadows cast by the dying sun.

Emmit sighed. "I have someone watching your apartment."

"Of course you do."

Before Mira could say anything else, Gabriel got her attention and wordlessly asked her to pass over the phone.

Shrugging, Mira said nothing, but gave it to him.

"You've done something to the apartment, haven't you?" Gabriel accused.

Mira couldn't hear Emmit's response.

"Yes, I felt it. You could have hurt someone." There was a lengthy pause before Gabriel said, "You're such a dammed prick sometimes."

Mira couldn't help but grin at him whenever he cursed.

He followed it up with, "Fine, make it fast," before he ended the call and passed the phone to Mira.

"What did he do to my house?" Mira asked, not able to hide the smile.

"I don't know," Gabriel said. "This was exactly the type of thing I wanted to avoid tonight."

Her smile fell and she felt her heart try to seize up. This is never going to work, is it?

She wanted to say the words out loud, but was terrified he'd agree.

"I can come tomorrow and get this stuff on my own," Mira said.

"You shouldn't come here on your own. Harker is right about one thing—it's probably not safe."

"Sorry to start the night out like this."

"It's not your fault. Harker is the one that did… whatever the hell it is he did."

Lights emerged from around the big house as a black Escalade drove up.

"We're here for magic, though." She spoke softly in case the mention of magic made him run.

Gabriel shifted, looking uncomfortable. He didn't say anything as a man in a black suit climbed the stairs while another walked around the garage.

"Good evening," the man said.

Mira and Gabriel watched as the man put on a thick glove, and then slid his hand over the doorframe. He pulled his palm back holding what looked like a small pale stick with a patch of hair wrapped around it. He stored the thing in a small ornate box before moving aside Mira's welcome mat and picking up another object similar to the first.

He didn't take off the glove and continued to hold the box in that hand.

"Mr. Harker said that you might need assistance packing or moving things to your new living arrangements." It was as though he was pretending that the box didn't exist.

"Did he curse my apartment?" Mira's voice came out in a screech, but she didn't care. "That complete ass." She took out her phone again and called Emmit. He didn't answer. "Coward," Mira mumbled, putting her phone away. "Thanks for the offer," Mira said to the waiting man, "but I think we can—"

"Actually," Gabriel interrupted, "if they took your stuff over to my place until we got there, it might be safer. Then we could enjoy the evening."

Mira's mouth opened to disagree, but then she closed it again. The idea of someone having access to her spell books unnerved her, but it would make her feel better to know her books and potions weren't locked up unprotected in Gabriel's trunk.

"You're right," she said at last, "that would be great."

The other man appeared from around the garage. He was also wearing a large glove and carrying something.

"We'll join you inside whenever you wish," the man said before going downstairs.

Gabriel opened the door and Mira hurried in, long past ready to get out of the cold. Once inside, she could only stop and stare forlornly around the room. It was so quiet without Alchemy and Oracle. The apartment felt empty.

It didn't help that the bad memories were starting to outweigh the good. Gabriel stood behind her and rubbed her arm, which helped soothe the melancholy her apartment caused.

"At least the heat was left on," Mira said. She was reluctant to dislodge Gabriel's arm, but it was time to shrug off her coat and get to work.

"Is this the first time you've been back?" Gabriel asked.

"Yeah, I wanted to come yesterday, but Emmit talked me out of it. Before that, I didn't see the point."

"Where do you want to start?"

"I have some luggage in the closet. The stuff I need to pack is everywhere. Most of it is downstairs, though."

"Let's start there, then."

Mira wanted to tell him he could stay on the second floor if he wanted to, but the fact was, she didn't want to be alone down there.

Gabriel got the suitcase and followed Mira downstairs. She froze in the doorway, Gabriel almost walking into her.

"What's wrong?" Gabriel asked.

"This place is a mess," Mira said. "I think someone's been in here."

CHAPTER 14

GABRIEL LOOKED AROUND HER and studied the room. "Actually, I think we left it this way. Sorry about that. Harker needed supplies and we were rushed."

"That's a relief," Mira said.

"We may have broken a few things."

"No big deal." Mira was still having a hard time forcing herself into the room. She used to love her workshop. Yet now, she just wanted out as quickly as she could.

"You don't mind?" Gabriel asked.

Mira gave him a weak smile before going to her workbench. "Mind that you two were in a hurry to help me? No, I don't mind."

Gabriel sat the suitcase on a chair and started looking around while Mira weeded through her supplies.

"I thought I'd invite Ian and Della to my place for drinks after dinner," Gabriel said before sniffing the contents of a bag.

Mira had already started making two piles. "That sounds like fun."

"Yeah, I need something normal tonight.

Mira winced. "You can wait upstairs if you want to."

"I'm good. Is there anything I can help with?"

"Not yet, but maybe later." After a few minutes of quietly working, Mira said what she had been dreading. "I didn't realize you were so against magic."

"What do you mean?"

She couldn't look at him, but could feel him watching her. "I mean tonight. The need for normality and wanting to avoid anything magic."

"Oh." He came over to her, taking a bottle of what could have been beetles and setting it aside before holding her hand. When she still didn't look up at him, he put his hand on her cheek. "I didn't mean for you to think I don't like magic. Your magic is normal."

Mira's loved the feel of his hand on her, but she felt her eyebrows rise in disbelief.

"To me, I mean. Your magic is normal to me because it's a part of you. Things about you didn't make sense before I found out you could do magic."

"Then what is it? Because something's bothering you."

He took his hand off her face, which she immediately missed. "I think the bookstore got to me. That's all."

She waited, but it didn't seem like there was more to come. He said he didn't mind her magic, but did she believe him?

Even to herself, she couldn't give a definitive answer. She was missing something, and that was a certainty.

"And, you don't believe me," he said as though reading her mind.

Mira shrugged, trying to play it off. "I guess I just don't understand what happened."

He sighed. "It's not you, it was that stupid book."

It felt as though he was going to let go of her hand, but she gripped it tighter so he couldn't. "The book about the Ether?" Things still weren't adding up for her. "Because the words changed?"

"No, it's because they didn't change for me. I could read it."

Comprehension dawned, Mira's eyes widened, and a smile spread across her face. "You could read the book? That's great."

He shook his head and pulled away. "It's not great to me."

"Oh, I see." She let her arm fall by her side, suddenly depressed. She didn't understand his aversion, not really.

"We should get to work if we're going to make it to Della's on time."

"Right." She turned to her workbench, determined to ignore the fact that Gabriel seemed intent on ignoring the world around him. Maybe she too needed a normal night.

A normal date, anyway. The realization that it would be a date cheered her up some.

Mira opened two drawers a few inches. On the side, she twisted one of five decorative pieces, and then reached behind her workbench and pressed hard on a piece of wood that fit seamlessly into the surface. Up front, a thin drawer between two regular drawers slid open.

"That's something I didn't expect to see," Gabriel said, moving up behind her to watch over her shoulder as she pried the drawer out.

"You don't know what's in it yet," Mira said. "This drawer was always tough to budge."

"I mean that you opened it in front of me. Unless this is one of the ones that wouldn't matter if people knew about it."

"No one knows about this except me and the furniture maker."

"I didn't expect to see any secrets that I hadn't been able to find on my own."

Mira grinned and turned to him. "Did you expect to find them on your own?"

He was smiling as well. "Maybe."

"Why do you want to search for my hiding places?"

"I'm curious."

"You might regret that when you start seeing what I keep in some of these."

"Why are you letting me see?"

She hesitated. Why was she opening her secrets to him? Then she shrugged. "I trust you."

"Because I'm an angel?"

She rolled her eyes. "I'm sure angels are normal people, like any other supernatural. I trust you because you're Gabriel. You're still you, even when you sprout wings."

He chuckled.

Mira felt uplifted by his change of mood.

"There's something else I'm curious about," he said.

"What's that?"

He put his arms around her and kissed her. His lips were soft and pressed against hers delicately. She was almost as hesitant as he was, feeling like if they moved too quickly their small world would crack and tear them apart.

When he broke the kiss, they remained wrapped in each other's arms. Gabriel stared into Mira's eyes and she never wanted to look away. She was dazed, but she didn't care. They had been talking about something, but that didn't matter either. What mattered was this moment.

The room was silent, but their eyes spoke volumes to each other and spoke of future promises. When he kissed her again, she let herself forget everything except Gabriel. As the kiss deepened, Gabriel pulled her closer and her insides ignited.

As their breathing became faster and more urgent, Gabriel slowed things down until their lips released each other again, but he didn't let go.

"Are you still curious?" Mira asked playfully.

"Even more so." He cupped her face in his hand and brushed it down her neck, making her shiver. "But, we have some people waiting for us."

Mira wanted badly to let them wait, but she also remembered where she was. The room didn't have a plethora of warm, safe memories. Postponing their exploration made the most sense.

Besides, she told herself, I'm going home with him.

"What?" Gabriel asked.

"I didn't say anything."

"No, but you have a glint in your eyes that makes me think I should hold onto you a little longer."

"Do you need an excuse?"

"No." He kissed her again.

Mira broke out into a wide smile and put her hand on his

chest, gently pressing him back. "No, you were right. We should pack some stuff up and get over to Della's.

Feeling light and dazed, she turned again to her workbench. Gabriel stayed so close behind her that she could have laid her head back onto his chest.

It took her a few moments to refocus on the task at hand. Feeling Gabriel's charged presence behind her wasn't helping, but she wouldn't have given it up for the world.

"Is there anything I can do to help?" Gabriel asked.

She almost said no, but decided against it. "Sure. I'm taking a bunch of different things with me, so I'm going to need some boxes I keep under the stairs. Can you grab one of them?"

"Sure."

She missed his presence as soon as he stepped away, but while his back was turned, she used the opportunity to fan her face and take a deep breath before pushing aside thoughts of a more carnal nature.

When Gabriel returned with the box, he wrapped one arm around her waist as he moved up next to her.

"Do you know what you're bringing with you?" he asked.

"I know what I'll need right away." She started sorting glass, metal, and plastic containers of various sizes.

"So, you have some spells in mind?"

"A few. I haven't done any magic since... well, since we got back."

Gabriel shifted. "No spells at all?"

Mira sensed a shift in the atmosphere. "Nothing."

"In the Eth—where we were, you had spells already put together, but not fully cast. Like the lightning."

The smell of burning tar seemed to ghost around the room and Mira cringed at the memory. "Yeah, I put one like that together there as well. The fire."

"You have more like that ready, right?"

"Not yet."

He shifted again and seemed to tense. It might have been Mira's imagination, but it felt as though he disapproved. That was a surprise, coming from someone who wanted a magic-free evening.

Out of the first secret drawer, Mira was taking with her more items than she left behind. While she separated out ingredients in the next spot, she had Gabriel carefully pack up what they were taking with them.

It took a little while to scavenge all she wanted from the workshop. Upstairs was a little more difficult. She only kept a couple of books downstairs, but had a small library upstairs. There were other, more important things to get as well.

"We are still alone in here, right?" Mira asked.

Gabriel twitched a curtain aside. "Yeah, they're still in the car."

"Good." Mira went to the laundry room and was surprised when Gabriel didn't follow. He stood in the middle of the living room, holding the box and looking unsure as to what he should do. "You can leave the box."

He set the box down but didn't hurry on his way over. "I wasn't sure if you wanted me to come with you."

Mira grinned. "You're always poking around, trying to see if you find one of my hiding places."

"That was different."

"How so?"

"Then, it didn't matter as much if you thought I was nosy."

"And now it matters?"

"I just don't want you to feel pressured to show me everything."

She chuckled and started to feel a flutter in her chest. He really did seem worried. "Trust me, I don't feel like I need to show you everything. Rest assured, you are only seeing a small portion of my hiding spots. This one, though, I should have shown you before. Come on."

She ushered him inside and closed the door. The laundry room was a decent size, but even without wings, Gabriel took up a lot of space.

"There's no one here," he reminded her. "You don't have to close the door."

"Actually, I do. You could investigate the area all you want and you'd never find this space unless the door is closed." She gently nudged Gabriel into the corner and crouched down.

"How many hiding places do you have?"

Mira carefully lifted up a long section of baseboard and set it out of the way before pausing to count them all up in her head. "Um, I think there are around nineteen."

"Wow, I never would have guessed."

"This one is the most important, though." Mira stuck her hand into the wall and pressed down on something. A tile directly in front of the door popped up.

"Why are you showing me the most important one?"

"Because it has the most important stuff. And probably the most dangerous." Mira lifted the tile and then the one next to it. She carefully picked up a small wooden puzzle box. After a few twists, turns, and slides, she had the box open. Inside were three snow-white feathers. "I should have given these to you long before this." She took them out and held them out to Gabriel.

He didn't look happy about it and didn't reach for them. "Why are you doing this now?"

"I shouldn't have left them here this long without being around."

"Keep them," Gabriel said stiffly.

"It might be better if you—"

"Can we not?" Gabriel waved them away. "Not tonight."

"Sorry," Mira said, feeling stung. "I just didn't want to leave them behind."

He squatted down next to her and his voice softened. "I get that." He picked up one of the feathers and ran a finger over. He brushed it across his hand and then held it up for closer inspection. After a few moments of what looked like deep contemplation, he returned the feather to Mira, taking the opportunity to stay in contact with her. "Keep them. Once this case is over we can talk about it, and then you can tell me what to do with them."

Mira felt a little better with Gabriel's hand lingering on hers. "Sure. I'll keep them close until then."

Gabriel turned his attention to the gaping hole she had opened up in her floor. "What's this?"

To Mira, it appeared as though he grabbed something at random for a distraction. She only had to glance at it to know what he held. "Blood."

Gabriel's eyebrows rose and he lifted up the bottle for closer inspection. "Whose? Wait, maybe I don't want to know."

Mira bit her lip. "I think her name was Heidi."

Gabriel seemed to freeze and concentrated on the bottle, not looking at Mira.

"She was a heifer," Mira said, trying to let him off the hook.

"If you're name-calling—"

"Heifer. As in cow."

"Sorry," Gabriel said. "I should have known you wouldn't have human blood."

"I do," Mira said. Seeing the look on Gabriel's face, she hurried on. "I have my own." She reached into the hole and grabbed a jar, holding it out to him.

He didn't take it. "Isn't it dangerous to keep something like that around? From what you said—"

"It's dried, so it's not as bad, and occasionally I'll make a spell that needs dried blood as opposed to fresh."

She waited for him to cringe or say something, denouncing the whole thing. Instead, he peered into the hole again and took something else out.

Mira took Heidi and returned her to the hole in the floor. She rummaged around and took a few other things out before turning to Gabriel. He was carefully pulling back black velvet from an item.

"Which one do you have?" Mira asked, leaning over for a closer look.

"You have more stuff wrapped in cloth?"

"A bunch of stuff. That's—" she saw the glint of gold and slapped the cloth over it quickly, almost knocking Gabriel over in the process.

"Sorry," he said quickly, handing it back. "I didn't mean to pry."

"It's not that. There's a reason some things are wrapped up, though. Sometimes it's just to cover it up. In this case, it's kind of to hide it. Take a look." Mira carefully held out the object and lifted up an edge for Gabriel to see.

"It looks like gold."

Mira grinned smugly. It was rare that she was able to show off her treasured pieces. "It is. Not just any gold, but leprechaun gold."

"Leprechauns? You're telling me there are leprechauns?"

"Well, yes and no. There used to be leprechauns. The coin has been in my family for ages."

"Why keep it hidden?"

"If there is anyone around with leprechaun blood in them, they'll be attracted to it like bears to honey. They'll then steal it and won't even know why."

Gabriel was quiet for a while as Mira got what she needed and started to close things up.

"Is something wrong?" she asked.

"Yeah." He wore a bemused smile. "I just never would have guessed such a thing existed."

He stood up and backed out of the way until Mira could open the door. She stowed the new items in the box and after a few moments of hesitation, put the feathers into her pocket. She wanted to keep them close. It wasn't that she didn't trust Reinfield's men, but she didn't know whom else they might be working with. They'd been guarding her for a week now, several of them even watching over her while she slept. She cringed at the thought, though she trusted them to an extent.

"You okay?" Gabriel asked.

But she didn't trust anyone to keep those feathers safe.

She smiled at him. "Yeah, you know, I think we've got enough for the night. Let me grab some clothes and we can get out of here."

CHAPTER 15

I AN WAS ALREADY AT Della's when Mira and Gabriel arrived.

Della gave her a quizzical look when she let them in the back door. "Ian's in the kitchen," she gestured to Gabriel, "we'll be right behind you."

When they heard Gabriel and Ian start talking, Della turned to her best friend. "What's going on?" she asked.

There was so much happening that Mira had no idea even where to begin. "With what?"

"You look—I mean, what happened? I haven't seen you in ages and you show up looking... Is everything all right?"

Light dawned and Mira patted her hair. "Geez, do I look that bad?"

"Not bad, just... disheveled, I guess."

"I'm fine. I was in a car accident last night, but I'm okay, really. Emmit's car has a thousand airbags." None of which helped the driver. She tried to push that thought away.

"You were with Emmit? Are you and he—"

"No," Mira jumped in before she could say anything further. "Definitely not."

"Good." Della gave her a wicked grin. "I got the idea that someone else was interested. Are you sure you want to go out tonight?"

"Yeah, I think it's a great idea."

"Wait," Della said as Mira moved toward the kitchen, "I heard about the trouble with the witches, but I don't know what's going on."

Mira looked at her friend. So much had happened in the past few weeks that what Della didn't know stood like a mountain between them.

"Let's not talk about it tonight," Mira said, still unsure if she should tell Della anything about what was happening. "We can catch up later."

"If you're positive," Della said.

"I am."

Della grinned. "Let's go see what the others are up to, then."

Mira admired the way her friend could seem to turn away a subject and jump into another as though switching from hot water to cold.

"I think we're ready to go," Della announced. She went over to Ian and put an arm around his waist. "How about you two?"

"Yeah," Ian said, all eyes on Della.

Mira's move toward Gabriel was much more awkward. She had no idea what to do. Should she hold his hand? Stand close?

Was this a date, a real date, with Gabriel?

"What are we doing tonight?" Mira asked.

"We thought dinner and drinks at Kalliopē," Della said.

Mira raised an eyebrow but said nothing. It was a great place, but maybe not the best for a non-magical evening. The owner was a supernatural, although Mira had never met her, so it was possible there was no actual magic involved.

Della must have noticed. "It was Ian's idea."

"I've never been there," Gabriel said.

"You'll like it," Ian said.

The warmth of Kalliopē beat away the chill from outside. When Mira and Gabriel arrived moments after their friends, they managed to make small talk while the waiter served drinks and took their order. When they were alone, an odd silence overcame them. They all knew each other but had never really been together socially as a group. There was always a case between them that bridged the silence.

The case was still there, but with a no-magic night, a case full of supernatural occurrences doesn't mix well.

"Have you started car shopping?" Della asked.

Mira was grateful to have a topic to talk about. "Not yet. I hate car shopping at the best of times. In the winter, the cold makes it downright miserable. How's work?"

"I'm taking some time off in a couple of weeks," Della said.

Mira beamed. Della was a workaholic, so it was good to see her take a vacation. "That's great. Do you have any plans?"

Della smiled at Ian. "Maybe. I'm hoping to get down to the islands. Anywhere warm would work, though."

Ian grinned as well. This was obviously something they'd been discussing. Mira had the distinct feeling that Della wouldn't be going alone.

"Getting out of the city sounds great," Mira said. Just the thought made Mira envious. With the hell she'd been through in the past two weeks, she was ready to check out of her life for a while.

"You could join us," Della said. "There's plenty of room."

Suspicions verified.

If Della was talking about the islands, she was thinking about her family's villa, where there was plenty of room. There was no way Mira would tie her friend down with a third wheel on her first real vacation in ages.

"Thanks, but I'll have to pass. I need to start looking for a job."

"You're not reopening the store?" Della asked.

Mira shrugged. "I'm not really sure yet, but it doesn't look like it. I may keep the mail order part."

"You have a job for now, at least," Ian said.

Mira's confusion must have been evident.

"The case," Ian said. "We still need you for that."

"I'll help," Mira said, "but I need something that pays."

"We put in for you to be paid as a consultant," Ian said. "Although, we haven't heard back. I'm surprised the other side isn't paying you."

"The other side?" Mira asked, not wanting to look at Della to see what her friend thought about his comment.

Ian shrugged. "Seems like you've given up a lot of time for everyone else. I'm surprised they aren't paying you something."

"It doesn't work like that," Mira said.

"No," Della interrupted, "he has a point. Well, part of one, anyway."

"Most people won't even speak to me." Mira carefully avoided the word witches, but still glanced at Ian to see if he thought the conversation was going downhill.

"Only the witches," Della said. "The community is larger than one group."

Mira shook her head. "I can't ask for money just for helping. It's almost like asking for money for a spell," Mira said as she winced.

Della kept going. "But people pay you for what you spend out of pocket. I'd say you're out of pocket big time while working on our behalf."

Mira put her hands under the table to wipe her suddenly sweaty palms on her jeans. "Maybe. I'll think about it."

"I'd say you don't have to worry about rent," Della said. "But you're not exactly staying in the apartment right now, so it's a moot point."

The conversation was making Mira feel as if she had her hand out, begging for money.

"We should hear something in the next few days," Ian said.

"And staying at Emmit's is convenient while you don't have a car," Della said.

"I'm not staying with him anymore," Mira said without thinking.

"Did you move back home?" Della asked, looking happy about the idea.

Mira could feel a blush creeping into her cheeks. "Not yet."

"She's staying with me," Gabriel said.

"When did that happen?" Ian asked.

"At about three-thirty this morning."

Looking up, Della caught Mira's eye. Her friend was giving her a look that suggested she was thrilled for Mira, but for all the wrong reasons.

Thankfully, the food chose that moment to arrive, giving Mira the distraction she desperately wanted. Although, as they ate and started on other small chat, she saw Ian grinning at his partner from time to time.

Gabriel either didn't notice or didn't care.

By the time the four reached drinks and dessert, they were starting to talk how they had chosen their particular career paths, and Mira found that she really enjoyed getting to know Gabriel better. She and Della managed to sidestep talking about the magic in their past by focusing on the more mundane adventures, which were usually more fun anyway.

They talked, laughed, and shared for another hour before deciding keeping the table for any longer might cause someone waiting to be seated to go postal on the place. They bundled up and as soon as they reached the frigid outdoors, Ian wrapped his arm around Della's waist, keeping her close.

"Is your car this way?" Ian asked.

"Yeah," Gabriel said, falling in step behind the couple.

Mira fleetingly wondered if she should take Gabriel's hand, but the after-dinner drinks had her feeling mellow so she linked her arm in his instead. Gabriel didn't shrug her off, which she took as a good sign.

"This was fun," Della said. "We should do this again."

Mira's phone chimed, alerting her to a text. Reluctantly, she unhooked her arm from Gabriel's to dig out her phone.

"Yeah," Ian said, "we could meet up after work sometime next week."

Mira peeled off a glove and fell a few steps behind. As she typed in her pin, she also took a step toward the curb to put some distance between herself and Gabriel. Her mind flitted through people who could be texting.

Seeing who the message was from, she stopped. Lance of all people was texting her, and the whole thing looked more like a short letter than a text.

Hello Mira. Levi has asked me to reach out to you on his behalf. He would like to make an appointment to meet with you at a neutral location. In an effort for you both to feel more comfortable—

"What's up, Mira?" Della called. They stood by the corner, waiting for her.

"Sorry, just a sec," Mira said.

—comfortable, he requests that you bring one of the detectives with you. I have offered my house for your use, but he mentioned that the hospital might also be fitting. Please reach out to me with your decision. Thank you. Lance.

"Coming," Mira said, stowing the phone in her pocket.

She took a step and then a truck thundered by. The deluge of ice and water rose high and cascaded over her.

It felt like a slap across the face. Mira sucked in a shrill breath and froze, almost quite literally, as the water soaked through to meet her skin. More water and icy slush slid down the back of her neck and down the front of her shirt.

Gabriel grabbed her hand and pulled her away from the road.

"Aaa," Mira rasped.

"Oh, my god, Mira, are you hurt?" Della asked.

Mira blinked and tried to think past the way the cold bit into her skin. "I-I-I'm okay." Her teeth chattered and her muscles clenched up against the cold.

"Let's get to the car," Gabriel said.

"I hope your heater is good." Della sounded worried as Gabriel hurried past with Mira. "Let me know if you need anything!"

Mira gave a wave instead of trying to talk around her chattering teeth.

In the parking garage, Gabriel rushed to the car, opening the passenger side before running around to the other side. By the time Mira shut her door, Gabriel had the car started. He adjusted the heating vents, but Mira didn't hold out hope that it would get warm quickly.

Gabriel stripped off his gloves and ran his hands over her arm. "You are completely soaked, aren't you?"

Mira had her arms wrapped tight around her and nodded.

"Take off your coat," Gabriel said as he shrugged off his own.

Mira was slow moving, but managed to get her coat off. Gabriel threw it in the back and handed over his. She didn't put it on, but used it like a blanket.

"Are you all right?" Gabriel asked.

"Cold," Mira managed.

Gabriel reached across her and pulled her seatbelt on before his own. Then he popped the car into reverse and hurried toward his house.

"I'm sorry," he said once they reached the street. "I didn't sense anything. Why didn't I sense anything?"

Mira shivered under the coat and pulled it tight to her. "I didn't get hurt."

"At least not until the pneumonia kicks in."

Mira curled up tighter at the thought, but she was already starting to feel a little better. "I'm all right. It's getting warmer."

"Yeah, that's what everyone says before frostbite settles in." Gabriel ran his hands over the vents, checking for heat. "I should have been able to stop that."

She shrugged, feeling miserable—hating to end their first date on such a bad note.

"We're only a few minutes away. Get out of those clothes as soon as you get inside."

Mira raised an eyebrow in his direction. That also wasn't what she wanted to hear on her first night at Gabriel's—at least not for the reason he intended.

"I mean because they're wet," he said quickly.

Mira chuckled and tried to relax, but the cold seeped into her bones and she could only shiver.

"You can take a hot shower."

By the time Gabriel pulled into his driveway, Mira's skin felt as though it were burning in some areas. Mira stiffly pulled on his coat, dreading having to open the car door in the garage.

She wasn't waiting around for the garage door to shut, though. She got out of the car when he did and followed him hurriedly into the house. Alchemy and Oracle were perched like statues on the washing machine and watched them breeze by.

"I'll get the water started," Gabriel said, disappearing down the hall.

Mira had a momentary pang of guilt when she took off Gabriel's coat and realized it was wet. She didn't take time to dwell on it, however. The coat could wait—getting warm couldn't. She kicked off her shoes, took a moment to leave them in the laundry room, and went in search of heat.

The hallway bathroom was empty, so she followed the sound of running water. She stopped at the open door of a bedroom and saw light spilling out from around the corner, but she felt unsure about invading Gabriel's private space. He appeared from around the corner, looking flustered.

"Come on," he said. He took her hand and led her to the rapidly filling bathtub. "Um, towels, soap, everything is here. Let me know if you need anything else." He glanced around the room before he disappeared, closing the door behind him.

Mira hesitated for a moment, feeling like a stranger. The large, rapidly filling tub called to her. She stripped off her shirt, but her jeans had to be peeled off. When she dipped her foot into the water it felt scalding, but she turned off the water and eased into the tub.

It didn't take long for her skin to feel warm, but the chill deep inside took time to go away. She leaned back. Telling herself it could have happened to anyone was no good. It was true, but the cloud of bad karma clinging to her made sure she was the one it always happened to.

The knowledge that things were bad but could still get much worse was hard to dismiss.

As the heat began to penetrate deeper and chase away the cold, Mira relaxed in the tub, closing her eyes. Who knew a day ago that she would be in Gabriel's house? Probably no one, especially since he had left her at Emmit's, more than hinting that she should stay cooped up inside.

The thought agitated her, but it was an easy one to thrust aside, especially since she was sitting in his tub and would spend at least a few nights at his house.

There was a scratching at the door, which made Mira sit up. A sharp meow announced that a closed door existed that one of her cats was opposed to. Mira should have asked Gabriel about Alchemy and Oracle. They had just gotten swooped up in the move. She knew Gabriel liked them, but she wasn't sure how long that would last if they started clawing up his doors and shedding on his couch.

Feeling better, Mira went ahead and drained the tub, eager to prevent cat damage. She used the hand-held showerhead and quickly showered. Remembering that the cold slush that accosted her had come from the street, she washed her hair twice, just in case. She didn't want to think about the muck that had been thrown on her.

She toweled off and looked around. Putting on the clothes she had been wearing was out of the question and there was no robe. The thought of going out in the towel made her hesitant, but it was large and fluffy, so she made it work. Using her fingers, she combed through her hair, secured the towel, and grabbed her clothes before she poked her head out of the bathroom. Gabriel's bedroom was dark and devoid of him or the cats. The plush carpet allowed her to pad quietly out of the room and into the hallway.

Where she all but ran into Gabriel.

"Oh," he said, stopping short, "sorry." His gaze traveled down. "I should have thought of having you grab clothes. I, uh, made hot chocolate. He held a mug in his hands but didn't seem eager to pass it over. "How are you feeling?"

"Much better," Mira said, glad her blushing was hidden behind skin already pink from the hot water. "And warm." While his eyes roved over her once again, the warmth spread. "Thank you."

He caught her eye and Mira held her breath, wondering if that look in his eye meant he was contemplating kissing her again. Or maybe— hopefully—more.

A quiet meep, followed by a cat rubbing against her leg, broke the moment. Oracle was winding around her legs, then Gabriel's.

"I hope it's okay that Alchemy and Oracle are here," she said.

"Of course," Gabriel said, reaching down to scratch Oracle behind the ears. She noticed him glance at her feet and she wiggled her toes. "I'll get out of your way."

He stood aside and Mira walked past, feeling him watching her until she disappeared into the guest room, Oracle on her heels.

It wasn't until she started rummaging through her luggage that she heard Gabriel walk by again, heading to the kitchen. She started pulling on jeans but paused when she glanced at the clock. It was well into the night. She tossed the jeans aside and settled for something more comfortable.

Despite Gabriel's new tendency to check her for shoes, she settled on socks. The hallway was empty this time, but Gabriel waited for her in the kitchen.

He slid a mug across the counter to her. "I don't have any tea, but thought you might want something warm to drink."

"Thank you." She couldn't keep the smile from her face, but tried to tone it down so she didn't look like a grinning idiot.

"Reinfield's men dropped off your stuff, and I moved everything to the other bedroom for now."

Mira nodded and drank with her hands wrapped tightly around the mug. She didn't think she'd ever get too much warmth ever again.

"And, um, I grabbed your coat. Your phone fell out." He pulled it out and slid it across the counter as well, but much slower than he had done with the hot chocolate.

"Thanks," she said. She pressed the power button and saw several notifications pop up.

"It rang while you were getting dressed."

Sure enough, one of the messages said she had multiple missed calls.

"Twice," Gabriel said.

She punched in her code and found that she had actually missed three calls. All from Emmit. Her nose wrinkled up. She didn't have to guess that Gabriel had seen the caller ID.

CHAPTER 16

I'LL GIVE YOU SOME privacy." Gabriel's voice was measured and even.

"You don't—"

"It's late," he said, not giving her the chance to protest. "I should get ready for bed."

After he disappeared quickly down the hall, Mira shook her head, but then dialed Emmit.

"Sorry to reach out so late," Emmit said. "Thank you for calling me back."

Mira looked down the hall where Gabriel had disappeared. "It's no problem."

"I only wanted to check and make sure everything was going well."

"I'm fine," Mira said.

"It was my understanding that you had a rough evening."

Mira shook her head and turned to her hot chocolate. "Just a cold one."

"And you're settling in well?"

"Yeah, but it's getting late."

"You should get some sleep. We'll talk soon. Goodnight."

Mira hung up and checked her messages. She returned a text to Della before opening the text from Lance. She was just starting her reply when Gabriel returned. She glanced up, back to her phone, and then up again for a second look. Gabriel was wearing a t-shirt and pajama pants. The only other times she'd seen him in a t-shirt was when they had been running for their lives.

It was a good look. One that made her wish for the end of winter.

"Can I get you anything?" he asked.

"No, thank you, though."

He once again moved to the other side of the counter, putting distance between the two of them.

The evening was beginning to have more low points than high ones. Not a good mix. Mira took up her mug again and finished the drink, thinking she'd go to bed before things got any worse.

She quickly rinsed out the mug, and when she turned, Gabriel was right behind her.

When he wanted to be, he was quiet and seemed almost as quick as Emmit. She almost said as much, but bit back the words, knowing it would cause the evening to end in disaster.

He looked uncomfortable, which was something she hadn't really seen much in Gabriel. Even when she expected him to be uneasy, he was usually unflappable.

Except, she realized, when it came to Emmit.

"Are you—is everything okay?" Gabriel asked.

"Yeah." She wondered if telling him that Emmit had just called to check on her would make things better or worse.

If anything, he looked more anxious.

"Everything covers a lot of ground," Mira said. "I can't be truthful when you say 'everything'."

His lips turned up slightly, but it only lasted a moment before he put on a more serious face. "You're right. It's none of my business anyway."

He had used that phrase before, and even then, she thought that maybe it was his business. She watched him and bit her lip. It was better to get it over with, right?

"Ask me anyway," Mira said.

"Is your relationship with Emmit completely over?"

She had thought she might have to wheedle the question out of him, but he hadn't even hesitated. "I'm still friends with Emmit." Mira wondered briefly if there was a way to emphasize the truth to Gabriel. "And I don't think that's going to change unless he does something really stupid."

Gabriel rolled his eyes. "When does he not?"

"If you're asking me if we are still dating," Mira continued, ignoring the remark, "I've already told you we aren't seeing each other."

Gabriel nodded but didn't look any happier about it. "I'm not trying to say you shouldn't see him—or anyone else—I just need to know how things stand."

"I don't want to date Emmit," Mira said. "That's not going to happen again." She tried to put some sort of energy or power behind the words but had no idea how to do that—especially without a spell. "Besides," she said, trying to bring something more positive to the discussion, "I really like the direction things are going."

He finally cracked a smile.

"You don't have to worry about Emmit. Ever. There wasn't even much between us to begin with."

"I'm really not trying to say you can't see other people."

"Are you seeing anyone?" The curiosity had the words out of her mouth before she really thought about them.

"No."

"This is new," Mira said. "We just need to be honest with each other. I think that's all we should expect, don't you?"

He smiled wider and moved closer. "I'm good with that."

If Mira so much as leaned forward, they'd be pressed together.

"It's getting late," he said.

"It is," Mira agreed, although her fatigue had disappeared.

Mira's cell phone chimed. She ignored it.

"Do you want to get that?" Gabriel asked, though he didn't move away.

Mira bit her lip to try to stop from grinning again. "No."

The minuscule gap disappeared. Mira's heart fluttered when she found herself pushed against the cabinet with Gabriel's lips joining her own. Her insides melted when he pressed into her, his eagerness apparent.

She wrapped her arms tightly around him and began exploring the muscles of his back. The next chime from the phone barely registered over her mounting passion.

Gabriel's hands reached under her shirt, and a tickle inside spread with the anticipation of his exploring hands on her skin. His hands settled on her waist when he pulled away. His eyes drew her in.

"That could be important." He kept his voice soft and his hands on her.

"Hmm," Mira murmured. "What could?"

Gabriel cupped her face with his hand before moving it to the back of her neck and pulling her into another kiss. His strength made her shiver.

Sadly, he pulled away again. "I have something for you."

She raised her eyebrows and grinned playfully. "Do you?"

"You see who it is that can't wait till morning to text, and I'll be right back." He brushed his lips lightly against her in a quick kiss before leaving.

Mira didn't push herself away from the cabinet immediately. She heard Gabriel retreat to his room. When she felt as though her legs were steady enough to support her, she grabbed her phone and unlocked it.

She popped open the texts, her mind still on Gabriel.

It's time.

Mira's glow started to die as she read the string of texts.

Your store in one hour.

If you don't come, we start taking members of your family in your place.

Tyler dies and your angel disappears.

If you're late, it's going to be so much worse for you.

I promise.

Mira started shaking, and somehow the cold seemed to be creeping back. John was going to go after her family. It was a threat, like the one before, but this one felt more real. More immediate.

A high-pitched squeal started in her ears as blood pulsed faster and she read through the messages again.

"I should have given this to you earlier." Gabriel's voice came from a distance, down the hall. "But the time didn't feel—" He took one look at her and stopped. "What happened? What's wrong?"

Mira swallowed hard, trying to get the rapidly forming lump out of her throat.

"Let me see your phone," Gabriel said.

"I don't know. It's..."

He shoved something in his pocket and took her hand. She had a death grip on the phone until he touched her, and then she let it go.

She could feel his cool energy erupt, fragment, and crackle around them, which contrasted greatly with the professional mask that fell into place.

"You should get some sleep," he said in a much calmer and more coherent than she could manage.

Mira shook her head, not trusting her voice.

Gabriel went to grab his own phone, and Mira instantly missed the closeness, despite the barrage of manic energy that came with it. He made a call, and after a minute, blew out an air of frustration. He hung up and made another call.

"Sorry, man," he said, "but we have movement on John."

"Yeah."

"We might have to."

"See you soon."

He hung up and called another number. In moments, he was shaking his head again and hanging up.

"Mind if I use your phone to call Harker?" he asked, holding her phone out, her screen black.

She stepped away, not wanting to take it, and instead gave him the pin.

He called and started to pace.

"How many people do you have outside?" Gabriel barked into the phone without introduction. "I don't give a damn, Harker. Just answer the question."

"Right." Gabriel glanced at Mira. "Send a few more, just in case. And Tyler?"

"Yeah, he wants her at her store in an hour. Probably closer to fifty minutes now. What about Mira's family?"

Mira felt her breath grow shorter at the thought of her family.

Gabriel listened for a while.

"Ian will be here in ten."

Alchemy jumped on the counter next to Mira and stood there, keeping an eye on Gabriel. The cats knew not to jump on counters, but right then, Mira didn't care.

"Right. Yeah." Gabriel hung up and returned to Mira, giving her phone. "We have company coming, so I'm going to get dressed. Do you have any shoes besides your wet ones?"

"Sure." Her phone pinged in her hands, and she jumped as though stung.

Gabriel took it, read the message—glaring daggers at it—then handed it back.

Fifty minutes.

"This sucks." She hadn't meant to say it out loud, but it was true all the same.

"This is good," Gabriel said. "For once, we know exactly where this asshole will be."

Mira nodded while feeling that no part of the situation was good.

"Get hold of Mr. Singer," Gabriel said. "Ask him to spread the word and make sure the witches are on guard. All of them."

Mira nodded.

"Do me a favor," Gabriel said.

Mira looked at him expectantly.

"Shoes?" The was a note of pleading in the single word.

The idea of getting pulled into the Ether sent another shiver through her. "Yeah, I'll go get dressed."

First, she needed to text her sister. The threat against her family had her heart in her throat.

Take the kids and go to Dad's.

She wasn't sure if her sister would acknowledge that, so while she followed Gabriel down the hall, as far as her door, she sent another message.

Mr. Singer will call soon, but go now. Someone is threatening you and them.

Mira knew that Robin would take any threat to the kids seriously.

If you can, get Mom to go too.

The last line would make her stand up and listen. The idea that Mira would even suggest her parents get together under the same roof meant serious business.

This was not how she wanted the night to go. Far from it.

Mira flipped on her light and looked around before stepping into the room. Closing the door didn't seem like a good idea. It felt as though someone was watching her, even though she knew the room was empty.

"I almost forgot," Gabriel said from behind her.

The only reason she didn't jump at the unexpected voice was because she was frozen to the ground. She took a steadying breath before turning around.

"Sorry to startle you."

"I'm fine," she managed, trying not to let her shaky breath show. "What did you forget?"

He held out a small white box. She took it while at the same time wondering if this was really the moment for gift giving. As she opened it, Gabriel started talking.

"My first thought was a necklace," he said as she peeled away the tissue paper. "Because that's what you used to have, and what you made for me and Ian."

A glint of silver caught her eye and she pulled out a ring. "It's beautiful." She turned it around in her hand, inspecting the band of Celtic knot-work.

"Emmit is the one that suggested the ring. He said it was perfect for a ward because it always touches your skin."

Now that she knew it was a ward, she checked more closely to get a measure of the magic it held.

"I had planned on making it myself, but he helped."

The magic was dense and heavy, and it flowed through the knots like tiny rushing rivers.

"Do you like it?"

"I love it," Mira breathed, unable to take her eyes off the ring.

"I wasn't sure of the size."

Mira slid it onto one of the fingers on her right hand. It fit perfectly. "It's wonderful."

"You'll wear it, then?"

"Of course. Thank you."

He took her hand, rubbed a finger over the ring, and then kissed her. "With everything going on, I feel better knowing you're wearing it." He squeezed her hand and, without looking down, said, "At least I will when your shoes are on."

She grinned. When he was gone, she stared at the ring. It had managed to push away the rapidly building fear. The power it held was immense, but so tightly controlled that it seemed like a little supernova weaving a net around her finger.

Feeling safer, she shut the door and before she forgot, she made the call to Mr. Singer.

She was blunt and to the point. Chris's explanation, that Mr. Singer had done this so her next actions wouldn't count against her, were still in the forefront of her mind, but being shunned still sucked and she wanted to make sure Mr. Singer knew she wasn't happy about it.

Once she had his assurances that her family would be told immediately, she hung up and tossed the phone down on the bed. Mira rubbed her finger over the smooth surface of the ring, which helped ease the irritation caused by talking to the old witch.

She heard movement in the hall and quickly dressed.

When she left her room, she followed the voices into the living room. Ian was there, and one of Reinfield's men—a second glance told her it was Eric—stood by the door.

Gabriel and Ian were both wearing their side arms openly on their belt. Usually, she never saw their weapons, but tonight, the detectives looked serious.

"Emmit will be here in a minute," Gabriel said, looping her into the conversation.

Her phone pinged at the same time the doorbell rang. She hesitantly took out her phone while Eric let Emmit in. She woke up the screen to the message: Forty minutes. If you aren't there, I will make sure you live to regret it.

"Is everyone ready?" Emmit asked.

Gabriel read the message over her shoulder, and the same frantic energy rose and crackled like electricity around them.

Emmit watched him closely while moving with what seemed like exaggerated slowness. "Mira, may I see that?"

Mira numbly held out the phone. Emmit walked past her, putting himself between her and Gabriel. Only then did he read the messages.

The explosion of power lasted only a moment before it was bottled up again. Mira gasped and clutched at the ring on her finger, which seemed to hum with the stimulation.

"I see," Emmit said. He turned off the screen and, after a moment's hesitation, handed it to Ian. "I think you should be entrusted with this. If he continues to send a countdown, let us know that. The rest is irrelevant."

Mira expected Gabriel to disagree, but he didn't. She did, however. "I can keep my phone, thanks."

"We might need it this evening. Are we ready? Good," he said, not waiting for a reply. "Let's go."

"I can carry the phone as easily as Ian can," Mira said.

"You should wait here," Gabriel said.

"But—"

"It's police business," Gabriel interrupted. "We can't take you with us."

Mira's eyes narrowed. "But Emmit's okay?"

"I'm not worried about what will happen to Harker. You'll have people inside and outside the house."

It wasn't that Mira wanted to go—she had no inclination to face John again. But even more so, she didn't want Gabriel out of her sight.

"I thought we were sticking together." She couldn't manage to put any accusation into her voice.

"We won't be long," Gabriel said.

"You can take this phone," Emmit said, handing her one. "Reinfield's men will be here for your protection."

Mira nodded. Gabriel was all business and didn't even try to get around Emmit to say goodbye. She watched him leave without saying anything else.

Emmit didn't move until Gabriel was out the door. "Will you be up when Gabriel gets home?"

"I doubt I'd be able to sleep even if I tried."

"Good," Emmit said. "Be sure to wait up and talk with him tonight. I think it will be important to do so. And I shall call tomorrow."

"Sure," Mira said with no real feeling.

Emmit nodded and followed the others.

Mira went to the front window and watched the group walk to Reinfield's trucks, which were waiting for them on the street.

"It will be safer if you stand back from the windows," Eric said.

Mira waited long enough to see the trucks start down the street before she took Eric's advice.

She felt at a loss for what to do. Alchemy and Oracle sat side by side on the coffee table, watching her intently. They were good at sensing her mood, but they seemed as much at a loss as she was.

"Can I get you anything to drink?" Mira asked. She checked the phone and saw that it wasn't password protected, and a quick scroll showed her it was blank.

"No, thank you," Eric said.

"Can you let me know when they get close to my shop?"

Eric paused before saying, "I can give you updates along the way."

Mira nodded and went to the kitchen in search of tea or anything that might calm her nerves. She opened and closed a few cabinets before she realized she wasn't really seeing anything. Her mind was fixed on the threat ahead. Thoughts of John and what he might be doing had dug themselves in and taken root.

"Detective Flint would like to know if you've been able to reach Mr. Singer," Eric said, interrupting her blind search.

Mira latched onto the conversation. "Yes, I called him earlier and he's warning the witches. He said he'd call my family first."

Eric nodded and said nothing.

"Do you need to pass that on?" Mira asked.

"It has been passed on," he said, more formally than his grin conveyed. He tapped under his ear.

Mira nodded. With Eric's conversation seemingly exhausted, she had to return to her search as a distraction. Her chest ached with an intense need to feel useful, and searching Gabriel's kitchen wasn't helping. She let a cabinet door slam shut and rubbed her temples.

"Do you need assistance?" Eric asked.

"Where are they now?" Mira asked.

"They're still en-route to your store."

Mira nodded and looked blankly around the room. Oracle bumped into her shin before winding herself around and through Mira's legs. She patted the cat causing the beautiful new ring to catch the light. It was smooth when Mira glided her finger across the surface. The power inside made her feel a bit steadier for a moment.

Then she wanted to kick herself. Emmit seemed indestructible by any normal means, and she knew he would look after Gabriel and Ian. If anything happened to Ian, however, she'd be screwed and she knew it. Ian also still had his ward, which was more than she could say for Gabriel. That, at least, was something she could solve.

CHAPTER 17

WHEN MIRA LEFT THE room without a word, Eric was on her heels, quick to stop her when she put her hand on the door to the spare bedroom.

"I'll need to clear the room." He didn't actually nudge her out of the way, but he seemed to cast an aura that made her pull away all the same.

She rolled her eyes and shook her head, but waved him on. Unlike in Emmit's apartment, it only took Eric a moment to search the entire room, mostly because he had to walk over to the closet. As she entered, he dropped the blinds and curtains in the room, blocking out the empty darkness outside.

At least Mira hoped it was empty. She firmly pushed that thought aside and started to raid the boxes scattered around the room. The ward would need to come first. Whatever she chose, it would need to be soaked in purified water to release any contaminants before she cast the spell.

Before long, Mira had another necklace with a pendant soaking in a smooth dark glass bottle.

She was at a loss as to what to cast next. Everything seemed important. A few weeks ago, she never would have thought about having offensive spells at the ready. Recently, though, they'd saved her life more than once, so it seemed a good place to start.

Spark was becoming her lucky spell, so she pulled out everything she needed and began grinding ingredients together in her mortar.

"They've reached their destination," Eric said.

"You mean they're at my store?" Mira asked.

"A few blocks away."

Mira bit her lip. She imagined a number of scenarios where Gabriel and the others stalked the darkness of the streets, combing the area between themselves and her store.

For some reason, that made her think of Lance. Dark deserted streets seem like a fitting place for a vampire to hang out. But the thought came from vampires you see in the movies. She knew Lance at least tried to be a people person—he knew everyone on the list of victims from the case.

He was also setting up a meeting between her and Levi. Whatever kind of supernatural the reclusive man was, Levi needed help. The person in the hospital even more so.

Once Spark was ready, Mira grabbed a few other items. She didn't need to know what type of supernatural Levi was. Mira had hidden her inner self from an angel. Something similar might work to hide whatever Levi was from witches.

The room was too small to use as an area for casting. Gabriel's bedroom had the space, but it would feel presumptuous and invasive to use it. Mira grabbed her things and moved to the kitchen, then hesitated there before bypassing it for the living room.

"Any news?" Mira tried to thrust away the incessant worry that filled her, but she wasn't having any luck. She put everything down on the coffee table before pushing it aside.

"They are approaching your store from different directions," Eric said. "It's going to take a while before everyone gets in position."

"Do you know where they are on the countdown?"

"Less than fifteen minutes."

"Any more messages?"

"It's my understanding that the messages are still arriving."

Mira waited for more. When nothing came, she raised her eyebrow at Eric before taking out a long strand of undyed cotton yarn.

"Ian hasn't told anyone the contents of the messages," Eric finished.

Mira let the yarn trail down to the ground. This house had never had a circle cast, so the thread didn't cement itself to the ground the way it would have at Mira's. She had to nudge it into place here and there, and wasn't completely happy with the finished result, but it was circle-ish, which would have to do.

"Are there a lot of people listening into our conversation right now?" Mira asked.

Eric looked uncomfortable with the question. "It's important that others know our status, just as it's important we know theirs."

Mira shook her head and gathered her supplies around the inside edges of the circle. "That's a yes, then."

His grin had a worried edge to it.

"Are we being recorded?"

"Generally speaking, we don't record everyday activities."

"Hmm, another yes, right?"

He sighed and nodded.

"I need you to turn off the listening devices."

"That's not the best idea."

"If we are visually being recorded or seen, I want that turned off as well."

Eric shook his head. "They're requesting the audio stays on."

"I'm not saying you can't listen to them, but I'm about to cast. I'm not letting others listen in on this."

"We are very discreet."

"Good, so you can discreetly turn off the audio."

"The request is being denied."

Mira lost her calm, which was never a good thing before spell casting. "You're lucky I'm not kicking you completely out of the room."

Eric gave her an amused look that seemed to say, I'd like to see you try. "Keeping contact is for safety."

She crossed her arms, tired of people telling her what could and couldn't happen in her life. She readied herself to argue more, and then she realized she didn't have to.

"What?" Eric asked.

Mira hadn't noticed that she'd started to smile. "If you don't turn them off, I will."

He gave her a quizzical look and held out his hands, palms up, silently asking what she was talking about. "Reinfield has denied the request."

"Reinfield himself? I didn't know he did that kind of thing. You don't have any witches on your team, do you?"

"Not that I'm aware of."

"I can tell. Look, I'm not trying to be difficult. Really, I'm not." Mira settled down on the ground inside her circle. "But if it's not turned off, I'll short it out. It could take your cell phone, too. Sorry in advance."

"Why?" Eric asked, forgetting any formality in his confusion.

Mira sighed. "It's a witch thing. The whole being burned at the stake off and on throughout history has made us a little skittish."

Eric's expression showed his dawning understanding.

"Are you turning it off?" Mira asked.

"For how long?" Eric asked.

Mira looked at what she had spread before her. "Forty-five minutes, give or take?" When she saw the look on Eric's face, she continued, "You can turn it on between spells. Let's say, fifteen to twenty minutes."

"Let's try to stick with fifteen." Eric put a finger in his ear. "Outgoing audio is off."

"Thank you."

"Could you really short this thing out?"

"Sure. You'd be surprised at what a witch can do, especially when motivated."

Mira charged her circle, and then closed her eyes and tried to concentrate on the first spell. Getting her mind clear wasn't easy. She shifted on the unfamiliar floor, and then moved her legs. After the second time she fidgeted, her eyes popped open, and she noticed Eric was watching her intently.

"I'm not going anywhere," Mira said. "The bad guys are outside."

Eric chuckled and moved to the window to peek out before taking up a spot next to the front door.

This time when Mira closed her eyes, she sank straight into her spell. She had cast Spark so many times that the spell came quickly to her, which was why she had decided to start with it.

Magical energy swirled around her, comforting her like a friend. She'd been away from magic for far too long. Somehow, it made her feel better—safer—to be in the flurry of her own power. It was as though Eric, the room, and the rest of the world folded itself away, settling snugly into the back of her mind.

This time around, she tied the spell to a small piece of copper wire. When creating a spell to hold, one not fully cast, it used more energy than going ahead and casting it immediately. You had to freeze the magic a few moments before it was set to be released, and then anchor it to something. When she was ready to finish casting the spell, she'd break the anchor object and finish the incantation.

If she had cast the spell for someone else to hold, it would probably only last a day or two. Since she was holding this for herself, her own power would surround it. The strength inside wouldn't fade as quickly, so the spell might be good for several days. A week, if she was careful.

When she opened her eyes, Alchemy was sitting directly in front of her, outside her bubble of magic. She stretched and dropped her barrier in order to give Alchemy attention. Apparently, though, he just wanted to watch and objected to being touched.

Mira didn't push it. When she looked around, she didn't immediately notice Eric. He was at the window again, peering out.

"Everything okay?" Mira asked.

"Yes," he said without moving.

He didn't sound remotely convincing.

"What's wrong?"

"Nothing." He drew away from the window again. "I'm starting the audio again."

"Wait, I feel like I'm missing something. What's happened?"

Eric seemed to ignore her and turned the audio back on.

Mira looked at him suspiciously before shaking her head and going back to her work. She was making something for Levi next. As she laid out the materials in front of her, her mind naturally returned to Gabriel.

Her heart seemed to skip a beat and she quickly looked up at Eric. "Are the others all right? Have they reached the store?"

"They have."

She waited for more, but it didn't come. "Well, what's happening?"

"I'm afraid we've lost contact with them."

Mira stood up. "Why, what happened?"

Eric held up a hand to stem the barrage of questions Mira was ready to throw at him. "It only means that they've turned off their audio. It's not uncommon."

"So, they're okay?"

"They're out of touch. That's all."

It wasn't a solid answer, but it was one Mira would accept. She looked down at the materials for her next spell, wondering if she should continue. Then again, the thought of her pacing the house, wringing her hands and wondering what was happening didn't sound like the best use of her time.

"This spell is going to take longer." Her voice was as hesitant as she felt.

"It's not the best time to turn off audio," Eric said. "Mr. Harker and Detective Flint will want an update as soon as they are able."

Mira knew it was true, especially since she wanted the same thing from them. "How is it they can turn off audio and I have trouble getting mine turned off?"

Eric didn't answer.

"Fine, give me five minutes. I'll work silently for a while, so the audio can be on. When I start working, though, I want it off. Will that work?"

"Five minute intervals. No matter what you're doing, I'll only go silent for five minutes at a time."

Mira didn't argue—she knew it was the best she was going to get.

When Eric turned off the audio, she didn't get to work. "Why is it so important? The audio, I mean."

"Believe it or not, it's not every day we watch over someone that is actively in danger of being killed."

Mira shifted uncomfortably at the thought.

"And our team hasn't worked directly with a Harker for any substantial length of time."

"You knew about Emmit before you met him?" Mira asked, surprised.

"Everyone in the company knows about him, but very few work for him for long periods of time."

"Why not?"

"The Harkers don't call on us often."

"Then why do you know about them?

Eric shrugged. "We keep track of the family. That's the way Reinfield set it up."

"What do you do when he's not around?"

"Mostly the same thing we do when he is around, just less of it—there's a whole lot more travel, and shit doesn't get so weird." After a moment, Eric looked as though he wanted to suck back the last statement.

Mira smiled, though. "I could do with a lot less weird myself."

"Don't worry. We've got you covered."

"Hopefully after tonight there won't be a need anymore."

"We'll still have you covered."

"Emmit's not likely to stick around once everything here gets resolved."

"You probably won't have someone looking out for you twenty-four, seven, but we'll still be around. Mr. Harker already has it arranged."

Mira's eyes narrowed. "Has what arranged?"

"For the agency to have someone in the area."

Mira rolled her eyes and shook her head. "Of course he does."

She turned to her spell. "He probably has you watching all sorts of people. Does he drive people crazy like this wherever he goes?"

"People being watched, yes. People being protected, no. This is only the second request of protection he's made. You, Tyler, and Gabriel will be guarded."

"Only the second? Who's the first? His sister?"

"I'm not at liberty to say, but his sister is a Harker. We work for her the same as we work for him."

"Really? Do they spy on each other? That could get complicated."

"A Harker's business isn't shared with anyone, not even another Harker."

"Why are you telling me all this, then?"

"You're an anomaly for us. That and I haven't given you details."

"I guess not."

"Also, it gives you an idea of why you'll be seeing us around so often."

Mira thought that over. She didn't particularly like the idea of someone looking over her shoulder all the time, but it seemed like a small concession with someone trying to kill her.

"Audio's up," Eric said.

Mira started. She'd been so absorbed in their conversation that she had lost track of time.

She turned to her spell, wanting to give Reinfield and his men a few minutes of audio before starting, so she rearranged things in her circle and thought over what she was going to do.

To help Levi, she didn't feel the need to purify the chain she used. In fact, purification might actually hurt the spell instead of help it. When she found nothing else to distract her, she charged her circle and began.

Not knowing what Levi was made the spell a little trickier than the one that she had used to hide herself from Gabriel, but it wasn't too different. The basics were all there.

The first part of the spell did take about five minutes, just as she had anticipated. When she went quiet, she began to draw invisible symbols into the carpet. Since she was a witch, it only made sense that she would know how to hide someone from a witch. It wouldn't be perfect, but at least she'd have a starting place.

Mira lost track of everything except the task at hand while she was surrounded by magic. She went through the remaining incantation. It wasn't until she was wrapping up that she realized the spell had taken longer and used more power than she had anticipated.

After she dropped the circle, she stretched her stiff limbs. Eric was once again at the window.

"Any news?" Mira asked.

"Detective Flint is on his way here," Eric said.

"He is? Did they find John?"

"He wasn't there."

Her hopes that the disaster would finally be over evaporated. "Well, at least everyone is safe."

Eric didn't say anything.

"Everyone is okay, right? I mean, if John wasn't there..."

"Something else was there. Two men were injured, nothing serious."

"What do you mean something else?"

CHAPTER 18

THERE WAS ONLY ONE thing that came to mind when Mira thought of 'something else,' but she had to be wrong. More creatures from the Ether couldn't be here. But she knew it was true, so she didn't ask the question.

Instead, she began to clear away everything that she used for her spells and asked a different question. "Who was hurt?"

"Two of Reinfield's men," Eric said.

Two more hurt because of me. "I'm sorry to hear that." She wouldn't look at Eric. She wasn't sure she could look any of Reinfield's employees in the face right now. One dead and three injured.

"I need to take us live." Eric didn't wait for a response, but turned on the little device in his ear. He immediately began to talk, letting them know Mira was done.

Mira began to take her stuff to the bedroom. She had hoped to get a little space, but Eric followed just as closely as he always did. Wordlessly, she stored the supplies. It felt strange to have some of them out in the open, but there were no hiding places in Gabriel's house.

Spark was in her pocket. Since the nightmare wasn't over, she had a feeling her spell wouldn't leave her side, even when she slept.

"Detective Flint has been dropped off out front," Eric said.

Mira hurried out of the room and met Gabriel in the living room as he walked in the door. Without even thinking about it, she wrapped her arms around him and hugged as though he might try to leave again. Gabriel returned the gesture, but not with as much enthusiasm as she expected.

She pulled back and looked him over. The erratic power that had been around was still there.

"What happened?" Mira asked.

"He didn't show up," Gabriel said.

"I gathered that, but what happened?"

Gabriel glanced at Eric but didn't seem inclined on sending the guard away. "Two creatures from the Ether were there."

Mira gripped his arm. Hearing the truth forced her to face the reality of what Eric had said earlier.

"You should get some rest."

"Yeah, like that's going to happen."

Gabriel ran his hand through his hair and stepped away. "You should at least try."

Emmit's words before he left waved a flag in her mind. "We should talk."

"Not tonight." The erratic energy seemed to get stronger.

Mira sat down on the couch, ignoring him. "Those things. Are they dead?"

"Yes, you don't have to worry about them."

Alchemy and Oracle jumped on the couch. Oracle planted himself on Mira's lap while Alchemy sat rigidly beside her.

Mira absentmindedly scratched Oracle behind the ears. "Does anyone know how they got through?"

"No."

"Did Emmit say—"

"Look, if Harker knows something, he's not telling anyone," Gabriel snapped.

Alchemy's hair stood on end and he hissed at Gabriel while Oracle moved to perch himself next to his brother.

Gabriel looked at them in surprise before sinking down in a chair opposite Mira. "Sorry, I'm just frustrated. I thought this would all be over tonight."

"Me, too," Mira admitted. "But I'm glad you're not hurt."

"Not everyone was so lucky."

"I heard." Not able to look at Gabriel due to her own guilt, she concentrated on the cats, which appeared calmer, but still ill at ease. Mira's guilt only grew while Gabriel stayed silent. "Do you think those things came through in my shop because you and I ended up there the first time we left the Ether?"

"It's possible."

"So Lance's house may have issues as well." Mira glanced up at Eric, not willing to say more with him in the room.

"I'm more worried about Barney's apartment."

"Is someone watching it?"

"They are now. Barney's place, your shop and apartment, and this house."

"And my family?" Mira looked again at Eric.

Gabriel answered, "Someone is looking out for them and Tyler."

Mira looked down at her hands and tried not to get upset. "This is such a mess."

"Can you give us a minute?" Gabriel asked quietly.

She looked up in time to see Chris move into the kitchen and tried to force a smile when Gabriel sat down next to her. The cats stared at him, their tails flicking anxiously.

"It is a mess." He put his arm around her and she leaned into him. "That's what has me frustrated. Mostly, anyway."

Finally giving their blessing, Alchemy and Oracle jumped off the couch. Oracle rubbed against Gabriel's leg before they disappeared.

"Mostly?" Mira asked.

Gabriel grimaced. "I'm such a hypocrite."

"Meaning?"

"I don't want anything to do with being an angel until I want to use it. I spent the entire night trying to step away from that part of myself, only to end the night trying to make the whole supernatural stuff work."

"You used your voice on the creatures?"

"I tried to. I only ended up feeling like an idiot for thinking it would work here."

Mira bit her lip and hesitated before taking the plunge. "It will work here. I'm sure of that."

"What makes you think that?"

"I've seen it."

"When Harker was sending me to the Ether? That doesn't really count since I was part-way there already."

"Not just then. You've helped me with it." When she saw Gabriel about to argue, she rushed on, "I've sensed it, too. Loads of times. It's as though the power builds up around you, but isn't directed or aimed."

Gabriel seemed to think that over.

"It happens a lot when you argue with Emmit."

"Well, I wouldn't actually want to do anything to him. I can't stand the guy, but like it or not, we need him."

"He likes you," Mira said.

Gabriel snorted.

"No, really. He's worried about you."

"Even if my powers did work over here, they're not going to if I spend all my time ignoring the fact that I'm not who I thought I was."

Mira was willing to let the subject of Emmit drop. "You are, though. You still don't get it. Nothing about you has changed. You're still the same person, you just know a little more about yourself."

Gabriel hugged her closer. "Maybe."

"It's true. If I decided today to give up witchcraft, I'd still be me, right?"

He smiled down at her. "Yeah, you'd still be you."

Mira beamed, thinking maybe, just maybe, he'd get past this hurdle.

Then he kissed her, and all thoughts of angels and witches flew from her mind. Mira melded to Gabriel. Their lips pressed together gently at first. She felt his hands on her skin under her shirt and she breathed deeply, feeling some of the tension unwind.

Gabriel increased the urgency of the kiss as a tingling fire built in Mira. She let herself be pushed down on the couch, Gabriel over her. When he pressed into her, she craved the feeling and wanted more.

Shattering glass yanked them out of their haze of lust. Mira was just taking in the fact that the front window was broken as she noticed the bottle which had broken it.

Gabriel's mind was clearly working much faster than hers was. He yanked her to her feet and pushed her toward the kitchen as the curtains caught fire.

"Eric!" Gabriel hollered into the house.

There was a deafening crash from the back of the house, which rattled the whole structure.

A guttural screech came from one of the bedrooms.

Mira's breath caught in her throat. "What the hell—"

"I didn't have any idea this was coming," Gabriel said, interrupting her.

The sound of breaking glass nearby grabbed their attention. A sickly green talon grasped hold of the doorframe to her bedroom. What emerged could have been something almost human, if not for the color and lack of hands.

Eric shot it three times, in what might have been a chest, and the creature crumpled to the ground.

Flames were beginning to billow in earnest from the living room. Mira sensed some magic at play, but she couldn't tell if the magic was creating the fire or just egging it on.

"Garage," Gabriel said.

"It's too close to the fire," Mira said. "Magic's fueling it."

"Dammit!" Gabriel clenched his fist into a tight ball.

Eric grabbed Mira's arm and pulled her farther into the house. The smell of burnt tar began to fill the air. Her mouth went dry when they approached the wounded creature as it twitched on the ground.

Eric added another bullet to its head before stepping over the figure. Sluggish dark fluid was leaking out onto Gabriel's floors.

Mira jumped when Eric fired more shots into the house. His hulking form hid whatever he was firing at, but the shriek that followed indicated he had hit his target. He rushed into the spare bedroom, quickly assessed the area and dragged Mira in behind him.

Gabriel followed with gun in hand and slammed the door shut.

Mira scanned the room herself. Her heart raced and her chest threatened to seize up. But in this room, she was surrounded by magic—her magic. She began running through possibilities, but then she froze.

"Alchemy and Oracle," Mira squeaked. "Oh, my god." She moved to the door, not even thinking about what might be on the other side.

Eric slipped a new clip into place and grabbed her arm. "Don't even think about it."

Mira's eyes bulged and filled with tears. She began to shake and looked toward Gabriel, who was already opening the door, inspecting the hall.

Gabriel checked one way, and then opened the door wider to check the other way. Mira called for Alchemy and Oracle. Gabriel fired twice while Mira's frantic cats ran under his legs into the room and straight under the bed.

Gabriel fired again before slamming the door shut. "How in the hell did these things get here?"

He wasn't asking anyone, but Eric replied anyway. "I'm getting no response from outside. More people are on their way."

Mira covered her mouth. "The guards are—"

"Not responding," Eric said.

A voice called out from somewhere else inside the house, "My lucky day!" All noise sounded muffled through the walls. "I followed an angel and I found he has my witch."

"Can you get her safely out of here?" Gabriel whispered to Eric.

"I'm not going anywhere without you," Mira whispered as forcefully as she could while trying not to let anyone outside the room hear.

"I can't ensure anything until backup arrives," Eric said, ignoring her. "There's no way to know what the situation looks outside."

"How far away are they?" Gabriel asked.

"Three minutes," Eric said. "My best guess is that the police are seven minutes away."

The doorknob turned. Gabriel pushed against the door and fastened the lock.

"From the Ether, I've seen the doors that houses have in this age." John's voice was quiet, almost thoughtful. Louder, he added, "Give me the witch and I'll spare the rest of you."

"Not a chance," Gabriel said.

"He's not going to give up," Mira said.

Gabriel looked at her. She couldn't tell if he was alarmed or startled, but he moved to her and wrapped his arms tightly around her.

Eric moved between them and the door.

She felt better with Gabriel close by. They had survived worse than this. Together, they could make it through.

The door slammed open. Eric opened fire.

Mira caught sight of a beast with tufts of fur matted randomly around its body. It roared and disappeared.

"There will be a car out front in less than a minute," Eric said.

Gabriel pulled Mira over to a window and opened it, pushing out the screen.

He looked around outside and jerked his head up when Eric started shooting again.

"When you hit the ground, run for the street," Gabriel said. "Don't stop for anything."

"I'll wait for you," Mira said.

"No, just run, I'll be behind you."

Mira bit her lip and nodded. She glanced nervously at Eric as he stepped out into the hallway. Shaking, she sat on the windowsill and let Gabriel lower her the few feet to the ground.

"Come on," she hissed.

Gabriel had one leg out the window. "Dammit, Mira, run to the car!"

She turned and ran as though demons were chasing her.

Maybe they were.

She heard noises behind her and shots from outside the house. There were sirens in the distance. She tried to turn and see what was behind her but found she couldn't.

Fury took hold, trying to nudge fear out of its way. Gabriel had made her run.

Out in the front yard, there were four armed men approaching the house. They stepped aside as she ran past them and to the truck waiting at the street.

It was only then that she could stop and turn. She saw Reinfield's men rounding the corner of the house. The front was engulfed in flames.

Someone grabbed Mira's arm and pulled her into the backseat of the SUV.

"Wait! Gabriel's coming!" Mira screeched when the door was shut.

The truck started moving before she could reach the door handle.

"Wait!"

Something pinched her shoulder while she tried to open the door. It wouldn't budge.

Mira's world began to spin as she watched the fire fade away behind her.

CHAPTER 19

IRA WOKE UP TO the sound of Emmit yelling. Despite feeling as if she had been raked over hot coals, she smiled. Only Gabriel made him yell like that.

Sitting up was a chore, but she forced herself all the way to her feet. The fact that she was in Emmit's apartment wasn't a surprise. The fact that she was alone, however, was.

It also made her nervous. She'd seen all the things that go bump in the night and knew enough to be scared. Tiptoeing down the hall, she sought out Emmit.

One man stood outside the door to the library.

When he noticed her, he stood up straighter and tapped his ear. "You don't want to go in there."

"I need to see them."

The man shook his head.

"Is Eric okay?" Mira asked.

"He will be."

Mira didn't press, not yet wanting to know how bad it was. What she needed more than anything was to see Gabriel.

She opened the door and poked her head inside. The two men didn't appear to notice her arrival. She closed the door softly behind her and looked around the room, not taking in what the argument was about. It was between Emmit and Reinfield.

Mira's heart tried to seize up as her gaze darted around the room. She didn't see him.

"Is Gabriel..." She couldn't say dead. The words wouldn't leave her mouth.

They stopped arguing but continued to glare at each other.

"They have him," Emmit said.

The words made Mira lightheaded. She sank into a chair, not wanting anyone to notice that she was so unsteady.

"You shouldn't be up," Emmit said. "The doctor is on his way."

Mira shook her head. "I don't need to see a doctor. I need to see Gabriel. What happened?"

Emmit hesitated—something she'd only rarely witnessed.

"Don't lie to me or tell me to go away," Mira said before he could respond. "I want to know what happened. This time, I am demanding an answer from you."

Emmit's lips twitched as though frustrated, but trying to hide it. "And if I refuse?"

The room seemed to grow darker and shadows spread thickly out of the corners.

Mira glared at him and stood up. "Try me."

She had no idea what she could do. She had Spark with her, a spell that hides someone from witches, and Gabriel's feathers. Nothing that would hurt Emmit in the slightest.

"Knock it off," Reinfield snapped.

Emmit blinked and glared at him, but the darkness in the room seemed to dissipate. Mira tried not to let out a sigh of relief. Emmit could probably snap her in two if he wanted to, spells or not.

"Gabriel was followed home," Reinfield said. "At least, as far as we can tell he was."

"The house was guarded," Mira said, "inside and out."

"That was my first point as well," Emmit said.

Reinfield shrugged, not looking the least abashed. "My team is only human."

Mira wanted to yell and rage at the man. When she saw Emmit's face grow redder, she guessed that he already had.

"Were the guards hurt?" Mira asked.

"Only one man outside was injured. The rest were just knocked out. We think it was magic. We'll know for sure when they wake up."

Mira's eyes narrowed. "Speaking of knocked out, how in the hell did I end up here?"

Reinfield shifted. "That was an unfortunate necessity with police arriving."

"Necessity?" Mira glared at the man. "I don't think so. They drugged me. If anything like that happens again, someone is going to pay, karma be dammed." She wanted to shake Emmit—aggravated by his seemingly passive attitude to her being drugged.

When neither man commented, she continued. "What happened after I got out of the house?"

"We don't know," Reinfield said. "Eric saw Gabriel make it out the window. We heard shots, but no one saw anything else."

"And Gabriel was gone," Mira said, sitting down again. "The fire?"

"Took most of the house and part of one next door," Reinfield said. "The firefighters had a hell of a time putting it out."

"Magic was involved," Mira said. Her mind started to get closer to a subject she was dreading. "Eric got out, though, right?"

"With passengers," Reinfield said.

Mira frowned at him.

"Two black felines," Reinfield said.

Part of the stress on Mira's chest lifted. "They were found?"

"They seem to be uninjured," Reinfield said. "We took them to a vet, just in case."

Mira had tried not to imagine them being hurt. Even now that she knew they were safe, she was having a hard time letting it sink in. "What do we do now? How do we track Gabriel?"

"We don't have to track him," Emmit said. "We know where they took him."

That sounded like progress to Mira and she perked up immediately.

"We had eyes on a few spots," Reinfield said. "Your pal Barney's apartment and your old store are areas where the space between worlds gets a bit thin."

"Thin?" Mira looked at Emmit. "Does Reinfield know about everything?"

"As much as any of us know," Emmit said.

"Anyway, we lost contact with our team watching Barney's apartment. It looks like the creatures slipped through that way," Reinfield said.

"Slipped through," Mira said, dully. "You mean to the Ether. John and those things took Gabriel to the Ether." She remembered the ward she had started for him. It wasn't done yet, so he had nothing but his voice. They would have stopped him from being able to use that the moment they took him.

Mira shivered at thoughts of how they may have silenced Gabriel. She closed her eyes, but nightmares had permanently entrenched themselves in the darkness of her mind.

"When can you get me there?" Mira asked.

She hadn't noticed they had started talking until she interrupted.

"We won't," Emmit said.

"We can't," Reinfield said at the same time.

Mira glared at Reinfield. "I already know he can." She waved a hand in Emmit's direction. "He sent Gabriel there the last time and he brought us back."

Reinfield sighed and shook his head at Emmit. "You can't be subtle with anything, can you?"

Emmit's gaze narrowed on Reinfield. "I did what I had to do."

"It should only take me a few hours to have a few spells ready," Mira said.

"A couple of spells might help even the odds a bit," Reinfield said to Emmit.

"What could you make for me?" Emmit asked.

"I was going to make Fire and Gust. Possibly another Spark, but I planned on creating them for me," Mira said.

"We're out of options," Emmit said. "I'm the one going over."

"You said if you went over you couldn't come back," Mira said.

Emmit nodded.

"No way," Mira said. "Send me over—I know the place. I'll get Gabriel and meet you at Lance's house again."

"Not this time," Emmit said.

"Going over there isn't going to help if you only have half a ritual," Reinfield said.

"My ancestors never had a ritual," Emmit said.

"No," Reinfield snapped. "They had the witches."

"If you need the help of a witch," Mira said, "you just have to take me with you."

"I'll go over and send Gabriel back," Emmit said.

"If you can send Gabriel here, you can come back yourself," Mira said.

"You won't survive for more than a few minutes, and you know it," Reinfield said.

"I'll do what I can," Emmit said.

"If you—"

"This is happening." Emmit didn't sound angry when he cut Mira off, simply adamant. "I do need assistance on this side, naturally. I would appreciate the assistance of you both, but if I must get it elsewhere, I will."

"And you won't take me with you?" Mira asked.

"It is not an option," Emmit said.

"And you'll find Gabriel?" Mira asked.

Reinfield made an exasperated noise and shook his head.

"I'll do what I can," Emmit said, ignoring Reinfield.

Mira wasn't instilled with confidence. It didn't sound like enough. Not nearly enough.

Maybe if I stall for time.

"What do you need us to do?" Mira asked.

"I would appreciate if Reinfield and his men ensured that your shop is clear and set up," Emmit said. "The world is thin there, which should make it easier to cross over."

"You're set on this?" Reinfield asked.

"I am," Emmit said.

"I'll gather those available and see what we can do."

"Thank you," Emmit said, shaking the man's hand.

"And me?" Mira asked as Reinfield left the room.

"You've had a long night. Are you up for more?" Emmit asked.

"Of course."

"When we brought you and Gabriel back, the witches didn't have the spell. Instead, I directed their magic."

"Mr. Singer mentioned it."

"As I will be going to the Ether this time, I cannot direct the magic."

"You're asking me to send you over there?" Mira asked.

"You know what lives in the Ether. I trust that you wouldn't attempt to use the spell for foolish reasons. You are also strong enough to cast the spell on your own."

Mira wasn't sure how she felt about having the spell to enter the Ether. She knew how she felt about actually sending Emmit to that horrible place, and it didn't sit well.

"There is something else," Emmit said.

"Yes?"

"You mentioned making spells for yourself. Is it possible for you to make them for me instead?"

She thought about trying to use his query as an excuse to get him to take her with him, but it didn't seem like the right time. "Of course."

Mira spent the morning poring over Emmit's notes. She'd be the first witch in hundreds of years that would know how to get to the Ether.

No, she corrected herself, witches started this mess.

It's true that the witches may have had human encouragement, but witches had gone there when they shouldn't have.

Someone had been visiting the Ether. Mira shook the thought out of her mind. She still had no idea who went there, so there was no way to get that witch to help.

Trying not to think about what might be happening to Gabriel was about as effective as a piece of paper surviving an open flame. She wasn't confident that Emmit would bring Gabriel back. Emmit seemed to be on some sort of death march, intent on sacrificing himself.

Now that Mira had a feel for the Ether, the spell to send Emmit there wouldn't pose much of a challenge. Emmit and Reinfield both suggested they could bring in more witches for support, but Mira declined. Only a few witches knew what was happening, and for what she was planning, she'd need them on this side of the Ether.

Once Reinfield's team had gathered her ingredients, she began to cast the spells that Emmit intended to take to the Ether. This part would have been tricky as well, if other witches had been around. She created the spells, and then tore the object holding the spell in half before freezing the spell in place. She pocketed half and gave the other half to Emmit.

Emmit's spells had to be real and as effective as possible, just in case her plan didn't work. She wanted to give Emmit every chance at returning.

If things went the way she hoped, however, Mira would be the one making this journey. Since time of day didn't matter in the Ether, they planned on sending Emmit over from the burnt husk of Mira's store that evening. Mira's mind was on her spell, though she couldn't guess where Emmit's mind was.

Still, she probed where she could.

After she cast the spells and held them, she sought out Emmit, finding him exactly where she'd expected, going over his plans in the library.

"Where's Reinfield?" she asked as she entered.

"He left early," Emmit said. "He's ensuring we aren't disturbed while you're casting. Are you comfortable with the spell? Is there anything you need?"

"What's that?" Mira asked, turning his attention to the paper in front of him. The sheet showed three points with one in the middle. She had seen one before, here and on the cover of one of Chris's books.

"This is frustration personified," Emmit said.

"I thought that's what I was," she said.

Emmit's rigid look went soft and he smiled at her. "This has you beat."

"The day's not over yet." Mira grinned in a way she hoped he took as her joking. "What is it?"

"The remnants of a very old ritual. It takes four people, three around the one in the middle."

"This was the ritual Reinfield mentioned."

"Yes, his family and mine tracked it down through the centuries."

"What does it do?"

"It kills a god."

"A god?"

"Not really a god, of course, but the creature in the Ether. The one that destroyed the balance. This is supposed to kill it."

"Where did it come from?"

"No one knows. Not really. The first information we found on the ritual said it was discovered in the Library of Alexandria.

There had been an earthquake and the scholars were preserving the scrolls, moving them to a sister library while repairs to the building took place. They copied it before returning the original back to the original library. At least that's the way we understand it. It's been pieced together through hundreds of different stories."

"I thought Reinfield said you had half the ritual. You only have those two pages, though."

"He was being kind. The truth is we have no idea how much more of it there is. We do know, however, that this alone doesn't work."

"If you had the rest of the ritual, would the ritual work?"

"That depends on whether there is a translator. It took the family around a hundred years to find one for these two pages, but now we have no record of the original language."

"So, if you had the ritual and the translator, would you be able to stop that thing?"

Emmit sighed. "If we'd had those things a month ago, we would have stood a chance. Now? I wouldn't wait to find out. That's where Reinfield and I disagree. He wants to hold the line, but I don't want to take the risk."

"If we stop John, what risk would there be?" Mira asked.

"The world is too thin here. The creatures that have attacked you needed help getting here. But the monster you describe in the city only needs power to cross over."

"Which is why John wants me." The thought didn't sit well with Mira.

"I'm surprised they needed more than Tyler, but the beast must have been diminished all these years with only the smaller creatures to feed on. Now it's growing in power."

Mira shivered. She would not feel sorry for those things.

"It's nearly time. Are you comfortable enough with the spell to send me over?"

Hold the line, Mira thought. If I get Gabriel and the book, we can fix this.

"We can review again if you'd like," Emmit said.

"What?" Mira said. Then she replayed what he had said. "I think I'm good with the spell, though I would like to change it slightly."

"We can't change the spell. There are too many unknowns," Emmit said.

"Actually, I think you'll agree with this change. I want to make a double circle."

Emmit looked thoughtful. "My reaction this time shouldn't be as volatile as it was when you performed the other spell." He seemed to be rolling the idea around. "But we will be close to the Ether."

Mira mentally crossed her fingers.

"You're right. It's a good precaution to take. Once I'm through, I'll try to find Gabriel, and I'll do what I can to return him to you."

Mira nodded. "But getting us back isn't the same spell? I mean, it didn't seem the same."

"No, I'll need you or three other witches on this side to make it work."

"Why can't you just come with him?"

"When I cross, my presence will be known to anyone in the vicinity. I can hold them at bay for a short time, but it won't be possible to return."

Mira dug into her pocket. "Speaking of holding them at bay, I have a few things that will help." She laid the contents out. "Spark is the thin wire. Twist it, and it should break in two fairly easily. Close your eyes when it breaks, and if Gabriel's with you, make sure he's close by or he could get caught up."

"What will it do?"

"Shock anything around you. The Ether eats away magic pretty fast, and I won't be there to fuel this, but it should still be powerful enough to kill for the first ten-twelve hours." *I hope.*

She pushed the thought away. She'd be the one there, so it would turn out fine. "The thick wire is Fire. It won't be as easy to break as the other will, but that's for good reason. Break it and it does what's marked on the label. It's big, strong, and it arcs out. Gust should be about the same. It's the string. Untie it to release the spell. With any of them, make sure Gabriel is close behind you."

Emmit gestured to the necklace that Mira had pulled out and set aside. "What's this?"

"I made that for someone else. I should probably ask one of Reinfield's men to deliver it. It hides the wearer from witches."

"It makes them invisible?" Emmit looked skeptical.

"No, it hides what the person is—it hides their essence."

"That sounds as though it might be useful for someone. May I?"

"Go ahead. Anyone can touch it or wear it. Witches will just sense the person differently."

Emmit held it up, inspecting it. "I sense your power in it. It's beautiful work."

"Thank you," Mira said, blushing slightly.

He handled it as though it was a delicate heirloom.

"Would you..." Mira could feel her face grow redder and tried to start again. "Would you like to keep it? Kind of like a, uh, good luck charm."

Emmit surprised her by pulling her into a hug. "This will make me luckier than you know."

It hit Mira that, if what she planned didn't work, Emmit would essentially be walking straight into his death. She hugged him fiercely, trying to hold back tears.

It will work. Mira had to repeat it over and over again.

There was a light rapping on the door as though someone was very worried they might be heard. Emmit pulled away. When he did, all of his emotion disappeared inside as well. "Thank you." Louder, he added, "Come in."

A man entered, holding a phone out as though it were a peace offering. "Your sister is available, sir." He was young and nowhere near as stoic or battle worn as Reinfield's other employees.

Emmit took the phone. "Would you mind going ahead and setting up? I'd like to take a few moments in private." He held up the necklace, looking it over again. "There's a lot I need to discuss with my sister and little time."

"Of course," Mira said. "I'll see you there."

In the hall, Mira almost turned to tell Emmit not to tell his sister that he was going into the Ether to die. If he knew what she was planning, though, Emmit would never let her go through with it.

CHAPTER 20

AT THE STORE, MIRA was tempted to tell Reinfield about her intentions, but the man was too much of an unknown. It would put an end to her plans if he told Emmit what she intended.

Instead, she set up as instructed, with the addition of the extra circle. Reinfield was in a foul mood anyway, so Mira told herself it was better that she said nothing.

"My sister will be here in two days," Emmit said as he walked in. "She will pick up where I left off, if needed."

Reinfield crossed his arms. "You know if she follows the same path you're taking, that's it, right? No more Harkers."

"You'll have to find the rest of the ritual." Emmit sounded completely unconcerned. "If it eases your mind, I will try to return. If I'm able, I'll at least make the attempt and we can hold the line as we think of another plan."

"Then send me," Mira tried again. She was starting to get nervous about the idea of altering a spell this old. Emmit was right; there were too many uncertainties.

"Not an option," Emmit said. "I don't think a lone witch would last long. Let's get started."

Mira wrung her hands and looked over what she had put together. Emmit walked around the outer circle, inspecting everything.

"The outer circle doesn't need to match the inner one," Emmit said.

Mira swallowed. "I thought it might amplify the center." What she didn't say was that it didn't copy the inner circle, it mirrored it.

"The bottle?"

"Put it in your pocket. If I had a bigger bottle, I'd use it. Trust me, you're going to want it if you're there for any time."

Emmit nodded. "Very thoughtful."

Mira patted her coat, feeling the bottle reassuringly inside.

Emmit stepped aside, saying a few words to Reinfield before they shook hands and Emmit entered the circle. Mira stepped into the outer circle. She wiped her suddenly sweaty hands on her jeans and looked at Emmit, wondering what was appropriate to say at this point.

He appeared to be struggling with the same issue but trying to hold it back.

Once again, she thought of telling him the real changes she made to the spell. The thought of backing out also arose. But no, she knew she needed to do this.

"If this doesn't work, we'll think of another way," she said. "In twenty-four hours, we'll start checking for you every hour."

"For three days," Emmit finished when she didn't add the length of time she should try to look for him.

Mira wasn't excited about the three days part, but since the plan was about to change, the point was moot. She glanced at Reinfield, who still didn't look happy about the situation. Once again, she ran her sweaty palms over her jeans.

"I'm not sure what to say," Mira said, feeling quite choked up. If her plan didn't work, this would be the last she saw of Emmit.

"It was an honor to be your friend," Emmit said.

Mira entered the inner circle and hugged him fiercely. He returned her embrace, but then peeled himself away.

"It's time to start," Emmit said. "Gabriel is waiting."

The idea that Gabriel had been suffering in the Ether all day caused Mira's heart to constrict. Closing her eyes, she charged the circles and started the spell.

It was part spell and part ceremony, really. Once Mira was deep in the flow of her magic, the anxious and stricken feelings disappeared. She was in her element.

The spell couldn't be rushed. Power rose around them in waves and arched over the bubble that held Emmit. Mira allowed the faintest of static to leak out into her own circle, readying it. The path to the Ether began to thin.

Mira opened her eyes. Emmit was watching her.

With her power streaming around them, she looked into Emmit's eyes, which were now a rich, shining green. "I'm sorry."

He nodded, knowing the time was close.

It bothered her more than she thought it would, that he thought she was apologizing for sending him to the Ether instead of asking for forgiveness in messing up his plans. He didn't have Gabriel's gift of telling if she was lying, which was a good thing, but she hated not telling him the truth all the same.

The barrier between the Ether and their world thinned an impossible amount. Mira caught flickers of changes within Emmit. He seemed to spread out and become thin.

It only took a moment to freeze Emmit's circle, allowing it to stay for a few moments beyond her departure. Then, with a monumental effort, she flipped the spell. The world around her tore away.

Her stomach lurched at the sudden change. It was as though the pressure bounced her around slightly. The thin strands of sound that issued a curse could be ignored. Emmit was in the real world—she had bigger problems to contend with here.

Now that she was in the Ether, she realized she never thought beyond the need to get to Gabriel. He would be at the church, she was sure about that, but she needed to find him without being discovered or confronting John.

Mira gathered her fear and stuffed it away into the corner of her mind, and then she took inventory of what items she had at her disposal. The moment she started, she noted the bright glow around her ring. It had already begun to burn away the haze around her.

With the ring on, she stood out—probably for miles around. Without it, however, she'd probably never survive. Remembering what she had Gabriel do with his ward, she worked the ring off her finger. Putting the ring in her sock seemed like a horrible thing to do with such a beautiful ring, not to mention, horribly uncomfortable if she stepped on it.

She dismissed putting the ring in her pocket. If she ran into John, he probably knew enough to have her turn them out. Instead, she snugged the ring into her bra. Still wasn't the best or most comfortable place to put such a treasure, but better than the alternatives.

One of the two Spark spells stayed in her pocket for easy access. The other spells she decided to hide in her sock. It would hide the glow and she didn't think anyone would think of checking her feet.

The feathers joined the ring.

Her coat was starting to get hot, so she took it off and wrapped it around her waist. She rolled up her pant leg and undid the sheath holding her athame. She secured it in a better spot and unsheathed the blade. She felt better being in this world with a weapon in her hands.

Turning to the door, she took a deep breath. Before she could think things through, worried she wouldn't be able to leave if she focused too hard on what could be outside, she cautiously opened the door a few inches.

The haze seemed thicker than it had been the last time. She tried to see if there was anything around, but she could make things out half a block in any direction.

Maybe it's the city. She sincerely hoped the air would clear the farther she got away from the city.

It took a great amount of willpower to slip out of her store. The atmosphere was a little disorientating at first, but she pictured the city in her mind and chose her direction.

A squeal pierced the air.

Mira's breath caught, and she looked around for the source. She took a step toward the safety of her store but froze when something large fell on top of her, slamming her into the ground. Pain lanced through her arm and head and the high-pitched voice filled her. She barely had time to react, raising the dagger.

Two large hands gripped her aching head and slammed it into the sidewalk.

The world dimmed and winked out.

Sounds and occasional voices broke through Mira's consciousness. Each time, pain came with the noise, causing Mira's mind to flee once again into darkness. It wasn't until she heard a god-awful wail that she exerted enough strength of mind to break into the world of the living.

The world of demons, Mira thought when she opened her eyes. The first thing she saw was a coral-colored creature that yipped when it saw her open her eyes. Then it ran at her.

Mira tried to scramble back, but the way was blocked, and movement made her feel like she was going to throw up.

The thing's mouth opened and shut rapidly as it made a noise worse than any little yapping dog Mira had ever heard. The real issue was the razor-sharp teeth it exposed.

It bounded closer, then seemed to hit a wall and bounced off. It tried again a few times before growling and running away.

She watched the door where the little creature had disappeared. Nothing appeared to move in the hall. The noise died away. Only then did Mira take a slow look around the room. When she tried to move her head fast, vertigo gripped her and she felt as though she was falling over.

Hardwood floors wore a layer of dust thick enough that she could see where she had been dragged into the room. When she looked behind her, she saw that what she had been leaning against wasn't a wall. It was the same invisible barrier that had stopped razor-thin teeth ripping flesh from her bones.

She shivered, wishing she hadn't thought of it in that way. Carefully, she moved to the center of the circle, if that's what it was. Her pounding head wasn't making it easy for her to get a good feel for her surroundings.

"You are awake."

Mira's head whipped around at John's almost jovial voice. It was instant regret. Her head wobbled and the arm holding her up slid out from under her.

"Come on in here," John called down the hall.

Mira lay dazed on the floor for a moment, but when John stepped into the room, she pushed herself painfully up.

Two stick-thin women waited in the hall, watching John.

"I was hoping you'd make it through to this world on your own," John said. "I'm surprised you survived my lookout. Pleasantly surprised, of course."

Mira closed her eyes tight and tried to pull her mind together. "I came to trade."

John chuckled, making Mira want to punch the mirth out of him. "You have nothing to trade."

"Myself," she said, "I came to trade myself for Gabriel."

"Why would I want to trade?" John asked in mock confusion.

Mira gritted her teeth and didn't reply.

"I have you both. There's nothing to trade." He looked out into the hall and one of the women flinched. "Drop the barrier."

Distantly, Mira sensed a small flow of power fade away from around her.

"I don't think you came to trade," John said, moving closer. "This little dagger here tells me you had other intentions. Not to mention the wire."

"That's not—"

John kicked out.

Caught off guard, Mira couldn't block the blow. She screamed and when she fell back against the floor, she clutched her head which radiated pain from being knocked onto the ground yet again. When she opened her eyes, she couldn't see straight. She couldn't be certain if the tears were what blurred the room or pain.

John kicked her again in the stomach, which didn't hurt as much as she'd expected. Still, she shut her eyes and grimaced.

A smell entered her nose, making her gag. The blur could only be Johns face, up close to her own.

"You see, you're mine now. Right along with your feathered friend." The blur disappeared. "Take her to the hall."

Mira's head lolled to the side as she was dragged into the hall by her arms. She expected them to stop there, but with a grunt of effort, the woman slid her farther and maneuvered her through a set of double doors.

Blurry images of pews sailed by Mira in a surreal way. She saw the women again and was confused, because it felt as though she were still moving. Everyone was standing still. They got no further away, so she must have stopped while the room continued to spin.

Mira wished for darkness. Closing her eyes, she searched for it. Why had she come here?

Gabriel. Her eyes snapped open again. He was here somewhere.

She stared at the ceiling, willing her body at least to support movement. Her vision cleared after a while and she dared to look around a little.

John was still there, talking with some... thing—which had brown tufts of hair.

"For christ's sake, someone get her cleaned up," John snapped when he noticed her looking at him.

The woman who had flinched in the hall came up from behind her and knelt between Mira and John. Another walked up.

"Sybil?" Mira asked when she got a closer look at the standing woman.

"Not both of you," John snarled. "You go stand over there and watch."

Sybil made no response to her name. When John told her to move, she did. There was no light behind Sybil's eyes.

The woman crouching down next to Mira had a dirty piece of cloth and smeared it across Mira's face.

Mira gasped and drew away the moment the woman touched her head.

The woman grabbed her arm and yanked her back. Mira took a good look at her. There was fire raging behind this woman's eyes.

"Don't move and don't talk," the woman said in the lowest of whispers. Even as close as Mira was, she had to strain to hear the woman.

"Who are you?" Mira asked, trying to talk just as low.

"Doesn't matter anymore. I just do what I have to."

"Because he says so?" Mira seethed.

The woman glared at her. "While he has my kids. Yes."

Mira's eyes widened.

"No talking," John yelled. "Dammed witches." He came up behind the woman and smacked her on the back of the head.

The woman gritted her teeth and made no other reaction. After a moment, she continued to wipe the grimy rag over Mira once again.

"Talk again and I'll drag your husband out."

The woman froze, terror marring every feature.

Mira wasn't sure if the threat meant she couldn't talk either, so she kept her mouth shut. After seeing the stark fear the woman had shown over the words, Mira didn't want to know what it meant.

John kept a watchful eye on them.

When the woman stood and backed away, Mira tried to sit up again.

"In a hurry to get up?" John asked. His burned face was starting to decay giving his smile a melted quality that made Mira want to look away. "Good. Strap her to the board."

The woman and Sybil moved forward again.

"Not you!" he yelled at Sybil. He nodded to someone else and watched Mira. "He'll help."

The woman took Mira's arm and tried to lift her on her own. When Mira saw the brown, leathery monstrosity that moved toward her, she scrambled and tried to get to her feet. Leaning heavily on the woman, Mira managed to stand.

Mira tried to back away from the thing. Her body felt cold and didn't want to respond. Thick fingers wrapped around her wrist, and she couldn't help but cry out when the grip threatened to grind her bones to dust. Mira was thrust backward by the creature where she fell against a wooden plank leaning behind her. The woman holding her stumbled as she tried to soften Mira's landing.

John laughed.

Mira breathed in short small bursts. When the creature stepped away, she felt mildly better. It wasn't until the woman started to bind Mira's hand to the board that Mira realized she'd missed an opportunity when John had been distracted. The woman had to be Mrs. Henderson, but she needed to confirm it before she did anything else.

"What the hell is this?" Mira called out to John. Fear tinged every word.

"Your friend Tyler didn't tell you?" John asked.

"What are you doing?" Mira asked, ignoring the question.

"You are taking our place," John said.

"I don't know what that means."

The woman began strapping her other hand down, making Mira feel like she was angled back on display for everyone to watch.

"It—" John stopped when something in the hallway clanged loudly.

Mira took her chance after John looked around. She leaned forward and whispered. "Mrs. Henderson?"

The woman had a short sharp intake of breath, which told Mira all she needed to know.

"Let's get this over with," John said. "Get away."

Mrs. Henderson fled to the back of the hall.

John moved forward. The cocky stride he always seemed to have was gone. He moved behind Mira, and after a few moments moved back into her line of sight.

Frowning in concentration, he dipped a gloved finger into a bowl.

"What is that?" Mira asked, pulling away as far the restraints would allow.

He leaned over, drawing something on her forehead. "I told you. You're taking our place."

Mira couldn't help but notice he wouldn't look her in the eye. When he was done, he stripped off the glove and quickly moved back. Everyone except Sybil had moved farther away, toward the center of the hall. Sybil stared into nothingness as if unaware of anything happening around her.

The sound of a tree creaking in the wind was the only sound in the room. Mira twisted her hands in her binds, trying to slip free. The sight of John watching her, almost reverently, made her blood run cold.

Something touched her arm and she jerked, trying to reel back. A thin tendril wound its way over her, slipping under her shirt and wrapping around her arm.

More joined the first, gliding across her skin. She shivered, feeling something slide up around her calves from the bottom of her pants leg.

Her breath came in short sharp bursts, and the creaking grew louder. She clamped her eyes and mouth shut when she felt thin roots dart across her face.

Movement ceased. The creaking stopped.

Mira dared to crack her eyes open, trying to see what was happening. She couldn't move any part of her body.

She shuddered but breathed a little easier when nothing happened. Everyone else in the hall seemed to hold their breath.

The vines around her tensed, then tightened around her hard, causing her to cry out in surprise.

A breath later, the searing pain started, forcing a scream out of her.

CHAPTER 21

WHITE-HOT FIRE SEARED IN strips across Mira's body. She writhed and screamed. Thin tendrils of metal stabbed into every nerve in her body and made her blood feel as if it was boiling.

There was nothing but agony.

Then there was sound. A roar from the city filled the room. The board Mira was strapped to vibrated under the assault. The sound drowned out her screams. It found passage through her, straight to the bone, causing even her marrow to dance until she thought she must surely shatter.

The searing threads followed the new channels, touching every cell in her body.

Mira wanted to die.

Or maybe this was death, because she knew no person could withstand this.

The fire began to retreat, leaving cold emptiness behind. It took Mira a while to realize that the noise had stopped. Her screams had stopped.

Maybe she couldn't scream anymore.

Maybe there was nothing left to scream with.

Maybe oblivion had finally taken her.

She blinked, numbly surprised that she still had eyes with which to do so.

Some part of her brain registered voices, but they came to her in a disjointed, hazy way.

"Give her a drink and take her to a room."

That was... John. Right. John.

"The same room?" The voice was trembling and unrecognizable.

Was it her own?

"No, give her a bed and let her rest." There was despair in his voice that Mira had never heard before.

Couldn't be John.

"Water?"

"No, no, save the water for later. She'll need it then." Whoever sounded like John seemed solemn and regretful.

Mira had no idea where she was. There was light and shapes and voices, but she couldn't make sense of anything. She closed her eyes, feeling they were useless, and concentrated on the sounds.

Shuffling of feet and a sense of emptiness opened up before her.

Mira wasn't sure if she fell asleep or if she just became numb to the world around her.

At some point, Mira felt someone approach.

Her eyes shot open and she tried to pull away.

"It's me."

Mira found Mrs. Henderson's face, but didn't feel any better about it. The woman had tied her to the board. Mrs. Henderson and the monsters were one and the same.

"You know who I am."

Mira took note that the woman didn't move any closer.

"There's... there's nothing I could do."

Nothing she could do? Mira's gaze turned hard and locked on the woman... no—the thing—in front of her, because no real human would have done this.

"They have my kids. They used to let me see them—they were here, in the building. But now..."

"Andrea and Kevin." Mira wasn't surprised to hear the croak in her voice. She was more surprised that there was a voice to be had.

"Yes."

"He doesn't have your kids."

"I have a drink for you."

The woman stepped closer and Mira tried to pull back into the board. The woman stopped.

"There's nothing I could do," the woman said again.

"He doesn't have your kids."

"He won't put the kids in here. I'm almost sure of that."

"They aren't here."

"He won't hurt you anymore, either. Not really. Threats. He'll make threats, but that's it."

"Because he knows there's nothing worse he could do."

The woman said nothing.

"And you're helping him."

"He has—"

Mira didn't want to hear it or anything else from her. "He may have your husband, but he doesn't have your kids."

"He doesn't have my husband." The woman hung her head. "No one does."

"Then you're helping him for nothing." Feeling was starting to come back to Mira. The numbness faded.

"He took us all."

"Andrea and Kevin escaped last week."

The woman's head snapped up and she glared at Mira.

Mira kept on. "I was here. Gabriel and I got them out."

"He took them somewhere else. After Tyler—"

"We took Tyler out of here, too." Something clicked in Mira's memory. "And Andrea and Kevin said they hadn't seen you. They didn't know if you were still here."

It took the woman a little longer to respond. "They didn't see me. He let me see them to make sure I knew the threat was still there. Tyler died after—"

"Tyler's alive." Mira winced. "At least he was when I left."

The woman started breathing heavier. "My kids aren't here?"

"Gabriel and I rescued them." Mira put as much scorn into the words as she could, wanting to condemn the woman who had helped John do this.

"Wait here." The woman disappeared.

"Like I have a choice, you stupid woman."

She appeared again moments later and unstrapped one of Mira's hands.

The arm hung limply. Ghosted pain spread across her chest. Wishing for the numbness to return, Mira realized what she had done.

This was her fault. She had come here instead of letting Emmit. It was hard to remember why. She stared at her useless arm and began to weep.

Mira had been trying to channel the blame to the woman, the thing, which was in front of her, but it was Mira's own fault.

Why? Why had she come here?

With tears running down her face, she watched the creature disguised as a woman. It was pouring a thin vial into a cup but seemed to be having difficulty.

Agony, whether real or remembered, once again receded.

The woman shoved something in her pocket and came to Mira again. Mira couldn't even muster the strength to glare at the woman.

"Drink this."

Mira only stared at her.

"Look, he'll leave us alone for a short time, but he will be back. This will help."

"Help me or him?" Mira asked.

"Us. You and me. He doesn't know I have it. He makes us... make things. I put this together with what I could manage to sneak past him."

Mira shook her head.

"Wait, look." the woman put a hand down her own shirt for a moment.

Mira's nose curled up as the woman seemed to grope herself.

Seeing Mira's face, the woman started to blush. "He won't search a woman. Not really. It's... strange. Anyway, he made me search you, and I found this." She held out Mira's ring.

Fresh tears welled up and Mira wasn't able to take her eyes off the gleaming metal.

"I figured it was important and I could see the magic." She slipped it on Mira's finger.

Mira found the strength to lift her hand and her eyes locked on the shining silver.

"I have the feathers, too, although I have no idea what they are."

"Give them to me," Mira demanded.

The woman seemed taken aback by the fierceness in Mira's voice, and then she held out the cup. "Drink this first. I added Relief or the best version I could make of it."

It seemed a small price to pay for the feathers, so Mira reached for the cup. The woman had to help her hold it.

The viscous fluid made it into Mira's mouth. She gagged and choked. The woman pulled it away before Mira dropped it.

"I know it's awful, but it's all we have. There's no water here. Well, there's a little that he brings in, but that's all."

"This… this isn't water. What am I drinking?"

"I… I… I've been afraid to ask. I don't want to know. Just drink it, quickly."

Mira took it once again and downed the foul concoction.

The woman set the cup aside and began to untie Mira's other hand.

"The feathers," Mira demanded.

The woman unbound Mira and handed over the feathers.

Mira bit her lip and began to shake. After staring at them, she shoved them into her pocket.

"We have to go," the woman said.

"I'm in no rush to be shoved into a room somewhere."

The woman looked surprised.

"What?" Mira asked.

"That bastard doesn't have my kids. We're getting the hell out of here."

Mira stared at the woman but allowed her arm to be put around the woman's neck. The woman helped Mira to stand and immediately began to move.

They didn't head toward the entrance to the hall, as Mira had expected, but behind a tattered-looking curtain and through a door behind. There was a small office and another door, which led them to freedom.

"Your name is Mira, right?" the woman asked quietly, looking out the door before helping Mira outside and into the open.

"Yes."

"I'm Jean Henderson, but I guess you already knew that."

Mira didn't say anything. She was starting to feel a little stronger and was beginning to walk more on her own. When Jean got them to an alley, Mira pulled back, steady enough on her own.

"Where are we going?" Mira asked.

"Away."

It was good enough for Mira. At least at the moment.

Two blocks away, they started down a new alley. Every muscle in Mira's body seized as phantom pains scorched their way through her. When her body started to return to some sense of normalcy, she found herself lying on the ground, panting, with Jean standing nearby, keeping watch at the alley entrance.

Mira let her head fall back and watched the sky while she worked life back into her limbs.

"Can you still walk?" Jean hissed.

"I... I think so." Mira used the wall to help push herself up.

"We need to move. Fast," Jean said then grabbed Mira's arm and urged her forward.

Mira staggered before catching her footing and walking again, but there was nothing fast about her pace.

"Here," Jean said, leading Mira to an alcove made between a building and an add-on garage. "Sit, rest for a few minutes. We're out of sight here."

The pressure to move on made Mira hesitate, but in the end, she wasn't sure she could. Mira sat on the ground, pulled her knees up, and rested her head on them. Her muscles felt weak and watery.

"It gets easier," Jean said.

"Easier? Did you... did they put you through that?"

Jean looked uncomfortable. "They needed someone to complete their spells. Since I wasn't a real witch, they chose me. But I saw the others, Sybil and Tyler, go through it."

"It didn't look like Tyler was having an easy time." Mira couldn't help but let scorn eke into her voice.

"The... aftereffects. It gets longer between incidents."

"It goes away?"

"I'm not sure."

Mira closed her eyes. "I need Gabriel."

"I think we can find a way out of the Ether—"

"He's here. Where would they keep him? Back at the..." Mira couldn't bring herself to say church. There was nothing church-like about that place.

"I'm not sure I've seen him." Jean was keeping her voice very careful.

"He's a big guy. Tall, blondish hair, he has an over six foot wingspan."

"Wingspan?"

"Mostly white wings. Your daughter is a big fan of his."

Jean looked stricken at the mention of her daughter.

"She's safe," Mira said, softening her tone, "but Gabriel isn't."

"Before you arrived, they did mention someone, though I don't know if it was him."

"What did they say?"

"They were ordering everyone, everything, to stay away."

The first hope Mira had felt since being in the Ether started to kindle. "From where? Stay away from where?"

"I don't know."

"Think! What exactly did he say?"

"Um... uh..." Jean looked around nervously. "Something about... something about him not being able to get out. John said he'd be at home at the place and killed some of those creatures there."

"Gabriel doesn't kill," Mira snapped.

"I'd kill them."

"These things don't count."

"It counts to them."

Mira laid her head back against the wall and looked at nothing. "You're right."

They sat quietly for a while. Mira tried to get her mind away from what had happened to her and instead concentrate on Gabriel.

"Do you know where he was when he killed them?" Jean asked after a while.

"Everywhere he had to." Mira thought through all the nightmares they had faced together. "He may have killed some of them last night at his house, back in our world."

"Could they hold him there?"

"I doubt it. Lance's house wouldn't work either. Mine for the same reason. There's no way Gabriel wouldn't be able to get out."

"The place must be important in some way. Where did he kill most of them?"

"The street. Or maybe Lance's."

"And the most recent ones were at his house?" Jean asked.

"Maybe. Also my store, earlier that night."

"Is there a place in your store?"

"The freezer, maybe, but I doubt it. Is there any place that you've noticed them avoid?"

Jean shook her head. "They only take me where they want me to work. Where was he when he killed his first... thing?"

"The street, I think." Mira thought back and realization struck. "No, it was a parking garage."

"Those are open spaces."

Mira pushed herself to her feet, her body protesting. "But it was at the police station, where he works."

"Is it nearby?"

"A couple miles, maybe," Mira lied. She knew they were over five miles away. Whether she was trying to fool herself or Jean, she wasn't sure.

"They'll be out looking for us by now," Jean said.

"Do you have any idea how long I've been here?" Mira asked.

"I've lost any sense of time in this place. There's no day, no night, no weather, no seasons. It doesn't help that some minutes feel like hours, but some hours go by like seconds, especially when they leave you alone."

"I have no idea how long I was out of it." Mira touched the spot where her head had been slammed against the ground. "We should go."

"Can Gabriel help us leave this place?" Jean asked.

"He can help keep us alive while we're here."

Jean didn't look convinced. "We don't have any magic or weapons."

"I'm not going anywhere without him." She kept the fact that she had magic to herself. As much as she wanted to, she couldn't fully trust Jean. There was no way she could trust the woman who had helped strap her to that board. Just remembering that made her take a step away from the woman. "Let's go."

Mira didn't wait for a response. At the alley entrance, she watched the street for a while before darting across. Jean stuck close by.

Everything they did seemed painfully slow. They were always looking over their shoulder and trying to find any hints of a pursuit. Even with the paltry progress, it wasn't long before Mira needed a break. This time, she stayed on her feet, only allowing herself to lean against the wall for a short time before moving on.

They were granted a brief reprieve when Jean spotted movement in the distance. The two took cover, taking a chance on one of the buildings. Going inside was something that Mira wanted to avoid. It was not only possible that something was claiming the place as home, but it was leaving the buildings that bothered her most.

They listened closely while Mira sat in a corner, close to the door, trying to focus on nothing but getting to Gabriel. If she concentrated on him, there was less room for the jumble of emotions that welled up when she left even the tiniest of space for them.

The strange light and haze of the world seemed even more unnatural inside the buildings as well. It seemed as if there was no difference between inside and outside.

"When we find your friend," Jean whispered, "do you have a plan for how to get out?"

Mira was hesitant to tell Jean that someone would be waiting for them at Lance's house. There was a slight possibility that Jean knew where the house was—or in this world, where the house used to be. Trusting Jean was out of the question, but like it or not, she needed the woman.

"Don't you want to go back for your husband?" Mira asked. "And there's Sybil to consider as well."

"My husband is gone."

"But John said—"

"His body is still there." Jean seemed to shiver and made herself smaller. "After... well, after Tyler started to weaken, my husband was the one that took his place." Jean's face scrunched up as if she were in pain. "He didn't last long." Her voice cracked.

"I'm so sorry," Mira said softly.

"But they thought his body might be of use. They had already tried once on Sybil, and it didn't work on her, so they tried my husband."

"Tried what?" Mira wasn't sure she wanted to know, but she didn't want to leave anyone behind. She needed to understand.

"John's body was badly damaged. He needed help on the other side. Help he could trust. They tried to possess another human's body."

Mira put a hand to her mouth, feeling ill.

"No one is sure what happened to Sybil. The woman Sybil was, is gone, but the creature that tried to possess her... it seems to be gone as well. Only a shell of a person is left."

Jean was shaking and Mira wasn't going to push her any further, but after a while, Jean continued on her own. "With my husband, the creature survived... in a way. It was as though the bodies fused together instead of their minds. The... the... thing that was created screams almost nonstop and mutilates itself and anyone around it. They keep him... it, chained up."

She sank to the floor and wept, although there were no tears. It had probably been a week since the woman had much in the way of water.

"I am so sorry." Mira felt it was a weak reply, but what could she say? What could anyone say in the face of something so horrendous?

They sat in silence, each trapped in their own thoughts. Mira had no idea how long they sat there, but Jean's nightmare had caused horrible visions for Mira and she needed some time to push them aside.

When she had her mind firmly on Gabriel again, she pushed herself to her feet and took the chance to peek outside. She even studied what she could see on the neighboring rooftops.

"We should go," Mira said, keeping her voice low and her eyes on the street.

Wordlessly, Jean got to her feet and followed Mira. They ran softly to the next alley entrance and began to make their way through the maze of streets.

Mira held up a little longer after their break, but being on constant guard was wearing her down. She knew they were getting close, so she forced herself to go a few more streets. Again and again, she told herself one more block, one more, another...

Without warning, her body seized. She wasn't sure if she managed to stay quiet—she tried—but there was nothing but agony. Even thoughts of Gabriel were swept from her mind. It built and built until it felt as though every nerve ending was on fire. She wanted to black out, be knocked unconscious, anything to take her away from herself.

The feelings began to ebb. This time had felt like more than just phantom remembrances of pain. When mental processes began to coalesce again, Mira realized she was on the ground, curled into a little ball sobbing.

It took more than a few steadying breaths before she could get herself under control. Jean was nowhere to be seen, but at that moment, Mira didn't care. There was something wrong—something seriously wrong inside her. She didn't know what it was, but the ideas of what it could be frightened the hell out of her.

Shakily, she moved to a wall and leaned against it, closing her eyes. At the sounds of running, they shot open again and she jumped to her feet. The wall was the only thing that kept her standing, but it felt better than being on the ground.

Seeing Jean running forward, Mira leaned down and took her piece of string and wire out of her sock. She pushed the wire into her pocket and balled the string up in her hand so that the light glow of magic looked as though it was coming from her ring.

Jean looked behind her several times, tripping over her own feet in the process. Mira could see fear in the woman's eyes, but she couldn't see a cause.

"We have to go," Jean whispered fiercely to Mira.

"What happened?"

"I went to check the area," Jean seemed to blush and didn't look at Mira, "Just in case. And I saw that."

She pointed toward the sky before tugging on Mira's hand. Mira stumbled, but caught herself and started to move with Jean—slowly at first, and then with more confidence once she confirmed her body was working correctly.

"I don't see anything," Mira said.

"It's there, the sky, the whole area."

Mira looked and saw the same endless haze and dim light radiating everywhere.

CHAPTER 22

"THERE'S A MASS OF darkness and shadows." Jean stopped and looked at Mira uncertainly.

"What is it?"

Jean's eyes were wide and her hands were shaking. "I've never seen anything like it. But, but… you do see it. Don't you?"

"I don't see anything." Jean's uneasiness was spreading. Mira looked behind her one more time, striving to see even a speck in the sky. "Let's get moving. Tell me what it looks like on the way."

"It's a shadow, a pillar of shadow moving through the city."

Mira started moving faster, her heart beating quickly. "The thing from the city?"

"I don't think so," Jean said. "I've never seen this."

They took more twists and turns than necessary. Mira tried to keep moving, but she was beginning to slow and lose steam fast.

"It's following us," Jean hissed, tugging on Mira, trying to urge her onward.

Mira looked back, still seeing nothing. Her muscles were shaking from exhaustion now. They crossed a wide street, never moving in a straight line. At the cross street, Mira couldn't continue and fell against the wall.

"We can't stop," Jean pleaded.

"Where is it?" Mira asked.

"It's not far behind us. We have to keep going."

Mira stared at the sky, still seeing nothing. When she tried to push away from the wall, she found she couldn't.

She bit her lip, fear and frustration welling up.

"Come on." Jean moved around the corner but came back when Mira didn't follow.

"I can't," Mira said.

"We're almost to your friend, right? He can help us."

They were close.

But not close enough.

It was time to take a stand. "Whatever John has sent after us," Mira said, "I think I can slow it, or them, down."

"Dear god, it's coming around the corner." Jean dodged around the corner herself, peering around.

"Stay there," Mira said. "Keep out of sight."

"You have to see it." Jean once again sounded as though she were pleading.

Mira shook her head, saving the effort of speaking for the work ahead.

"Maybe... maybe there's nothing there," Jean said, a tincture of hope trying to peek through.

Mira considered what she said. The woman had been here for a long time. Would it be a surprise if she were starting to crack?

"You could go on ahead." Mira didn't look at Jean, afraid the woman might sense that she silently pleaded for her to do the opposite.

"And go where?"

"I—"

"There it is," Jean hissed before she disappeared.

This time, Mira did see something. Even through the haze and bad lighting, she couldn't miss it.

Emmit, scowling deeply, jogged out into the street. He slowed to a walk when he saw her.

Mira began to cry again. Emmit could fix this. He looked like he wanted to tear seven hells out of someone, probably her, but she didn't care. It took two tries before she could push herself off the wall.

"You," there was acid in his voice, but again Mira didn't care, "how could you—"

She staggered up to him and hugged him, cutting him off short.

He stood rigid, clearly startled by her reaction. After a moment, he wrapped an arm around her.

"You," he snapped.

Deliriously relieved, Mira wasn't even startled at his outburst.

"What's happened?"

Mira looked up, not sure what to say, but she saw that he was pointing at Jean, who looked frozen and caught in his gaze.

"That's Jean," Mira said quietly before resting her head against his chest. "Jean Henderson."

Emmit looked down at Mira and lifted her chin with his finger, searching her face. She didn't know what he was looking for, and she didn't care. She didn't care that he looked angrier than she had ever seen him.

Emmit released her chin. "Jean." Mira was impressed at how level he managed to keep his voice. "Come here."

"Mira?" Jean's voice wavered, unsure.

"He's a friend." Mira peeled herself away from him, but he kept a protective arm around her.

Jean approached, looking like she might run the other way at any moment.

"What happened to her?" Emmit asked.

Mira started to feel cold.

"She—"

"Nothing," Mira said, cutting Jean off. "I mean," she tried to make her voice sound normal, "I hit my head. Um, something hit my head. John had me and Jean helped me escape." She reluctantly stepped away from him.

Emmit glared at her. "What did he do?"

"When I left my shop, something jumped on me." Mira felt she was talking too fast, but couldn't seem to slow herself down. "I hit my head when I fell to the ground, but then it... it slammed my head into the ground again and it knocked me out."

This time he looked uncertain but no less unhappy.

"Jean?" Emmit said, putting a demand into his voice.

"She was unconscious. I don't know for how long," Jean said.

"Leave her alone," Mira said. It looked as if Jean would tell him everything if he pushed even a little.

Emmit looked like he was going to argue or explode. Jean stepped back.

Then he shook his head. "Why did you do this?" His voice was closer to normal this time. He began examining her wounds as he spoke.

Mira reluctantly let him, figuring that if he saw the evidence, he'd drop it. "We need to get Gabriel first."

"You know where he is?" Emmit asked.

"Ouch," Mira said when he hit a sore spot. She slapped his hand away. "I have an idea of where he is. How did you find me?"

Emmit handed her a pentagram pendant hanging from a chain. It had been her ward for many years—useless now, but sentimental all the same.

"Who spelled this for you?" Mira asked, turning it over in her hands.

"Mr. Singer obliged when I told him I needed to find you."

"You don't happen to have the ingredients for another, do you?" Mira asked.

"For Gabriel? I thought you knew where he was."

"I think I know. Come on, I'll explain on the way. We're almost there."

Mira led the way, her fear almost extinguished now that Emmit was with them. She told him what Jean had heard and what she suspected. Jean herself stayed behind them. When Mira turned around, she noted that the woman was pale and shaky, her eyes wide, and she was hugging herself.

Seeing Emmit had revitalized Mira. It was short lived, but when the police station was in sight she forced herself to it, eager to find Gabriel.

"This seems too easy," Emmit said.

"Nothing about this place is easy," Mira said.

"But there are no guards," Emmit said. "And I've run across very few creatures since I've been here."

"There are less of them," Jean said.

Mira turned to her as Emmit moved toward the building. "What do you mean?"

"There have been fewer around. John was in a rage about it not long ago. He—well, there are fewer."

"From what I understand," Emmit said, "Mira and Gabriel have taken a toll on their numbers."

"They've also been used to feed that thing in the city… when other food isn't available," Jean said.

Mira wanted to get off that train of thought. "I wonder if they'll have any guards inside? It seems unlikely that they would. Gabriel could just force them to release him."

"If he can still talk," Emmit said.

Mira blinked at him. She tried not to think of that. There was so much someone could do to stop a person from talking. Her heart skipped a beat and she gazed at the building, her breaths becoming shorter. What could they have done to him? Was it possible, even from here, that they could have done to him what they had done to her?

With a jolt of speed, Mira raced to the door. Emmit stepped between her and the building, but she only had eyes for the door. He had to bar her way physically before she even noticed him.

Mira opened her mouth to yell at him, but he put a finger to her lips, looking stern. "We don't know what's inside."

She lost steam and could only nod in agreement. The little burst of fear and panic left her tired.

Nevertheless, she was still determined. "Let's go find out."

"Maybe you and Jean should wait out here," Emmit said.

He wanted to leave her alone. Alone in this god-awful place. He was going to leave her behind.

Emmit must have seen at least some of the abject terror in her face. "Never mind," he said. "We'll go together."

Her nod was needy, but she didn't care at this point. The only thing that mattered was getting to Gabriel. If she could manage to do that with Emmit by her side, she felt all the better for it.

Still holding her arm, Emmit went inside. "Do you know where he might be?"

Mira wasn't sure if he was holding her arm to ensure she didn't run ahead or to keep her on her feet. "I'm not sure. I think there are cells on the main floor, but I'm not positive."

Emmit seemed to inspect every inch of the room.

"We get inside over there," Mira said. "I had to be buzzed through in our world."

"My guess is the door is always locked except when it's in use." Once Emmit seemed satisfied they were alone, he strode across the room, taking her with him.

Looking back, Mira saw that Jean was still following, but seemed like she could bolt at any moment. Emmit tried the door, not appearing surprised to find it locked.

"Most doors are unlocked in this world," Mira said.

"If I understand the way things work here, if the door remains locked the majority of the time, you'll find it remains locked here."

When Emmit let go of her, she stepped back, watching as he studied the door. He gripped the knob and pushed. Nothing happened.

"You should check on Jean," Emmit said, not looking back at them. "She seems unnerved by my presence."

Mira couldn't help but agree. "Are you all right?" she asked softly as she approached Jean.

Jean shook her head vehemently.

"It's okay. He's a friend of mine."

"What... What is he?" Jean asked, almost too low for her to hear.

The squeal of metal on metal made Mira turn. It was hard to say how he managed it, but Emmit had pushed the door open.

"He's a friend," Mira said. "That's all that matters."

Emmit disappeared and she heard another door under strain. Mira rushed through the first in time to see Emmit slam the second shut, with him on the other side.

Mira's heart jumped to her throat. He had shut her out. It was startling to feel so lonely with just that one door between them. It was as though he had turned off a light and left her in darkness.

Hearing shrieks on the other side of the door brought her up short when she went to follow him. A reedy scream reverberated around the building. Growling joined the cacophony. Just as suddenly as Emmit had slammed the door, the noises stopped.

Mira approached the door uncertainly. It opened before she had a chance to try opening it on her own.

"Forgive me," Emmit said. "That was rude. It seems, however, that Gabriel was not left on his own."

Peering around him, Mira saw scorched and withered bodies of multiple hues. Emmit held up the broken wire as explanation.

It wasn't as strong as Mira had hoped for, but it had done the trick. The three moved through the room, moving wide around to avoid the worst of the mess.

The desks in the room had the same blurred edges that Mira remembered from her first trip to the Ether. Looking directly at them made her uneasy.

They had almost reached a door on the other side of the room when they heard a skittering sound, as though an insect were stuck in a heating duct. Instinctively, Mira looked up but didn't see anything.

Emmit appeared to be on high alert, trying to watch all directions at once. "Stay close behind me."

Mira had to grab Jean's arm and coax her forward. She tried to drag the woman forward, but she didn't have the strength. Jean seemed to sense that and hooked her arm around Mira's dragging with her closer to Emmit.

The next door swung open easily. Emmit froze in the frame. "We're in the right place."

The noise was louder here. Peering around, Emmit didn't

give Mira any clue as to what might be causing the noise. At the moment she didn't really care. Up ahead, she could see cells. The police station was old and the cells looked like they were the originals.

Mira tried to push past Emmit but only succeeded in getting him to move forward. The cells appeared empty. When they reached the corner, though, Mira saw that there were two halls lined with cells. The one in front looked empty.

The other...

"Gabriel?" Mira called, not as loudly as she had wanted to. The other noise was a constant, and she was afraid of what might hear her.

There was something in one of the cells, but it didn't move or respond.

Between them and the cell was a sea of black running toward them. Mira looked up and saw the same thing on the ceiling.

Jean pulled Mira back, causing her to stumble and fall. They both crashed to the ground. Thousand, maybe millions of insects surged toward them.

Emmit grabbed Mira and put her on her feet. He fumbled in a backpack. "A circle," he said quickly, "can a circle keep them back?"

Mira wasn't a hundred percent sure, but she grabbed the proffered skein and unwound a large amount.

They backed quickly down the other hallway, keeping the cells in view. Mira didn't want to lose sight of what might be Gabriel.

It was messy and not as sturdy as it could have been, but Mira dropped the circle and charged it. She concentrated hard on making sure it was as strong as possible under the circumstances.

The ground beneath them began to shake. Then thousands of insects met her circle. Some died when they touched the magic. Others were able to crawl up a few feet before perishing and falling back to the ground.

Up above, tiny pops sounded like rain on a tin roof as insects fell. The dark wave broke in half and surrounded the three. The ground heaved and shook, but still, the circle remained.

Then, the insects fled. They ran through the door into the room Mira and the others had just left.

Emmit looked confused. "That was not what I expected as a sentry."

"They eat their dead," Jean said, shivering. "My guess is they caught the smell and..." she trailed off as she waved her hand in the direction they had disappeared.

Mira was clinging to Jean's arm at this point. She didn't want Emmit to know just how much support Jean was giving. With the ground still turning under their feet, she hoped it looked like she was just trying to keep her balance.

"I think it's safe to let go of the circle," Emmit said.

Mira looked at the ceiling one last time, just in case. Then she let the circle drop. A small hill of tiny corpses surrounded them, and Mira stepped gingerly over them. The ground stopped moving. Mira breathed a sigh of relief.

Emmit cautiously moved toward the shape in the cell ahead.

"Gabriel!" Mira cried out. Closer, she could see white feathers on the figure.

He twitched and raised his head.

Mira's heart felt full and she had eyes only for Gabriel. He didn't quite look the same, but it didn't matter. It was him.

Emmit was still being cautious, which made Mira frustrated at the slowness of their pace.

He was there. She found him.

A roar ripping through the city beat the air, assaulting them all.

Every inch of Mira's body seemed to pulse. It felt as if the roots were there, wrapping themselves around her, digging into her flesh, pushing their way inside, invading her. They pulled on her essence, straight down and into the bone.

Her screams rivaled that of the creature in the city until she got what she wished for. Mira fell into darkness and there was nothing.

CHAPTER 23

THE ARGUMENT HAD STARTED. Mira could hear the two voices rise and fade.

Would they ever get along?

The noise went away and Mira fell with it; her mind hummed blankly, drawing her back down.

"There's no time for this," she heard Emmit yell.

She could feel the heat of his frustration.

"You're going to make the time!" Gabriel's cool anger greeted Emmit.

"I'm going!"

Going. He was going. Mira's breathing quickened. He was going to leave her. They would leave her alone. Her eyes snapped open and she jolted up.

The world spun, and it wasn't her world. The Ether was all around. The nasty haze of the air was being pushed back, though. Gabriel had a soft glow about him, burning the air clean.

Emmit looked the same, but once again, the air appeared as if it was clearing.

Had it been that way before?

Her mind felt disjointed and spacey. She watched the air around her friend become clear.

She stared, not noticing Gabriel move until he kneeled down beside her.

"What?" she asked, knowing she had missed something.

He brushed the hair off her cheek. The moment he touched her skin, the feeling of thousands of tendrils spreading across her face made her unsure of where reality began and imagination started. She started to shake but felt frozen to the spot.

Was anything in the Ether reality? She had already missed what he said, but she looked into his eyes and latched on to her reality. Gabriel was real, feathers and all.

But he looked...

"Oh, my god." Her hands reached up to his bruised face, lightly touching skin that was purple and caked with blood from wounds on his head.

He took her hands in his. "Can you hear me?"

She nodded. "What did they do to you?"

He drew her into a hug that she never wanted to end.

"Take her to Lance's," Emmit said. "Get her home."

He turned to leave.

"No!" Mira broke away from Gabriel and rose unsteadily to her feet. "You can't go."

He had frozen at her demand but didn't turn around. "This has to be taken care of now."

"It does," Mira said. "That's why I came. The book. We need Chris's book."

Gabriel wrapped an arm around her waist, for which she was grateful.

Emmit turned, looking confused before addressing Gabriel. "The witches might be able to help, but take her to see my sister. If there's anything that can be done, she'll arrange it."

It was Mira's turn to look confused, but when he turned to leave again, she started yelling, "You have to stay!"

"Ssshhhh," Gabriel said, trying to sound soothing.

Mira glared at him. She wasn't amused when he smiled at her softly in return. "Damnit, Emmit, will you just listen?"

"Hold up," Gabriel said, keeping his voice light and even. "A few minutes isn't going to hurt."

"You don't know that," Emmit said, but there was defeat in his voice.

"I know that we could use a little rest," Gabriel said, watching Mira. "Come on. We'll sit and talk it over."

Mira looked at him suspiciously. He was being too calm, but she sensed him storming underneath.

He sat down with her, pulling her as close to him as he could. "Tell us what's going on."

Mira felt safe and protected in a way that she had never felt before. His wings behind her were soft and curled forward slightly around them.

"I'm not sure—"

"Emmit," Gabriel said, in the same tone, "shut the hell up and sit down."

Mira grinned up at Gabriel. The word hell on the angel's lips always seemed to be able to crack a smile out of her.

"I don't want—"

"Emmit," there was a touch of steel in Gabriel's voice this time, "let her say what she needs to say."

The cool energy whipping around Mira made her shiver. She was surprised that there was no matching response from Emmit. Instead, Emmit sat down opposite from them. He looked uneasy and unsure of himself, something Mira had never seen.

Gabriel cupped her cheek. "Tell us what happened."

Mira frowned and felt confused. "What happened? No, that's not what I'm talking about. That's not—" She stopped and looked around the room for Jean.

It was the first time she had actually taken in the room they were in. It was like a small box. They had pushed the table and chairs aside. Looking around, Mira realized she'd been here before. They were still in the police station, but upstairs.

"Where's Jean?" Mira asked.

"Jean is in the room next door," Gabriel said. "She felt... safer over there."

Mira shot a glare at Emmit, figuring he had scared the woman off. "She's all right, though?"

"At the moment, we're all okay." Something under Gabriel's calm demeanor felt like it was going to erupt.

Mira glanced at Emmit, wondering if he felt the same volcanic energy coming from Gabriel. He was watching Gabriel closely but didn't seem concerned.

"Now," Gabriel continued, "we have time. Talk to us, and then we can decide on what happens next."

Emmit's eyes looked pinched around the edges.

"Tell us what happened," Gabriel said again.

"That's not what I was talking about," Mira said.

She looked up at Gabriel. It was his secret to tell. He had seemed so upset when he'd found out he could read Chris's book. It was possible that he wouldn't want Emmit to know, but what needed to happen was more important.

She bit her lip and turned to Emmit. "You said there was a way to end this. Permanently."

He was already shaking his head. "I can put it to sleep, possibly for a few centuries. You won't have to worry about it waking up in your lifetime, or even your children's lifetime."

"It needs to die," Mira said with more force than she'd intended. She took a deep breath, making sure to rein in her anger as much as possible.

"We know," Gabriel said.

"But there is a way to do that," Mira said. "With the book. Chris's book."

"No one knows how to kill it," Emmit insisted. "I'm sorry, Mira. We've searched and there's no way. The ritual has been lost for centuries."

"The ritual you mentioned," Mira said. "You had a page that showed a point and three others around it. I've seen a book that had that exact same diagram on the cover."

"That's why you swapped places with me?" Emmit said.

To Mira's surprised, Emmit was angry—even more upset than he was when she first found him.

Gabriel hugged her closer.

"Why didn't you tell me?" Emmit asked.

The room seemed to flicker, and Mira blinked, looking around for the source.

"It doesn't matter what you found," Emmit seethed. "I thought you understood that. You stupid witch! It's written in a language that can't be read. Why would you do this?"

"Hey!" Mira yelled back at him. "I did it because I needed to! You were ready just to walk in and die!"

Again the room seemed to stutter and the strange light of the place seemed to dim. Shadows grew in the corner.

"Shut up!" It was one solid, demanding phrase.

Both Mira and Emmit stopped talking. Mira glared at Gabriel, remembering that he had done that to her before, the night he had been taken. He'd told her to run, making her do so.

Gabriel took a deep breath. His energy was beginning to feel erratic and wrong.

Mira glanced at Emmit. It seemed like he felt the difference.

Mira put a hand on Gabriel's chest. He took another deep breath and patted her hand before, lightly holding it in his.

"Get a grip on yourself, Harker. This book," Gabriel said, softening his voice for Mira, "is it the one that we saw together at Chris's?"

She nodded.

He stared at her for a few moments before shaking his head. "And you didn't tell Harker because you thought I'd be upset."

The only response she could think to give was to shrug.

There seemed to be a great flexing of energy across the room.

"As I said, it doesn't matter what you found. It can't be read." Emmit glared at Gabriel. "Don't try that again."

Gabriel seemed unconcerned by Emmit's threats. "It can be read. That's why she didn't say anything. I can read it."

Emmit was quiet for a while. The whole room fell quiet. The shadows that had stretched across the room began to fade.

Now that it was out in the open, she laid her head against Gabriel's chest and closed her eyes.

"She should have told me," Emmit said.

"Shhh," Gabriel said, "let her sleep."

They spoke in soft, muted tones. Mira wasn't quite asleep, but wasn't quite awake, either. Her body needed the rest, but her mind was afraid to actually fall asleep. The idea of sleeping in the Ether, even in Gabriel's arms, freaked her out. Especially now that she knew how bad the place can be.

"This might be what we need to kill this thing," Emmit said.

"It will die," Gabriel said, "one way or the other."

They were quiet for a while. Mira enjoyed hearing the sound of Gabriel's heartbeat and concentrated on the warmth of his skin,

"Do you know how angels fall?" Emmit asked.

Gabriel sighed deeply. "Give it a rest, Harker. I'm sure this can wait."

"I'm not certain it can. Anger and vengeance can weigh any man down. For an angel, it can permanently chain him."

Gabriel tensed. "You don't think this thing needs to die?" The buzz in his energy made Mira shift uncomfortably.

They were still for a few minutes.

"Of course, I agree with you," Emmit said, "but then, I don't have to worry about the fall."

"Some things are worth it."

"But some things," Emmit paused and Mira sensed movement, "some things are worth more."

Worried that the movement meant Emmit was going to try to leave again, Mira wearily opened her eyes. The rest didn't do anything to revive her.

"You should eat something," Emmit said. "You both should." He dug around in his bag and pulled out some sort of protein bars, handing them over. "And here." He passed Mira a bottle of water.

A longing sigh escaped her before she could stop it, then she blushed and took the bottle. "You've been here longer." She held the bottle out to Gabriel. "You first."

Gabriel shook his head. "After I eat. You go ahead."

Mira took a few sips of and the water felt cleansing and cool on her throat. She forced herself not to drink too much. "We should give some to Jean. You have any more food?" Mira asked.

This was met with stony silence.

"What's wrong?" Mira asked.

"Nothing," Emmit said. He seemed rather reluctant to Mira.

She pulled away from Gabriel to look up at him. "What am I missing?"

Gabriel jammed a power bar into his mouth instead of answering and pulled her to him again.

"Well, if you don't have anything else," Mira said, "she can have part of mine."

"I have more," Emmit said. Then he smiled and stood up. "I'll go give it to her."

"No." Mira put a hint of warning in her voice. "You scare her. I'll go instead."

Gabriel automatically stood when Mira did. "What do you see when you look at Emmit?"

Mira gave Gabriel a puzzled look. "He looks like he always does. He looks like Emmit."

She took the food and the bottle of water. Before walking out of the room, she peeked outside. Seeing the hall was empty, she stepped out. When she moved to the room next door, Gabriel followed close behind.

Mira stopped. "I've got it. She knows me."

"I don't want to leave you alone with her."

"What—"

"With anyone," Gabriel corrected. "I don't want you alone with anyone."

Mira shook her head. "You have a lot of nerve saying that."

He frowned. "Why—"

"Run," Mira snapped. "You told me to run. You know I had no choice, right? You made me run away and leave you behind."

"Mira, I—"

"I know." Mira put a hand on his arm. "I get it, but I'm not happy about it." She ran a hand over his face again. He looked agitated. "Are you hurt? You look like they beat you. What happened?"

"You first," he said.

Mira froze and her hand started to shake. He hadn't compelled her to say anything, but even the idea of trying to explain what happened to her made her skin turn cold.

The flash across his face made her know he regretted what he said. "Shit, I didn't mean that. You don't have to tell me anything you don't want to."

Her hand dropped and he engulfed her, wrapping himself tightly around her. She stood rigid for a while, but then let herself melt into him, pushing the whole thing out of her mind.

"I don't know what happened," Gabriel said. "They dragged me out of the house. I shot one of them, but there were others. They knocked me out. I came to once, but they didn't let me stay that way long. Then I woke up here. Alone. Mostly alone. Those bugs were outside the cell, but they kept their distance."

"I'm sorry that happened to you," Mira said.

"Next time, we stay together."

Mira nodded and pulled away. "I'm going to go see Jean."

"Together?"

She shook her head. "Being in the next room over doesn't count as being apart unless we're being kept apart."

"I'll wait outside."

"Go talk with Emmit. Make sure he doesn't run off on his own."

Gabriel refused to leave until he checked the room. Mira appreciated the gesture but closed the door firmly behind him when he left. She wasn't actually upset with Gabriel, not after everything else that had happened to them.

What she needed now, though, was to talk to Jean alone for a few minutes.

Jean was sitting in the corner with her head leaning against the wall. She didn't look up at Mira and hadn't taken notice of Gabriel as he inspected the room.

"I brought you something to eat and drink," Mira said, settling in next to her. "You don't have to sit here alone, you know."

"The more I'm out of their sight, the better for everyone."

Jean seemed unsure if she should take the proffered food, but relented when Mira pushed it at her.

"The water may need to last a while."

Jean drank a little before passing it back. Mira put it behind her. Seeing the water was too much of a temptation to drink it.

Mira gave Jean the chance to eat a little before she asked the question that was on her mind. "Do you know what happened? Downstairs, I mean."

"Your friends asked me the same thing."

Mira stifled a groan. "What did you tell them?"

"I told them I don't know. Not really, anyway. I gave them an idea of what happened."

"Crap," Mira said, not quite under her breath.

"I didn't dare give them details. They were... upset, and very, very unhappy with me."

"You didn't tell them your part, did you?"

"I couldn't."

"That's good, at least. So what do they think happened?"

"They just know that John hurt you. I told them there were side effects, but I really don't know what it all means. They're understandably concerned."

"So what drove you in here?" Mira asked, wondering what had been so bad that the woman would rather be alone in the Ether.

"I felt safer in here. The other room felt crowded."

That made sense, at least. Any time Emmit and Gabriel were in the same room arguing, it could easily feel like the space wasn't big enough for anyone else.

"We're going to leave soon, I think," Mira said.

"Back to our world?"

Mira felt bad about squashing the look of hope on the woman's face. "I think we're going to go get something first."

The sound of raised voices outside the door made Mira roll her eyes and shake her head. Jean, on the other hand, looked as though she might try to become one with the wall.

Mira got to her feet. "I'll come and get you when we're ready to leave."

When she pushed the door open, eyebrows raised at the men outside, their conversation ceased.

She closed the door to Jean's room, and not feeling comfortable in the open, went back to the room they had been sitting in. Gabriel followed closely behind.

"Are we going for the book?" Mira asked.

"We can't even be sure it has shown up in this world," Emmit said.

"It'll be there," Mira assured him.

"Then I'll go get it and bring it back here," Emmit said.

Mira shifted uncomfortably. "I don't think that's a good idea."

"It's the most sensible," Emmit said.

"I'd feel better if we stuck together," Mira said. "How do you feel about it, Gabriel?"

Gabriel tentatively put an arm around her. "To be honest, I'm torn. I want to take you home and then come back to finish this. But then, I can't leave you back home. Not again. Not now."

"Then we go together," Mira said. "Emmit, you said they'd notice you right away. We need to do something about that first."

He smiled at her. "You already have." He indicated the chain around his neck.

"What is it?" Gabriel asked.

"It's something I made for Levi," Mira said. "It hides someone's inner self from witches. You're saying it works on those things as well?"

Emmit nodded reverently. "They don't see me for what I am."

"Then let's work out what we have and make a plan."

Mira was pleasantly surprised that they had more than she'd ever had in previous ventures into the Ether. She still had most of her spells, and Emmit had his as well.

"We are moving closer to the inner-city area," Gabriel said to her, once they had a loose semblance of a plan. "Are you going to be okay?"

Mira's automatic response of yes died on her lips, knowing he'd be even more worried if she lied. "I don't know. What I do know is I feel better with you two close by, and I want to get this over with. How about you?"

He looked puzzled for a moment, and she put a hand to his face.

"It's not as bad as it looks," Gabriel tried to assure her.

For a moment, Mira wished she had Gabriel's power of lie detecting. She could only take him at his word and move on from there.

"Let's get Jean, and we'll go."

CHAPTER 24

I N THE LOBBY OF the building, Mira tensed. "The lack of windows in this place really sucks."

Gabriel took the lead. He carefully opened the door and looked around before stepping outside.

The moment the door swung shut behind him, Mira's heart started beating faster, and she moved to follow him. Emmit caught her arm, holding her back. She cast an anxious look at Emmit, but his attention was fixed to the door. He looked as though he was seeing through them.

Moments later, he relaxed, and Gabriel swung the door open again, gesturing for them to follow. He took Mira's hand and they led the way. Emmit was adamant about walking behind, watching their backs.

Jean looked small, uncomfortable, and lonely in the middle. After they had walked a few blocks, Mira mentally cursed herself as she began to slow and falter. She didn't want the others to notice, so she reluctantly left Gabriel's side and fell back to walk with Jean.

"Are you all right?" Mira asked softly.

"I won't be until I get home and can see my children," Jean said.

"If anyone can survive this place, it's us."

"I'm afraid I feel rather useless."

Mira hadn't even thought of that. She dug into her pocket and handed Jean the piece of string tied in a circle. "Take this.

It's Gust. Magic is strong in this world—if the air hasn't eaten it away, at least—so make sure we are close by, but behind you when you use it."

"You have the spell trapped in the string?" Jean held the circle, inspecting it.

"Something like that. To finish the spell, you just untie the string in the direction you want the spell to go."

"Thank you," Jean said, closing her hand around the string. "This is really nice of you." Jean seemed to stand a bit straighter, armed as she was now. "We should rest," she added, looking Mira over.

Mira shook her head. "I'd really rather not."

Jean hooked her arm around Mira's, letting Mira lean against her, as she needed.

"Thank you," Mira whispered.

Two blocks later, Mira's body seized up. She crumpled to the ground, and Jean, trying to keep her up, fell with her. Attempting not to cry out as the phantom pains assaulted her senses, Mira lost track of everything else around her. She didn't see or hear anything. Her world was the agony that traveled through her.

As normal sensations returned, she found her muscles felt weak. She also realized she wasn't on the ground as she had expected. Numbly, she opened her eyes and saw that Gabriel, glowing softly, had her in his arms.

They were sitting alone in the doorway of some old store. It was inset into the building, so they couldn't be seen immediately from the street.

"Where are the others?" Mira asked.

Gabriel started and looked down at her. "Thank god." He pulled her as tightly as he could to him. "Mira, you have to tell what's happening."

"It's passing. I just need a few minutes."

"I'm taking you out of here. Rest while you can, then we're leaving."

"We can't do that."

"Then tell me what the hell is going on!"

It wasn't an order or demand that she'd be forced to obey. If it had been, Mira probably wouldn't have forgiven him. She didn't want to talk about it, but if she got it over with—

"Don't." Emmit stepped into sight.

"You don't get a say in this, Harker!" Gabriel began trembling, and once again, the energy around him became erratic.

"While we're here, I do." Emmit kept his voice even and level. "Let's do what has to be done."

Mira winced as the atmosphere became charged.

"Emmit, can you give us another few minutes?" Mira asked.

"Don't—"

"Now," Mira interrupted.

A flash or irritation marred Emmit's face briefly, and then he turned and left without a word.

Mira knew she needed to get Gabriel back on track. She hugged him tightly and he clung to her. It took a few minutes before he stopped shaking. That sharp energy he radiated remained palpable.

Letting go with one hand, she drew her hands lightly down his feathers, concentrating on their softness. His wings twitched. She did it again and watched them shiver.

"Stop that," Gabriel said.

Mira chuckled.

"That tickles and it's not funny."

"I'm pretty sure you mentioned that the first time we were here too."

"It wasn't funny then either."

"That's because you can't see yourself twitch." She pulled back enough to make sure he could see her grin.

"Right after that, I almost killed you," Gabriel said.

"And you've spent the last few weeks saving me over and over again."

"But this time you're not going to let me help you."

"You are helping me. I wouldn't be able to go on if you weren't here."

"Is it crazy to say that this was easier the first time we were here?"

"It might have been easier." Mira wiggled around on his lap a little. "I like this spot better, though."

His smile looked forced, but at least he seemed like he was trying to make the effort. "It would even be better if you let me take you home."

"We were in a pretty good spot on the couch back home. If we take care of things here, we won't have to worry about interruptions."

"I really like the sound of that."

"We should go away with Ian and Della," Mira suggested.

"When we go back, are you going to be okay? I don't know what's happening here."

Mira sighed. "I don't know what's going on, either, but I do know I'll feel better if we can stop that thing."

"Is there anything I can do for you, at least?"

"Yes, make sure you and Emmit stay close by—at least one of you. I don't want to be alone here."

"That, I can do," Gabriel said. "I promise—"

"No," Mira said, putting a finger to his lips, "we said no promises here, remember?"

He took her hand. "I lied. I promise to do whatever I can to make sure you aren't alone while we're here."

A silvery cord connecting the two shimmered for a moment before disappearing.

Gabriel kissed her on the forehead. It wasn't good enough for Mira. She pressed her lips to his and kissed him. He squeezed her to him once again, and for a second, Mira tried to forget that they were in the Ether.

The erratic power around Gabriel had returned to its normal cool and serene flow. Eventually, they had to pull apart and come back to reality.

Mira disentangled herself from Gabriel's lap and they both got to their feet. As much as she could, Mira tried to hide her unsteadiness.

When Gabriel frowned, she knew she had failed. She was worried he would become agitated again, but he hooked his arm with hers and didn't say anything when she leaned against him.

Emmit and Jean weren't in sight.

"Where'd they go?" Mira asked.

Gabriel looked around, and then to Mira's surprise, looked up as well. "Harker is a block or so that way."

"How do you know?"

Gabriel shrugged. "He stands out here. Jean's probably with him. They can catch up."

Arm in arm, Gabriel and Mira started slowly on their way again. Every now and again, Gabriel would search the street and sky. Mira assumed it was for signs of Emmit.

A few blocks later, Emmit did catch up. Jean was with him, although she kept her distance.

Emmit said nothing, but Mira felt his eyes on them. Each time she looked, he was inspecting either her or Gabriel. If Gabriel noticed, however, he ignored it.

"We should take a break," Emmit said after a while.

It was a suggestion that Mira could get behind. "How far away do you think we are?"

"We might get there in an hour or so," Gabriel said, walking with Mira to the sidewalk.

Mira immediately sat down and leaned against the wall.

Emmit handed over the water bottle, but Mira passed on it, preferring to close her eyes for a few minutes.

Jean took the offered water before sitting next to Mira. When Jean leaned against her, Mira opened her eyes and found the woman had fallen asleep. Mira almost envied her ability to sleep in this place. Gabriel and Emmit were standing in the street, talking and watching the area.

Mira nudged Jean awake. "We should go." Then she struggled to her feet and joined Gabriel and Emmit.

"It's been too quiet," Emmit said. "Gabriel, do you want to go ahead a bit and make sure the way is clear?"

"Jesus, Harker, we just talked about this," Gabriel said.

"You are the only one with a weapon," Emmit said. "I'll stand guard at the rear."

Gabriel held out his arm and his sword appeared. "Here." He passed the sword to Emmit.

Emmit looked thrown off guard and took the weapon. He winced and held the sword aloft. Smoke rose around his hand and Mira thought she could hear the faintest sizzling noise.

"I don't think this is going to work," Emmit said, though he still held the sword, inspecting the hilt.

"Emmit, drop it!" Mira said. "Gabriel—"

The sword disappeared.

Mira took Emmit's hand and saw blisters. "Give me the first aid kit."

"There's no need," Emmit said, seemingly unconcerned.

"There's some bandages..." Mira let her voice drop away as she heard another sound.

A wailing noise came from the city. Then it was joined by another. Close by, a squeal pierced the air.

"That's not good," Mira said.

"It's the smell." Gabriel tore the arm of his shirt off. "Wrap your hand in this. We need to move. Now." Two paces and the sword and shield were already in Gabriel's hands. "Mira and Jean, stick close behind me."

Jean looked pale and rushed to do as she was told. Mira stayed back a little farther, making sure Emmit didn't get left behind.

"Perhaps we should make a stand here," Emmit suggested.

"Not unless we have to," Mira said. "I think we'll be safer at the store."

"What makes you say that?" Emmit asked, easily keeping pace.

Gabriel was trotting now, with Jean right behind him.

"It was something Chris said." Mira fought to keep herself moving at the same speed as the others, but she was already feeling the effects. "Something about the books being hidden."

Gabriel slowed and turned a corner. Mira's heart felt squeezed when he was out of sight, but she forced herself to move quicker. Once she rounded the corner, her heart fluttered at the sight of Gabriel. She didn't want to lose sight of him.

"We're maybe a mile away," Gabriel said.

The thought of going a mile seemed insurmountable to Mira. As they raced up a hill, Mira became sluggish.

The world seemed to slow. There was only Gabriel in front of her and a long tunnel between him and her. With each step she took, he seemed to get farther away. Then he looked back, saw her, and stopped. Mira kept going, and it seemed to take forever to get to him.

"They are close," Emmit said.

"We just need to push a little farther," Gabriel said.

"What does the store look like?" Emmit asked.

Gabriel began to move again as he explained the exterior of the store.

Without thinking, Mira leaned against Emmit. She tried to make herself move but she wasn't getting far.

"I'll take Mira. Meet us there," Emmit said.

Mira didn't immediately notice that she wasn't on her feet, but she felt pressure and air rushing around her. She numbly wondered if the movement was her own. It only lasted a short time, though, and she found herself on her feet again, standing in front of the old bookstore.

"Is this the place?" Emmit asked.

"His store is kind of inside this one." Mira looked around, trying to find Gabriel. "What happened?"

"Show me," Emmit said.

"Gabriel—"

"Is down the street. He'll be here in a few moments." Emmit took Mira's arm and escorted her inside.

There were no books in the outer room. The empty shelves stood tall, although they had the same blurry outlines as the other furniture in this world.

"You should go back and grab Jean and Gabriel," Mira said.

"I don't see that happening."

"But—"

"Can you imagine Gabriel allowing me to pick him up?"

Mira couldn't help but laugh at the picture the statement created. "I guess not."

"Besides, I promised Gabriel I would keep you in sight when you're not in his, and right now, I want to do what I can to keep Gabriel happy."

Mira led him into the next room, although she was leaning heavily on him.

"Why's that? It's not like you two even get along." She followed the wall and rounded the corner.

"Gabriel is slipping. We need to prevent that."

"You mean he's falling," Mira said.

"In a manner of speaking, yes." He stopped, halting Mira at the same time. "Which is why you cannot tell him what happened here."

"He was pretty upset."

"Not a fraction of what he will be if he finds out."

Mira frowned at Emmit and glared at him. "How do you know?"

"Because if he knows the details, he will fall and walk through the fires of hell, if necessary, to destroy that creature."

"What makes you think that?"

Emmit sighed. "Because I am rather fond of you and I know my plans. Gabriel isn't just fond of you—he loves you. He'll seek vengeance if he knows."

"Jean told you," Mira said, flatly.

"I didn't give the woman much of a choice."

"Harker!" Gabriel yelled from the other room.

"We're here," Emmit responded calmly.

"What in the hell are you trying to pull?" Gabriel asked as he stomped through the store. He rounded the corner, saw them, and faltered.

"You know where the entrance is?" Emmit asked.

Gabriel nodded, looking unsure of himself.

"Were you seen coming in?" Emmit asked.

"No," Jean answered. "We could hear them, but they hadn't spotted us yet."

"Then let's find what we're looking for," Emmit said. "If it's not safe here, we might have to move on."

"This way," Mira said. "The door's right down here." It wasn't until she started to move that she realized how much strength she had actually lost. Emmit was practically holding her up.

When they reached the door, Emmit tried to open it, but it wouldn't budge.

"We always had to use a key," Mira said.

"There aren't any keys in this world," Gabriel reminded her.

Emmit pushed on the door. Mira could feel his muscles straining, but the door remained ridged. He stepped back, pulling Mira with him. "Maybe the key is special?"

"Let me try," Gabriel said. He leaned against the door, turned the handle, and almost fell when the door swung open.

"Or maybe the door is special," Emmit said.

Gabriel stepped into the room. Mira was surprised to find the beaded curtain was in this world. It seemed like such a temporary thing which didn't belong here. Smoke encased them as they moved into the room, but then, to Mira's surprise, the air cleared leaving the room looking much like it did in the real world, complete with books, though not as many.

"Don't touch the books," Gabriel said.

"Do you mind?" Emmit asked.

Mira didn't know what he meant, but she was happy when Gabriel took her arm. He smiled at her, still looking unsure, and she wrapped her arms around him. She wanted to feel better holding on to him, but the truth was she felt awful. Even the books weren't keeping their usual fascination over her.

"The room looks different here," Gabriel said.

Mira perked up and looked around. "The air is fresh."

"Look at the walls," Gabriel said.

The smoke drifted over them. This wasn't the haze of the world outside the room, but actual smoke. Mira reluctantly pulled away and touched the rough walls. "That's an interesting design." Rough grooves went through the walls, as though making a pattern, but not quite a uniform one. "It's not stone."

Gabriel, hovering behind her, ran his hand over the wall. "It feels warm. I haven't felt anything here actually feel warm."

"These are fascinating," Emmit said.

Mira saw that he stood next to a shelf of books. He had his hands clasped behind his back as if holding them away from the temptation.

"The one we're looking for is down there." Gabriel indicated the direction. "You'll know it when you see it."

Emmit tore his eyes away from the books but didn't rush to the one he needed. Instead, he examined each book as he went past.

"Where's Jean?" Mira asked.

"Over here," Jean said softly. She had found herself another corner and was keeping her back to the wall without actually touching the wall or the smoke. "Resting."

She looked almost as beat as Mira felt.

"I think we're safe in this room," Mira said. She wasn't as confident about that as she had been outside. The room felt okay, but something about it was making her senses itch.

"Safe or not," Gabriel said, "I think we should get out of here and home as soon as we can."

Noticing that Gabriel still hadn't made a move toward the book, Mira took his hand and led him that way. She glanced at the books as she passed, noting the soft clean glow that came off them, but like Gabriel, she just wanted this nightmare over with.

Looking at the cover of the book made Mira uncomfortable. The symbols seemed to shift under her gaze.

She reached to open the book, but Gabriel's hand caught hers.

"I don't think you should," Gabriel said.

"If you say so," Mira said. "It's your book."

"It's Chris's book."

Mira shook her head. "I don't think it is. Not really."

"Have you noticed that the shelves and pedestals are solid in this room?" Emmit asked.

"Yeah," Gabriel said, "I don't know if that means it's been here a long time or what."

Mira hadn't realized things appeared more solid, so she looked around the room more carefully. "There are rugs in the room as well."

"Interesting," Emmit said. "I wonder if we are truly in the Ether here."

"Where else would we be?" Mira asked. "It's definitely not our world."

Emmit didn't elaborate.

Mira left Gabriel with the book, which he had opened, and sat on a stack of rugs. It was almost comfortable. Nothing in the Ether had ever been comfortable.

"I think we should get to know Chris better," Mira said, more to herself than anyone else.

Gabriel snorted. "Easy for you to say."

Mira saw his smile.

"I know why he'd be interested in spending time with me."

CHAPTER 25

Mira chuckled, thinking of Chris teasing Gabriel.

Gabriel grabbed the book and settled down beside her.

"This place feels," Emmit looked around as though searching for the right word. "Scratchy."

Mira laughed, startling a look from both of them. "I was thinking itchy."

"I think it feels wonderful," Jean said from her nearby corner where she was laying.

"Me too," Gabriel said. "It's like the whole room has a warm glow."

"Interesting," Emmit murmured.

Thinking Jean looked comfortable, Mira shifted and used Gabriel's lap as a pillow.

"What does the book say?" Emmit asked.

"It's going to take a while to read," Gabriel said.

Mira closed her eyes, and in the safety she felt from Gabriel, she fell asleep.

The Ether was full of nightmares, but Mira had none of them while she slept. She felt that it could be because there were too many horrors walking around while she was awake.

Maybe the Ether was where nightmares lived.

It had been a deep, heavy sleep, and she felt revived—even lighter—when she woke up. And since she woke up next to Gabriel, she felt happy as well.

He had sprawled out beside her, and it looked as if he had fallen asleep while reading. One of his wings lay over her.

It creeped her out a little that she had fallen asleep in the Ether, but maybe, as Emmit said, the store didn't really count as the Ether.

Up until this point, she had felt like she had been a hindrance while here. When she woke up, for the first time since she'd crossed over, she felt more like herself. Restless, she slipped out from under Gabriel, stood, and looked around.

At least one of the books drew her attention, but she knew better than to touch it—especially the one that seemed to sing to her. She passed down aisles, going to the opposite end of the room where they had found Chris standing in their own world.

Mira wasn't exactly sure if Chris was a witch, but he seemed to know a lot about them, and he obviously had dealings with Mr. Singer.

Behind where Chris usually stood, the wall design had changed. There was a large, round, smooth stone, much larger than Gabriel's shield, which appeared to be embedded in the wall. She didn't remember seeing that in the real world.

This area had more rugs, but also other items. There was a chest in the corner, ornate metallic pitchers, shiny items that could have been candleholders, and glass jars in beautiful colors.

Even more than the books, these felt like Chris's things. The idea of touching them felt invasive, so she concentrated on the shelves nearby. Mira wasn't looking for any of the items she saw in the open, although the chest in the corner looked promising since she was looking for spell ingredients. If he were a witch, even a witch on the fringe, he would have magic supplies close by.

"Are you looking for something in particular?"

Mira spun and tripped. If it wasn't for Emmit catching her by the arm, she would have fallen across some of the glass jars.

When Mira's heartbeat returned to normal, she shook Emmit off.

"I apologize for startling you."

"I didn't realize anyone was awake," Mira said.

They kept their voices low as to not bother Gabriel or Jean.

"I thought it prudent for someone to keep guard."

"I'm awake now if you want to rest."

"Are you feeling better?"

"Yeah," Mira said. "I think I just needed some sleep."

Emmit cupped his hand under her chin.

Mira narrowed her eyes at him when she realized she couldn't move her head. Since he seemed to be looking into her instead of at her, he didn't seem to notice.

After a few moments, he let go and looked at the shelving as though nothing had happened. "Can I help you find anything?"

"I doubt it." Mira put as much testiness into the words as she could manage. "I'm looking to see if Chris might have some spell ingredients around."

"Chris isn't a witch," Emmit said.

"Have you met him?"

"No, but I've seen enough here to know he isn't a witch."

"But he deals with witches. Maybe he keeps more than just books for them."

"What kind of spell are you wanting to create?"

"I don't know," Mira admitted. "Something that could help us out."

"We both still have spells. Those should assist us on our way to Lance's."

"To Lance's? I thought we were taking care of this thing?"

"No, it will have to be done here in the presence of the creature in the city."

"So it's easy to do?"

"Surprisingly, yes," Emmit said.

"Great, so we can do it and go."

"No."

"We have to come back again?" The idea made Mira feel tired all over again.

"I will come back again."

"What? Why? If it's easy, why can't we just do it now?"

"The ritual requires four people."

Mira looked at him as if he was crazy. "We have that."

"People that I trust."

Mira felt affronted. "Gabriel and I are your friends."

"This ritual deals with a lot of power. Perhaps more than we can handle."

"Perhaps? You mean you don't know?"

"It is quite possible that it will kill everyone involved."

"Oh," Mira said, feeling less excited by the idea, "but you don't know."

"I know the risks."

"What is the ritual, exactly?"

"Gabriel only skimmed the book to get an idea of what we might face. The thing in the city is a parasite of sorts. A magical parasite. The book calls for several ways of killing it. The first is to take away its food source."

Knowing what the creature ate made Mira shiver.

"To do that, every beast that roams this world would have to be moved into ours."

"Those things wandering around in the real world? I'm pretty sure banishment would be the least of my problems if that happened."

"Another way of killing it is to cause it to expend all of its energy. It won't survive if it uses all the magic."

"What does it use the energy for?" Mira asked.

"Growing and getting food. It also seems to be trying to access our world. Although the magic is weak there, it is a fresh source."

"We definitely don't want it to grow anymore. How else can you get the magic out?"

"Absorb it."

Goosebumps raised on Mira's arms. "Absorb the thing itself?"

"Only the power. That's the third ritual. It takes three people and a conduit."

"That's what you're planning on doing, then?" Mira asked.

"Precisely. I will connect to the creature and the other three will be able to pull the energy through me."

Mira unconsciously took a step back. "Connect how?"

"When I remove the necklace you gave me, it should want to come for me."

"That only hides you from witches."

"With the amount of witch energy that the thing has collected through the years, it is almost as much a witch as you are."

"That's not funny."

"It wasn't meant to be," Emmit said solemnly.

"We know John has been feeding witches to that thing. Are you saying someone else has been too?"

Emmit shifted. "It fed on them all on its own, though probably not well through the years. I think my ancestor was able to put it into hibernation. Fresh witch blood woke it."

"Because John sacrificed them? No, wait. He didn't do that, though. They were other supernaturals at first."

"The others were a change of diet that didn't work. No, it wasn't John, but the creature inside him that caused this. When they tricked Sybil into this world, they woke the parasite. It wanted more witches and this world's hell grew rapidly after that."

"So they came to our world and brought back witches to feed it." Mira pressed a hand to her stomach. "That's sick. Why couldn't they just starve it again?"

"John brought the fresh witches to take the place of the people here."

"But it only eats..." Mira stopped. "That's not possible. All of those things... they're monsters, not witches."

"Most have forgotten what they once were. A few of the stronger ones, like the one living inside John, still felt the pull of the hibernating creature. They remember that many, many years ago, they were witches."

Mira shook her head. "You're saying that witches lured Sybil here."

"Through John, of course."

"Why him? Why John?" Mira asked.

"I think he disliked supernaturals, so he had no problem killing them. When that didn't work for the parasite, sending witches here was just the next step. Of course, by that time it wasn't really John."

Mira rubbed her temples. "Why did they take me? In the beginning. They said I sided with you."

Emmit sighed. "I did my best to make the path between worlds stronger. When you helped me, they felt that they had been betrayed by one of their own."

Mira wasn't ready to believe Emmit. The monsters here were cruel and vile. If they were witches, the amount of bad karma they must build...

Was enough to keep them trapped in the Ether.

She shook her head to dislodge the thought. "You can't know all this."

"I assure you that it is the truth."

"They don't look like people."

"The parasite has twisted them, keeping them alive, but continuously feeding off them. They've probably been encouraged to breed—"

"Stop!"

"Mira?" Gabriel was at her side in an instant. "What's going on?"

"Nothing," Mira snapped, glaring at Emmit. She stalked back to the rugs and fished through Emmit's bag for the water.

"You have such a way with people," Gabriel said, clapping Emmit on the back.

Mira rolled her eyes but didn't look up.

Emmit sighed. "It's a knack. Did you find anything in the book beyond those three rituals?"

"Those three are the only ones that have anything to do with the thing in the city."

"What else does the book say?" Emmit asked.

"Nothing relevant."

"I guess that leaves getting details for the ritual we discussed. Let's make sure this can be done."

Mira had inadvertently woken Jean up. They all listened to Gabriel read the text.

To Mira, it sounded like the text droned on forever. From the glazed look on Jean's face, it looked like she might be feeling the same. Emmit, however, was soaking up every word.

The part where the conduit connected to the parasite sent shivers down Mira's spine. If the person was connected and the other three didn't do their part, the creature fed off the conduit. Mira pulled her knees up to her chest when the book started to go into detail about what feeding the creature does.

The book told them that the parasite grows, changes, becomes more powerful, and although it takes time, it would eventually leave a husk of a person behind.

Mira tuned out as much as she could. Even Emmit appeared uncomfortable. Jean hid her face and Mira could hear her unsteady, raspy breath.

For the ritual, when the three completed their part, they would pull the power through the conduit. It was a blood ceremony, of course. The three connected themselves to the conduit by blood once the creature made contact.

"We should look again at making the creature use its own energy," Gabriel said when he was done. He flipped through the pages of the book.

"That won't be possible with a parasite of this size. No," Emmit said. "We have what we need."

"We don't have anything," Gabriel said. "What are we supposed to do next?"

"Go back to Lance's," Emmit said. "That's our next step."

"The ritual to remove all other creatures from this world sounded complex," Gabriel said. "But maybe we should go through it again to see if it's possible."

"We don't have anything we need for that," Emmit said. "Even for the small part you read."

"There has to be some way to kill this thing," Gabriel said, growing frustrated.

"Why don't we perform the ritual?" Jean asked.

"Even Harker doesn't deserve to be served up like that," Gabriel said.

"And to be willing to do that, I have to trust that everyone else will do their part," Emmit said, looking at Jean.

"If we kill the creature now the other witches will be safe," Jean said. "My kids will be safe."

Emmit frowned.

"I know you don't trust me, but believe me when I say I'll do anything to keep my kids safe," Jean said.

"Gabriel," Emmit said, not taking his eyes off Jean, "is she lying?"

"I will do my part," Jean assured him.

"It doesn't matter," Gabriel said. "This thing will feed off you. None of us knows what we're doing. We need to try something different."

"Do you have any other ideas?" Emmit asked.

"Hack it to pieces," Gabriel suggested.

Emmit raised an eyebrow at Gabriel.

"Okay, maybe not that," Gabriel said.

"If we kill the creature, this ends," Emmit said. "Once the ritual is done, everyone is safe."

"You don't know that," Gabriel said, but he sounded like he was caving. "Do you really trust me for something like that?"

Emmit looked at Gabriel as though the angel was slow on the uptake. "You are trust personified."

"You can't count on me for something like this," Mira said. "There's no way I could let that thing feed off you."

"I trust you more than Gabriel," Emmit said.

"Do you really think I could watch something like that?" Mira asked, internally cursing Emmit for not seeing the obvious. "You think I could be a part of that ritual?"

"I think you, more than anyone, will do whatever you can to make it stop," Emmit said.

Mira shifted uncomfortably and grasped at straws. "There are hundreds, if not thousands of other creatures here, ready to kill us. Do you think they're just going to sit idly by while we do this?"

"Actually, I have a plan for that," Emmit said.

Knowing that all the dark and twisted creatures that roam the Ether were witches made Mira's stomach churn at the thought of them being killed. Sending Emmit alone into the city didn't sit any better with her, but he was determined to do both.

Emmit disappeared, heading toward the church. He planned on luring the creatures out, and then devastating their population, leaving the remains to provide a feast for the rest.

Mira tried not to think about it.

She went with Gabriel and Jean to a park, deeper within the city. Parks in the Ether just meant a space not covered in concrete. A strange mold grew in patches, but there was no other vegetation.

Using his sword, Gabriel carved a large circle onto the ground. Mira and Jean took the yarn Emmit brought and walked in opposite directions around the circle, creating a shell meant to keep creatures out.

Gabriel dug out three other circles—much smaller than the first—a triangle connecting the three, and then drew a line to the center.

Mira felt exposed, especially this close to the tendrils that had wrapped themselves around the buildings of the city.

"Are you okay with this?" Mira asked.

"Not even a little," Gabriel said.

"Then why are we doing it?"

"Because as much as it pains me to admit it, Emmit is right."

"Before you woke up, he said the power would be too much. That it could potentially kill us."

Gabriel looked toward the mammoth roots rising through the towers in the city. "I don't think he'd go through with it if he thought it would kill us."

"He's already given me up for dead once."

Gabriel looked hesitant. "If we don't do this, I'm not sure there's anyone else he could bring back here to perform the ritual. His sister maybe, but there's no one else around strong enough to help." Mira bit her lip and Gabriel took her in his arms. "You'll survive this. You'll be fine."

She shook her head and pulled away. "I'm not worried about that." She was having trouble putting into words how she felt about Emmit having to endure that creature. "He just shouldn't have to do this."

"Nonsense," Emmit said, appearing in the field close by. "This is what I'm here for. This is what Harkers do."

Mira put her hand on her hip and glared at him. "You'd let your sister do this?"

Emmit's look faltered slightly. "If I go back and leave this behind, that's exactly what she'll do. Nothing anyone could say would stop her. I'd really rather avoid having to make that sacrifice."

It was Mira's turn to feel unsure. How would she feel if it was between her and Robin?

"Let's do this, then," Mira said feeling defeated.

Emmit walked around the circle and inspected their work. He said nothing but examined every inch before moving to his spot in the center.

"Mira and Jean, when you're ready," Emmit said, facing the city.

Mira looked at Jean and nodded. They both leaned down and charged the outer circle.

"That—" The ground started shaking, cutting Emmit off short. In the city, tendrils seemed to flex and the big tower crumpled under the creature.

"My sister was in there," Emmit said.

"Our world is reflected here," Mira reminded him, "not the other way around."

Frowning, he stared at the city, and then studied the symbols Gabriel had carved into the ground. Despite the shaking, they were still aligned correctly. Then he looked critically at Mira.

"Drop the circle," Emmit snapped.

"What?" Mira said. "No!"

She didn't see him move, but he was directly in front of her, in her face. "Drop it!"

Mira looked for Gabriel, whose confusion mirrored her own. Then she shrugged and dropped her circle.

She folded her arms and glared at Emmit.

The ground stopped shaking and Emmit turned toward the city. "Jean," he called, "hold your circle."

He stalked back to his spot.

The ground erupted below Mira. A root the size of her wrist jumped up, sprouting tiny shoots along the way. The roots spread out encircling her entire body.

She was sure her heart stopped. Her entire body froze, realizing before her mind did that she was well and truly screwed.

Before Mira could scream, the roots began to wither. She felt them fall away and she was yanked forward.

Gabriel had cut the root.

The scream that erupted from the beast in the city reverberated through Mira, who answered the wail with one of her own. Another root sprung up, grabbing her. This one didn't matter. Every cell in her body already radiated the agony caused by the creature's feeding.

There were yells around her.

It could have been moments or an eternity—they were both one and the same. The pain dropped away and numbness took her. Looking down, she saw the root was still attached to her. She was bleeding in several areas and was beginning to feel lightheaded.

Looking around, she saw Gabriel standing back in his spot for the ritual, gripping his sword for all he was worth. His gleaming white feathers looked gray in her hazy brain.

Jean was there on her spot with something behind her. Looking the other way, Mira saw Emmit. At least she thought it was Emmit. The shape was shrouded in shadow, and the inky blackness seemed to send out red waves of static.

It should have scared her, but she knew it was Emmit. She could feel him.

The lightheaded feeling sputtered and she was filled with excruciating pain once again. It was like a pulse that reached into her marrow and lit a fire along the way.

Mira felt that she was on the ground. The root was there. She wanted to hack it away. When she grabbed it, new shoots danced across her hand.

The pain was gone, but Mira wasn't sure how long that would last. She reached into her pocket and grabbed the hard piece of wire. She knew something had gone wrong—there was a push and pull of energy going on inside and around her. The shifting made her ill.

Of course, it had gone wrong. The moment the creature came for her it had gone wrong.

Jean was no longer doing her part. That part of the triangle felt absent. The others weren't going to be able to drain the creature, although they were still pulling. Mira could feel the struggle of Emmit and Gabriel working—unwilling to give up.

Lying on the ground, Mira watched the sky for a moment. It was time for this to end—before her friends hurt themselves. Before there was nothing left of herself.

When the flow eked back the other direction the flourish of pain was less pronounced. There was a battle of energy raging around her.

Ignoring it, she jammed the little wire which held Fire into the thick tendril. She slammed her hand down on it, ensuring to pierce the skin fueling the spell with her own blood. Then she let Fire roll away from her, sending it into the creature, much the same way it had sunk itself into her. She gripped the root for all she was worth.

The pain rose again. The scream that came from the city made her twist and writhe on the ground, but even when she felt the fire inside her, she didn't let go, shoving Fire deeper into the creature.

If you want magic, choke on it.

Stars danced across her vision, but she bore down. Her body wanted to quit but pure determination kept her gripping the thing.

Her bindings began to slacken. When the creature tried to drag itself back into the ground, she wouldn't let it go.

She could smell smoke. Looking down, she saw that she held the fire. It felt no different from what the creature had filled her with, so she ignored it.

At least until she was pulled away.

Blinking up into Gabriel's face, she smiled fuzzily at him before the world went black.

Someone squeezed her hand, and she yelped and sat up, smacking heads with Gabriel along the way.

"Ouch!" Mira snapped, glaring at Emmit standing in front of her. Once again, she could only tell that it was Emmit because she sensed it—she only saw the erratic shadow of a person, which dimmed the entire world around him.

"It's the smell," Gabriel said, pulling her to her feet.

She was irritated beyond belief and glared at Gabriel as well. Her head was splitting, and she hurt from head to toe.

"Can you give me a minute?" Mira asked.

"I'm afraid not," Emmit said.

The haze was especially thick around them. The city was on fire. In some cases, the ground erupted flames. Looking down at her hand, she realized that she had also been on fire.

"Is it dead?" Mira asked.

"I've got her," Gabriel said. "Grab Jean."

"Jean. What's wrong with Jean?" Mira asked.

"It attacked her," Gabriel said.

"Oh, my god," Mira said, trying to look around and catching a face full of feathers. "Is she hurt?"

"Unconscious," Gabriel said. "Come on, we've got to go."

"Is it dead?" Mira asked again as Gabriel helped her across the field.

"It stopped moving and every part we can see is on fire," Gabriel said.

"Then why are you dragging me across a field?"

"Don't you hear them?"

CHAPTER 26

MIRA LISTENED. SHE HEARD the pounding of her heart, the steady beat of Gabriel's, and the sound of his and her feet beating against the ground.

It wasn't until they reached the edge of the park that she heard the howls and growling. It seemed to come from everywhere at once.

"I can't keep going like this," Mira said, knowing she was well past her limit.

Gabriel dragged her across the street, pushed open a door, and ducked inside with her. Mira immediately went to sit, but he leaned her against the wall instead. He thrust up her sleeves and ran his hands over her arms. She was about to ask him what the hell he was doing, but he carefully took her hand and peeled back the cloth.

She gritted her teeth and sucked in a breath. When she saw the burns, she winced and looked away.

"Keep it wrapped," he said, folding the cloth gently around it again. "Where else are you hurt?"

Mira closed her eyes and laid her head back against the wall. He lifted up her shirt and ran his hands over her stomach.

"What are you doing?" Mira asked, trying to push him back a little.

"They smell blood," Gabriel said.

Mira grabbed his hand with her good one—she was surprised to find him shaking. "Where are Emmit and Jean?"

"I don't care," Gabriel said, pulling off his shirt. He ripped it, making a long strip and then wrapped it tightly around her arm.

"Are they okay?" Mira asked. "I thought they were behind us."

"We were," Emmit said. Mira saw that he looked like himself again. "I went around through the back with—"

Gabriel spun around and punched Emmit in the face.

Emmit staggered back. Gabriel went to punch him again, but Emmit stepped out of the way.

"What are you doing?" Mira asked. She pushed herself away from the wall and grabbed Gabriel's arm before he could lash out again.

He turned fiery eyes on her, but she didn't let go.

"I didn't agree to that!" Gabriel raged.

"None of us did," Mira said, trying to keep her voice calm. "I'm not sure what happened—"

"He put you in his place!"

Mira looked at Emmit, his face a blank slate, his stance defensive. He had taken off his necklace at some point, maybe to lure the thing away. Regardless, Mira knew he hadn't intentionally put her in the line of fire.

"Not on purpose," Mira said.

Emmit appeared to let out a deep breath, and some of the tightness around his eyes relaxed.

"He should have known," Gabriel snapped.

"It was the magic, wasn't it?" Mira asked.

Emmit gave a curt nod but wisely said nothing.

"This wasn't Emmit's fault," Mira said.

"You're siding with him?"

Mira looked into Gabriel's face, which was twisted up in anger. A tiredness fell over her mind, almost as much as it did her body.

She dropped Gabriel's arm. "I'm done."

Emmit took a step to move toward Mira and found Gabriel's sword pointed at him, blocking the way.

"I'm fairly certain that will actually kill me," Emmit said.

Mira stepped away, and with her good hand, dug around her pocket. She had two spells left. It wouldn't get her to Lance's, but maybe as far as Chris's.

She tucked one away and held the other for easy access. Ignoring the others, she went straight for the door. When she opened it, Gabriel slammed it back shut.

"What are you doing?" Gabriel asked.

"I told you. I'm done. You two can go at it and kill each other, but I'm not waiting here to watch."

Gabriel didn't say anything, but he didn't move, either.

"Get out of my way," Mira said.

Gabriel's wings twitched and some of the fire died from his eyes. "You're still bleeding."

Mira was unfazed. "Bleeding is the least of my problems."

"It won't be if you step out the door," Gabriel said. "Come on."

Mira begrudgingly allowed herself to be led away from the door to a place where she could sit down. "Is Jean hurt?" Mira asked Emmit, who still hadn't moved.

"I think she will be." He glanced at Gabriel, who was studiously ignoring him and wrapping Mira's other arm. "I'll check on her, but I'll be just in the next room if you need me."

Mira nodded.

Gabriel said nothing while he wrapped her arm. "The other cut is on your side."

Mira lifted her shirt and saw that, sure enough, she was bleeding.

Working with the remains of his shirt, Gabriel tried to tie it around her waist. He gave up, struggled with his t-shirt until he could get it off, and then wrapped it around her waist.

Mira bit her lip, trying not to grin. She tried to remind herself that she was mad at him, but that didn't seem to be working.

Gabriel was still scowling. "What?"

"Nothing."

"None of this is funny."

"You're right." Mira tried to keep a straight face.

His scowl seemed to deepen.

"It's just that, I finally got you to take both your shirts off."

He blinked at her, as though not believing what she'd just said.

Trying to lighten Gabriel's mood, she added, "I think it was worth the trouble."

He shook his head and pulled her into a hug. "I promise never to wear a shirt again if it keeps you out of trouble."

"You know what promises mean here, right?"

"Oh shit," Gabriel pulled back, looking for the telltale line of silver, but nothing appeared.

"I think that means it's going to be impossible to keep me out of trouble."

He smiled weakly and shook his head. He settled down next to her before moving her onto his lap where she shifted to get more comfortable.

He held one of her arms out, checking the wrappings.

"That better work. You're out of shirts, and you can't have mine."

"I really hated doing that," Gabriel said.

"I really hated you getting so upset," Mira said.

"What we did—"

"What that thing in the city did," Mira corrected.

"I thought we were going to lose you."

Mira rested her head against his chest.

"I'm not sure why I didn't know."

"Know what?" Mira asked.

"Everything, really. From the moment they set the house on fire, it felt as though something was missing. I should have known beforehand that you would get hurt. I could have stopped it."

"Maybe the promises wear off?" Mira suggested.

"Maybe," Gabriel said. "This time I'll work on the wording."

"It could also have something to do with that." Mira gestured to his wings. "Have you seen them?"

"It's not something I regularly look at, no." He spread them wide behind them.

The feathers at the top were still pure white, but they cascaded down to gray. At the bottom, the tips were dark.

"That didn't happen until here," Gabriel said.

"I don't think so. I think it started that night you went to my store, hoping to find John. Your energy was all erratic. It's been that way here, too."

"Well, it's over now. Maybe it'll go back to normal."

"Emmit might know." She wished she could take it back the moment she said it.

"Maybe I'll ask him later," Gabriel said, surprising her.
She smiled.

"I said maybe," he stressed. "How are you feeling?"
She thought about it and opted for, "Tired."

He seemed to be willing to accept that—he didn't push anyway. "Let's get home."

"How long have we been here?"

"Too long."

"True, but do we still have a way home?"

"Let's go find Harker and find out."

Mira was reluctant to let go of Gabriel, but she forced herself up, and they went into the back rooms where they found Emmit and Jean.

"Is she okay?" Mira asked.

"She's not awake yet," Emmit said, getting to his feet.

"Will we be able to carry her?" Mira asked.

"That won't be an issue," Emmit said.

"Is there someone still at Lance's? Waiting to get us out, I mean."

"There should be someone there."

Mira's heart sunk. "But not guaranteed?"

"We've been gone for more than two days, but they should still be checking every hour. I'm not sure we can wait there for that long, though. It's too exposed."

"His house is big," Gabriel said, "but it's not that big. We had no trouble last time," Gabriel said.

"Yes, but in this world, Lance's house—along with a large part of the neighborhood—has been destroyed."

Mira rolled her eyes. "I left a few walls."

"Did you leave them on fire?" Emmit asked.

Mira ignored him. "You opened the path here. We have two witches—at least we will when Jean wakes up. With our help, can you open the way back?"

Emmit shook his head. "I can only find the reflection. Going to the reflection of this world would be a mistake."

"There's another—never mind," Mira said. "Lance's it is."

"How's your hand?" Emmit asked.

Mira scrunched up her nose. "I'm trying not to think about it."

Emmit handed her the water bottle, which was almost empty. While she sipped, he looked her over.

Mira passed the bottle to Gabriel.

"You take it," he said.

"We have a long way to go," Mira reminded him. "I have two spells, and then I'm useless."

Gabriel shook his head.

Mira relented. "Emmit, your turn." She hadn't seen him drink anything since they'd arrived, but it was something easily missed. He was still inspecting her. She shook the bottle at him.

Once again, he moved with unsettling speed. He gripped her under her chin and stared into her. Through her. This time she didn't glare. He was frowning and looking for something—though what it was she didn't know.

"Harker." There was a warning tone in Gabriel's voice, but only a trace of anger.

Emmit's frown turned to Gabriel. "You will keep a close eye on her?"

"What do you think?" Gabriel asked.

Emmit stepped away again. Mira felt unsettled. She didn't know what he was looking for. It's possible he was trying to determine if she could make the trip. Mira hoped that was all it was. With everything that had happened, she wasn't sure she wanted to know if he was searching for anything else.

They all three ate something, but to Mira, it only seemed to remind her of how hungry she actually was.

It took Emmit a while to figure out the best way to carry Jean through the city. Mira was concerned about the woman not waking up, but at least Jean was alive.

They moved slowly at first, but then with more confidence when nothing stirred around them.

Mira couldn't help but look back every now and again. The city burned, but what did that mean in a reflected world?

The first two miles were slow. The third even slower. Gabriel led, but never moved too far away from Mira. When she pushed herself as far as she could, she called for them to stop.

Her hand throbbed, and little stabs of pain made her very aware of the fact that she had several cuts. She intended to lean against the wall for a short time before moving on, but even the thought of pushing herself away made her more tired.

"I don't suppose you all know of any witches that live in this area of town?" Mira said, forgetting her plan to stay on her feet. She cradled her hand to her chest, trying to ignore the thudding of her blood rushing under the burns.

"Most of them tend to live away from the city," Emmit reminded her.

With Gabriel's help, Emmit sat Jean on the ground.

"Tyler's house isn't too far out of the way," Emmit said.

"There's nothing there," Gabriel said. "We tried last time we were here."

Mira closed her eyes. She would do just about anything for a warm, safe bed.

"I could take her ahead," Emmit said.

"No," Gabriel said. "Maybe we should detour back to Chris's and get some rest."

"We need a witch's house and a reflection," Mira said, not opening her eyes.

"You made it back the first time through a reflection, right?" Emmit said.

"Yeah, Mira had a piece of a black mirror at her shop," Gabriel said.

"I'm assuming that Tyler's house had the magic removed when he was taken," Emmit said. "Does anyone know where they took it?"

"Jean said she never went far," Mira said. "Maybe they have stuff at the church?"

"I'm afraid I left a bit of a mess in that area," Emmit said. "Every creature for miles is there, except for the ones that were attracted to the city."

"We're back to Lance's, then," Mira said. When she opened her eyes, she took note of Emmit and frowned. "You're going shadowy."

Emmit took a step back and drew the chain out from under his neck. The glow was less prominent than it had been.

"I'm out of time," Emmit said.

"Can it be, I don't know, recharged or something?" Gabriel asked.

"Not from here," Mira said. She struggled to get to her feet and took Gabriel's hand for help. "How far away is my house?"

"At our pace, it'll take hours to get there," Emmit said. "I need to get away from you all. Gabriel, you'll need to carry Jean?"

"Can you make it to Lance's house?" Mira asked.

"They check once an hour," Emmit said. "If I have to wait, I'll attract every beast from miles around. It's possible that no one else could get through." He looked toward the city. "I'll go back the way we came. It will lure everything away and give you all the best chance."

"You can't do that," Mira said. "You won't be able to get to Lance's."

"That was the original idea," Emmit said.

"No, we'll stick together and go to my house." Mira didn't wait for a reply, but started to move in that direction.

"You can carry Jean?" Emmit asked.

Mira turned around. She pursed her lips, but when she went to cross her arms, she bumped her hand and her face reflected her agony.

Gabriel winced and moved beside her, rubbing her shoulder in sympathy. "Do you have anything for pain relief at your apartment?"

"I can make something—as well as something to keep us awake. But to do that, we need to get moving."

"I can carry Jean," Gabriel said. "You and Emmit go ahead."

"We should all stick together," Mira said.

"I can move faster on my own with Jean," Gabriel said. "I'll catch up."

"When I take off the necklace, they will come for us," Emmit said. "Being inside a building isn't going to stop that."

"She has a strong circle," Gabriel said, sounding resigned. "Maybe that will help."

Emmit lowered his voice and leaned toward Gabriel. "I may inadvertently distress Mira when I'm no longer hidden."

"I'm standing right here," Mira complained. "And I've already seen you with the necklace off."

"This is hard enough," Gabriel said. "Help me get Jean situated, then get going."

"I don't like the idea of splitting up," Mira said. "You'll be alone with Jean to watch after."

"You two need to look out for each other." Gabriel pulled Mira close and kissed her.

"I don't want to leave you out here alone," Mira said, her voice cracking.

"He needs you," Gabriel said. "I'll catch up. I promise."

Emmit helped situate Jean so Gabriel could still have use of his sword, then Gabriel took off at a trot.

"Are you ready?" Emmit asked.

Mira watched Gabriel moving quickly away. "No, but we should go anyway."

"We have farther to go than last time. This may be a bit disorientating."

Mira shrugged. "It can't be worse than anything else today."

"That shouldn't have happened."

"None of it should have happened," Mira said. "But the sooner we get out of here the sooner it will be over."

Disorientating wasn't a strong enough word. Emmit had Mira on his back. She tried to keep her eyes open for a few moments, but the shadows and colors that didn't quite belong made her stomach churn.

Mira was surprised when Emmit stopped before they reached her house. Emmit was out of breath and looking pale.

"Are you all right?" Mira asked. "We can walk for a while."

"I don't think the magic will hold out," Emmit said.

"Will it really be that bad?"

"I would rather us not wait to find out."

The next stop they made was outside of Mira's apartment. Mira slid off Emmit and had to hold on until the vertigo dissipated.

As he steadied her, Emmit looked around. "It appears that your apartment has suffered damage on this side."

She looked at the large hole where a door used to be. "John has quite a few options when it comes to monsters willing to help him." Then she saw that the arm holding her up appeared to be more shadow than flesh.

Emmit noticed her taking a closer look and pulled back.

She reached out, seeing the red static begin to stretch out. He stepped away before she could touch him.

"Let's get to the circle before the magic fails altogether." Emmit went inside and inspected the room before moving to her workshop.

The door to the workshop was leaning in place rather than acting like a proper door. Emmit set it out of the way. He didn't take time to search the workshop. Instead, he went straight for the circle.

"Will you be able to hold the barrier?" Emmit asked.

"You need to pass me the necklace first," Mira reminded him.

Emmit hesitated, then took off the chain and laid it on the table. Without turning around, he went to the circle.

"It will need to be strong," Emmit said, stepping inside. "But if anything approaches, you must drop the circle."

Mira leaned against her worktable, wondering where she would get the strength to do any magic. Della had had the right idea when she'd suggested a battery of power.

"This seems to be appropriate," Emmit said.

"What does?" Mira asked.

"The amount of power. It should hold."

"I haven't…" Mira moved forward and put her hand out, trying to get her too-tired brain to figure out what had happened. The magic was rough and unfamiliar. "No, no, no."

Emmit turned to her. She saw a shape under the shadows and dark eyes.

"What's wrong?" He shifted. "If you want me to go…"

"Get out of there." Mira's mind started to fire in fits and bursts. She ran a hand over the shell, looking for flaws that she might be able to exploit.

"If you drop—"

"I didn't charge this. This isn't me."

Mira knelt down on the floor and examined the base of the circle.

"Stand back," Emmit said.

Mira moved back over to her worktable and frantically began pulling out items. There were things that could weaken magic, even after it had been cast. She just hoped like hell that she had something.

A crackling pop behind her made her turn around. Inside the circle, Emmit appeared to disperse slightly before slamming into the barrier. The magic glowed brighter momentarily and Emmit fell back. He tried again and again, each time his movements seeming a little less desperate. He was slowing down—worn out.

When his form sunk to the ground, Mira's heart began to race. Had he hurt himself? His body didn't appear solid enough to be harmed.

"Mira," Emmit said, "you need to run."

"What?" Mira turned back to her workbench and looked for anything that could leech magic off something. Obsidian shards, no. Hematite, maybe.

"Go to Lance's or find Gabriel. Whichever, but you have to go now."

Moonstone, no. Redwood? Hmm, maybe Redwood. Ammonite would just make it worse.

"Mira!"

Mira jumped at the harsh voice. "Shut up, I'm thinking."

The red static dispersed more rapidly. "What?" His voice was dark and raspy. The shadows grew darker, but only inside the circle.

"And you're scaring no one," Mira snapped. "I'm working on a way to get you out."

"If I save enough energy, I can break through. Go. Now!"

"You can't. Each time you hit it, it gets stronger. I don't know how."

"That's because no witch alive truly knows magic." John's voice preceded him down the stairs.

Mira froze.

When he stepped into the room, the smell of rotting flesh seemed to build thickly around him.

"This wasn't exactly what I expected to catch," John said. "But having a Harker will definitely do the trick."

Emmit banged around his little prison.

John chuckled.

"Let him go," Mira said.

"In time, perhaps," John said. "That's all going to depend on you."

"Look, the thing in the city is dead. You don't have to worry about that anymore. You won't have to… I mean, it can't…"

"I'd like to know how you did that," John said. "It was a nifty trick."

"You don't need any more witches," Mira said. "And you certainly don't need Emmit."

"That's where you're wrong." John moved quickly around his prisoner.

Mira backed away, not letting the man out of her sight, even though the stench made her gag.

John made a whistling noise. Mira didn't see anything else around, but she sensed movement outside the room.

"Your friend here is going to be your incentive. If you don't willingly turn yourself over, I'll kill him."

Mira glanced at Emmit. The shadows seemed to settle down in the center. After a few moments, he began speaking, but in a language, Mira wasn't familiar with.

Mira felt a breeze begin to flow through the place.

John laughed again. He reached into his pocket and pulled out something that looked like a string bracelet with multiple colors. He grabbed one of the threads and pulled. Emmit's bubble shrank until it was barely the size of a doghouse. There wasn't much space that wasn't filled with Emmit's form.

John toyed with the thing and all noise from inside stopped.

"What did you do?" Mira said.

"He's still alive… for the moment. How long that's true depends on you."

Stall, I need to stall until Gabriel gets here. "Why are you doing this?"

"Quite simply, I want your body."

Mira's nose curled up in disgust and she backed toward the garage.

"You see," John said, moving to intercept her, "this one is used up. Thanks to you, there's no way this one will work out in the real world."

"You tried that already," Mira said. "It doesn't work."

"The issue that we've been faced with is that the bodies we've tried just don't want to be cooperative. John invited me in. Now you're going to do the same."

CHAPTER 27

"THAT'S INSANE," MIRA SAID. "You're insane."

She backed up to the open doorway. There was no way she was going to run and leave Emmit behind, but John didn't know that. She needed to do whatever she could to stall for time.

When she stood in the doorframe, something in the garage growled. She turned around and stepped backward, not wanting whatever it was to attack her from behind.

Nothing moved into the room. When she turned back to John, he was right next to her. He grabbed her hand.

Pain shot through her arm setting off echoes of pain radiating through her. John, taken by surprise, let go and stood back.

Mira fell to the ground, clutching her burned hand.

"You've damaged your body," John said with a sneer. "Stupid witch. It doesn't matter. We can work with that. Get up."

Mira's vision blurred from exhaustion, pain, and fear.

John kicked her, not hard, but enough to make sure she knew he was there. "Get up!"

Slowly and painfully, Mira got to her feet. He doesn't want to damage the body any more than it already is. Is there a way to use that to my advantage?

The only advantage Mira could see would only make things worse. She'd had enough pain for a lifetime, so she certainly wasn't going to inflict any more on herself.

At least not without a good reason.

"Why do you need me?" Mira asked, panting between words.

"This brain worked for a while, but let's face it; this body was human to start with. A few flashes of insight are nothing compared to what I'll be able to do using you."

"Why would I help you in any way? You'll just kill Emmit if I'm gone. And Gabriel's going to come and kill you."

"Gabriel has promised to protect that body," John said. "Letting him and Harker fight it out is just going to add to the fun."

Mira wearily smirked at John. "That wore off. That promise doesn't work anymore."

"Is that what you think? This is going to be even more enjoyable than I thought. You make the switch, and Emmit and Gabriel live. Unless one of them kills the other."

"And my friends and family?" Mira asked, wondering where the hell Gabriel was.

"Safe."

"Why should I believe you?"

"Because I don't care enough to do anything. In a witch's body, I'll be able to do my own magic again. Witches today can't do crap. Even you. But with me using you, I'll be revered among your kind. We will be revered."

"You've said that before, that witches today don't know magic."

"You tie everything to yourself. Even your magic circle." John gestured to the shadowy form of Emmit. "If I hurt your circle, I hurt you. It's weak."

Of course, all your spells are tied to yourself. "So you're going to do, what? Show witches how it's done so they'll like you?"

"No, I'll show witches how to be great again. Then we'll take our rightful lead in the world."

"You want to expose witches? No one's going to let you get away with that."

"And you don't have to worry about what happens."

"Why do—"

"Enough!" John yelled. "You, for him. It's time to decide."

"You can't have me."

John pulled on the string that made Emmit's cell smaller. "You're sure?"

If what he said is right, then that string was tied to Jean. She had to have been the one to create it.

"Stop!" Mira yelled.

Jean made all his spells.

John grinned. "Second thoughts?"

Jean had bonded to Mira with blood as part of the ritual. All three of them had.

"Let him go first." Maybe she had something to work with, since she had their blood. Mira wrapped her arms around herself and gripped down on the cut on her side.

"That's not the way this works."

"How does this work?" Mira turned away slightly and worked her hand under her bandage enough to wipe the blood across her hand. This action would have been so much easier if she knew where Jean had cut her.

"You relax and invite me in."

She shifted and gripped her arms. Pain radiated across her burns, and she had to bite back a gasp when new waves of pain arrived. "How can I relax? There's no way to relax here."

"You'll have to," John snapped.

"And you are already in a body. I can't invite a body into mine." What else did she have?

"Stupid witch. I'll leave once you've given me permission."

"And if I take it back?" She had Spark.

John seemed to hesitate. "Once you've given me leave, it won't matter. We will seal the deal in blood."

Mira turned completely away. "I'll need something." She rubbed her hands together, now sure that she had Jean's blood along with Gabriel and Emmit's on her hands.

Spark was in her pocket. Now she had to figure out what the hell she could do with it.

"I've grown weary of this," John said. "I'll kill this one and bring the angel in. Maybe I can pluck his feathers out one at a time until you agree."

The only power he had was what he held in his hands. That power could take away Emmit's life, but he had to have a chance to use it.

Could he even kill Emmit? Mira put that idea out of her head. That dangerous guessing game was one she didn't have the brainpower to play.

What would Gabriel do if he were here?

"You can't have Gabriel, we just left him." Gabriel's feathers were also in her pocket. How could she have forgotten about them?

"I assure you, he is under my control."

Gabriel would have pulled out his sword and taken John down.

Mira hung her head. "You've given me no choice." The quiver in her voice was real. The blood of four people was on her hands, and she only had permission to use her own.

How did Gabriel call the sword to him? Mira wished she could believe that Gabriel's sword would come to her aide, but she knew that was his. But, with his blood and feathers, along with the power of Spark and the other blood…

"Come here and we can finish this."

"At least I know you'll end up with bad karma. You may have a hard time staying alive long enough to enjoy being me."

John's cackled. "Where do you think that came from? I can push it off to someone else once I join with you."

Mira turned and gaped at him. "You did this?"

"It had to go somewhere."

Someone had done this to her once before. Pushed their karma off on her until it had almost been enough to kill her. How could she not recognize it when the same thing was happening again?

"Jean cast this spell for you?" Mira asked, her anger raising enough to combat her fear.

"She's been useful, but now I won't need her."

A few seconds would be all she had. With Jean's blood, she could cancel the spells, right? It was so tricky with the woman being a hedge witch—Mira didn't have much experience with them.

"It's time," John said.

"Can I say goodbye?" Mira asked, gesturing to the clouded circle.

Mira had nothing to power a spell, or even a spell negation, but she held items that were power in their own right. Perhaps a transfer of power would work better.

"You've wasted enough time," John snapped.

Ignoring him, Mira walked around the circle, brushing a hand against it, fingers trailing as she did. John noticed the gesture, but with any luck, he didn't spot the hint of blood added to the enclosure.

Looking meek as she approached might be difficult—Mira seethed beneath the surface. Her fear was still real, so letting that show would hopefully be good enough.

John looked as if he was going to start yelling, but his demeanor turned smug when she turned toward him.

The smug look helped.

"We swear on blood—yours not mine—to seal the pact," John said.

Mira walked up slowly, her bloody hand extended. John had the strands that controlled Emmit's prison in one hand, and he extended the other.

Mira balled up her fist and with every ounce of her strength, she brought her arm around and caught John across the face with her elbow, then brought up her knee. John looked more shocked than hurt by her attack.

Her knee to the groin did nothing. A hazy thought of dead body and dead nerves flitted through Mira's mind. To add more strength to the attack she grabbed her arm and swung around again catching him hard.

John reeled.

Mira grabbed the strands of cotton from his hand as snarls and growls erupted from the stairs and garage simultaneously.

"You bitch!" John yelled.

Mira ignored him. Not paying attention to the sound of talons on concrete was harder.

Mira scrambled back, then grabbed Emmit's necklace from her workbench.

"Bring her down!" John's rage hung heavy on the words.

Heart racing, Mira jumped behind the enclosure, buying herself seconds. In blood, on the concrete, she hastily scrawled three symbols. Necklace and strings in hand, she slapped them on Emmit's prison and wrote one final symbol. That of reversal.

Emmit's cage sizzled and bulged.

Mira screamed when she felt something grip her leg. She dropped everything and scrambled in her pocket as something started to drag her away.

As Emmit's bubble burst, Mira grabbed the little copper wire. Spark sprang to life and worked its way around the room like a ball of lightning.

The creature that had her by the leg clamped down harder for just a moment before going limp.

Shadows filled the room and the eerie glow of the Ether winked out

The shrill screams that followed in the darkness would haunt Mira. Emmit's voice held more than enough menace to cause any sane person to bolt. He began yelling in the unfamiliar language that she had heard before.

The perverse thrill of beating up John was falling away. With the last vestiges of her strength, she pushed herself into a corner of the room. As she reached the spot, her panicked spell casting and fear caught up with her, leaving her muscles slack and useless.

Mira was fairly certain that more creatures were coming into the room, but the darkness was absolute, so she couldn't be sure.

When she tried to pull her knees up to make herself less prone, her body was uncooperative, even when a fierce curse close to her caused her blood to run cold.

Since there was no difference in what she saw with her eyes opened or closed, she closed them and tried to block out sounds. The shrieks and growls were cut off one by one, but mixed in between she could hear bones break along unnatural, wet tearing noises.

Time was hard to track in the Ether. She could have been there for minutes or hours.

A subtle shift in the atmosphere told her the room was emptying. She heard a voice outside in the distance. Mentally, she cringed at the idea that John might have gotten away.

When a hand touched her face, she jolted back, smacking her head on the wall.

Emmit was crouched down next to her, his face a tight, angry knot. It took her a moment to realize that he looked like his real world self again. The chain was once again around his neck.

"You're okay?" Mira asked.

"It got a little tight," he admitted.

Mira smiled wearily. "Well, I wanted to see how far your immortality could be pushed."

He raised an eyebrow. "Not much further, in all honesty."

"It's good to know you have your limits." Mira's nose curled up as the stink of the scene began to sink into her awareness. She tried to look around Emmit, but he blocked the way, not letting her see anything.

"We should go upstairs," Emmit said, looking her up and down. He shifted to examine her leg, ripping back her jeans to expose the wound.

Mira could hear him suck in air. He pulled off strips of cloth from his shirt and wrapped it tightly around her leg quickly, saying nothing. She winced as he tightened the knot.

He looked weary and worried, something Mira was unaccustomed to.

"Let's move," Emmit said. "Then I'm going to need you to work a bit of quick magic."

She looked at him blankly. Before she could say anything, he stood and pulled her to her feet, still trying to block the room from view.

Emmit gripped her arm. The strength of the hold increased, bearing down on Mira.

"What's wrong?" Mira asked, trying to shake him off, though she was exhausted and couldn't muster any strength.

Emmit said nothing.

When Mira glared up at him, she saw something in her eyes that surprised her and her face softened. His eyes showed exhaustion, but the fear took her by surprise.

"Emmit?"

"Go upstairs and wait for Gabriel," he said, and then gripped harder.

Mira harshly sucked in air and tried not to curse the man.

The pressure released and Emmit wavered. Mira grabbed hold of him, trying to keep him steady.

"You need to sit," Mira said.

Emmit's body went limp in her arms. She tried to hold him up, but she fell with him.

CHAPTER 28

S HE PUSHED HERSELF UP—TIREDNESS had been replaced by dread.

"Emmit?" She ran a hand over his forehead and cheeks, but Emmit was unresponsive. "Shit." Mira started to look Emmit over expecting to find blood or a wound somewhere.

When she moved to check his legs, the full carnage of the room came into sharp focus. Mira slapped a hand over her mouth and tried to breathe steadily through her nose. The acrid scent burned her nostrils.

It took her a minute to really understand what she was seeing. The tar-like blood of the creatures was splashed across her entire workshop. There were… parts.

Mira's stomach heaved. She turned away from Emmit and the room in time to throw up against the wall. With so little food and water, stomach acid roiled up with the remains of her last meal.

She closed her eyes and sat back. Her leg radiated pain and the darkness greeted her with images of torn leathery flesh. Furry portions of limbs were seared into her conscious. It didn't seem to matter if her eyes were shut or open. Therefore, she looked down at Emmit in an effort to focus on him instead of the remains.

"Emmit, you need to wake up." A sob escaped her and she held back more, swallowing them down before talking again. She put her face close to his until she felt his breath across her skin.

A puddle of inky liquid had reached Emmit's other side. Mira desperately wanted to pull him away from the blood, but there was nowhere to move him.

Mira wanted to shake him to try to get him to wake up, but she was afraid of what that might do. She couldn't see any marks on Emmit, but internal injury was a possibility.

She got to her feet and steeled herself to look around the room again. Maybe there was some indication of what happened to him.

The disaster in front of her made her swallow hard. She couldn't help but glance down at Emmit, knowing he been responsible for this butchery.

A hint of lighter color could be seen in several places in the room. She even caught sight of something that looked remarkably like human flesh.

Movement in the garage made her cringe back, trying to meld into the wall.

Gabriel stepped into the doorframe and froze. Mira let out a relieved sigh, letting go of the breath she had been holding.

After scanning the room, Gabriel locked eyes with Mira. He lurched forward a step and stumbled, having been tripped up by something Mira didn't want to see.

"Are you okay?" he asked hoarsely, his voice almost a whisper.

Mira shook her head. "I need help. Emmit… I can't move him."

Gabriel looked bleakly around. "We need to move upstairs. Have you… has he been upstairs?"

"No, I don't think so. It was… it…" Mira swallowed hard trying not to break down, but her eyes filled with tears.

"It's okay," Gabriel said, his voice still soft in the silence. He carefully walked into the room, towards the stairs. "We can take Jean upstairs and I'll come back for Emmit."

Mira watched him carefully try to avoid what he could. Jean, still unconscious, was on his back now.

"Come on," Gabriel said, waving her over. "Just go slow and stick as close as you can to the sides of the room."

Mira began to shake. The idea of leaving Emmit alone was one she couldn't handle—not here, surrounded by the dead.

"Mira, I'm not leaving you down here. Harker will be okay for a few minutes."

"I don't think I can." She not only didn't want to leave Emmit behind, but she wasn't sure she could get across the room on her own.

Gabriel rubbed his forehead. "Okay, I get it. Don't move."

Mira held her breath when Gabriel moved through the door to the steps. Moments later, the air whooshed out again as Gabriel reappeared, sans Jean.

"She's on the stairs," Gabriel said, starting to work his way towards her.

More than once, Gabriel had to look away or squeeze his eyes shut tight so he didn't have to look at something he was trying to push aside with his feet.

When he reached her, he pulled her into a fierce hug, which Mira returned, laying her head on his chest.

"We should move Emmit," Mira said, not letting go.

"What happened to him?" Gabriel asked, breaking contact and squatting down over Emmit.

Mira's breath became short and sharp when she realized Gabriel's wings touched the ground. Trying to ignore it, she took a deep breath and concentrated once again on the person in front of her.

"John set a trap," Mira started. "Emmit was caught in a circle. John was trying to…persuade me to turn myself over to him. When I said no, he shrank the circle, squeezing Emmit inside."

"That man is sick. Where'd he go?"

Mira looked at the bloodbath behind Gabriel and he took the hint.

"That's one less worry," Gabriel said, not sounding as though he regretted the loss. "How did Harker get out?"

Trying to keep it short, Mira gave Gabriel an overview of what happened.

"I see the problem," Gabriel said. "What happened to him?"

"John's prison was pressed down pretty hard. I'm worried something serious is wrong."

"I think you're right. Normally, I wouldn't want to move him, but we have to. We can't stay here."

"What do you see that I don't?" Mira asked.

Gabriel picked up the pendant that was hung around Emmit's neck. "You might not be able to see it without seeing him as he is. Let's get him upstairs."

More carefully than she expected, Gabriel eased Emmit off the ground.

"It's better to move him only once," Gabriel said as he made his way to the staircase. "We can take him straight upstairs."

Mira looked down at her leg and gingerly put weight on it. She gritted her teeth against the pain, and leaned against the wall, then her workbench, trying to relieve as much pressure as she could.

"Can you get around Jean?" Mira asked when Gabriel reached the door.

"I'll manage. Stick close."

"Right behind you," Mira said, to avoid lying.

Gabriel was halfway up the steps when Mira reached them. She grabbed the banister and carefully tried the first step.

She couldn't take a step. Only the banister stopped her from falling.

"I'll put him in the living room," Gabriel said, not looking behind him.

"Good idea," Mira said, trying to keep the agony out of her voice.

Gabriel disappeared upstairs and Mira sank onto a step. When she was little, she had scooted up steps, one at a time. She sat down and using her good leg and her arms, she moved up a step.

"Mira?" Gabriel called in a croaky voice.

"I'm coming." One at a time. Halfway up, her strength gave out. She leaned against the banister and rested her eyes, listening to her own breathing.

Gabriel's footsteps soon pounded down the stairs. "Are you okay?" His voice was quiet, but she heard the hint of panic.

Mira forced her eyes open. "Tired. And my leg… I think something bit me."

"You should have said something," Gabriel grumbled, delicately picking her up.

Mira shrugged and leaned against him, happy to soak up his warmth.

"Sit next to Emmit," he said, setting her down. "I'll get Jean."

He rushed away before she could say anything. He was back much faster than she anticipated.

After laying Jean down, he sat next to Mira and looked at her leg.

"How bad is it?" Gabriel asked as he started to untie Emmit's handy-work.

Mira was thankful she could give him an honest answer. "I have no idea."

"Are you hurt anywhere else?"

She stuck with honesty. "There's nothing else that's new."

Mira winced when Gabriel pulled back the cloth.

He sucked in sharply and his feathers twitched.

Now worried, Mira leaned forward. "What's it look like?"

Gabriel quickly covered it again. "It's not good."

He looks even more tired than I am. "You need to rest."

"Not here."

Mira knew that sentiment. "We need to find a way to get Jean and Emmit to Lance's."

Gabriel looked bleakly from Jean, to Emmit, and then to her. "Unless you have a magic carpet stashed somewhere, there's no way and no time."

"No carpets," Mira said, "but I haven't heard anything coming close since…" She waved her hand towards the basement door, unable to say what had happened another time. "We should at least have some time."

Gabriel looked so deep in thought, she wasn't sure if he had been listening.

"If we mask the smell, we might be safe for a while," she said.

"The first time we were here, you took something. Relief, I think it was. It healed your leg."

"It didn't heal me. It only made me feel better. It's not going to fix my leg or the burns. Some of the cuts, it might help with, but we need to get out of here and to a hospital."

"I don't think there's time, and I'm not sure they can help."

It felt as though a pit were opening up under Mira. "Why not?"

Gabriel shifted and took her good hand. "Do you know what bit you?"

"No, I don't know what anything here is." A touch of hysteria tried to break into Mira's voice. "Emmit said they were once witches, but whatever they were, that's not what they are now." Mira looked down at her leg and shook off Gabriel's hand so she could remove the covering.

Gabriel stopped her. "Careful." He patted her hand before letting go. This time, he was mindful about what he was doing. Slowly, he pulled back the cloth.

Mira could only stare. That's not me. Her flesh had been stripped away but the wound itself had turned black. Under her skin, black veins stretched out, turning green and returning to normal a few inches away from the bite.

Staring longer, she thought she saw the area around the bite mark pulse.

Gabriel dressed the wound once again.

It was a figment of your imagination. Telling herself this over and over again didn't help.

"Is there something that can heal? A potion or a spell… anything?"

She felt disjointed. "Heal is a difficult potion in the best of times." Her voice sounded hollow, even to herself. But that was okay, because some part of her mind was screaming and another was freaking out about parasites and monsters. Outwardly, Mira began to feel numb. "I'm not sure I have everything."

"We have to try." Gabriel looked at the others. "It might help the others too."

Mira stared at Emmit for a minute.

"We need to get this started, Mira." Gabriel stood and helped her to her feet. "Where do we start?"

"I don't think I have—"

"Let's focus on where we start. We can substitute what you don't have."

"I'm too tired to focus. Let's start with some Awake. I have a feeling we might need a lot of it before we get home."

"I'm not sure we have time."

"There's some already made in the kitchen. It might be stale, but the magic should still be strong enough to be mirrored on this side."

Gabriel wrapped his arm around her, making her lean on him as much as possible on the way to the kitchen. Once he settled her into a chair, he appeared to study her eyes for a moment.

"Tell me what to do," Gabriel said, taking her hand again.

"Anywhere else and that might sound like fun."

Gabriel raised an eyebrow at her and she forced a grin.

"Try the cabinet next to where the refrigerator should be," Mira said. "There should be a few packets in there."

"In the open?" Gabriel asked, checking it out.

"Sure. There's nothing illegal in it. It's like tea. In our world, it's almost like caffeine that lasts longer. We're going to need water as well," she added when he found the packets.

He left and returned quickly with the backpack. Mira took the water and after a few more instructions to Gabriel, she had everything she needed to make a paste out of the Awake.

"This is going to taste awful," Mira warned.

She and Gabriel both used their fingers to scoop up the concoction and took it. Their faces twisted up at the flavor.

"That's so much better as tea," Mira said.

"I'm going to try to give some of this to Harker. Maybe it will help."

"Not too much."

Gabriel hesitated at the entry to the living room, but after a moment, hurried in. Mira was surprised at how fast he returned.

"You should make sure he doesn't choke."

"I'll watch him from here," Gabriel said. "I don't like letting you out of my sight."

Mira smiled at him, a warmness spreading inside her.

"It would be easier if I still knew when something was going to happen to you. I need to make a new promise," Gabriel said.

"Actually, I think it's a spell blocking the previous link."

Gabriel looked at her appearing confused and a little hurt. "It was something John said. I think he did something to hide the connection. I think Jean can break it."

"The sooner we get her on her feet, the better, then. Until then, I want to be able to see that you're safe. Well, as safe as we can be here."

Mira shook her head, but felt closer to normal after his show of affection. "I'm going to have to send you out of the room. Maybe even out of the apartment."

"We can go together," Gabriel suggested, but he wasn't excited about the idea.

Mira squirmed in her seat. "Some of the things I need are downstairs as well."

"Right," Gabriel said, sounding defeated. He stared into the living room. "Maybe we can wake Harker up now."

"If we can find everything, we might be able to wake him and Jean."

Gabriel nodded. "If you know everything you need, we should try to get as much as we can out of the first floor now. The smell will eventually attract something."

"We should get started then."

With the Awake in her system, Mira started thinking more clearly. She put Gabriel to work, first gathering items from everywhere around her apartment, including her bedroom where very little was stored. Once everything was gathered, Gabriel began using the mortar and pestle to grind herbs together.

There were ingredients missing, but she knew that before they started. She made substitutions where she could.

While Gabriel worked, Mira poured over a few of her spell books, trying to find ways around the items she didn't have. It might have been easier if she had a pencil and paper. She was used to jotting her notes down as she went.

When she found that bloodstone might be a decent substitution for calcite, at least in this situation, Mira sent Gabriel back down to the basement.

She could hear Gabriel downstairs as he worked to get into one of her secret compartments. It bothered her to send him into such a vile place. Mira watched the door to the basement and absentmindedly scratched her leg.

The wound pulsed. Mira sucked in air as fire seemed to burn through her veins, radiating from the bite.

She gritted her teeth. Each cell in her body ignited in a way she never expected after the death of the creature in the city.

Holding back the scream wasn't possible. The intensity increased and the only thing that existed for Mira was the pain.

CHAPTER 29

T HERE WAS NO WAY of knowing how long she lay on the floor. As the agony leaked away, her awareness began to return. All of her muscles had contracted so that she was curled up.

Slowly, she began to relax, afraid that moving too fast might end up causing another flare.

"Mira?"

Gabriel was hovering over her, pale in the face, but trying to maintain a stoic expression.

"I need a minute," Mira said, her hoarse voice now matching Gabriel's.

"What happened?" Emmit's voice was tight.

Mira looked around, happy to hear his voice, despite his tone. She saw he was slumped against the wall and he wasn't looking well.

"Lie down before you hurt yourself," Gabriel snapped.

To Mira's surprise, Emmit followed the suggestion without argument.

"I didn't expect… I mean, the thing in the city is dead. Isn't it?" Mira hated to have to ask the question.

"I don't think it has to be alive for the symptoms to continue," Emmit said.

With Gabriel's help, Mira sat up. "It'll continue?"

Emmit's eyes were closed when he responded. "Not for long."

Mira noticed Gabriel's face fall. She could only hope that it wasn't because Emmit was lying.

"Did you check her leg?" Emmit asked.

"Earlier," Gabriel said.

"Check again."

"Don't go back to sleep," Gabriel said.

A strained smile crossed Emmit's face, but he didn't open his eyes. "I'll do what I can."

Mira held her leg out and watched Gabriel closely as he pulled back the wrapping. When he tried to block her sight of the leg with the bloody cloth, she took his hand and eased it away.

A mass had formed over the puncture wounds and the darkness had spread.

It was impossible for Mira to stop the small whimper that escaped her, but she held back the remaining ones.

It was enough of a response to cause Emmit to sit back up and move to Gabriel.

Mira folded her good leg up to her chest and grabbed, before hiding her face. This isn't happening. She mentally repeated the mantra again and again.

Gabriel began wrapping her leg. "It's okay. Your potion will heal your leg."

Mira lifted her head up and looked at Emmit. "If it doesn't, I can't go home, can I?"

Gabriel answered. "Of course you can. We're getting out of here."

"The choice will be yours," Emmit said.

"But whatever this is, it might spread to others. Or…" She couldn't finish it, but in her mind, she was worried that whatever she had, it would do worse than only killing her. "It might spread," she repeated.

"It will," Emmit said.

Mira looked down.

"Let's just make the spell," Gabriel said, as he secured her makeshift bandages. "There's no use inviting the worry in, if the spell works."

Without looking at anyone, Mira used her chair to push herself up and back into her chair. She stared blankly at her books for a short time, before beginning to flip through, not really seeing the pages.

"I found the blood stone," Gabriel said.

Mira nodded numbly.

"What should I do with it?" Gabriel asked.

"It needs to be crushed up somehow, but by itself. I usually use a hammer, but I doubt we'll find one here," Mira said.

"I'll take care of it," Gabriel said. "What else do we need?"

Mira shook her head.

"We're missing several other ingredients," Mira said uncertainly.

"What are they?" Gabriel asked.

"Lavendar, medical-grade water, olibanum, and several other things…" Mira trailed off as she thought about the missing items. "We can use what little water we have, but I can't think of replacements for the others."

"So, you can't make it?" Emmit asked.

"Usually I have Tyler to bounce ideas off of when I'm stuck. Can you think of anything that might have a purifying kick to it?"

Emmit looked around the room, and then stared at Gabriel for a while.

"What?" Gabriel asked after too long under scrutiny.

"It's not something I would normally suggest, and nothing that I would ask for," Emmit said, "but in this case, I don't think we have much choice."

"Just spit it out," Gabriel said.

"Help me up," Emmit said.

When Gabriel dragged Emmit to his feet, Mira was unsettled by the amount of assistance Emmit required. Even after Gabriel sat him in a chair, Emmit had to lean against the table to stay up.

"If we can find your lightest colored feather, it might help," Emmit said. "One that's pure white certainly would."

"They're pretty gray," Gabriel said, twisting around as best he could.

"Which may make things worse instead of better," Emmit said.

"I've screwed things up, haven't I," Gabriel said, studying his wings.

"If things settle down, they'll return to normal with time," Emmit assured him.

"We don't have time," Gabriel reminded him.

Mira pulled out a rather grubby feather. "I guess I'm the one who messed things up." Even holding it, she could see that she was contaminating it further.

Emmit leaned closer to her, examining the feather. "The dirt won't hurt the quality, but how did you end up with it?" He held his hand out, silently requesting the feather.

Mira started to hand it over, but stopped and glanced at Gabriel. "Is it okay?"

"Anything to help," Gabriel said. "At this point, I don't think Harker's going to do anything to it or me. Not while we're here."

Nodding, Mira handed over the feather and told Emmit about her enthusiastic grip on Gabriel their first time in the Ether.

Emmit smiled weakly. "This will work as a substitution."

"Good," Mira said.

"We will want to make sure that it has nothing from this world on it. No blood from any of those creatures. I'm not sure what it might do if you took anything that held their blood at this point in time."

"What about adding blood to the spell?" Gabriel asked.

Emmit passed the feather back to Mira. "I just said…"

"I mean, from us. It amplifies the spell, right?" Gabriel asked.

"It might not hurt to have the extra boost. Let's try without first. We can see how well it helps and go from there."

The actual casting took another few hours. Emmit had what was needed for the circle, but there were no shortcuts this time. Several times, she heard shouting but dismissed it. With Gabriel and Emmit in the same room for any length of time, it was expected.

Mira fell deep into her magic. It was stronger than she remembered, but the Ether always seemed to make things that way.

Despite having the Awake still in her system, Mira began to falter before the spell was complete. She was cold, which was something that she wouldn't expect while in the Ether. By the time she was done, she was swaying where she sat.

Once again, she made a paste, enough for all four of them. She sat unmoving for a while, taking some small comfort in the flow of her own power, and then she broke the circle.

When the magic stopped, she began to shake and vertigo set in. Before she said anything, she pushed the paste away and laid down.

Emmit was once again on the floor, seemingly unconscious. Gabriel had moved Jean into the room as well. Her heart skipped a beat when she saw that the angel himself was absent.

The little jolt of adrenalin that Gabriel's disappearance caused, allowed Mira to sit up. "Gabriel!" Too late, she realized that this might not be the best place to yell.

Gabriel appeared in the room, sword and shield in hand. He rushed over to her and sat down before pulling Mira into a hug.

"I think we're okay for a minute," Gabriel said.

Mira leaned against him. The angel was breathing hard and he was sweaty. She took note of the fact that his sword and shield were right next to them.

"How's your leg?" he asked.

"It doesn't hurt," Mira said.

"We should check."

"Later. I think it's done."

"Have you taken any yet?"

She sat up a little straighter so she could look him in the eye. "I wanted to see you first."

Gabriel pushed back a few stray hairs from Mira's face. Then he pressed his hand to her cheek, and then her forehead. "You're burning up. You need to take this now."

"If this doesn't work, I'm not going back."

"This will—"

"I want you to let my family know what happened, and that I love them. Will you do that?"

Gabriel looked at her for a few moments, looking as though he wanted to argue further. "We'll ask Harker. He can pass on the message. If you stay, I stay."

"No way. I couldn't ask you to do that."

"You didn't ask. My choice, remember. It's your choice if I'm inside with you, or waiting around outside."

Mira sniffed. "Inside—always with me."

There was a noise in the other room.

"Shit," Gabriel quickly moved Mira and jumped up. "Take the potion. Give some to Emmit as well. We're going to need him."

Gabriel dashed out of the room. Moments later, Mira heard a growl and then Gabriel ordering something away. Now that she was listening, there were other noises as well, but they all remained below them. The basement door had stuff pushed against it to prevent it from opening.

The front door slammed shut and she heard Gabriel shifting stuff around in the other room.

Mira grabbed the Heal and scooted across the floor over to Emmit. If things were bad enough that Gabriel admitted to needing Emmit, then it was past time to get Emmit back on his feet.

Shaking Emmit did nothing, so Mira lifted his head and set it on her lap.

"This would be so much easier if you would wake up," Mira said, hoping to get some sort of response. She took a minuscule amount of the paste and rubbed it inside his mouth.

Gabriel came in, but stayed in the doorframe, keeping an eye on the living room and kitchen together. "Is it working?"

"It's too early to tell. I don't want him to choke."

"And you?"

"I wanted to get Emmit up, so he could help you."

"Take it," Gabriel said. "The sooner you're feeling better, the better for everyone."

"What did you give me?" Emmit asked. He looked like he was barely awake.

Mira looked down and smiled weakly. "Heal. At least a version of it. You need to take more."

"Perhaps you could help me," Emmit suggested.

"Stow it, Harker," Gabriel said.

Emmit smirked.

"You're obviously feeling better," Gabriel said. "Now take the rest of your part." His head jerked to the living room. "She hasn't taken any yet, so make sure she does." Gabriel disappeared.

Emmit was sitting before Mira even noticed he moved. "Was I your guinea pig?"

Mira started to protest, but then saw his smile. "No, I think Gabriel needs help."

A screech sounded in the living room and Emmit sighed. "This place is beginning to wear my temper thin."

"That's my job," Mira said.

"One in which you are very skilled at. Don't think I've forgotten how you ended up here."

"Sorry."

The look on Emmit's face softened. "We couldn't have succeeded without you. Now, you take your medicine, and I'll take mine so we can get out of this wretched place."

"I'd like that." Mira wanted to put off taking the potion. She was sure the outcome would mean that she would have to stay in the Ether. She wanted to keep hope alive for as long as she could.

Emmit, however, wasn't going to let her stall. Under his watchful eye, she took the Heal and Emmit followed suit.

Once the spell was out of her hands, Mira leaned against Emmit without thinking. She felt cold, tired, and her mind was fogging over from exhaustion and fever.

They heard Gabriel clash in the other room.

"I made some for Jean and Gabriel as well," Mira said.

"I'll take care of it," Emmit said.

Mira felt him move but she fell asleep before giving him instructions for the Heal.

CHAPTER 30

M IRA WAS PLAGUED BY nightmares, the worst of which was when she was turned into one of the creatures. When she did, Gabriel didn't recognize her and killed her. The dreams of fighting and arguing were almost a relief compared to the others.

At one point, someone poured something foul down her throat. It was worse than the Heal had been and her dreams shaped around it, implying that she had drunk the tarlike black blood.

When she woke up, she had no idea how much time had passed. It took her a while to realize she was awake, because a black cloud hovered around her, blocking much of the ever present light of the Ether. It didn't help that she had no idea where she was.

At the center of the inky fog, there was a form. It radiated thin strands of red static. She knew it was Emmit, but she said nothing for a while, and simply watched him, amazed at his difference in appearance.

The black haze stretched into the sky, but it was also as though the rest of the world dimmed around him. If the Ether had a sun, Mira was sure the shadowy form would block it out.

Emmit seemed to realize she was awake and in the center, his more solid form shifted away.

"How long have I been asleep?" Mira asked.

He stopped moving away. "For quite a while, but it's good to see you awake now. I don't want to cause you any distress so I'll wait outside until Gabriel returns."

"The only thing that would upset me is if you leave."

Emmit seemed to hesitate. "I don't worry you?"

Mira felt weak, but pushed herself into a sitting position and looked around. "You don't worry me, Emmit. I know you're not going to hurt me." And the fact that your accent remains doesn't hurt. Mira grinned at the thought.

"That's true." He was silent for a while and Mira knew he was watching her. "How do you feel?"

Mira thought about it. "Better." She looked at her hand and saw that the burns were almost gone. Fresh cloth—or at least unbloodied cloth—was wrapped around her leg, but she couldn't steel herself enough to check under it.

"Is that the truth?"

Mira grinned. "I thought I was a bad liar?"

It was amazing how exasperated an almost shapeless form could seem.

"It's the truth." Mira held up her previously burnt hand and inspected it. She had thought it was going to be useless, but even now, it seemed to be healing further. "I'm tired and hungry. Starving really. But I feel much better. It looks like the Heal worked."

"Gabriel earns some credit to that. Once Jean broke a spell, he could sense you once again. It looked as though the shock might kill him. Once we had him on his feet again, he took the Heal, added his own blood and mine along with more blood stone and gave you the new potion."

"Where is Gabriel?"

"He's scouting around Lance's house. He looked unsettled, so I asked Jean to join him."

"He's okay, though? And Jean?"

"They are both okay now. We all are."

"And my leg?" Mira asked.

"It's healing."

It felt as though a huge weight was lifted from Mira. "I can go back home, then?"

The cloudy form shifted around. "We haven't checked your leg in a while. I'm sure it's healed by now."

Mira started to pull at the cloth, trying to unknot it.

"Careful," Emmit said, leaning forward. "We don't want it to start bleeding again."

"Can you help me?" Mira asked, feeling frustrated when the ties wouldn't budge.

"If you'd like me to."

He seemed to drift forward, but slowly—slower than she'd ever seen him move.

"I'm not going to run away," Mira said, starting to get agitated.

"I wouldn't blame you if you did."

"I would. I take it the magic of the necklace wore out again."

Emmit closed the gap between them. "It did."

"I'll have to work on the spell. It should last for much longer."

"Even with the parasite dead, magic still seems to leak out here."

While Emmit worked on the knots, Mira took the chance to study him in this state. She could see his eyes. They were dark, but with hints of red. The red static appeared to be just that. A thin, constant, red electrical charge radiating out and dancing around his cloudy form.

This close, she could also see that he wasn't solid at the core. Despite what he appeared at a distance to look like, she could see his inner self swirling as though caught in a breeze.

Emmit cleared his throat and she came back to her senses. She couldn't help but think he was beautiful in the Ether. Strange and uncanny, but he held a rare beauty that she knew she'd never see again.

She turned her attention towards her leg.

"It looks even better than it did before. I'm sure that you'll be fine in no time."

It did look better. The black was starting to turn green in her veins. The color also didn't run as far away from the wound as it previously had. Even around the punctures, the skin appeared to be healing and the dark color appeared more fleshy toned than it had before.

"How much more time do we give it to heal?" Mira asked as Emmit covered the wound again.

"As long as it takes."

Mira sighed.

"I don't expect it to be too long," Emmit added.

"Where are we?"

"I think Gabriel intends to take you back as soon as the way is open. We are at the closest house to Lance's that is still standing in this world."

"How do you feel about that?" Mira didn't want to say it herself, but she hoped Gabriel would take her home immediately. It sounded like a bad idea in every way, but she longed to be back in her own world.

Emmit drifted back a little. "Magic is stronger here, which has its advantages. If you went back without being fully healed, we would want to keep a close eye on the damage."

"If it doesn't heal, would I have to come back here?"

"With nothing pulling our worlds together, I'm not certain the pathways will be easy to travel for long."

"That, at least, is a relief. If it's harder for us to get here, it will be harder for anything else to come into our world." Mira reached for the backpack lying not far away.

"There's no food or water left," Emmit said, beating her to the bag.

"What's in there, then?"

A loud bang sounded somewhere in the house and Mira jumped. Heart pounding fast, she scrambled closer to Emmit, forgetting the bag.

It was a surprise to Mira that Emmit still had a hand. It was a little warmer than she anticipated, but he felt solid when he squeezed her reassuringly.

"Time to go!" Gabriel yelled.

Mira relaxed a little, but she still felt anxious when Gabriel opened the door to the room and froze.

It looked as though he was shocked to see her there, although it was equally possible that he was surprised to see her awake. It didn't take him long to recover. He strode across the room and scooped her up in his arms.

Emmit gave them space the moment Mira dropped his hand. Mira and Gabriel held each other. Time was almost impossible to track in the Ether. They could have held each other for hours, though, and Mira wouldn't have thought it was long enough.

When Gabriel finally loosened his hold, it was to tell her it was time to go home.

Mira glanced at Emmit, then back at Gabriel. "I'm not sure my leg is all the way healed."

"It'll heal back home. Emmit's offered to help us out until you're better."

"You're okay with that?" Mira asked.

"As long as we're back in our own world, I can handle anything, even living with Harker."

When they walked through the charred surroundings, Jean took the lead. The realization that her children were closer to her than they'd been for over a week had taken hold of her.

Mira and Gabriel walked together with Emmit close by. They paused once or twice quietly to watch the city burn.

Barney was once again the lookout that helped them find their way back to their own reality.

Mira wasn't surprised to see Mr. Singer there as well. He didn't seem inclined to bring up her being shunned, but Mira decided to avoid him all the same.

The thing that did shock Mira was the high pitch squeal that rang out when Emmit stepped through, instantly retaking his normal form.

A woman with dark hair and a pink dress flung herself at Emmit and began asking a barrage of questions. Mira couldn't follow the litany, but she took note of Emmit's relieved smile, along with slight embarrassment that they were the center of attention.

Emmit stemmed the rapid-fire interrogation, and along with the woman, joined Mira and Gabriel.

"Mira, Gabriel, I'd like you to meet my sister, Anastacia."

"Anya," his sister corrected with a smile. "Or you can call me Bunny."

Although Mira would never admit it, she had expected any of Emmit's relatives to be rigid and uptight. She had also thought a certain level of arrogance; after all, she was Emmit's sister.

"Anya, this is Mira and Gabriel, they're… they've been assisting me while in the city." Mira noted the name Bunny never passed Emmit's lips.

"We're his friends," Mira amended.

Emmit appeared to appreciate the correction.

They shook hands with Bunny, and Mira noticed that as they spoke, Emmit's sister seemed to drift towards Gabriel, much like Emmit always appeared to do—unless the two men were arguing.

It didn't take long before Renfield's men had the group rounded up and on their way. Jean opted to go with Mr. Singer, who assured her she would be taken to her children immediately.

Mira felt jittery on the car ride, and even though she wanted to, she couldn't sleep on the way to the apartment. It was a relief to see that Gabriel didn't have the same issue. He had done so much in the Ether that she figured he'd sleep for a week.

When they reached the apartment, she was immediately proven wrong. Emmit and Gabriel excused themselves to talk with some of Renfield's men. Bunny mentioned dinner and disappeared into the labyrinth of an apartment.

Mira went straight to her bedroom, which Emmit intended for her to continue to use. She peeled off her clothes, shoved them in the trashcan in the bathroom and then took the hottest shower she could manage.

It felt wonderful to get the Ether scrubbed off of herself. Seeing that her leg still wasn't fully healed was a little disturbing, but the coloring was almost back to normal. Before long, she figured it would look like any other cut or bruise.

At least she hoped that would be the case. In an effort to get it healed as fast as possible, she took her time, cleaned it, and wrapped it.

When she stepped back into her room, Gabriel was waiting for her. It looked as though he had already showered as well and was wearing a sweat suit that must have belonged to one of Renfield's men.

"That was fast," Mira said, glad that she had put on a robe before entering the room. "I thought you and Emmit had things to talk about."

"The less I know about what he's doing, the better," Gabriel said.

"Why's that?"

"Emmit thinks it will be neater all around if the case gets closed. I can't say I disagree."

Mira sat on the edge of her bed. "How will you close the case?"

Gabriel looked uncomfortable. "We, uh, brought back evidence from the Ether."

"What? How? I thought Emmit was adamant that your work had to stay in this world."

"It still does, but we needed John here. Or, at least enough to identify him."

Mira scrunched up her nose, not liking the sound of the idea.

"Don't worry about it," Gabriel said. "Renfield's men know what they're doing. Not that that makes me any happier about the issue. We brought them what they need to make it happen. How are you feeling?"

Mira latched on to the change of subject. "Tired, how about you?"

"Same. Harker has a room they're setting up for me."

Mira smiled. "I'm glad you'll be here."

He returned the smile. "Me too."

Mira patted the bed next to her and Gabriel sat down, putting an arm around her. It didn't take long for them to fall asleep, wrapped in each other's arms.

Hours later, Mira woke when she heard Gabriel talking softly with someone.

Moments later, Gabriel slipped back into bed. Mira slid over to him, and he put his arms around her and pulled her close. When they kissed, they were interrupted by Oracle jumping on Gabriel and Alchemy curling up close behind Mira so she couldn't move.

Happy as she was, she wouldn't have moved for anything.

Writing the last book in the series was so difficult! It was hard to leave the characters. The last few chapters were redone more times than I care to admit, but with some wonderful feedback, I think we have a satisfactory amount of detail and our heroine is with the man she loves. I'm not saying I'll never return to these characters, but I don't expect to see them for a while.

If you enjoyed this book, please leave a review on the site where you made the purchase. Leaving a review helps the reader and author in many ways. Your support is appreciated!

Thank you for reading!
Amanda Booloodian

Interested in information on upcoming releases?

Sign up for the Hidden World Newsletter to receive information on upcoming releases, news, and more!

Complete works by Amanda Booloodian:

AIR Series on Amazon (In Reading Order)

Stonecoat: Novella 0.5 (AIR Series Book 0.5)
Shattered Soul (AIR Series Book 1)
Redcap (AIR Series Book 1.5)
Broken Paths (AIR Series Book 2)
Stolen Sight (AIR Series Book 3)
Fenrisúlfr: Novella 3.5 (AIR Series 3.5)
Fractured Worlds (AIR Series Book 4)

AIR Series Box Set on Amazon

AIR Series: Books 1-4 with AIR Case Files (AIR Series Box
Set)

Spellbound Murder Series on Amazon

Oath Bound (Spellbound Murder Series Book 1)
Grim Magic (Spellbound Murder Series Book 2)
Fallen Witch (Spellbound Murder Book 3)

Spellbound Murder Box Set on Amazon

Spellbound Murder Complete Trilogy

ACKNOWLEDGEMENTS

TI find myself really lucky to have as much support for my writing as I have. My friends and family are always cheering me on from the sidelines, or even getting involved. I'm grateful for everyone's support.

JD Book Services went out of their way to provide me extra feedback for this novel. This was the first completed series I've finished and I appreciated their feedback on the book. Also special thanks to Frankie Sutton for fitting me into the schedule on short notice! The final edits turned out great.

Deranged Doctor Design has done another amazing job with this series! They've provided the books with wonderful covers. I love their work and their flexibility.

For all the people who gave reviews online, you are amazing! Thank you so much for taking the time to leave a review.

ABOUT THE AUTHOR

Amanda Booloodian lives in Missouri with her loving, and often times peculiar, husband. In 2006, she took part in Great Beginnings and was awarded first place in the Mystery/Thriller category. Amanda has been passionate about the written word throughout her life. Now, much of her spare time is spent at the computer, delving into worlds accessible only through vivid imagination. In warm weather, when she isn't pounding on the keyboard, she can often be found wandering through the wilderness. Occasionally she gets it into her head to SCUBA dive or to sit back at home and make wine, which can have interesting results and inspire her writing.

You can find out more about Amanda and her writing, including upcoming releases, on www.Booloodian.com. You can also find her on Facebook: Amanda Booloodian - Author, Twitter: @ajbooloodian, and Instagram: AJBooloodian.